WITH BLOOD IN THEIR EYES

WITH BLOOD IN THEIR EYES

THOMAS COBB

THE UNIVERSITY OF
ARIZONA PRESS

TUCSON

The University of Arizona Press
© 2012 Thomas Cobb
All rights reserved
First issued as a paperback edition 2014

www.uapress.arizona.edu

Library of Congress Cataloging-in-Publication Data

Cobb, Thomas, 1947–
With blood in their eyes / Thomas Cobb.
p. cm.
ISBN 978-0-8165-2110-4 (cloth : acid-free paper)
I. Title.
PS3553.O194W58 2012
813'.54–dc23

2012000988

Manufactured in the United States of America on acid-free, archival-quality paper containing a minimum of 30% post-consumer waste and processed chlorine free.

17   16   15   14   6   5   4   3   2

I have tried to be true to the facts of the "Power Affair" as they are known, working from two main sources—Tom Power's *Shoot Out at Dawn*, and Darvil McBride's *The Evaders*, as well as contemporary accounts. But this is a work of fiction, and I have filled in gaps in the story and recreated the characters and events whenever the story seemed to require it. Though the vast majority of events and people in this novel are true, they are also fictional.

Map by Susan Rowe

To Donnie Dale,
more than friend, brother.
And to Warren Knowles, Tom Randall, and Jim Todd,
who walked the walk.

WITH BLOOD IN THEIR EYES

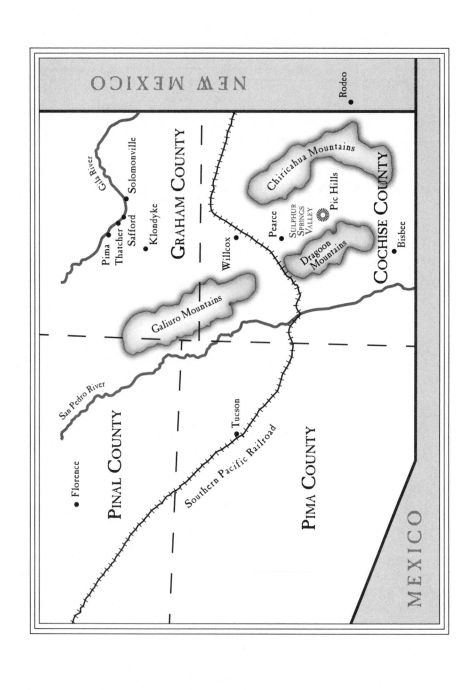

NEW MEXICO

Rodeo

Gila River

Solomonville

Chiricahua Mountains

Safford
Klondyke

Pima
Thatcher

GRAHAM COUNTY

Pic Hills

Pearce
SULPHUR
SPRINGS
VALLEY

COCHISE COUNTY

Willcox

Bisbee

Dragoon
Mountains

Galiuro Mountains

San Pedro River

Tucson

PINAL COUNTY

Florence

Southern Pacific Railroad

PIMA COUNTY

MEXICO

February 10, 1918

John Power woke to the sound of bells and horses' hooves. He rolled out of bed, not quite sure what was going on, just that it wasn't right.

"Lion," his father said. "There's a damned lion after the horses."

"Lion," his brother said.

John had his feet on the floor as his brother Tom stumbled over him, rifle in hand, heading for the door.

Jeff, still in his union suit, rifle in his right hand, pulled the door open.

"Throw up your hands," someone said.

"What the hell?"

John heard the shot then and saw his father take a step back before he lurched forward, through the door and outside.

More shots.

John went to the door where his father had stood only seconds before. There was more shooting, and he could hear bullets going past him. Tom ran behind him and went to the window at the far end of the cabin.

John saw someone move ten yards beyond the cabin door and took two shots, unsure whether he hit anyone or not.

Glass shattered and Tom yelled, "Sons of bitches, sons of bitches." John turned and saw Tom hunched over against the wall, blood coming down his face. He made a move toward him, and Tom waved him back.

He saw the movement beyond the door, sighted and shot quickly, and saw the body drop like deadweight. Something blew up in front of him, and then his face, his left eye, went to fire. He was blind now, blood in both of his eyes.

John heard more glass breaking, and Tom fired out the window.

There was more fire coming at him from in front of the door, and John continued to shoot blindly until Tom came up behind him. "Got one at the window," he said. Tom continued to fire out the door, though his face was also a mask of blood.

Then there was no more firing except theirs. Both Tom and John stepped back from the doorway and hunkered down on the floor, waiting for more fire to come.

When it didn't, they moved slowly out the door. The Old Man, Jeff, lay in front of it, face down.

John knelt down. He had wiped blood from his right eye, and he could see now that the Old Man was bad shot. The back of his union suit was thick with blood, and more pulsed out of the wound on his back. He turned the Old Man over. Jeff's eyes rolled in their sockets, and John could see that he was struggling to control his eyes and look at John. The hole in the upper part of his chest whistled, and blood oozed from that, too.

"How is he?" Tom said.

John only shook his head.

"Jesus," Tom said. "You shot in the face?"

"I don't think so," John said. "Something in my eye. Did I get shot in my eye?"

"I don't think so." Tom cradled John's chin in his hand. "My God. You got a chunk of wood in that eye. Big as my finger."

"Bastards," the Old Man said, his voice only a little beyond a whisper. Tom Sisson walked up to where the brothers crouched over their father.

"Who the hell are they?" John asked.

"That right there is Kane Wootan," Tom said. "I'd say you shot him all to death. Wish it had been me."

The Old Man began to cough blood out of his mouth and nose.

"We got to get him to the doctor," John said.

"No," Tom said. "He don't need no doctor. Wouldn't live to see one. Get a blanket on him. Try to keep him warm. I'm going to check these others."

Sisson handed John the blanket from around his shoulders.

"You all right, Sisson?" John asked. Sisson only nodded.

"Holy Christ," Tom said. "We just killed us the Graham County Sheriff's Department."

"Are there any more?"

"Not that I can see. Don't know, though. Don't go standing up, just in case. Where the hell were you, Sisson?"

"In there." Sisson motioned toward the cabin with his head. He had a .30-06 in his hand.

"You shoot?"

Sisson nodded. He had the glassy look of a man who has seen what he feared most in the world.

"Hit anything?"

Sisson just stared down at the Old Man. "Dying," he said.

"Guess that's right," Tom said.

"What are we going to do?" John asked.

"Get out of here," Tom said. "We got to get the hell out of here."

"We can't leave the Old Man here."

"Got to. We can't take him."

The Old Man looked from Tom to John, back to Tom, and then to Sisson. He looked surprised. Sad and surprised. He nodded. "Go," he said.

"We won't leave you," John said.

The Old Man shook his head. "Go." Then he raised his right hand slowly and pointed toward the mine. "Mine."

"Yeah," Tom said. "That's the mine. Our mine."

"He wants to go to the mine," Sisson said. "He don't want to stay here. He wants to go to the mine."

"That what you want, Old Man?" Tom asked.

Jeff nodded. "Bastards," he said.

Tom wasn't sure who the Old Man referred to. "Sisson, you want to help me carry him to the mine?"

"I'll do it," John said.

"You should go clean yourself up. You look worse than dead. We got to look at your wounds."

"No," John said. "I'll carry him."

Tom started to argue, then said, "Get his feet. I'll get his arms."

They carried him the couple hundred yards from the front of the cabin to the entrance to the mine. They laid him down just inside the entrance. "You still alive?" Tom asked.

The Old Man wheezed, and more blood came out of his mouth.

"I'm going to get some water for you. You want food?"

Jeff shook his head. "Water."

"I'm going to get that."

"What are we going to do about these ones?" Sisson asked.

"Nothing," Tom said. "Leave them be."

"We killed them."

"That's right, and that's all we're going to have to do with them."

"I better go find the horses," Sisson said.

"Fast as they was going, they're miles gone now," Tom said.

"Got to find them. Can't walk out of here."

"Well, do it, then."

Tom went back into the cabin and poured some water from his canteen into a tin cup for the Old Man. He looked around. There wasn't much there. Some clothes and their guns. A little food. They had been eating out of cans since Ola May died. Better take it all, he thought. He saw the leather folder for the mine papers and picked that up and put it in his pocket.

"I thought I told you to wash your face," Tom said when John came back.

"I did."

"You're bleeding like a pig."

"I know. You too."

"All three of them missed us. Still messed us up, though."

"Bastards," John said.

"Bastards."

"Got horses," Sisson said. "Two horses and a mule."

"Not ours."

Sisson nodded toward the dead lawmen. "Theirs."

Tom shrugged. "Ours now."

Tom took the water and papers to the Old Man inside the mine entrance. He held up Jeff's head so he could drink a little. Jeff coughed most of it up, mixed with blood. Tom put the papers under the blanket on the Old Man's chest. "We ain't going to need these. You neither, I guess. But it's your mine. Probably always was."

He looked at the Old Man and thought the Old Man was going to cry. "They hurt you pretty bad, Old Man."

Jeff just coughed some more. At just a whisper he said, "Go."

"We are," Tom said. "Don't want to leave you here, but we got to go. Got to get out of here."

The Old Man raised his hand an inch or two and twitched it. Good-bye. Tom walked out of the mine and up the hill toward the cabin. The bodies of the lawmen were spread evenly around. He sighed. It had started to snow.

CHAPTER ONE

1918

Tom Power had glass splinters in his eye. His brother John had a large wood splinter in his eye, and a piece of his nose had been blown off. Both were blind on the left side. The wounds were open and bleeding, and their blood mixed on their clothing with the blood of the dead and dying they had left behind.

They kept riding, moving forward. Tom Sisson, the hired man, followed them at a distance as they descended the Galiuro Mountains of southern Arizona, heading toward Redington and the northwest base of the mountains. It was Sunday, late morning. They were the only ones left alive.

"I think we ought to get rid of Sisson," Tom said. John said nothing. "I'd leave him, except he's the only one who can see worth a damn." John plodded forward in silence. "He didn't do us no good back at camp, and I doubt he will do us any good today," Tom added.

"He did his part," John said.

"He's no man in a fight."

"He held his own. He can see. We can't."

"And that's the only reason I'm keeping him on. He can see." Tom let his horse pick its way through the rock and scree of the draw they were descending. "I think he had something to do with Ola."

"Do what with Ola?"

"Whatever he done," Tom said. "Whatever. Somebody did something to her, and I think it was him."

"I don't think he done nothing," John said.

"Well, you wouldn't. Thinking ain't what you're good at. And somebody did something to that girl. I think he fucked her and killed her."

"He didn't do neither. And he can see. We need him."

"Then why ain't he out in front then?" Tom asked.

"No one told him to. Sisson don't do what he ain't told to do."

"And I guess that's right. No one told him to shoot anyone, so he just stuffed his big ass under the bed and let us do all the work."

"He was shooting. I know that."

"The hell. Sisson. Get up here and take the lead. You got two good eyes."

Sisson spurred his horse forward until he made his way up even with the brothers. "Where we headed?" he asked.

"Out of these mountains and away from Thems that got ropes and a need to see us hang. Someone's found those bodies by now. There might have been another that got away. We don't know."

Sisson, a big man, old, in his forties, with big, drooping moustaches, nodded and spurred his horse forward and on down the draw. The rocks were getting bigger now, rocks that had rolled a long way down the draw in the spring thaw. Sisson was a former army scout. He knew this territory as well as any other white man did. He turned back to Tom and John. "Mexico?" he asked.

"Suppose," Tom said. "Any way we go but south, there's going to be more of Thems, looking for us. And there ain't going to be nothing left for us up here. Mexico. Mexico's where we can start over."

"Can't be posses yet. Probably no one's found out about it yet. It takes a long time to get to Safford, which is where they would go."

"No," Tom said. "Klondyke. There's a telephone in Klondyke. If Thems don't know yet, Thems is about to find out. And when Thems find out, Thems is going to be on us like hornets. It won't take Thems long to find out and to let everyone else know."

"Telephone," Sisson said. He shook his head. He didn't know much about telephones, except that he didn't like them. He had known the telegraph operators at Fort Grant, and he figured they were out of work now because of the telephones. Now he had to outrun the damned things. He wished they had never been invented.

The snow that had begun a couple of hours earlier was easing off now. They had been riding in it all the way down the mountains from Kielberg Canyon, a ragged upheaval of rhyolite, treacherous in summer and worse in winter, especially in snow. But whoever was going to report the fight to the police, and someone was going to report it, would go the other way—east and north to Klondyke and then to Safford. They wouldn't come this way, west, toward Tucson, and the law in Tucson wouldn't be as anxious to take them as the law in Safford. And the law in Tucson wouldn't try to hang them.

The horses moved slowly, picking their way down the canyon. The men wanted speed, but, blind, they needed the horses to go as they would. Even with Sisson, clear-sighted and in the lead.

The mountains, the Galiuros (locals pronounced the name "glurrows"), were rugged and steep. There was a road on the east side through Rattlesnake Canyon that the Powers and Sisson had cut through to bring in mining supplies and to take out the ore they had mined. They left the other way, though—the way without roads, the way that was safest for them. The Galiuros had been home to Tom, John, and their family for years. It was hard country, but they were hard men. They had expected to become rich up there in Kielberg Canyon. They had not. And now only the dead were left up there in the canyon. They were leaving the Galiuros, and they were not coming back.

"We should have stayed with the Old Man," John complained. Often enough, he picked up on Tom's thoughts, though he was the dumb one and Tom was the smart one. "We shouldn't have left him there to die alone."

"More dead than alive," Tom said.

"It wasn't right."

"You want to die, don't you?"

"Nah, I don't want to die."

"You keep coming up with ideas that lead to the same place—you and me and Sisson here, dead. When Thems come up and find all of them dead, killed by Gentiles, Thems is going to want us dead. Going to get us dead, if they can. The only way that ain't going to happen is if we can put enough distance between us and Thems to keep ourselves alive. You want to go back and see to the Old Man and take your chances? You want to see if Thems is going to forgive in that holy way that Thems got? You think we got ourselves a chance?"

"No. The Old Man shouldn't have to die alone, though."

"We all die alone. That's how it works," Sisson said. Both Tom and John looked at him as though his horse had begun to speak to them.

"That's right," Tom said. "We got one chance, and that's with me, and it's down to Mexico. That's our chance. Otherwise, we're dead, too. We keep riding. The Old Man is dead by now. That part of the story has been told."

The fight had lasted only seconds, and now they were getting the hell out. The two brothers and Tom Sisson had headed west out of Kielberg Canyon and into Redfield Canyon down toward the San Pedro River Valley. They kept the mountains between them and any who would be following them.

"I don't think Sisson killed anyone. I think he had his big ass wedged under the bed," Tom said, after Sisson moved ahead.

"Maybe he did, maybe he didn't," John said.

"Those would be the choices," Tom said. "'Didn't' being the correct one."

"How many did you kill?"

"I don't know, one, I guess."

"I got one. That's two. Who got the third?"

"I don't know."

"Sisson. It's got to be Sisson. He's the only other one there."

"The Old Man could have got one."

"I don't think he ever got off a shot. They shot him as soon as he opened the door. So it's got to be Sisson who got the third one."

"And then he crawled under the bed, did he?"

"I don't know," John said.

"That's right, you don't. Don't burn a lot of food thinking. It ain't your strong point."

They rode on in silence, on the lawmen's horses, following Sisson. It was still snowing, but less now. It had begun to snow just after the fight was over, and it had kept up. It was a light snow that covered the scrub brush more than the ground and that glistened in the horses' manes. They were coming down in elevation quickly now, and soon the snow would be gone. That was good. Tracking them would get harder. Tracking them would be hard anyway. They knew the area well.

"Do you think the Old Man is dead?" John asked.

"Yeah. I think he's dead. He was bad shot."

"That was something. That fight just starting up like that. We can tell them that we didn't start the fight. Thems just up and started shooting. Shot the Old Man still in his underwear. Thems had no call. No call."

"You want to explain that to a jury? A jury in Safford? A jury of Mormons, most of Thems the dead's relations? You want to explain that to Thems? Even if Thems don't hang you before you even get your trap open?"

"I don't want to explain nothing."

"Well, there you go, then," Tom concluded.

"I wouldn't mind if you explained some things, though."

"Yeah? Like what?"

"Like what was that all about?"

"Maybe we can go back and ask the law," Tom said. "No, wait. They're dead. No use in asking."

"No. You. You explain," John demanded. He had a rugged perseverance that saw him through things, including arguments with his younger brother.

"Do I look like law to you?"

"No. But I think you know what they was doing there this morning."

"Must have been that draft business. They said they was coming for us."

"I don't know."

"You don't know what?" Tom asked.

"That draft stuff. That don't seem worth it."

"No, it doesn't. But that's law for you. Thems got their own way of looking at things."

"Kane Wootan was there. Why was he there?"

"Because he's a deputy sheriff?"

John snorted. They rode on a bit more. The snow had let up to just occasional flakes. "You know. You know that you know. You know a lot more about this than you're saying."

"I know a lot about a lot of stuff that I ain't saying. And I ain't going to say it, so leave it be."

"Where are we going?" John asked.

Tom sighed. The world would be a better place if you didn't have to spend so much of your life explaining it to the dumb ones who figured they needed to know things instead of just following along in silence. "Mexico."

"I know, Mexico. Where in Mexico?"

"We ain't even out of the canyon yet. Can't go nowhere until we're out of this canyon. Right now it's out of the canyon or be killed. Let's do this first."

"It's a long way to Mexico."

"It's a long way to anywhere with you running your yap all the way. When we get down out of the canyon, we're going to need better horses. I think I can do that at Carlink ranch. Then just down the river's a big mesquite bosque where we can get some rest."

"Posse ain't going to rest."

"That's because there's a bunch of them. There's only the three of us. We rest. When we ain't resting, we outthink them. You needn't be a part of that."

They came out of the canyon in the afternoon. The trail had become steadily more treacherous as they descended toward the floor of the San Pedro River Valley. Stones from boulder size to small enough to fit a man's hand littered the opening of the canyon. Worse were tons of scree that had come down the streambed carried by the spring thaw. The horses and one mule picked their way delicately through the obstacles, skittering now and then as a stone or deposit of scree gave way under their hooves.

Sisson's horse hit a pile of scree resting against a dead and rotting sycamore branch and lost its footing on the right side, going down heavily and sending Sisson hard into the rocks. The horse went down near his feet and stayed there for a moment, then, in a panic, struggled and righted itself, coming up bloody on the right side. Sisson lay still on the rocks, which were now spattered with blood.

"Sisson. Sisson. You all right, Sisson?"

Sisson groaned, then rolled from his side to his back. He came partly upright, braced on his left arm, his right arm held to his side. He sighed. "I don't know." Then, "I'm all right. I guess. I'm all right. How's the horse?"

The bay mare was bleeding from a cut on the shoulder and having a hard time putting her weight on the right foreleg, more trouble than one would expect from a cut to the shoulder. Tom Power touched the wound with his finger, and the mare snorted and skittered. "I don't know." He bent down and ran his hands up and down the mare's leg, stopping every now and again to put some pressure on the bone. "I don't think anything's broke. Something wrong up at the shoulder, though. May have knocked it out. Just have to see if she can walk and take weight. What about your arm?"

"It ain't broke. It's the elbow. My hand's gone numb. That shouldn't be too bad." He came over to his horse, took the reins from Power, and started walking ahead. The horse followed, limping but walking. "She'll get better. Or worse," he said. "We'll see."

They headed due west, then, toward the bosque, which would give them cover until nightfall. If necessary, they could hold off a good-sized posse from the cover of mesquite. Tom took the lead, with John bringing up the rear. Sisson, leading his horse, walked in the middle. The horse seemed neither better nor worse.

"I'm going to leave you two in the bosque while I take the horses over to Carlink. By the time I get back, it should be dark enough we can head out again. You all get rested up. It's going to be a long pull. We'll take the riverbed as long as we're able. Once we're out of there and onto the flat of the valley, we're going to need to beat it across fast as we can. We should be able to get into the Dragoons before they can get up any kind of posse." The Dragoon Mountains, rugged and rocky, would provide good cover.

"I don't think they'll want this horse," Sisson said.

"That ain't your problem. I'll take care of it. How's the arm?"

"No better. No worse."

"That's half bad, which is better than all bad, I guess."

"Usually. Not always."

"You'll be OK here," Tom said. "Just stay low and don't do anything stupid." They were deep in the mesquite bosque, a thicket of mesquite on the San Pedro River floodplain, thick and nearly impenetrable. No one could sneak up on them.

"We ain't going to do nothing stupid," John said. "You always think we're going to do something stupid. But we're not stupid, Tom."

"Not 'we.' You. Sisson, see if you can do something about that eye. See if you can get some of that wood out. It don't do much for his countenance."

Sisson looked up at him, part look, part glare. His big, drooping moustaches gave his whole face a baleful look. It was just his look. "I ain't a doctor. He needs a doctor, and so do you. You don't look a hell of a lot better than he does."

"We ain't going to be seeing any doctors for a while. We're on our own. And I don't have to look at me, just him. See if you can get that out before his whole eye festers and breaks open."

"He'll lose the eye."

"Eye's lost. So's mine. Take it out if you have to. We don't want to stop just because his dead eye is grieving him."

At the edge of the bosque he stopped and listened. It was moving into early afternoon now, and there wasn't much cover between the bosque and the Carlink ranch. He would have to keep to the sides of the hills where he would be blocked from some view at least. He chose to stay on the east side, figuring that if the posse came back down the canyon after them, they'd be a long while coming down. The larger the group, the slower the travel, and there were damned few who knew the canyons the way the three of them did.

He heard nothing except the rattle and clatter of the horses behind him. He sat the mule because it was the strongest of the three and would be able to keep a pace the unmounted horses, even Sisson's lame one, could maintain. He spurred the mule and exited the cover of the bosque.

Almost immediately, his skin began to crawl. He took out the binoculars and glassed the exit of the canyon and the valley floor to his east. There was nothing. He felt watched, though. He was reasonably sure he wasn't, but the feeling was a powerful and uncomfortable one. He had hunted all his life—glassing the landscape in front of him until he found the prey, then calculating the path toward it so he would not be seen until it was too late for the prey to escape. Now, he guessed, it was his turn. His only advantage was that he understood what they would be doing as they came after him. He could anticipate their movements, and then he could avoid them.

He crossed the plain, staying to the east of the small hills, avoiding his most likely threat, which would come from Tucson or Redington if anyone had had time to get to a telephone. It took him nearly an hour from the bosque into the outskirts of the Carlink ranch. He stopped at the first stock tank and drank and filled his canteen and water bags.

He saw the rider coming from several hundred yards away. There was nowhere to go. Even if he untied the horses and spurred the mule toward the lower hills, the rider would see him and know exactly where he had gone. He took the .30-30 from the scabbard on his saddle and stood behind the mule, watching the rider approach.

With one eye it was hard to judge distance. It would be a difficult shot, not knowing exactly how far away the rider was. But a single rider was not a great danger. The danger would come from a group of riders. No one was going to come for fugitives of a gunfight alone. They would travel in groups.

At a little over a hundred yards, he recognized the rider as Poke. And it was Poke he had come to find. It was as though things had somehow turned his way, though he guessed they hadn't. He had had bad days in his life, but nothing like this. The day had simply broke bad, and he guessed it was going to stay on that path for a while. A long while, he guessed.

"Holy God, Tom. What happened to you?"

"Poke. It all tightened down. That thing tightened, just like I figured it was going to."

"Well, goddamn. It did, huh? That's a hell of a thing. A hell of a thing." Alvin Blyer was a big, raw-boned cowboy. No one called him Alvin, only "Poke" for his fondness for cards. He was on the bad end of his life, pushing fifty, managing the horses for the Carlink outfit, still in the saddle when he needed to be in an armchair or at least an office chair. Sitting on his horse, he looked all right, but when he dismounted, you could see the wear he had taken in the long years of being a cowboy. He had been broken up more than it was good to think about. He wore a pair of battered spectacles, and his hands looked to be a thousand years old, the fingers all pointing off in different directions from being broken so many times.

"Anyone around here know about it yet?"

"This is the first I've heard of it. How bad was it?"

"Pretty bad. The Old Man's dead or right up on to it. And there's three more up there."

"Who's that?"

"The Graham County bunch."

"All of them?"

"I think so," Tom said.

"Well, I ain't heard a word of it, so maybe not. You killed two?"

"Three. The Wootan kid was there, too."

"Kane?"

"Yeah. Him."

"And Frank Haynes?"

"No. Not Frank. I don't know whether he was there."

"Damn," Poke said. "That's bad. The other way around would give you a chance. Not saying you should have killed Frank, but I don't think you want him running around."

Tom drew lines in the ground with the toe of his boot. "No. We don't really want Frank running around. Listen, Poke. I need to trade you some horses."

"I don't know, Tom. If there was law involved, I don't much want to be a part of it, though, you know, I side with you on this."

"I understand that, Poke. I don't want to draw you in on the trouble, but it would be a favor if you could just put yourself in our place for a couple of seconds. We just killed three of Thems, all law. It don't mean nothing that Arizona isn't a death state. Thems's going to make it one just on our account. Hell, Thems is gathering up rope right now. Posse catches up to us, we're dead. There ain't going to be no trial. Trial is the time it takes to tie a knot. If it weren't for that, we'd turn ourselves in. Hell, it was self-defense, Poke. But that ain't going to mean spit to Thems."

"It's a bad spot. That's for sure. Was this part of that draft business? I mean, I can't see anyone going up into the Galiuros for the draft."

"Wasn't no conversation, Poke. We was still in our beds. The Old Man got up and went to the door and fell out with a bullet in him. From then on it was all shooting. No talking. It might have been the draft business, but they didn't say. Thems will say it is. I do know that. We tried to sign up for that draft in Redington, but they told us we didn't need to. It might have been the draft, but it was probably gold, too. We was starting to pull some nice ore out of that mine. Thems can smell gold. Thems believes gold is for Thems and no one else. You know that as well as I do. I'm pretty sure it was the gold that started it."

"I don't know. It seems pretty bold on their part to just come in shooting and taking your mine. What about the whiskey business? You and Kane was in that together with Frank."

"Thems is a bold people. You know us, Poke. We don't go looking for trouble. But we don't abide others bringing it to us. We was just up there mining our mine. I was pretty much out of the whiskey business. We never did nothing to Thems."

"Well, that would be most right, too. These your mule and horses?"

"No, these is the law's. Ours got run off, and we didn't have time to go round them up."

"My God, Tom. You want me to swap you fresh horses for those of the ones you killed? They'll as likely hang me, too."

"I got that figured, Poke. You and me never had no conversation, never saw each other. You just come out here and found these animals. Later you noticed some of yours was gone. It would make perfect sense that we would just steal yours, us being wanted desperados on the run. And you can make a claim on ours up at the mine. You just tell Thems that you want our horses as compensation. Hell, you could end up six for three if Thems don't get their hands on these."

"I don't know, Tom. It's a bad spot. But you always been straight with me, and I believe you're straight with me now. And I don't want to see you killed. And I do believe they will kill you if they catch you. There's a small string right over yonder beyond that little hummock. They's about eight of them. Take what you want, and leave those behind. That one there looks pretty lame."

"Fell on her shoulder. Might have popped it out. I don't know. If you have to shoot her, it's still a good deal for you—five for three. And this mule is quality stock. And this one, it might just be bruises. I don't see you losing on this."

"Yeah. Well, I don't share your optimism, but I don't want to see your bodies in the back of someone's truck, either. You can handle the switch, right? I'm not sure I want to be that involved."

"Oh, hell yes, Poke. You know me. I can handle horses."

"Yes, you can. That's the truth. Where you headed?"

"Mexico. Not exactly sure how we're going to get there, but Mexico. Mexico will be good for us. That's the land of opportunity. Better than this place, where a poor man never gets a straight deal."

"Don't need to know, Tom. Don't want to know. As the Mexicans say, 'Vaya con Dios.'"

"You stay here, Poke. I don't want you with me if Thems should come up on me. Give me about fifteen minutes with the horses and then get on out of here. If you see someone coming, I'd appreciate a sign."

Poke touched the rifle in his saddle ring. "Lots of damn coyotes out here. I might want to thin that herd a bit."

"I appreciate it."

"You got it. I been meaning to tell you, next time I seen you, how sorry I was to hear about Ola May. She was a good girl. It's just a shame what happened to her. And now this. A shame."

"What is it they say? 'Didn't got bad luck, wouldn't got luck.' Must have been a Power first said that. But you go with what you got. Don't get no redeals."

"That's the truth. And if I ain't being too nosy, what was it happened to Ola May?"

"Rattlesnake, I guess. Didn't know about it until she was gone. She'd been out riding fences. Seems her horse got spooked by a rattler and dumped her right on top of it."

"A rattlesnake in the winter? Well, that doesn't make any less sense than a lot of the stuff we been hearing about it. Some folks have been saying some pretty nasty stuff, though I didn't take a lot of stock in that kind of talk."

"I'll bet a lot of folks is saying a lot of things. Ola May was who she was. She was my sister, and I loved her, but there was some who didn't. A lot that did, though."

"I guess that's right. She was something, all right. Did just as she pleased, no matter what anyone else thought. Kept true to herself. Looked like a woman, acted like a man. Hope that's all right to say."

"Hell, Poke. It's all right. Ola was who Ola was. We don't have no delusions about it. She grew up with men, except for Granny Jane, who was tougher than the Eighth Cavalry. There's no offense there. That's who she was."

"Well, all right then. I wish you luck. I'll do my best to get you a good head start. Vaya, friend, vaya."

"You doing all right?" Sisson asked John. They were deep in the bosque, hunkered down on a patch of ground Sisson had cleared of mesquite beans and sticks and cholla joints that the rats had dragged in.

"Did that really happen?" John asked. "I feel like I'm just waking up from a dream. A really bad dream."

"Afraid it did, John. Afraid it did."

"Crap. We should have stayed with the Old Man until he died. I been thinking on that. We should have stayed."

"I feel bad, too, leaving him like that. But you can't say that Tom was all that wrong. There's going to be a posse, and they're going to be plenty pissed about the killings. We hung around, we'd be killed, too. Your brother is right. We got to run. There's no other choice."

"Crap."

"Yeah. Crap. And here's more of it. I got to look at your eye. How's it feel?"

"Hurts, Sisson. It hurts like hell. But it will be all right. Just leave me be."

"No. It ain't going to be all right. It ain't ever going to be all right. I got to take a look. And it's going to be painful."

Sisson gathered up small handfuls of mesquite twigs and beans and made a fire just big enough to heat up the blade of his jackknife. "You ought to stick something in your mouth so you don't yell. We're pretty well hid in here, but we don't need no yelling."

John put the fleshy part of his right hand, between the thumb and first finger, into his mouth.

"Well," Sisson said. "Wouldn't a been my first choice, but I guess that will work."

The eye was swollen to the size of a teacup. The lid and the area around it had turned blue with coagulated blood. Sisson took water and a clean sock and gently brushed away the blood that had crusted John's face from his lower eyelid to his jaw. It was difficult to tell what had come from his eye and what from his nose. There was a wound half an inch wide across the bridge of John's nose, and Sisson could clearly see cartilage and bits of bone splinter. In the eye itself a wooden splinter—a quarter-inch-thick piece of pine dislodged from the cabin's door frame by the impact of a bullet—protruded almost three-quarters of an inch between the swollen lids of John's eye. It was easy to see that the splinter of wood had exploded off the door frame, gone across the bridge of John's nose, taking skin and bone with it, and then lodged in the eye. Sisson pried the eyelids apart the best he could with his left hand. The splinter had pierced the eye just to the outside of the iris. The white of the eye, hemorrhaged a bright cherry red, was swollen to nearly twice its size. John was biting deeply into his hand, and Sisson had barely touched him. Sisson sighed heavily.

"Don't cut it out," John said.

"Your eye? I'm after that piece of wood. I ain't going to cut your eye."

"Just don't cut it out."

Sisson looked back at the eye. It was a terrible thing to look at. He had cut the eye out of a heifer with a suppurating wound once, and the heifer had died a week later. He didn't know if he had killed it or if it was going to die anyway. He didn't want to cut this eye out. He was sure of that much. "I guess you better bite hard," he told John.

Holding the eyelids open with his left hand, he reached as gently as he could for the splinter. He wasn't sure how to do this—quickly, so that John wouldn't jerk his head back and make things worse, or slowly, to minimize the damage, which would then likely maximize the pain. He couldn't decide, so he closed his fingers on the end of the splinter and pulled. The splinter seemed to move, then stopped. John gave a muffled scream, and Sisson could see drops of blood where John's teeth had broken skin. Sisson's hand glistened with blood and other gore. He wouldn't be able to grab the splinter with his fingers again.

"I think I can get it out of there," he said. "You going to let me give it one more try?"

John looked up at him, a glare, a look of pure hatred. Then he relaxed and nodded his head. Yes.

Sisson made his way through the mesquite to an open area where they had stowed their gear, knowing that if a posse actually came into the bosque and found the gear, they would stop and likely talk, giving John and Sisson the chance to run or get ready for the fight. Sisson had a leather tool wrap tied to his saddle. Untying and unrolling it, he selected the only tool that would be of use—a pair of fencing pliers with wide, rounded jaws made for pulling fence staples from posts.

"I guess that little tug hurt pretty bad," he told John. "I'm regretful about that, and I'm guessing that this is going to be somewhat worse, though I'll do my best not to linger over it."

"Do it."

Sisson nodded. He knelt in front of John and pushed John's head back against the trunk of the tree. He took the leather tie from the tool kit and wrapped it around John's forehead and tied it off behind the tree, securing John's head. He kept the pliers down at his right side so John wouldn't see them. He had learned this working with cattle. "Shut your other eye," he said.

"No. I want to be staring you right in the eye, so I can curse you to hell, you bastard."

Sisson smiled. "Yeah, I guess you do." He put the thumb and index finger of his left hand on John's eyelids and slowly pulled them apart. The eye seemed to have swollen more, turned more red. He brought the pliers up, jaws wide open, quickly and efficiently to the eye, closed them around the end of the splinter, and pulled straight back. He could not see the splinter as he pulled, but John's eye seemed to explode as thick wads of blood and vitreous exited the wound as the splinter came out. He sat back and wiped some of the gore from his moustache. In the jaws of the pliers was a jagged cut of pine almost two inches long.

John unclenched his jaws and took his hand from his mouth, then put it back to suck the blood from the wound. He fought against losing consciousness.

"Hang in there. Don't go out on me," Sisson said. "There's more. It ain't done."

"There's always more."

Sisson went back to his gear, replaced the pliers, and then took a small bottle of pure grain alcohol from his saddlebag. He held it up for John to see.

"Give me that."

"No. You'll drink it. That ain't what you need."

"Oh, fuck no."

"Yes. It's what we got to do."

Sisson was a big man and strong, but John was wiry and strong as hell. Sisson took him down the way he would a steer, pushing his whole body weight into him and pulling John's hand down with a quick pull before John could fully tense his arm, and then he upended the bottle over John's eye and nose. When John brought his arm back up, Sisson pulled it down, dropped the bottle, and pulled open John's eyelids so the alcohol ran into his eye. When John's mouth came open, Sisson rolled his shoulder into it to muffle the yell. "It's over," he said. "It's over now. Calm. Calm. Calm. Come on."

"Oh, fuck me," John groaned.

"No. You already had enough fun for one day."

CHAPTER TWO

1889

The young couple had ridden nearly four hours through the tall grass and scrub of the Hill Country, heading for Junction, Texas, county seat of Kimball County. They were dressed in their best clothes, though her dress had become embedded with grass and thorns from the terrain, and her hair had long ago come undone and hung in long, sweated curls. His shirt, once laundered white with lye soap, was going brown at the neck and arms from the combination of sweat and dust.

Thomas Jefferson Power was twenty-four. His bride-to-be, Martha—Mattie—Morgan, was four years younger. He had their wedding license folded in the back pocket of his best trousers, going limp in the damp heat. They had nearly another hour's ride to Junction, where there was a preacher. They plodded forward, watched impassively by small groups of range cattle carrying a variety of brands. He had no doubt driven some of them. He was a cowboy, well known in the area as a hard worker and something of a harder customer. He took offense easily and was willing to throw a punch when he did.

In Mattie he had found a woman who not only tolerated his ways and quick temper but also brought the promise of stability and prosperity. Martha's father, Sebe, was a rancher who owned a small Hill Country spread. He was not a rich man, but he owned land and cattle, and that made him far richer than Jeff Power had ever been.

Mattie was anxious. It was growing late, the summer sun well into the west now, and they had a long way to go. She didn't want to stop and camp on the way. She knew the ways of men and their world. She had grown up around cowboys who were often tough and occasionally brutish, and she did not want to start her married life before the preacher had made it right. Jeff (never Tom or Thomas) was an honorable man, but he was a man and impatient about such things. She wanted things set right. Right from the beginning.

Jeff was a hard worker. Cowboys in general were hard workers. It was not an easy life. But Jeff also had ambitions that set him apart from most of the others who were content to trade their lives for food and shelter and the chance to go to town every couple of weeks and take their pleasures hard and fast. Jeff saw past the immediate. He would improve his lot in life.

They saw the other rider from nearly three-fourths of a mile away. He was coming toward them in no particular hurry but not ambling like a man out for an afternoon ride. Jeff reached back behind his saddle and untied the cloth bundle he had secured there. He brought it up and set it in his lap without unwrapping it. Inside was a Remington Navy .44 older than he was. The action was a little loose, but it was, all in all, serviceable. He did not expect that he would need to use a gun, but he took no chances. He was, after all, about to become a husband and assume the responsibilities of that position with all attendant duties, including protection of his family, or soon-to-be family.

"Afternoon," the stranger said as he pulled up closer to them. Jeff slid his hand under the edge of the bundle but made no move to touch the revolver.

"Afternoon."

"It would seem that you two have had a hard ride."

Jeff nodded. "A couple of hours. We've a bit to go."

"We're going to Junction City to find a preacher to marry us," Martha said, ignoring the sidelong glance Jeff shot her.

"Is that right? He works in mysterious ways, don't He?"

"How's that?"

"David Crane Brabson," the man said. "The Reverend David Crane Brabson of the Anointed Church of the Holy Brethren on my way to Austin to do the Lord's work."

"Could you marry us?" Martha asked.

"I could. In the eyes of the Lord, though, not in the eyes of Texas. You need a license for that. But if it's an emergency, the Lord's law supersedes the law of man, though we strive to honor it as well."

"We have the license," Jeff said, letting go of the Remington and pulling the document from his pocket.

"Well, so you do," the preacher said, reading over the license. "Official, from the state of Texas. I suppose we should dismount, though. It wouldn't be right to be too casual about the significance of joining a man and a woman.

"In the name of the Lord, under the law of the state of Texas, I now pronounce you man and wife. You may kiss your bride, Thomas, and you can remount and resume your journey, joined in matrimony and pleasing the Lord. Bless you both."

Later that night, in a boardinghouse in Junction, Texas, suckling like an orphaned calf on his new wife's nipple as his body shook and contracted, Thomas Jefferson Power fathered the first of three sons, the one who would be called Charlie.

Will Morgan leaned against the top post of the corral. "I don't know. Maybe that roan over there." He pointed.

"Uh-uh," Jeff Power said. "Look at the shoulders. Always look at the shoulders."

"Which one, then?"

"That sorrel back in the back. Solid through the shoulders and chest, and look how she keeps her ears up. That's a quality horse. That's the one you want."

"If you say that one, then it's that one. You're a better judge of horses than I am. You may be the best one in the country."

"May be."

"You know, we could do all right, you and me, if we turned this cattle operation over to horses instead. They don't graze as heavy, and there ain't as much up and down in the market. There's some good money in horses."

"Your old man is a cattleman, though. You don't move cattlemen off cattle."

"I know, I know. He's more stubborn than the cows. But if there was two of us working him, we might be able to turn him."

"Two of us. His son and the hired man. That's a heady combination."

"But what if you was more than just the hired man? Let's say you was the son-in-law?"

"You mean Mattie? Marry Mattie?"

"Why not? Neither of you is getting younger."

"I'm the hired man."

"But I believe she'd look on you with favor."

"I don't think so. She's nice and not at all hard to look at, but I'm just a cowboy. Rough as a shingle. You know that. She wouldn't want me."

"Rough don't bother Mattie. She's been around cowboys all her life. Cowboys, steers, bulls, mustangs—it's all the same to her. She can handle herself. And that would make you and me brothers, buddy. And that means we could take over this operation and make it into something. The old man, he knows what he knows, but time is coming up on him and passing him by. We'd be doing him a favor."

"I never thought of myself as the marrying kind, if you know what I mean."

"Time is coming up on you, too. You need yourself a better life, one with some ease about it, not just beeves and busted fences. You need a home to come to and someone to look out for you and maybe someone for you to look after. This cowboying, that's a young man's game if there isn't profit in it, and there's never profit in it for cowboys, only for ranchers."

"I guess that would be right."

"That is right. I guarantee it. If you was part of the family, we could take over this operation and run it right. The old man is living in a time that's just gone. It's a new world out there, and it's our world, not his. We need to take the lead on this one. This is our time, Jeff."

Mattie was dumping dishwater on the mid-May bean plants outside the kitchen door. It wasn't the best time he could imagine, but she was alone, and he was feeling more courage than he'd felt in a long time. He cleared his throat. "Miss Martha."

She stood up, surprised, then cocked her head and knitted her brow. "Jeff Power. What are you doing sneaking up on me like that? And why are you calling me 'Martha'?"

"Martha, I mean Mattie. Mattie. I have something to ask you."

"Before you waste both our times, I don't have any money to lend to cowboys. Now is this something I'm going to want to hear?"

He was becoming flustered now. "I don't know. I don't know if you want to hear it. If I knew that, this would be easier."

"It better not be of a lowly nature." She plucked at stray strands of hair and began tucking them behind her ear.

"Oh, hell. Beg your pardon. I don't know how to say things right, so I'm just going to say it and hope it comes out in some way not to give you offense. And I would appreciate it if you wouldn't laugh. Will you marry me?"

"What?"

"Marry me. I want you to marry me."

"You want me to marry you?"

"Yes, ma'am. I know I'm just a cowboy and all. And your pa owns the ranch. But I believe I got some prospects. I don't know. I work hard. I'm no angel, but I'm willing to give up some of the rough stuff and try to live better. I ain't a bad man."

She let out her breath in one long exhalation that kept going and going. He was afraid that she was going to deflate and end up on the ground like an empty balloon. "My goodness," she said at last. "He wants me to marry him." She moved over to the kitchen stoop and sat down. He hesitated and then followed.

"You want me to go away?" he asked.

She looked up at him. He looked down at her, realizing he was seeing her differently than he had seen her before. Her brown eyes stared back at him, unblinking, clear, and, he thought, beautiful. To others she was not a beautiful woman, but her features were regular and pleasing, and she might be thought beautiful if she were not a ranch girl. Her hands were red and calloused, but her wrists were small and delicate and somehow precious. She had thin shoulders, and that surprised him, having thought of her as sturdy and, maybe, stocky. Her breasts, which he had noticed many times before, were heavier than he would have thought for a woman who was actually slight.

"Yes," she said. "Go away."

He felt like a horse. He would catch her at the odd moment, looking at him, sizing him up, judging him. More often than not, she wore a frown. There was an occasional smile, a less occasional neutral look, but mostly her brows were down. He would straighten his back, lift his chin, take off his hat, and run his hand through his hair, become more deliberate in his actions and more self-conscious. Once or twice, he began to whistle a tuneless sibilance to indicate that he was not bothered by the scrutiny, or that he even welcomed it.

But he did not. It was not natural for a woman to eye a man that way—openly, critically. The smallest tasks became difficult for him. Once he tripped and nearly fell just walking to the barn. Another time he hammered his thumb and endured the pain silently, showing her his strength of character. Pain was not meant to be endured without swearing, and it confirmed a deep-seated suspicion that the overly holy were deficient.

He was soaping a bridle before putting it away when she came into the tack room. "And how do you feel about children?" she asked.

"Good day to you, too, Mattie. I like children. I used to be one."

"I wasn't looking for a smart answer or an entertainment."

"Yes," he said. "I guess I know that. I like children just fine, and I want to have children. A man should have sons to carry his name forward."

"And daughters."

"Yes. Daughters, too, though they do not carry the name forward."

"It will be a sacrifice."

"How's that?"

"Marrying me. It will be a sacrifice. A big sacrifice. You'll need to give up your pleasures."

"Marrying you won't be a pleasure?"

"Probably not the kind you're counting on. You will stay home. Friday nights you won't go out unless I go with you. The same for Saturday. And Sunday is for church."

"You don't go to church very often, Mattie."

"I will. And you will, too. And the drinking. And smoking. And swearing."

"My goodness, Mattie. You want me to turn preacher?"

"No. I want you to turn husband. My father takes a drink now and again, and he enjoys a cigar after dinner. I wouldn't deny you that, either, but I wouldn't tolerate that kind of cowboy drinking and smoking that seems to please you so much."

"A cowboy's life is lonely, Mattie. A cowboy takes pleasures where he finds them."

"You won't be a cowboy any longer. You will be a rancher, like my father and Will. But I suppose you already figured that angle."

"I won't lie to you. I have already thought about that. I'm prepared to take on my share of the responsibilities around here. I don't fool myself that I'm in for less work now. If I'm part of running this ranch, I will do the best I can. I would want this ranch to succeed for all of us, and for our children, too."

"That's why you want to marry me, isn't it? You want to be part of this ranch."

"No. That's not it. Not all of it. You're a handsome woman, Mattie. I could spend the rest of my life looking at you. You're pretty. Prettier than a beat-up cowboy like me is likely to find."

"I won't stay this way. I'll get old, and you will, too."

"I reckon I know that. I'm twenty-four years old. I've been a cowboy for about ten of those years. I'm getting busted up. Between horses and cows, a cowboy's life is about getting shaken to death, and for not much money at that. And I got nothing to show for it. I ain't got much family left. My mother. And brothers, though I got no idea where in hell one's at, and a baby sister. Pardon my French. Will is more brother to me than he is. And Sebe. He's a good man, not exactly a father to me, but someone I can look up to. And that leaves you. I don't want you to be my sister. I want you to be my wife."

"All right, then. I will."

"That's wonderful, Mattie, just wonderful. I will work hard to make you a good husband and a good life."

"Jeff?"

"Yes, Mattie?"

"You're a good-looking man, cleaned up. We'll have nice-looking children."

Chapter Three

1918

They were losing light when Tom made his way through the bosque to where they had camped. Sisson was sitting under one tree, John's body was on its side under another. Sisson had a rifle aimed at Tom, then turned it away.

"You all right?" Tom asked.

Sisson nodded.

"How about him?"

"He's had a rough go of it. Fell asleep awhile ago. Ain't stirred since. I got the splinter out."

"That ought to have been fun for the both of you."

Sisson nodded to where John still lay, unstirring. "You want me to take a look at yours?"

Tom looked back over to John. "Nah. I think I'll take my chances. You take the eye out?"

Sisson shook his head. "Just the splinter."

"I'll still take my chances."

He walked over to where John slept. The sleep of the dead. He couldn't help but think that. The sleep of the dead. He knelt down and shook John's shoulder. Sisson would remember the gesture as one of love and gentleness and that it hadn't surprised him. For all their bickering, for Tom's acid tongue, they were brothers and loved each other as brothers.

There was the older brother, Charlie, who had taken off just after they arrived in the Galiuros. He had taken up cowboying in New Mexico rather than staying with the family. And the family had a deep and seething resentment of that. A note had come nearly a year ago that Charlie had lost a hand, and probably his ability to make a living, in a mining accident in New Mexico. Tom had read the note aloud to both the Old Man and John. At the end of the reading, they had looked at each other, confirming that none of them was much interested in what had happened to Charlie. They went back to work.

"Come on, John. We got fresh horses, we got dark, and we got to ride. Now."

John came slowly back to consciousness and nodded as though he had been asleep only seconds, just nodded off. He rose, dusted off his pants, took a quick swipe at the line of scab and gore from his eye, recoiled, and went off to get his saddle and gear.

When the fight was over and the outcome was clear, Tom and John had dragged their father from the front of the cabin to the entrance to the mine. The mine was his dream, the cabin only a place to sleep.

While the brothers tended to their father, Sisson had gone looking for the horses that had been spooked just before the fighting started. Failing to find them, he took the two horses and mule that the lawmen had tied up just over the ridge from the cabin. He had packed their camp supplies and got them ready for the ride.

Tom Sisson was like much that surrounded the Power family—pretty well broken down. He had done time in the Arizona State Penitentiary at Florence for horse theft. He denied the charge that he was a horse thief for the rest of his life, but so did the Old Man, Jeff Power, who had a knack for acquiring horses.

Sisson had been released from the army in 1892 at Fort Grant, Arizona, some twenty miles from the Galiuros. The Apache Wars were over. Geronimo had surrendered to General Nelson A. Miles in 1886, and though there was an occasional skirmish later, the battle for Apachería had ended, and so had the career of Thomas Sisson, aged twenty-three.

He worked odd jobs around the Sulphur Springs Valley in south-central Arizona, cowboying when he could, laboring when that was what was available. He was illiterate and unable to sign his own name. He had learned both blacksmithing and wheelwrighting in the army, and he could often find work doing those jobs on a ranch or in a livery. He was a good farrier, but he lacked the initiative to do it on his own. He did not like being in the position of having to make decisions. Decisions tormented him. How someone could make a decision, not already knowing the outcome but somehow projecting out into the future, baffled Sisson. When he made a decision, it was usually wrong, so he tried his best not to make one. What he liked was being told what to do. In 1915 he was working in Aravaipa Canyon, finishing up some chores for a rancher there, when he ran into Jeff Power, who was rounding up a crew to build a road from the southern entrance to Rattlesnake Canyon and up into Kielberg Canyon, where he had a mine.

Sisson met Jeff Power a couple of times then as Power crisscrossed the Aravaipa Canyon area, picking up what able bodies no one else seemed to have a use for. He was like a junk collector, looking at the same jetsam four or five times, discarding it each time but the last, figuring it just had to be good for something. The younger men wanted nothing to do with Jeff Power. He was rough and acerbic, and he had the look of a man who examined another man just to see how best to cheat him. Almost worst of all, he loved to tell other people what to do. Sisson liked him immediately and signed on.

It took nearly two years to dig and scrape, cut and blast a road up Rattlesnake Canyon, which is often narrow and steep, so that the road had to cut back and forth across the creek several times. Much of the work done one year would be wiped out by the thaw and spring rains of the following year. Workers came and went, but Sisson stayed on. He never wanted to be the boss of a crew. He was well busted up, but he worked harder than most of the others and could tend to the stock—horses, mules, and donkeys—better than the Powers could. He never asked for more money. Jeff Power loved him.

As he saddled the horses and mule, he packed the items they would need, taking from the supplies in the cabin and mine. He took all the blankets and all the food from the cabin. A trip south, which was the logical choice, would take weeks, and there were few chances to reprovision along the route.

Finally, he gathered up the guns, both theirs and the dead lawmen's. They had three rifles—a .30 caliber Winchester, a .405 Winchester, and a .303 Savage. In addition they had five handguns—a .38 automatic, two single-action .38-40 Colt revolvers, an army-issue .45 Colt automatic, and a .30 Luger. He packed the entire six hundred rounds of ammunition the lawmen had brought with them.

They left the bosque from the north and followed the low ground to the bed of the San Pedro River. Sisson was in the lead this time. John, awake, though not completely alert, rode in the middle, and Tom brought up the rear. Each carried a rifle and at least one handgun.

The bed of the San Pedro was completely dry. The streams coming out of the Catalina and Galiuro Mountains had gone dry months before, and the spring rains and snowmelt were still weeks away. They moved in relative silence on sand and silt through the dry riverbed, staying close to the near edge of the bed, which was frequently overhung with mesquite, creosote, and acacia. The moon was moving toward the last quarter, and while it gave them enough light to pick their way through the riverbed, they were not visible from more than a hundred yards.

Mostly they moved in silence, or as much silence as three mounted men can move in. The horses' hooves made soft concussions on the sand and silt, and their tack creaked. The horses shook and snorted. Coyotes were yipping in the distance, and not too far to the east a great horned owl hooted.

The men talked little. There wasn't much to say. The events of that day, shocking and chaotic as they had been, had already settled into history and were now just the events the men were running from. They rode with a grim determination, away from the Galiuros and toward the Dragoon Mountains, some fifty miles away. Between themselves and the Dragoons was the Sulphur Springs Valley, some two hundred square miles of flat, open grassland. Once they were in the valley, they would be at their most vulnerable. A man with a pair of good binoculars could glass them from miles away, too far for them to know they were being watched. It was likely, Tom thought, that once they were making their way across the valley, they would be picked off before they ever knew someone was near. Tom was aware of his back now, feeling for the first time the gun sights on his back. It would become a familiar sensation.

He could see John's head nod, then come upright and begin to nod again. John could sleep in the saddle. Hell, they all could. They had done it hundreds of times in their lives. He couldn't make out Sisson, but he was pretty sure that Sisson was awake. He spurred his horse and came alongside John, who woke when he did.

"What?" John asked.

"Nothing. We're just riding. You're OK. Go ahead and sleep. I'm going up to talk with Sisson a bit."

"I wasn't sleeping."

"Right. And I ain't riding, either."

"I wasn't."

"All right. You wasn't."

He came up abreast of Sisson. "How far you think we can get tonight?"

Sisson hesitated. "We can make the Johnson mine, I guess. Plenty of places to crouch down around there."

"All right. We get up on the high ground there, we can hold them off for a while, maybe scoot out the west side and on down."

"Maybe," Sisson said. "We're leaving good tracks here. We ain't going to be hard to find."

"That's true enough, but I don't think it makes a hell of a lot of difference. We're going this way because it's the only way that makes sense. But it would take a six-year-old about four seconds to figure out that we're going to ride the riverbed south as long as we can.

"But we'll keep going for a while. Right now, I guess this is the safest spot we'll find. We can cut out of the river and head southeast at some point. Go a different direction. I'm thinking we can head for the Dragoons, then over the Chiricahuas, and then on to Mexico. There's people in the valley might lend a hand."

"All right," Sisson said. "Still, I'd like to not leave so many tracks. No sense to give them a clear trail."

"You're the best tracker in the state, I would guess."

"It won't take a good tracker," Sisson said. "Just one who can see."

They stopped under an overhanging mesquite, its exposed roots twisted and gnarled white in the pale moonlight. Sisson took a blanket from his saddle roll and began cutting it with a jackknife. He handed Tom two long pieces of the blanket. "Cut those into long strips, so we can tie these on." Sisson went on cutting the rest of the blanket into ten-inch squares. When he had cut two dozen, he doubled them, then cut one-inch slits into the four corners. He turned to Tom, who was still sawing at the blanket with his knife.

Sisson reached out, took the piece of blanket from Tom, and started pulling off long strips, tearing down the warp of the cloth. "I know you lost your momma early on, but you had a grandmother and a sister. Didn't you ever watch them work cloth?"

"Didn't need to. I had you."

Sisson nodded and grunted and began threading the long strips of cloth through the slits in the blanket squares. He handed several to Tom. "This part's easy."

When they were done, each horse had two pieces of blanket wrapped on each hoof, securely tied on by lengths of blanket. Instead of clear prints, the horses left soft, nearly formless depressions in the riverbed. "We should go this way a couple more miles. Let some of them get out of the riverbed here, keep the rest confused. Most will stay in the bed. So we'll need to get away from it in a bit."

It was past midnight when they came to the Johnson mine. They had been out of the river sand for over an hour. There was no light, no evidence of life at the mine, but somewhere, there was someone. At least a watchman would be on duty, though likely asleep. They stopped, watered the horses, which were still hoof-wrapped, and filled their canteens. While Sisson and John watered the horses, Tom crept up the trail toward the mine, looking for things they could use. He found only a shovel and, over the block of a gasoline engine that powered a generator, a canvas tarp, ten feet square. He cut the ropes that secured it, folded it, and put it on his back, securing it with his belt so his hands were left free. He stopped when he heard footsteps to the front and right. He crouched behind a creosote bush and waited, not moving. When he heard nothing else, he scuttled back to the horses.

They had nearly six hours of darkness left to them, so they abandoned their plan to rest in the hills above the mine, made their way back to the river, and kept moving nearly due south. They came back into the river nearly a mile from where they had left it, creating a gap in prints that would confuse anyone tracking them.

When they had gone several more miles, they spotted the train trestle over the San Pedro. They were now just twenty miles from the Little Dragoon Mountains, but that was too much distance to cover before daylight.

"What do you think?" Tom asked Sisson. "Where do we stop for the day?"

"There's no high ground between here and the Little Dragoons, only hills and ridges."

"Can we stay here? We're pretty tucked away under here."

Sisson shook his head. "I think this place is too good. Thems'll come looking here. Hardest thing about tracking Apaches was that they were always able to figure out what we knew about them and then do something else. I'd recommend the same. The last place I would look for three men on the run is out there in the middle of the flat. It's my mind to get out there and hunker down while they search out the good hiding places. We can get behind a little ridge or something and just stay low."

"That's a gamble."

"What ain't? It's all a gamble now."

"All right then."

"Do you think they know? Do you think they got a posse up yet?" John asked.

Tom started to scoff, but Sisson responded. "Hard to say. There's time for them to get up to the mine and back to Klondyke. Whether they been or not, I got no idea."

They heard the noise first, coming from the east, coming at them. They moved closer to the riverbank, right under the trestle, tucked under the chaparral. Soon they saw the light. Sisson jumped off his horse and motioned for the brothers to dismount as well. When they had, he took the horses and led them back down the bed toward a clump of mesquite.

The truck slowed and stopped, then slowly began to make its way across the railroad trestle, bouncing from tie to tie. It stopped on the trestle, just beyond where Tom and John crouched in the dark. Tom could see it was a railbed truck, and in the back was a number of men. He could hear them talking but could not get a count on them. There were a lot, though. Maybe ten. Maybe more.

"Some of you men get down there under that trestle. See if they're there."

Nearly simultaneously, Sisson and Tom pulled their rifles from the scabbards on their saddles. They held the rifles, not cocking them for fear of the noise but holding them at the ready.

"You want someone to go down there?"

"Hell, yes, I want someone to go down there."

"Well, I want to get this goddamned truck off the tracks before a train comes through."

"Well, I want the men who shot my brother. One of you ignoramuses get down there and look under the damned bridge. I want those bastards dead and buried before sunup so we can all get some sleep." Tom recognized this as the voice of Braz Wootan, Kane's brother.

They heard the rustling then of the man coming down the embankment. Tom levered back the hammer on his rifle. He looked back to see where Sisson was. He couldn't see him, but he heard the click of the lever action on Sisson's gun. That near froze him, but it didn't stop the man coming down the embankment for a second. He heard the thud of boots as the man made the last small way from the bank to the bed. Tom could just barely make out his outline.

Tom sighted the rifle. He had him. That was no problem. But the second he shot him, the ones on top of the trestle would go for their guns. And they would be shooting down. Tom and Sisson would be trying to sight and shoot up, a much more difficult job.

He felt the drizzle and recoiled instinctively. When he did, he lost his sight on the man who had climbed down the embankment and who was coming very close to where Tom was crouched in the darkness.

"Damn it all," the man yelled. "Who's pissing off the bridge? Stop that. Damn it all. I'm getting out of here before I get drowned in piss." And with that he turned and started scrambling his way up the embankment.

"Did you see anybody?" a voice asked.

"There ain't no one down there. And if there was, Lyman just pissed them to death. Damn, it's on my hat and everything."

"Well, come on then," the first voice said. "Let's get moving. We can still cut them off before they can get to the Little Dragoons. Let's get them sons of bitches."

Then the truck fired up again, and there was a general slamming of doors and creaking as men climbed into the bed of the truck, and then it started on its way, bumping from tie to tie on the trestle and then off and toward some road.

"God, that was close," Sisson said.

Tom was brushing the piss from his hat and coat. "Closer than you know, I guess. I'll be stinking of some Mormon's piss for a while."

"Well, it's better than bullets. You can't just brush off lead."

"I suppose. It ain't the first time I been pissed on by Thems, and I guess I know it ain't the last."

"Stink is better than dead, I'd say."

CHAPTER FOUR

1896

Jeff came up a small draw onto the mesa where he had seen the cattle. There were a number of them, maybe three dozen, grazing in the sweet grass. Of the three dozen, less than a dozen were his. He swore. This was the fifth time in three weeks he had had to ride out, hunt down the cattle, and separate his from the rest so he could drive them back to his grazing land.

Cattle naturally congregated in the best grazing areas, and cowboys came out after them, cut their own from the herd, and drove them back. A couple of ranchers let their cattle go where they would and cut them in the fall for market or to shelter over the winter. No one ever got back as many cattle as he set out. Cattle were stupid beasts that would get themselves poisoned, lost, snakebit, tangled in wire, picked off by lions or bears, or gathered up with someone else's herd and shipped to slaughter and turned into silver for another man's pocket.

Ranchers were fond of bemoaning all that as the cost of doing business. And for those who could afford to do business that way, Jeff supposed they were right. He wasn't one of those. The ten beeves he was running now were pretty much his entire stock, except for a couple of horses, a mule, and six goats. In the years since he had joined the Morgan family, a herd of two hundred had dwindled down to the ten that were inextricably lost among the rest of the free-ranging cattle.

It had not been his fault. Some of it was, maybe. But not all of it. There had been a decline in the market for horses not long after Jeff and Will Morgan had sold most of Sebe's cattle and bought horses. They lost thirty-eight horses to the sleeping sickness. It was a run of rotten luck. They had tried to wait it out, but while they waited on the market, the horses kept eating, foaling, sickening, breaking bones, and just dying off. Each new foal that increased the herd by one increased the expenses by some multiple of that. Sebe, it turned out, hadn't been as successful raising cattle as Jeff had thought. He was running a lot of debt, more debt than cattle. They had sold the Texas ranch and put the money into cattle in the high hills of New Mexico, close to Silver City, back when Charlie was still on the tit.

Sebe had not been happy. His son and new son-in-law, he was happy to tell anyone who would listen, were as ignorant as they were proud of what they supposed to be their wisdom, intelligence, and ambition. But what Sebe saw was only the greed, incompetence, and brash, unfounded confidence of the merely young. But he was old and getting bad busted up, gored by a bull two years earlier, the wound never healing right and leaving him slow and pained. The work got left to the boys and, with it, the management of the ranch. It was like burning money. He gave it all another two years, maybe three, and they'd all be broke, but he was pretty much done anyway, and if wanting had any power, he'd be dead by then, though he was fond of little Charlie and would miss seeing him grow up.

Sebe's pain and waning interest in anything that required him to get up or even wake up left a vacancy of intelligence and experience in running a ranch. Will and Jeff Power put their heads together and came up with a series of plans for their future success that put them all on a beeline for the poorhouse.

Nature, and that is everything you can actually think of, abhors a vacuum. So where there was no good sense or even common sense, the vacuum attracted intelligence, grit, and power. And that was Granny Jane Power, Jeff's widowed mother. Sebe thought her a holy terror and tried his busted-up best to just get out of her way.

Following the news of Mattie's pregnancy, Granny Jane had arrived at the Morgan ranch on a freight wagon with a trunk full of clothes, both men's and women's, which she wore indiscriminately, three cast-iron skillets, a Winchester slide-action 10-gauge shotgun, and four pounds of plug tobacco. She moved into the family, the kitchen, and the authority of the household easily and immediately, sending Sebe into a brooding silence on the front porch of the house, where he remained nearly constantly, except for dinner and supper.

When Jeff broached the idea that it might be time to sell the ranch and leave Texas and head west, Granny Jane simply declared the idea passed, with Jeff, Will, and Mattie in agreement with her. Sebe held the deed to the ranch, but he had no power to enforce his will over this new coalition that had arranged itself around the goddamned Powers and that was headed, or at least voiced, by Granny Jane, though Sebe was never sure whether ideas originated with her or with Jeff.

The first time Sebe had stood up to her and tried to enforce the idea that since he was the eldest male and held deed to the ranch, his was the natural, legal, and God-given authority for the ranch, Granny Jane had pulled the 10-gauge Winchester from the corner of the dining room where she kept it, jacked home a shell, and said, "Jeff don't care. I don't care. And this shotgun don't care what in hell you think about how to run this place." He moved out to the front porch with a bottle of sour mash and glared hard at the horizon. That and eating were his main occupations for the remainder of their time in Texas.

It was the natural stupidity of cattle that made for most of the work on a ranch. Cows couldn't figure what to eat that wouldn't kill them, wouldn't stay together, and wouldn't stay put. Jeff looked over the herd, riding slowly through them, trying to identify his cattle by brand. He found four of them together and a couple more some fifty rods away. But the rest were scattered among the neighboring cattle. He kept riding, picking out his beeves, driving them over to the others, only to have them wander off somewhere else to be rounded up again.

It was getting late, and he needed to get them back to his small ranch before the broker came by tomorrow. Finally, in exasperation, he cut fifteen cattle, eight of which were his own, and headed them back across the hills toward home. Three others just followed behind. The cattle were all branded, and he reckoned that the broker could sort them out, crediting each ranch with the proper amount.

The next morning the broker came. He went over the little herd carefully. Jeff was going to explain that some of the cattle were not his and that the broker could simply hold that money for the rightful owners. But the broker ran his hands over the mismatched brands and said nothing. In the end, Jeff got paid for eighteen head, six more than he actually owned. The broker's men came and took the cattle and headed them on. It was the most profitable transaction that Jeff had ever completed. He held on to the money for the six beeves that weren't his, and he waited a couple of weeks for neighboring ranchers to complain about the loss of their cattle. None did.

It seemed simply part of the cost of doing business. If the broker didn't give a damn about brands, Jeff didn't see why he should. He had had a prosperous year and would have the funds to double his run next year. New Mexico, he thought, less burdened by ethics and intelligence than Texas, was a damned good place to do business.

And he did well. He increased his herd by nearly triple in two years. His first boy, Charlie, survived the croup and the measles and thrived under the care of Mattie and Granny Jane. The second boy, John, followed soon after, in the spring of 1891. He was a big, raw-boned boy who sailed through the first treacherous twelve months of his life without much more than snotty noses and achy ears.

The news of the shooting came when Charlie was two and John one. Mattie was again pregnant. Two ranchers had gotten into it over the rightful ownership of a couple dozen cattle. What had begun as simply the vagaries of business and the laxity of the cattle broker had grown over the years until it became outright theft. While most of the ranchers running cattle around Duck Creek were willing to let some of their cattle be sold by a neighboring rancher while they sold another's cattle, so long as the numbers came out more or less right, the numbers were now getting further and further from right.

Jeff had been careful to increase his herd through the sale of other cattle only slightly, taking one or two cattle from other herds, rarely coming in with more than six or eight cattle that weren't his. It gave him a slight advantage in a highly speculative business, and it was just enough to not arouse a lot of suspicion. He was always careful to leave a couple of his cows on the range for others to pick up, just to keep the appearance of fairness. He was not making a lot of money, but he managed to increase the size of his herd and to turn small but steady profits each year.

Will knew what Jeff was doing, and they supposed Sebe knew as well. Sebe's knowledge of the business presented no threat, as Sebe, unless he was eating, sleeping, or shitting, was sitting on the porch alone, trying to stare down the horizon or whittling sticks until they were nothing more than an excuse to cut himself, whereupon he would throw the bloody stick away and start another.

But McCrory and Walters, two ranchers from just north of Silver City, both prosperous and fully expecting to become even more so, began to eye each other's prosperity, supposing that it came at their own expense. One of McCrory's men shot Walters's middle son near the stock tank, arguing that the Walters boy had been cutting McCrory cattle into his own string. Walters's son had, in fact, done that, but the McCrorys had always taken their share of Walters's cattle, too. A district judge in Silver City found the evidence too slight to indict a hand from one of the most prosperous ranches in the area.

Tensions mounted. There was no more killing in the winter of 1892–93, but the feed and supply in Silver City was stocking more and more barbed wire. In the spring, Mattie gave birth to their third son, Thomas Jefferson Power, Jr. He was born small and sickly but grew to be small and tough.

Jeff hated barbed wire. It was bad for business. But that spring there were crews out every day, stringing the damned stuff across the valley, sectioning out each ranch. Surveyors weren't used. Each rancher had a fair idea of where his ranch left off and his neighbor's began. But the ranchers never agreed on the boundaries and often argued that one ranch's wire cut into another's land.

Jeff tried to ignore the whole business, letting his cattle run where they had always run and leaving it to other ranchers' wire to keep them in more or less the same position. The problem was the stock tank. While Jeff had running water on his land, the water routinely gave out in late spring and did not come back until after the July rains. The stock tank had always been considered communal property, and all the ranchers contributed to its upkeep. Jeff had spent a good number of hours twenty feet off the ground, freeing jammed gears and straightening bent windmill blades. But the tank and mill weren't on his property, and he was given notice by McCrory that it was going to be fenced in with McCrory's land and that Jeff needed to make some other arrangements.

That meant digging a well and putting up a windmill, and that was a significant outlay of cash, especially for what had been free for as long as anyone could remember. While Jeff had more money than he had ever had before, the expense was going to be a heavy one, and he reasoned that McCrory ought to bear some of the burden of the new equipment. One afternoon he rode with Will and cut ten unbranded yearlings from McCrory's herd. That, he figured, ought to be just about right to make up for his new expenses. He spliced the fence back together at the post, doing a neat job so that it couldn't be seen unless you were right up on it. He branded the yearlings, went to town, hired two men, and set out to dig his well.

Next door, shots were fired. No one was killed, but McCrory's men, finding the yearlings missing and, later, the fence cut, took shots at Walters's men, and Walters's men shot back. As long as they were shooting at each other but not killing each other, Jeff thought things were going as well as could be expected, given that ranching was hard work.

But McCrory's foreman took a bullet to the hip, which crippled him. The law was called, and there was an inquest into the shooting and the rustling of the cattle. No one ever rode out to check his herd without a gun now. There was a lot of shooting going on, and Jeff, afraid to cut more cattle out of other herds, was seeing his prospects wither.

One day, in Silver City for supplies, Jeff overheard two men he didn't know talking about the difficulties of what was now being called "The Duck Creek War." He reasoned that the two strangers were hired men brought in to increase someone's odds as the shooting intensified. As the two threw names around, indicating who might or might not need their service, or might need to be "serviced," Jeff heard the name Power. He thought the old animosities would keep suspicion off him, but here, it seemed, it was. But maybe not. He didn't want to find out the hard way. Jeff thought it was time to leave Duck Creek. He had heard that there was good money to be made in lumber over at Cliff, New Mexico. He knew that cattlemen talked to cattlemen, and, sooner or later, no matter where he went, news of his sudden departure from the Silver City area would catch up to him, and he would not be able to get the stink of it off him.

Chapter Five
1918

Anyone else might not have noticed that the sky had lightened at all. But Sisson motioned to a thin ridge and tree line just ahead, and they rode for it, knowing dawn was just ahead of them and that they needed to be hidden before it broke full.

They hobbled the horses far apart. The horses didn't like the separation and neighed back and forth to each other. The separation was going to make remounting more difficult and slow, but three horses hobbled together were sure to attract attention. Opportunity was built on calculated risks. They took their saddles and packs with them and walked to the other side of the ridge. By first light, John's eye looked better, and Tom's looked worse. There was another streak of scab down John's cheek, but it was old and looked like the last blood had come hours ago. His eye had gone completely blue, but the swelling did not seem so bad. Tom's eye was also going blue and swollen now.

Sisson went through the packs and brought up a loose paper package. It was corn bread he had cooked. When? Not last night but the night before, when they were settled in the cabin and had thought about nothing except their aches and the need to get back into the mine the next morning. When he unwrapped the package, the corn bread had disintegrated into loose crumbs, some bits of it big, most of it just cooked meal. He took a chunk and passed it to John. They kept passing the package around, taking what chunks there were, then scooping crumbs together and pressing them into bite-sized pieces.

"Is this all the food we got?" John asked.

"There's some cans—meat and peaches and tomatoes. But we ain't got much. We'll forage as best we can."

"I'm really hungry."

"Get used to it," Tom said.

"You should have packed more food," John told Sisson.

"Yeah, and we should have brought a mule train, too, to tote our stuff. The stove would have been a good thing to bring, and the cots, too."

"Shut up, Tom. I'm just saying. We can have a fire. We ought to have something to cook on it."

"No fire," Sisson said.

"Why not? It's going on daylight. No one's going to see a fire out here."

"Look at what's around us," Tom said, indicating the grass and chaparral of the valley. "You see anything that's going to burn without sending up a column of smoke? This shit here's just smoke that ain't been lit yet."

"When we get to the mountains," Sisson said, "we can have a fire then. The trees will bust up the smoke so it won't be so plain. We're going to need it more then, too. We got a box of matches. That's it."

"Fucking Indian scout," John said.

"That fucking Indian scout is going to keep us alive. Don't you ever forget who's after us. And don't forget Thems wants us dead. Thems don't care nothing about law. The law's only an inconvenience to Thems. Thems thinks Thems're above the law, and Thems may be right. Thems catch us, ain't no law going to save us."

They took turns sleeping. John took first watch because he had slept most of the night as they rode. He took a spot near the crest of the ridge where he was partially sheltered by a pile of rock. He had a good view of the north and east where any posse was likely to come either from the northern road that went to Tucson or out of the riverbed to the west.

He had the binoculars, though he had to hold them to the side of his face so he could look through the left ocular with his right eye. Otherwise, the left eyepiece touched his swollen left eye, and he could barely stand the pain. Sweeping the glass from his right to his left, east to west, he saw only a few cattle grazing some distance away. There seemed to be no auto or horse traffic on the road. As he glassed back the way he had already looked, he saw movement. He reached down and touched the rifle beside him.

It was a herd of pronghorn antelope, a good-sized one, maybe a dozen or more, coming hard out of the east, not far from the playa, a dry lakebed that once or twice a year filled to a depth of a foot or so. Instinctively, he brought the gun up to await the approach of the antelope. Antelope was good meat, lean, stringy, but sweet, like deer meat. As they approached, John shouldered the rifle, only to take it down again. He was hungry, but he couldn't risk a shot, even if it meant giving up a good supply of meat for the run.

He thought what Tom would say. He was stupid. They were hiding in the middle of the desert in nearly plain sight, and John took to blasting away at some pronghorn. And they got caught. And shot. Or hanged. He was stupid. Only he had not done it. He hadn't shot the antelope. He wasn't so stupid, maybe. It didn't matter what Tom thought.

He wasn't smart like Tom. He had known that since they were little. Tom wasn't more than seven or eight when the Old Man had begun to favor him. It didn't matter that John was strong and tough and could outwork many full-grown men. The Old Man looked on Tom different. John would catch them exchanging words, sometimes even just glances, and would know that there was something that the Old Man and Tom understood and he didn't. It was like they could see, and he was blind, at least to some things. Or that they spoke some language that he didn't, though they all spoke Mexican pretty well.

And then one of them would up and say the thing he most hated to hear. "It's all right. Don't worry on it." Like he wasn't supposed to worry or even think. He was like a horse that chewed on the corral. It wasn't something you wanted it to do, but it done it anyway. Soon as your back was turned, it was eating the corral rails again. And the only thing you could do was to kick it. He was that horse. He couldn't stop thinking, because that was his nature, but he knew he wasn't supposed to be doing it.

Once when he was thirteen and Tom was eleven, Tom had come on John while he was working on the wheel bearings of a wagon that had busted down. He was struggling to get the bearing, washer, and castellated nut on when Tom had just come up on him from behind and said, "It don't go that way."

"What?"

"It don't go that way. You got it ass backward."

John did the work of a grown man. There was never any thinking that maybe he couldn't do something a man was supposed to do. Tom stayed around the Old Man, helping, watching. That's what Tom did—watched. John worked, Tom watched. Only now he wasn't just watching, he was telling John what to do.

"You want to do it?" John asked, flipping a pair of pliers at Tom.

Tom batted the pliers down. "I don't want to do it. You do it. Only do it right."

"You ain't the Old Man."

"No, I ain't. I was the Old Man and I had a kid as dumb and ugly as you, I'd a drowned it in the rain barrel first time I saw it. You don't know how lucky you are."

What happened next was something of a blur in John's memory, like he had brushed up against something and smudged it. He only knew he had Tom on the ground and was beating on him with his fists, trying to make Tom's face dissolve into the ground.

And when he finally quit beating on Tom because he had already beat all the fight out of his brother, John thought, for a minute or two, he had won. He was the older brother, and he was going to be treated like the older brother. But later, when the Old Man had seen Tom's busted-up face and dragged him over to where John was and pushed Tom forward like the evidence of something that got broke and asked, "What the hell have you little spitwads been up to?" John couldn't answer.

"Nothing," Tom said.

"Nothing, hell. Your face looks like the bottom of a stall after a good mare fuck."

"It wasn't nothing. We was just fooling," Tom said.

The Old Man glared at Tom like he was going to hit him, then just shook his head. "You little turds. I wouldn't mind so much if you was to just go ahead and kill each other, except for the trouble and expense of burying you."

The Old Man turned and strode off. Tom looked at John and just grinned. At that moment, John understood he had lost. He was the older brother, but he was going to spend the rest of his life doing what Tom wanted. Tom would figure stuff out, and John would be left to do it.

And that was the trouble. Tom was always figuring stuff out. This whole thing, the killing, the running, smelled like something Tom had cooked up. It didn't make sense any other way. John was not as smart as Tom, but he wasn't stupid, either. He didn't understand much about war, except there was one, but it was someplace else. Someplace over there. And he knew that he and Tom were expected to go, but they weren't going to go. The Old Man had said that when Thems came to Rattlesnake Canyon, Powers would fight for it. But the Power family would be damned in hell before they fought for England or France or any other people they didn't know and didn't give a damn about.

But that was no reason for the law to come after them, shooting. And the law had brought six hundred rounds of ammunition. It takes a long time to shoot up six hundred rounds. They had planned on a fight before they ever got to Rattlesnake Canyon, and they had planned on a long fight. He couldn't calculate why they planned on the fight. It didn't make any sense at all.

But Thomas "Kane" Wootan was in on it, and that made its own sense. Wootan was a cowboy, too, and the Power brothers and the Wootans kept getting thrown together. And lately Tom and Kane had been together more than usual, and that bothered John. Kane was trouble, even if Tom and his sister, Ola May, had favored Kane some. If Tom wasn't trying to kill Kane, he should have kept his distance from him. But they had been up to something together, Kane and Tom, and Kane was with the law when Thems came up Rattlesnake Canyon. However this ended, John was willing to bet big that Tom and Kane Wootan had a lot to do with how it got started.

Wootans and Powers weren't a good mix, though Tom and Kane kept getting themselves mixed together. Kane wanted what Tom wanted, easy money. And John knew easy money was always hard to come by. But Kane and Tom kept looking for some way to grab ahold of any money that could be the least bit loose.

John had run across Kane Wootan when he was riding out to get horses for a pack up to the mine. John had seen the lone rider in a cienega not too far from the Garden cabin, which was their home and base camp, though there wasn't nobody to live there now, except them, and John didn't think it likely he and Tom would be back there soon.

"I thought this might have been my horse," Kane Wootan had said, indicating the roan he had cornered between some rock and a great pile of deadfall washed down by the creek. Kane had worked out a lasso and was holding it at his far side so that maybe John couldn't see it. But John saw the lasso, and the gun, too.

"It ain't," John said.

"Yeah. Well, I see that now."

"I bet you do."

"Look, Powers. It's a mistake, and it's my mistake. All right?"

"It's 'Power,' not 'Powers.' I don't even know anyone named 'Powers.'"

"Well, damn, Power. I'm just full of mistakes this morning, I guess."

"You got a mistake in your hand over there on the other side. And there's another riding your hip."

"I made a mistake. All right? A mistake. I'm sorry."

"You're all full of mistakes, Wootan. The worst one is thinking you can just take one of our horses with not a bit of trouble."

Wootan brought his right hand up slowly and then carefully looped the rope around his saddle horn as if to show he no longer had use for it. But the same action also freed up his right hand in case he needed to go for his gun. "There," he said to John. "That make you feel any better?"

"I don't guess I'm going to feel any better until I can't see you anymore."

"Look. I lost a horse. It's a little roan, just like this one here, only it's got a bit of white under the right eye, which this one ain't. I see that now. You say it's your horse, it's your horse. And I don't mean any harm."

"What's going on here?" Tom asked, riding up.

"He says he lost a horse." John nodded at Wootan.

"And so he found one of ours," Tom said.

"It's yours. I got no argument. I also ain't got no idea who you stole it from, but it wasn't me, so it ain't any of my business."

"It's a horse thief calling us horse thieves, John. What do you think we ought to do about that?"

Suddenly, John was worried. He was apt to fly off the handle and cause trouble and violence, but when he calmed down, he didn't want trouble. Tom was the opposite. Tom thought about trouble before he started it. He was thinking about trouble right now. John could tell, and he didn't want any of it. "He says it was a mistake."

"And don't they always say it was a mistake? Life is just one big mistake for some people."

"Let him go, Tom. Just let him ride off."

"I ain't looking for trouble," Wootan said. "Like your brother says, Tom, just let me ride off."

"You don't want trouble, Kane, don't come out here."

"You're all talking pretty big, the two of you. If my brothers was here, you wouldn't be talking this big."

"We don't change our talking because of the company."

"All right, then. How about you meet us tomorrow down to Klondyke?"

Tom smiled and nodded. "We'll do that, then."

And they had. Both Tom and John took off at daybreak and made their way down Rattlesnake Canyon and then up Rattlesnake Mesa and back down to Klondyke. Both were armed, and John was about to throw up over the tension of it all. Tom rode easy and took a shot at a white-tailed deer but missed. It seemed like he was on his way to a social.

When they got to Klondyke, there was no fight. The Wootans were there, Joe, Braz, and Kane, and they were armed, too. But no one ever reached for his gun. There was bootleg whiskey there, and everyone had a couple of good drinks of that and talked about the weather, which was unusually dry, and someone, maybe Joe, had said some things about the war, which was pretty much the first time John had heard about the war over in France. And then they all just got on their horses and rode back the way they had come. No one talked about roping horses or cows or goats or anything. It was as though they had all come to town to sample the latest in illegal whiskey, which, perhaps, they had.

There were more antelope, small herds of them, crossing the valley. John badly wanted to shoot one. He was hungry, getting hungrier, and figuring that the prospects for satisfying that hunger weren't good. He had more of the corn bread crumbs in his coat pocket, and there were some beans back at the camp where Tom and Sisson were sleeping. The beans would be eaten cold, but that sounded fine to him.

Then there was another herd of antelope, only as it got closer, he saw it wasn't antelope but riders. He put the binoculars to his eye and glassed them. He recognized a couple of them, cowboys he had worked with a time or two, and Johnny, who worked the Klondyke store on and off. But what really caught his attention was the one riding lead—Braz Wootan, Kane's brother, the one who had been in the truck the night before. If they spotted John or the others, there would be a fight. There was no question. Braz wasn't the sort to wait on justice for Kane. He would try to settle scores right there.

There were five of them, heading west, maybe 250 rods, maybe a whole mile to the north. They were moving slow now, and John figured they were picking up tracks, though it was a traveled area with grazing horses and cows, and John's, Tom's, and Sisson's horses still had the blanket coverings on their hooves. Any tracks they left would be indistinct, but there would be tracks.

Then the group stopped, and someone, John couldn't tell if it was Wootan or one of the others, pointed down toward them and their grazing horses. He pressed himself harder in the basalt of the little ridgeline and kept the glass low and covered it with his left hand so it wouldn't shine out like a spotlight for the riders. They were having a confab, maybe an outright argument. The pointing one wanted to come down and take a look at the horses. John was sure of that. But the cowboy was getting an argument. It was like Sisson said. No one would think them stupid enough to camp out smack in the middle of the valley. The men argued a bit more, then John froze as they wheeled south toward him and the camp.

He scrambled down the ridge and into the flat, crabbing it on all fours, keeping his head and butt as close to the ground as he could. The binoculars bounced along the ground as he went. Tom was asleep, but Sisson was awake and sitting up. John pushed Tom's legs with his hand as he crawled over him to where Sisson was. "Five of them, coming this way."

Tom was awake now, his gun already in his hands. "Where are they?"

"Just north. Not a mile, I don't think. Coming this way. Not riding hard, maybe tracking as they come."

"Is it law?"

"Worse. It's Braz Wootan."

"Fuck me," Tom said. "Just fuck me."

John came upright then, sitting on his heels, waiting on Tom and Sisson, who were looking at each other, then back out over the landscape around them. John waited. He had done his job, and now Tom would have to give him another. There was only to wait.

"All right," Tom said. "Sisson, you and John crawl back up to that ridge where John was. I'm going to try to snake around the back over here and get to the other side of the horses. What I'm going to do is to pick off one of them, Wootan, if I can. That will spin them around toward me. You ought to be able to get at least a couple of them right off the break of it. I can move then and try to work for one or two more. If they're caught between us, we ought to take them."

"That will be some good shooting," Sisson said.

"It will, and I would rather not have to do it. Maybe they'll slip by us. Take your saddles and packs so they can't see them. I'll stow mine under that mesquite. Don't shoot until someone else does. Me or them. I think we'd be better off hid than shooting. That's our best chance."

Sisson nodded grimly, and he and John gathered up their gear. Tom threw them a couple of boxes of ammunition each, then scuttled off, low to the ground to get into the mesquite tree.

When John and Sisson had reached the ridge, the riders had come closer, but not a lot. They were moving slow, maybe still trying to find tracks, maybe being careful not to stumble into an ambush. John pushed himself hard into the basalt and kept his head down. He fought the impulse to just sit up straight, draw a bead on the lead rider, and fire. The odds on that weren't good, and it would certainly send one of the riders back the way he had come, and that would bring more riders and the rest of the posse down on them.

A fight was the last resort. He did understand that. What he was supposed to want was to see the riders skirt past them and on toward the Little Dragoon Mountains or, even better, farther east, away from the path they intended to take. As long as the posses didn't know their whereabouts, the posses would spread out and cover as much territory as they could. Once Tom and John and Sisson had been spotted, a posse would be bearing down, and it would be time to prepare to die.

Sisson was behind a creosote bush so that he could watch without being seen from a distance. There was no reason for John to raise his head at all. Still, it was a hard thing. It was what a rabbit did when it first sensed danger—just froze up and didn't move. But he was no rabbit, and he didn't like the feeling. He wanted to fight or run, but this was neither. It was a terrible thing to have a choice and have to choose the thing you least wanted to do. It was even worse because it might be the last thing he would ever do.

Sisson tapped him on the shoulder. John rolled over onto his back without raising up. Sisson pointed his hand toward the east and made a quick chopping motion, then raised his thumb up. They were moving the other way. Only then did John allow himself to raise his head just enough to finally see the riders going past them just to the east.

It wasn't over yet, though. Their horses were hobbled out that way. If the riders came up close to them, they could see the hobbles, or if they got close enough to spook the horses, they would figure it out. Then the fight would start, and John, Tom, and Sisson would be on the wrong side of the ridge, exposed to the south and east, where the riders would now be. John pushed himself back down into the ridge and waited, as he had done when he was a child, playing. He closed his good eye tight and waited for the shot.

But the shot did not come. Finally, John opened his eye and involuntarily moved his leg, dislodging some detritus. It clattered down the face of the ridge, and he pulled his leg up hard, dislodging even more. Sisson reached out and held John's leg, signaling that he should not move anymore. He could see the riders stop and turn around in their saddles. The riders were about three rods away, close enough to see them but far enough that they would be more shape than form. If the posse glassed the ridges, they could see them. Sisson turned his face toward the rock so his sweat would not cause his face to gleam in the sunlight, and John did the same. It was the childhood feeling again, the helpless waiting for what you could not foresee or control. And the tingling started at the back of his neck, the feeling that he was being watched, maybe through a rifle sight.

Sisson tapped him on the boot heel. John slowly turned his face toward the south to see the riders moving south, away from them.

"That was pretty close," Tom said. "How'd they get that close?"

"They just did," John said.

"They just did because you wasn't paying attention."

"No," Sisson said. "We ain't got no way to run. It's either going to be hide or fight for a while. You can't be glassing the distance every second. He was paying attention, and so was I. We saw them when we saw them. There wouldn't have been nothing to do if we'd seen them five minutes earlier."

"Shit. We're just out here in the open."

"We knew that when we chose the spot," Sisson said. "And it's as good as we're going to get until we reach the mountains."

"You chose the spot," Tom said. "Trying to think like an Apache, and you ain't no Apache."

"We all chose the spot. I made the suggestion, and it worked out all right. It worked out all right. They was within ten rod of us and went right on by. I'd say that worked out just about right."

"It worked, but it was a hell of a hard thing."

Sisson cast a baleful glance at Tom and snorted. Everything was hard. Sisson understood that. Tom was still learning it.

"All right," Tom said. "It worked and we're still alive. But we need to get up into those mountains where we can hide better and make a good stand if we have to."

"Wootan and them went to the mountains."

"I know that. But we can't stay down here. It's too risky. This trick ain't going to last forever. The Dragoons is big mountains. We got to get into them where the others ain't. That's all it is."

"I thought we was going to the Chiricahuas," John said.

"Eventually, but we can't get there right away. We can't spend a lot of time in the valley right now, and the Dragoons is closer than the Chiricahuas."

"How we going to stay up in those mountains without food?"

"How much we got, Sisson?"

"Not enough," Sisson said. "There's some cans of beans and some meat. That's about it. We can't stay up in the mountains in winter very long on that."

"All right," Tom said. "Before we head up there, we got to provision ourselves."

It was just dusk when they saddled up and headed southwest to the town of Pearce, ten miles away. The growing dark gave moderate cover. They would be able to see approaching cars or trucks from a long distance. They would be virtually invisible to riders at more than a half mile or so, but then, so would riders be invisible to them. They would rely mainly on their ears. There were fewer night sounds in February than there would be in just another month. The coyotes started up right away, yipping across the distances to mark their territories and passages. The owls would start up soon enough. Beyond that, it was quiet, save the concussions of horses' hooves, which were louder now, the muffles having been worn to shreds already and now discarded. There were trails to follow and roads, but they worked their way over them and parallel to them to avoid leaving clear tracks.

They were deep into the Sulphur Springs Valley now, rich grazing land and good, fertile soil for crops. It was the land of fences, and they used the fences to their own advantage, carefully prying out staples and holding the wire for the others to pass. One man could stand straight up on a bottom strand of wire and hold the top wires above his head, while the others could lead the horses through the fence. The staples would be driven back in their holes, and there would be no evidence that anyone had come this way. Besides, it was the right thing to do. Cowboys spent much of their lives riding and repairing fence lines. There were few men lower than the ignoramus hunters who came through land and simply snipped fences and left gaping holes that would have to be spliced and rehammered. And that could be done only after the stock, which had walked through the busted fence, had been rounded up and brought back to the right side of the fence.

Years earlier, John had caught two men, strangers, probably from Tucson or some other refuge of the worthless, driving cars across the valley in search of quail, snipping fences as they went, just driving right over and away from the ruins. When he had caught them, he had beaten the tall one with the stock of the little turd's own pretty shotgun, while the short one crouched inside the cab of the truck and whimpered. "I would appreciate it," John said, "if you was to go back where you came from and share that beating with the other worthless bastards you know who go around cutting fences so they can shoot a bunch of damn little birds." He rode off then, daring either of them to summon the courage to fill his back with birdshot.

They passed a couple of ranches, one with electric lights powered by a generator, chugging along in the early evening. If a ranch had electricity, it likely had a telephone, too, and they wanted none of that. Besides, ranches were full of dogs and chickens and other manner of noisemakers that could summon far too much attention.

Instead, they chose a small house on the edge of town where they could see the flicker of kerosene lamps sputtering in the windows. There were no wires going into the house. And they saw no dogs until they were almost to the front door, when an old black hound, maybe the oldest dog in the world, slunk toward them, head down, tail wagging. Tom went to the door and knocked while John and Sisson hung back, Sisson petting and rubbing the stinking old hound, whose tail wagged like a slow, creaking old metronome.

It was an old woman who came to the door, hair down, done for the day, and probably ready for bed. But she was still dressed and gave them a hard look, questioning the three riders, strangers, who had appeared at her doorstep after dark.

"Evening, ma'am," Tom said. He held his hat in his hands in front of him in a gesture of respect and decent intent in front of a lady.

"Has there been trouble?" she asked.

Tom's hand went up toward his damaged eye, then stopped. "I had an accident up to the mine yesterday. It was a cave-in. Some green timbers just snapped like twigs. We're heading south where we got family. We need some provisions. We have money. We can pay. We just lost all our food. I'm afraid the worst trouble is the trouble I'm causing you this evening."

"There are three of you?" She leaned out, squinting, trying to see and count in the dark.

"Yes, ma'am. Three. Me and my brother and our friend here. We're heading home. Get our people to go on up and help us dig it all out again."

"Your eye looks very bad."

"Yes, ma'am."

"You're not those boys they're wanting? From up in the Galiuros?"

"No, ma'am." Tom smiled. "I don't believe there's anybody wants us."

"And you want some food."

"Yes, ma'am. We have money, but there doesn't seem to be anywhere that's open to buy any. We're trying to get on down south. To our people."

"I have some bread and some beets and beans and tomatoes I put up last summer. I suppose you could have that."

"It would be appreciated, ma'am."

She turned then and went toward the back of the house, leaving the door open so that Tom could peer into the little house, which was neat and orderly and brought with it thoughts of his mother and Granny and even Ola May. A woman brought a sense of comfort and rightness to a place that a man didn't have on his own. But the women of the Power clan were all gone now. All three of them dead, and by now the Old Man, too. And Tom wasn't sure that there was a very good chance that he and John would live out the month. It was almost as if Thems' God had stood up and started to stomp the Power family right out of existence.

She came back then, a croaker sack cradled in her arms. She offered it, and he took it. "There's bread and beets, beans and tomatoes, some pickled cucumbers, a hunk of cheese, a big slice of ham I can't seem to get eaten, and half a can of coffee."

"Obliged, ma'am. We're certainly obliged for your help and kindness. How much money do we owe you?"

"I don't believe I'm owed. You need food and I have food. I don't see any 'owed' in that."

"That's a true kindness."

"I am a Christian woman, and I do my best to live that way. Others don't always, but I do."

"Yes, ma'am. I believe that's so."

"I do owe them at the store five dollars."

"It would be further kindness if you was to allow me to take that debt from you." He dug through his pockets and brought out five damp ones.

"I know who you are."

That froze Tom for a second or two.

"You're those Powers boys. The ones that shot the officers."

"'Power,' ma'am. Not 'Powers,' 'Power.'" He could kill her right now. It seemed what the situation called for. It would be an easy kill. There were lots of options. It wouldn't do to shoot her, not this close to the town, though that might work anyway. But a good blow from a pistol butt should take her down, or he could slice her throat with the knife in his back pocket. Or he could just reach out, grab her, and snap her neck. She was old and brittle. It would be no difficult task. She had only a short way to go to death anyway. "You're going to turn us in, then?"

"It seems that's what's right." There was a set to her jaw that reminded him of Granny Jane, who, having made up her mind about a thing, held on to it like a fox held a rat.

"Yes, ma'am. I suppose it does." He did not want to kill her. He had not wanted to kill the lawmen back at the mine. That was so much foolishness. But when someone tried to kill you, you did what it took to stay alive. He still found it difficult to believe that the business of yesterday had actually come down, since it was such a small thing that got it started. But that was the way of the world. Just a small shove got things started, then they went their own way. He considered taking her into the house and tying her up so that she could not tell until they were long gone.

That was better than killing her, but not much. It was a terrible thing to do to an old woman who was just doing what she thought was right, the way she had been brought up, believing all was good and evil. Tom just couldn't get himself to see things that clear.

"But I'm an old woman," she said. "I live alone and mostly mind my business. And I don't like to go out at night. When you get old, the dark isn't your friend anymore. The dark is for young people. You ever think on that? You start out afraid of the dark, and then, when you're young and strong and like to do those things that are best kept hid, you like it. But when you get old enough, you become afraid of it again. It's full of things that surprise you. So I don't go out at night, and I don't guess this night is a good deal different from any other. I don't want to trip over something or fall in a ditch and drown myself. I'll tend to my business when the sun is up."

"And that's another kindness, ma'am."

"No. It's just the way of the world. I don't think you should have killed those officers. I know that weren't right. But they ain't coming back, and I ain't quite ready to go where they are. I'll wait for the morning."

"A kindness," Tom repeated.

"Have it your way. There is kindness everywhere if you bother to look for it. It's free most of the time. You can afford to spend it because there's more of it left. It don't get used up like lesser things."

"Yes, ma'am. I suppose I don't always know the right place to look."

"If there's nothing further to do here, I would like to go to my bed now. You watch yourselves in the dark. There's not much moon up there, and there are irrigation ditches everywhere."

"So we have provisions, and we have the rest of the night. But they're going to know where we are in the morning," Tom said.

"Does that mean we're trapped?" John asked. "Wootan and his gang up in the Dragoons, the law coming at us down here?"

"Yes," Sisson said. "That means we're trapped."

"Getting trapped ain't staying trapped," Tom said. "A fox will chew its leg off to get out of a trap."

"Chew your own leg," John said.

Tom smiled. "Ain't going to be no leg chewing. A rat can swipe the bait out of a trap a couple of times before he gets caught. And that's what we're going to do."

Chapter Six

1894

Just outside of Cliff, New Mexico, they rented a cabin, too small for all of them. Jeff got on at the sawmill. It was hard work, but he liked it well enough. He had no known skill with the saw or any other dangerous equipment, and after he saw the second man carried from the mill with one less hand, he was content with his job of unloading logs from the wagons that came to the mill. The pay was not good, but his expenses were low. Their cabin cost a dollar a week, and there was plenty of game in the hills. Granny Jane was herself a decent hunter, nearly as good as Jeff. So though the rate of his prosperity had slowed, he continued to prosper, putting money into the bank every week.

In the winter of 1894, Mattie gave birth to a fourth child, though the third child, Tom, was still on the tit. This one, a girl, pleased her most. They named her Ola May, and while Jeff had wanted another son to increase the labor force, the entire family began to dote on the little girl. Even Sebe, who had given himself over to his dying, would ask Mattie to bring Ola to his bed, and he would hold her next to him, and the oldest of the family and the youngest slept away the afternoons. It was, Mattie thought, a blessing that Sebe spent his last few days cradling and loving a child rather than staring off into space trying to project his own bitterness onto the universe. When Mattie went to get Ola for her feeding one winter afternoon, the little girl was sleeping, cradled in the arms of her dead grandfather.

Mattie channeled her grief for her father into the care of her daughter, the quietest, happiest baby she had ever seen. Even by the time Ola May was old enough to crawl, she spent most of her time on Mattie's hip, and Mattie had learned to do just about everything one-handed. Mattie's life had moved from the last bit of Morgan to full Power like the silent, slow turn of a page.

Ola brought a certain softening to everyone else. The boys—Charlie, six, John, five, and Tom, two—played with and protected their baby sister as though she were as precious as the adults made her out to be. Jeff went for her first thing when he came home from the mill each evening, reeking of pine pitch. And Granny, who had maintained that they were doing the little girl a disservice by making her too precious, too delicate, found another side of herself—one she thought had disappeared some years ago—welling up again, and she began silently sewing dresses for the girl.

Cliff was prospering as growth settled on New Mexico, Arizona, and Texas. The sawmill added shifts, and Jeff took one of the new ones and added more money to his bankroll. But even extra shifts were not enough to keep up the new demand for lumber, a strong, cheap material. Workers were arriving in Cliff on nearly a daily basis, and new cabins quickly covered the hillsides.

A man from Nebraska named Ed Reed bought a small tract of land next to the Powers. He would work on his cabin in the afternoons and early evenings after his shift at the mill, eating supper most times with the Powers and sleeping in his unfinished cabin. As the demand for ponderosa pine lumber grew, so did the price of it. Trying to keep his costs in line with what he was earning, Reed found alternate materials for his cabin. For a ridgepole he felled a nice, straight alder nearly a foot in diameter. He nailed heavier than normal pine rafters to it, using the culls from the mill that were too warped, cupped, curved, or knotty to be worth shipping out.

He used the knowledge he had picked up in Nebraska and nailed thin sticks to the rafters, covered those with brush, and then covered the whole thing with sod. He had the only sod-roofed house in New Mexico.

"It's the finest material available," Reed explained. "It don't leak in the rain, holds the heat outside in summer and inside in winter, and can even be planted in the spring, so that a man can gather his supper simply by leaning a ladder against the roof of his house."

"How much does that damned thing weigh?" Jeff asked.

"Hell, I don't know. I don't have no plans to pick it up."

The boys were fascinated with the sod roof of the cabin and took to playing on it while Reed was at work. There were good rains that spring, and the roof had already greened and then turned colorful with delphiniums and, in the shade, red columbines. Mattie loved looking at it from her window, as their cabin sat some feet higher on the ridge. Granny thought the whole thing foolish and thought sleeping under flowers fit only for the addled and the dead.

"Mr. Reed," Mattie called from the empty doorway of Reed's cabin. "Mr. Reed, you have visitors, regretting any inconvenience to you."

They heard Reed coming through the woods before they saw him. He was a slight man, though wiry, strong in the shoulders and arms as farmers must be. He was wearing only a pair of overalls and an old pair of busted brogans that Mattie thought had surely been his church shoes at one time.

"If I thought I'd have visitors, I would have dressed myself some better," Reed said, wiping the dirt from his hands. "I'm clearing some stumps down there. You think cutting a tree is hard work until you have to pull the stump. That's when you understand what hard work is like."

"Mr. Reed, your house is a wonder. I never before saw a roof bloom."

"It's what I knew in Nebraska. But there, there ain't a lot of trees for cutting lumber, but there's God's own abundance of sod. So we build houses with it, walls, barns, whatever it is you need. I believe a good Nebraskan would eat sod if only it fried better."

"Well, it is truly beautiful, Mr. Reed. I believe you've met Mrs. Power." She gave a sweep of her hand toward Granny Jane as if introducing royalty.

"I have, most certainly," Reed said. "And it is a pleasure to do so again. And the lovely young lady in her arms there. She is growing up so fast."

"Ola is a year next month. The only girl in a pack of boys."

"That will prove a challenge to her in coming years," Reed said.

"She'll hold her own. A Power is a Power," Granny Jane added.

"That's so," Mattie said. "But we're hoping she's not the last daughter." She brought her hand up to her belly, which was just beginning to swell. "Of course, Jeff wants more boys."

"Well, of course," Reed said. "As I work them stumps down there, I have cause to regret my own lack of offspring. Especially boys." He looked over at Granny Jane. "But girls is good, too. I've known girls could hunt bear with a switch if there was the need."

"We brought you some things you might need. I'm afraid my husband is hanging on to the boys, though." She handed him a covered pan, then took Ola back from Granny Jane.

"Why, I thought I smelled corn bread."

"And here's a little rug that I braided myself," Mattie said.

"Why, that's a beauty, right there. That will brighten my life considerable. And it will keep my feet warm, too. Why don't you ladies come into my house? It's unmannerly for me to keep you standing out here. It's not much, just enough for an old bachelor such as myself. But perhaps you can choose a good spot for that rug. Ladies are better at that than men who have no calling for such."

"Why, this is a nice little cabin you have here," Mattie said. "Isn't it, Granny? It's almost as big as our cabin, and there's seven of us."

"Well, I ain't lost myself in it yet," Reed said.

"And you keep it so clean for a man alone."

"Well, here's the beauty of it. When your house is made of dirt, you can't tell what's dirt and what's house. If I was to polish too much, I might just wear it out."

"Well, right over here is where I would put the rug," Mattie said. She handed Ola May back to Granny Jane and unrolled the rug and went to place it next to the crude cot where Reed slept.

Granny Jane stepped forward, then back as she heard the creak and crack of wood. They all looked at each other as though this were the strangest and most terrifying thing they had ever heard. Then the ridgepole went on and broke the rest of the way, bringing the timbers and sod of the roof down on them.

Granny Jane bent forward, using her body to shield the baby from the avalanche of debris that came raining down. Reed jumped out the door and landed on the ground, rolling a couple of times before he came to a stop. Dirt and rocks and sticks came down on Granny's head, shoulders, and back. She brought the baby in tighter to her chest as she was buffeted by the falling roof. A chunk of sod came down and hit her on the back, sending her down into the pile of dirt on the floor of the cabin.

She lost consciousness and then fought back to it. Ola was still in her arms, and she knew right away that the baby was still alive. They were trapped, though, as Granny Jane had been driven to her knees and partially buried in the sod. What was holding her down was a couple of branches stretched across her back. She could not let go of Ola, so she twisted and pushed her back up, repeating these movements until she felt the force of the branches lessen. She held Ola in her left arm and began digging herself out with her right. Most of the sod had fallen in chunks on her, so though they were difficult to lift, once she got them up, she was able to get her legs free. She climbed over the debris to the door, still carrying Ola, and out to the sunlight.

Reed stood there outside the demolished cabin, mouth agape, his hands twitching and turning back and forth, like he was trying to shake something from them.

"The baby's all right," Granny yelled, trying to break the trance that held Reed. He didn't move. Granny Jane put Ola on the ground in a bed of pine straw and ran back into the cabin, clawing at the dirt with her bare hands. It was a mixture of clumped earth held together with roots and loose, silty soil. Some of the biggest chunks she could not move, the loose dirt just sifting between her fingers. The faster she dug, the more silt slipped back into the pile.

She clambered up and then out of the cabin and saw Reed just as he had been, and she ran next door, screaming for Jeff and Charlie. Jeff came on a dead run. Granny Jane did not frighten easily, and her fear frightened Jeff. When he got to the cabin, Reed stood there, mouth open, tongue slightly out, hands at his sides, twitching like a man who has just been hanged.

"Under there," Granny screamed. "Mattie. She's under there."

Jeff grabbed a shovel leaning against the door and began shoveling away dirt from the entrance to the cabin. "Where?" he screamed. "Where the hell is she?"

"Over there. Near the window."

He scuttled up the fallen roof toward the right side of the cabin and began again, shoveling toward his wife. He jammed the shovel into the debris, thought better of it, and, fearing he would hurt Mattie with the shovel, he fell on his knees and began clawing the dirt behind him, between his legs, like a dog.

He stopped that, took up the shovel again, and tried to push it slowly and carefully into the dirt so as not to cut or crush her if he hit her with the shovel.

This way moved the most dirt. He knew that. This was the most effective way, but it felt wrong, seemed to move too slow. It required him to move at a measured pace that did not fit his state of mind. His wife was buried under a ton of dirt, and he was methodically shoveling dirt away from her. It was wrong in some way he couldn't know. He threw the shovel aside once more and fell on his knees, clawing at the dirt with his hands. He screamed for Reed, he screamed for Granny and for Charlie. No one came. And then he saw that they were at his side, Granny and Charlie, not Reed. And they were clawing at the dirt, too. Even little Charlie, just five, but strong and fierce as a Power should be.

And it was Charlie who found her, or found the tiny floral print of her dress under his hands. He cried out, and Jeff and Granny began digging her out, exposing more of the dress with each scoop of dirt. It was a deep hole. Over two feet of the sod roof covered her body, and when they saw that it was her back they were uncovering, they knew but did not slow.

Their hands were raw and bleeding, all of them, even Charlie's, when Jeff was able to get his arms around and under her and to pull her back, her shoulders, and, finally, with a shower of dirt, her head. Then Granny and Charlie went to work on her legs and feet until Jeff was able to pull her free.

Her body. She was dead, as they had known she would be. Jeff, crying now, held her in his arms, her face covered with dirt so that her features were barely recognizable, her hair matted, her mouth plugged with dirt, and her body spattered with blood, which they would later understand was theirs, from their bleeding hands. Later, when they laid her out on the table in their cabin, undressed her, and washed her following Granny Jane's directions, they saw she had suffered no external wounds. She had been crushed and suffocated by the dirt suddenly coming down on her as if it were just one huge solid thing.

Jeff carried her outside the cabin and laid her on the ground, just beyond the door. Charlie knelt beside her, not crying yet, just touching her and brushing the dirt from her face, still not understanding what had happened. Granny Jane went to the pile of pine straw and picked up Ola May. She passed by Reed, who even yet was standing stock-still, eyes wide open, not blinking, staring beyond them at something they could not see, something immense, perhaps his own stupidity for trying to put a sod roof on green lumber or from using a just-felled tag alder as a ridgepole.

Jeff went back to the cabin, retrieved the shovel, and walked over to Reed. "You could have helped. You could have done something more than twitch. You killed my wife and child, and you didn't do a damned thing. Stop that twitching." He swung the shovel like a baseball bat, hard all the way around his body. It caught Reed on the shoulder, a tremendous whack, skittered upward, took off a couple inches of scalp and most of his left ear, and sent Reed sprawling onto the ground. Reed began to scream then, lying on the ground, knees pulled up to his chest, blood covering his face. Great wracking screams, not of pain but of some deeper agony. He had stopped twitching.

When her body had been washed, Mattie lay there on the table, naked, clean, and still, her hair wet from Granny Jane's washing with pine tar soap, her belly barely swollen with the baby she was carrying, their fifth child. Jeff ran his hand from her face across her chest, pausing at the swell of her belly. Granny Jane slapped his hand. "Get her dress. She's done with you now. Go on. Tend to your children."

Jeff hung in at the sawmill for eight more months. He bought a milk goat for baby Ola, and Granny Jane tended the children while he worked. He continued to put money by, raising his own food, keeping to himself. Ed Reed recovered, though he lost his ear, and his hair never quite covered over the thick, ropy scar. He apologized to Jeff and to anyone else who would give him a minute or even a few seconds. Jeff gave him only an icy stare in return, and the others learned to avoid him, especially in the evening when he had been able to drink and the whiskey pushed the guilt and grief out of him.

Finally, Reed just disappeared. No one saw him leave, no one knew where he went. He simply wasn't there anymore, and he hadn't been for some time that no one could figure with any precision. But the cabin remained, untouched since Mattie's death. For a while, Jeff seemed to take some comfort in staring at it, as if to stare it down like a bully and kill its power. Then one evening, after supper, not saying anything to anyone, he took a gallon of kerosene over to the cabin and burned the frame to the ground. They all watched it burn in the failing light, Jeff, the three boys, and even Ola May in Granny Jane's arms. And then they watched the embers glow in the darkness. No one said anything. When it was only the smell of smoke, they turned away, went back to their cabin, and slept.

Two weeks later, he gathered them up, put them in the wagon with a hastily built tent on the bed. Before he hitched the team, he went to Mattie's grave and promised her, "I'll come back for you." They began a ten-year journey from New Mexico to Texas, then Oklahoma, Kansas, Colorado, back to New Mexico, and then Texas again. Jeff worked whatever job he could find that paid a little money. He was a fine cowboy, but there wasn't enough money in cowboying to keep a family alive. So he worked as a laborer and a hand wherever he could. He was tight with a dollar. One of his friends claimed Jeff squeezed a dollar so hard the eagle farted.

In the winter of 1900, Jeff heard of good jobs in the sawmills of Alamogordo, New Mexico. He packed the wagon and family again in late February and made the cold trek to Alamogordo before spring, when he knew the rest of the itinerant laborers would get there. By mid-March he had a job unloading the log wagons as they came in from the mountains to the east. It was hard work, and though it paid much better than cowboying and was steadier, he worked harder than the pay he was getting seemed to deserve. He couldn't help notice that while he was unloading the wagons, the drivers disappeared and then returned when the wagon was empty and drove it off.

There were no openings for wagon drivers, and a foreman had told him that the company was tired of investing in wagons that broke down, in mules and oxen that broke their legs or collapsed from the weight they pulled, so they weren't likely to be hiring drivers. More and more, the company wanted to buy logs from independent loggers who would absorb the losses in stock and equipment themselves.

Jeff began buying raw lumber, especially hog lumber from the outside of the tree, usually barked and flat on only one side. He rebuilt and reinforced the wagon they had taken across country, the one they had lived in, and turned it into a log wagon. He bought two teams of oxen and talked four men from the mill into joining him in cutting and hauling lumber from the mountains to the mill.

Jeff's good eye for livestock served him well, and the teams of oxen, rotated between hauling and resting, held up and began making money soon after they started. His frugality proved valuable as well. By the end of the summer they had made a profit, socked some money away to expand the business, and split the rest. Jeff put Granny Jane and the children into a small house in Alamogordo, where the boys could go to school. Jeff and his new partners spent the late fall and winter building a base of operations at the four-thousand-foot level of the mountain, not too far from the tree line, where the pines grew, but not far enough up to be into the heavy snow, either. When weather permitted, they cut and hauled the lumber down, and when it didn't, they worked on the camp as best they could. By early spring, they had a good line cabin, corrals, and stables for the oxen and their horses. They began cutting and hauling full time again.

When Jeff returned from the mill in mid-April, only Melvin was at the cabin. The rest were looking for their sorrel mare, which had either jumped the corral or been stolen. They believed the latter. It would be difficult to find a stolen horse in these mountains. Gold and silver had been found at the base of the foothills, and it stood to reason that the horse had come down from the mountain itself. The canyons that drained the mountain's runoff were thick with prospectors and layabouts, trying for an easy strike. Any of a hundred or so could have taken the horse.

Jeff rode down one draw, looking for the horse, and then up the next. Sam and Melvin had given up the search, accepting the loss of the horse against the time spent looking for it, but Jeff was obsessed. The spring runoff was in full force, and he had to pick his way carefully, occasionally riding through streams swollen to near the height of his horse's belly.

On the morning of the fifth day, he came down a ragged little canyon and right up onto the sorrel mare, tied to a bit of scrub oak. A hundred yards farther on, he surprised a miner coming out of the brush, buttoning his fly.

"That horse," Jeff said.

"That horse, what?"

"Yours?"

The miner tilted his head at Jeff, a set to his jaw. "Yeah. Mine. What of it?"

"I don't think it's yours. I think it's mine."

"What are you trying to pull here, mister?"

"I ain't pulling nothing. I just want my horse back."

"That ain't your horse."

"You think it ain't my horse, but, by God, I know my own horse."

The miner turned and waved his hand at Jeff as if dismissing him for a fool. He took two steps forward to where his rifle rested against the trunk of a pine. Jeff saw where he was going, and as the miner reached for the rifle, Jeff let go with first one barrel of his 10 gauge, then the other. The miner was slammed into the brush next to the tree. Jeff did not need to look to know he was dead.

It was a hell of a thing. He had come only to collect his rightful property, and now there was a man dead, and there would be law involved. He was within his rights. The man was going for his gun, and he was a horse thief to boot. But the law was a slow and laborious process that was bound to cost Jeff far more than the horse was worth.

He was tying the sorrel mare to his saddle when he saw the small brush of white on its front leg. He brushed at it and knew that it was the horse's hair, not a dab of paint or lime. "Oh, fuck me," he said. "Fuck me, fuck me for a fool." He untied the sorrel mare, which he now knew was not his, remounted, and started up the trail to the camp when he thought better of it, turned around, and headed for Alamogordo.

"Pack up what you can," he told Granny Jane. "Leave the rest. I'll be back in an hour. As soon as the sun goes down, we're taking the children and getting out of here."

"What the hell have you done?" Granny Jane demanded.

"It don't need talking. It needs moving. We're out of here soon as it's dark."

Jeff went to the bank and took out half the money he and his partners had saved. When he didn't show up at work, Sam or Melvin or Zeke would come to the bank and find he had withdrawn his share and know he was out of it, fair and square. There should have been more, but they had spent considerable on improving the camp and the stock. He went back into the bank and withdrew half of the remainder. It was fair. They would have the business that he had come up with and had built himself.

After dark, the six of the Powers started west, back toward Cliff. It seemed as though they were wearing ruts into this route, following after good fortune, only to be pushed in the other direction by bad fortune. As good as Jeff was at business, he was worse at luck.

Chapter Seven
1918

Sisson took the lead then, heading them back toward the Dragoon Mountains and the Stronghold. It was a good place if they could get up there. For years the Apaches had used it as a place of refuge and attack. The Dragoons were the most rugged mountains in Arizona, and no one, except the Apaches, had been able to maneuver his way through them easily.

Sisson didn't like the odds. Tom Power was smart, but it seemed to Sisson that smart people had a way of getting too smart and doing things that were dumber than any dumb person would do. He thought of smart as a circle. Go too far toward smart, and you found yourself back at dumb. But there was nothing to do about it. It was just the way. You had to follow the smart ones just because they were smarter than you were. And even when you knew what they was doing wasn't smart, they was still smarter than you, and if you did something else, it would be wrong because you were dumb. You just had to trust them. Only thing was, mostly you didn't trust them.

The Dragoon Mountains are a series of pilings of weathered granite that look like they've been dropped down from above rather than pushed up from below. They are spectacularly rugged mountains with large spires and steep, narrow canyons from which rock had weathered and shattered. The great Apache leader Cochise had made his stronghold in the rugged, nearly impenetrable rocks and crags of the Dragoons. It was a good place to hide. It was a good place for anyone to hide. And if Braz Wootan and his gang of vigilantes had beaten them to it, they would be hidden away, just waiting in ambush.

Sisson had spent many of his younger years as an Indian scout. He boasted that he had scouted out the Indians that had killed Custer. He was too young to have actually done that, but he had helped chase the last of the Sioux back to the reservation, and that made his claim almost but not exactly true. There weren't many men in the state who had the knowledge that Sisson had about pursuit and escape. And his was all knowledge that came from the experience of having done it, not from reading about it. He couldn't read. He could only do things.

In Sisson's experience, the best way to avoid an ambush was to find your way around it. The next best way was to split up your forces in order to flank and ambush the ambush. Since they were only three, and two half blind, the second was no option at all. He would take the first option. He would go around to the north, as the vigilantes would be expecting them from the south. He would come around the north end of the mountains, come back up either from the north or from all the way around to the west. They would try to come up behind the ones who were waiting for them.

He guessed that Tom was thinking somewhat along those lines, too. That's what he guessed, but he wasn't good at guessing what Tom would do. And that put him back into the puzzle again. You couldn't tell the smart ones what to do, even if it was the right thing to do, because the smart ones were smarter than you, right or wrong.

That hadn't bothered him with the Old Man. In a lot of ways, the Old Man was like Tom. He was smart, and he was sharp in the tongue and quick to temper up.

You didn't want to cross the Old Man in any serious kind of way. He would take after you with a big mouth and a bigger stick. He was mean, but he didn't brood. Tom Power was a brooder. Sisson supposed that was because Tom had to grow up under the Old Man's shadow. It was not fun to be a grown-up dealing with the Old Man's temper. He could only imagine what it had been like for a young boy.

But the Old Man was gregarious in a way that Tom wasn't. Tom never dealt with anyone straight up. He was always a little ways off from everyone else, always a bit to the side, always figuring, always looking for the edge. Sisson supposed that, too, was the Old Man's doing. He'd known horses that would let you come right up to them, let you rub their ears, check their teeth, then, soon as you turned your back, they'd take a bite out of you. That was Tom. He didn't seem to trust anyone, and God help anyone who trusted him.

The Old Man, he was what he was. If he was going to take a swipe at you or fuck with you in any way, you saw it coming. If he was mad, he was mad, and he made no attempt to hide it. His temper would flare of a sudden, and you could get caught off guard, but not if you were paying attention. Tom would smile at you and then kick you in the balls before you finished smiling back.

If the Old Man was smiling, he was happy. He wasn't happy that often, but when he was happy, he *was* happy, and he was glad to share the feeling. He would stand a man a drink or a meal or slap him on the back. Of course, he would steal your horse or cow, too, if it came to that. But you knew that about him, and you kept an eye on him. And he didn't try to hide what he was.

The Old Man used to say that there were folks who hated a nickel because it wasn't a dime. But that wasn't his way. He loved currency of all kinds, and there was nothing he loved better than a free dollar. He would do the work of eight men to grab ahold of a dollar.

Nights up at the mine cabin, the Old Man was usually the entertainment. He would tell stories of when he was a boy or young man. Sisson would nod appreciatively at the stories, John would laugh long and hard like a hyena, and Tom would just sit and stare and sometimes crack just a smile.

Sisson remembered a story the Old Man told on himself from back in his Texas times, in the days before he met the boys' mother. He was courting a girl from up the road. And he was dirt poor, but he had come up with a couple of dimes, enough to take her to hear an accordion player in town. The trouble of it was that his pap wouldn't let him take the horses or even a mule to go to town because he wanted the animals rested up for the next day. His pap told him he could take a horse come May when all the planting was done.

But that sort of thinking was a curse on a young man. He was pretty sure he had caught that girl's eye, and, understanding something about girls' eyes, he knew he had to move now, not in May. So he scrounged around the barns and dumps, and he came up with enough parts to piece together a bicycle. Except for a back tire. He didn't have one of those. But he was a young man of cunning and invention, and he was able to make a tire out of a piece of rubber hose wrapped around the wheel rim and secured with a couple of turns of baling wire.

So on the big night he rode his new bicycle over to the girl's farm and picked her up. He put her on the seat of the bicycle, and, like a good gentleman, he stood in front of her on the pedals and did all the pedaling and steering. He supposed that it might not be the finest view she had ever witnessed, but he also understood that the sight of a boy's backside was not the least likely sight a girl could encounter.

"Now this was in the Texas Hill Country," the Old Man said. "And it's called that for the reason that it's full of hills. And I was huffing and puffing my way up one of those long hills, thinking that maybe I wasn't going to make it, and wishing I had found me a smaller gal. And all of a sudden we hit the crest of that hill and started down the other side. I stopped pedaling then, pulled my knees up, and kneeled on the handlebars while we went down that hill, which was long and steep. And free of the responsibility of pedaling, I began to whoop and holler as we went down that hill, just picking up speed so you could hear the whirring of the pedals as they spun all on their own. And she commenced to whoop and holler, too, and I was sure I was showing her the best time she had ever had, and all on my own homebuilt bicycle."

"But that wasn't the whole story of it, was it?" Sisson had asked, knowing how the Old Man's stories went.

"No, sir. It wasn't. Because this ain't that kind of story. It is, in fact, a story of great sadness. One of the worst things I ever encountered in my whole life." He looked over to where John was sitting, slack-jawed, and Tom was fighting off a smile.

"When we finally got to the bottom of the hill, I looked back and saw something whose equivalent I hope never to see in my life again. You see, that baling wire hadn't held. One side of it had broke off and let that rubber hose come free. That free end of the hose had kept spinning around and had just beat that poor gal to death. It was a terrible thing. Just terrible."

"Is that true?" John asked. Then Tom gave in and laughed and gave his brother a hard shove on the shoulder.

"That is the God's own truth," the Old Man said. "And if I ever catch one of you little fart-sniffers building hisself a bicycle, I'm going to beat the crap out of you, just to save some poor girl's life."

Sisson supposed that somehow the Old Man had pretty much brought on his own death, but he was going to miss him. And Sisson saw that his life was going to be harder now, following Tom rather than the Old Man.

It was a slow trek. The night was deeply dark, with only the thinnest sliver of moon for light. The country was level, flat as a frying pan, in fact. But it was full of small dangers: rocks, snakes out hunting at night, and an assortment of rabbit and squirrel holes for a horse to snap its leg in. But the worst danger was the miles of barbed-wire fences marking the boundaries of one ranch from another. A rider who was moving fast on a dark night and came up too sudden on a barbed-wire fence was going to be lucky if all he lost was his horse.

So they picked their way as quickly as they could but slow enough to avoid the most obvious of the dangers. Sisson rode lead still, being the only one with two eyes. There was no evidence that they were being followed or tracked, though they certainly were. It wouldn't do to show themselves any more than they absolutely had to. If the old woman on the edge of town knew about them, probably most of the three surrounding counties knew about them as well.

Sisson didn't much like riding at night. At nearly fifty, he had reached the age where sleep was the greatest pleasure he had any expectation of getting and the one he wanted most. He had spent most of his life in the saddle and had crossed more ground than most men ever get to see, but he had reached the hurting time in his life. His knees, hips, shoulders, and elbows hurt, and so did his back, especially after a long ride. His feet cramped, and his neck stiffened. His hands hurt, but, then, they always did. His fingers had started to ache with the arthritis. He thought sometimes it was easier to say what didn't hurt than what did. His ears didn't hurt. He couldn't hear a lot out of them, but they didn't hurt.

He began to see the faint outline of the Dragoons ahead and to the right. It was faint enough that he couldn't quite tell whether he actually saw them or only imagined them. It would be light pretty soon. They had maybe an hour, probably less, of good riding ahead of them, and then it would be time to look for a good hole to crawl into for the daylight.

He told that to Tom, reining in his horse and letting the boys come up to him.

"No," Tom said. "We're going to keep riding this time."

"I don't think that's a good idea. We know that Wootan's up in front of us, just waiting on us."

"And there's more coming behind us. I know where we're going to spend the day and where we're going to be safe. I was hoping we could make it under the dark, but we ain't going to make that. But we got to get there."

"Where?" Sisson asked.

"Up ahead."

"Where, up ahead?" God, he hated being treated like a child or an imbecile. He never wanted to be boss, but that didn't make him dumb, either.

"You'll know when we get there," Tom said.

Sisson snorted, wheeled his horse, and spurred it on. "You want to take the lead then?" he asked back over his shoulder.

"You're doing just fine."

They saw the riders at first light, and when they saw that the riders hadn't spotted them, they wheeled their horses and headed west, toward the Pic Hills. Though there was urgency, they rode slowly, letting the distances between them grow so as not to attract the eye as quick-moving riders or as the group of three riders that this posse was—it was dead certain now, no question—searching for. It was difficult to move slowly when you knew that you were being hunted. Your whole body tensed in anticipation of running, but you did not run, you ambled, and your stomach knotted.

Farther to the northwest they saw a dust cloud coming from a car or truck. This, too, was likely a posse, probably Wootan. In a car or truck there would be several pairs of eyes searching the landscape for them. That the truck was moving faster than the riders were made those eyes more likely to miss things. It was small comfort.

"They're to the northeast and northwest of us," Sisson said, riding back to Tom. John kept plodding on toward the hills. "And we know there are more southwest of us. We ain't exactly trapped, but we're close enough we don't need a debate on it."

"Not exactly 'trapped,'" Tom said. "All right. I ain't going to argue the point. The only direction that's open to us is southeast, and that's where the vehicle is headed. We want to head southwest, but then we'd be caught in a pincher. If we go where we was headed, we're going to run into those riders. So the only thing we got is to keep heading for the hills and keeping an eye on that vehicle and try to keep as much distance as possible between us and them. Maybe we should speed it up and try to beat them to the hills."

Sisson looked at the plume of dust in the distance. "I wouldn't. The rabbit don't get caught until it decides to run. I would keep going like we was, spread even farther, if we have to. If they get one of us, the other two still got a chance.

We look for a wash or a ditch or something to hide in. If it all works out, they will pass the hills before we get there. People chasing things look ahead. They forget to look behind them."

"Are you certain of that?"

"I ain't certain of anything. I'm almost fifty years old, though, and I'm still here. I think I guess pretty good." Sisson nodded and spurred his horse ahead, leaving Tom to come up behind. They moved that way for several minutes. Sisson kept losing sight of John, and that was good. It meant John was finding places to hide.

Both Sisson and Tom were riding flat on the backs of their horses now, trying to look like anything but the two mounted men they were. When he came to a small swale, not a wash or even a ditch, just a crease in the ground, Sisson rode in and dismounted. He saw John farther down the swale about twenty rods. John was dismounted as well and hunkered down on his heels. Sisson did the same.

They could see now that it was a truck. Whether or not it was Wootan, Sisson couldn't tell, but he assumed it was. It was a stake truck, and there were riders in the bed. They could see the truck, so it was not impossible that the riders could see them. And Tom was still coming up from behind. Sisson turned, still in his crouch, and looked behind him. There was no sign of Tom.

Since the riders in the truck were elevated from ground level, Sisson couldn't tell whether they could see past the swale where he and John crouched, but he thought the two of them were deep enough that the sight lines were more over their heads than at them. He was behind a small creosote bush, and John had a couple of yucca on the top of the ridge in front of him. His main concern was Tom. And then the men in the truck began to wave, first one, then the rest.

Sisson pushed himself farther down behind the creosote bush and rolled over on his back to see what was behind him. Twenty or thirty rods back sat Tom, on his horse, waving nonchalantly to the truck as it went past. The men in the truck waved back. Tom turned his horse and headed it north, slowly, steadily. A cowboy out riding fences or herding strays. Nothing out of the usual.

Sisson turned back onto his belly and crawled around the creosote bush and looked out toward the truck. It had slowed, and there was some interest in the lone rider heading north—a bit of pointing, some looking. Then the truck geared down and lurched forward to curses and laughter from the men riding in the back. The dust plume got larger. Sisson stayed prone for a good while, keeping his head down. He looked up every now and again, watching the plume go farther and farther south. He was just scooting onto his knees, ready to get up and go get his horse, when something slammed into his butt.

He spun around, pulling his revolver and pointing it at the grinning, still-mounted Tom, who threw up his hands in mock horror. "Damn," Tom said. "Just when I thought it was safe."

"Goddamn, Tom. I could have shot you."

"I know. I just passed up a bunch of opportunities to get shot. I been doing a lot of that these past days. Least we didn't get pissed on this time."

"You fucking waved at them."

"And they waved back. Neighborly folk."

"What if they had stopped to chat?"

"I would have been in a hell of a fix, wouldn't I? Whatever I done, I would have led them away from you two. And I don't appreciate any notion that I would have done different. I got caught 'cause I was bringing up the rear. I knew where you two was, and I knew they didn't. If I was to try to get to where you was, they would have seen you, too. I done what any cowboy would do—I waved at them. When they waved back, I knew we was all right."

"That was damned close," John said, leading his horse up to where Tom and Sisson stood. "I started to feel the noose tightening on my neck."

"It was close," Tom said. "But it was only close. We're all right. No one's getting hanged yet."

"It was too close," John said.

"We better get on toward the hills," Sisson said. "This ain't the time to relax or argue. It's broad daylight now. We're going to stand out like rummies in the church choir if we just stay out here on the plain."

It was ten more miles to the Pic Hills. They had to move cross-country. There was no road, and that was their advantage and disadvantage. It would be slow going, but if they were followed by a vehicle, the terrain would be more likely to slow or even stop the vehicle than it would the horses.

They rode closer now. They were in no less danger of being seen, but they were also more likely to spot trouble coming than they would have in the early morning light. They rode at a steady pace, just below a canter, trying not to send up clouds of dust that could be seen from a goodly distance.

"So, where was we headed when the truck came by?"

"Down by Rock Creek. There's a good place to hide the horses while we get up into the Cochise Stronghold. Once we're in the Stronghold, we're safe. The army never got Cochise out of there, and I don't figure a bunch of cotton farmers and shop clerks can get us out of there."

"And what if they're up there first?"

"Then we're dead."

They rode on. Sisson rolled a cigarette, took a couple of long drags, then passed it on to John and Tom. "Can't remember all the important stuff when you're in a hurry. I left a whole can of tobacco under the cot in the cabin."

"It would be a good thing to have more tobacco," Tom agreed. "It occurs to me that if Thems would take up smoking and drinking, it might keep them occupied so that they wouldn't be inclined to mind the business of others who ain't doing Thems harm."

"Guess people take their entertainment where they find it," Sisson said.

"Besides, Thems didn't come after us because Thems was bored," John said.

"No," Tom agreed. "Thems wasn't bored. Smelled gold, that's what it was."

"You sure that's all it was?" John asked. "I got a notion it was more than that."

"You got a notion, do you? Ain't that dandy? Maybe if we pass a post office, you could write a letter to the newspaper. They favor notions. Always glad to hear about someone's notions."

"All right," Sisson said. "This ain't the time."

"Tell him that," Tom said. "He's got something gnawing at him. Let it gnaw its way to the outside so's we can see what's what."

"No. I mean it. This ain't the time. Lookit back there." Sisson nodded to where the dust plume had reappeared, growing larger now as it got closer.

"Shit," Tom said. "Flat out for the hills?"

"I don't think so," Sisson said. "I don't think they have us yet. Probably coming back for a look at the waving cowboy. I think we should spread out and make for the hills at a steady pace and try not to make much noise or dust. That's our best chance. John, you go now. Tom, wait a minute, then you go. I pull up the rear and try to keep an eye on them. Even if they was to catch up to me, they might not know who I am. That sound all right?" He turned to look at the brothers, and John was already gone by two rods. Tom just nodded. "All right, then. We'll meet up to the first hill."

John rode ahead, his horse holding a quick trot but not wanting to break into a gallop or a canter even. But he held him back. The dust they kicked up was their most likely undoing. He liked that word, "undoing." It confused him, though. If you were "done," that was bad. Shouldn't "undone" be good, then? But it wasn't. It was bad, too. It seemed there were a lot more words for bad than for good. Or maybe he only knew the words for bad. He didn't seem to have a lot of need for words that meant "good."

He had spurred his horse before he was aware of hearing the charging hooves behind him and Tom, coming up hard, yelling to him, "Let's git."

On the other side, Sisson crouched low in his saddle like a man expecting shots to come at him from behind, and John crouched, too, lowering his head to the neck of his horse and spurring, though the horse, caught between two other horses at full gallop, needed no prodding to break into a full run. They were heading dead at the hills now, just making it an out-and-out race. He wanted to know if those in the truck had seen them and were coming for them, but that seemed stupid. He guessed it was. He turned his head to look back, but he saw only dust.

He gave himself over to the race, pushing farther down, laying his shoulder into the horse's lowered neck. His body was tense, nearly horizontal, and his heartbeat sped up to match that of his horse. There was no controlling the horse now. The horse was in full run, operating on a combination of terror of whatever was behind them and the desire to outrun the other horses. The horse was far beyond any commands a human might give it, and that suited John fine. Once the decision to let the horses run had been made, there were no other decisions to be made. He pressed himself into the horse, trying to make himself one with the animal.

They were on flat, rolling prairie, with little to impede the horses—small stands of mesquite, bits of saltbush, but mostly grass. The horses ran into and out of small swales in the landscape, but there was no protection here—but no obstacle, either. There was no shelter or camouflage or deceit, only the full-out run to save their lives.

John was not even looking ahead. Half the time, his one good eye was blinded with dust from the other riders. He looked up once in a while to see the hills growing closer, to see the mesquite trees go by, and then he put his head down again. He heard the explosion of breath, probably a curse from Tom, and that brought his head up, and he saw the danger. A three-wire fence. And he was out of his saddle and standing in the stirrups, bracing himself. Whether the horse saw the fence or felt John come up out of the saddle, he couldn't tell, but they were flying over the fence, and then he was flying over the horse until he hit the ground hard and rolled several times.

He lay stunned on the ground. He rolled over onto his back and tried to catch his breath. His wind had been knocked out, but he couldn't tell if he was hurt or not. Just ahead of him, the horse, on its side, was just beginning to move its legs. Still fighting for his breath, he rolled back to his side, knowing now that his shoulder hurt, and tried to get back on his feet. As soon as he put weight on his left leg he went back down. He stayed down then, fighting the panic of not being able to pull air into his lungs, and he watched as his horse awkwardly kicked and struggled to get its legs under it and right itself. He began to cough then and knew he had his breath back, but he could only watch as the horse, up and tentative for a bit, seemed to remember the panic of the last several seconds and took off with a start, riderless, after the other horses. He pushed himself up, took a step forward to go after the horses, and went down again, hard into sand, rock, and grass. He pushed himself back up onto one knee and felt then the pain bloom through his left side. He watched the horse go and did not try to rise.

He was able to get up by pushing himself with his arms and taking the weight on his right leg instead of his left. Upright and wobbly, balancing on one leg and using the other as only a stop against falling to that side, he watched his horse going after the others. He took a small step, more hop than stride, and stopped again to rebalance. He put a little weight on the left side. It hurt, but it also hurt without the weight, so he managed a couple of slow shuffle steps over to where his hat lay in a bit of low-growing saltbush. Once there, it took him a couple of attempts to bend down and pick it up.

He looked back the way they had come. He couldn't see any dust plume, but he had never seen it, had only taken off when Tom and Sisson had. He looked both south and north and may have seen a small swirl to the north, but he couldn't be sure what it was or how far away. Looking with only one eye, it was very hard to gauge distance. He turned and took slow, steady steps toward the east where Tom, Sisson, and his own horse were retreating into the distance.

He had gone twenty deliberate steps when he saw the lone rider heading his way. He stopped to wait, then went forward instead, limping heavily on his left leg. When he looked up, he saw it was Tom, come back for him.

"You're supposed to stay with the horse, you dumb shit."

"The horse is supposed to clear the fucking fence."

"You all right?"

"No, I ain't. I don't think anything's broke, though. How's the horse?"

"Really can't say. When he got you off his back, he took off like he was champion of the world. I didn't know you was down 'til he went right past me and Sisson both. For a bit I thought you was doing some top-notch riding there. Then I remembered who you was." Tom leaned down, extending his arm for John. John grasped Tom's arm at the bicep, and Tom took a similar hold of John's arm and, leaning back, pulled John up and into the saddle. Tom stood in the stirrups and crouched down, and they took off, back toward Sisson and John's horse.

"You think they actually saw us?"

"Can't say," Sisson said. "There was a lot of them, heading right for us. Could have seen us."

"Yeah," Tom said. "I'm sure you could find a Republican or two who could stare you in the eye and prove that it would be impossible for ten men, looking right at three riders, to actually see them, but yeah, I think they saw us."

They were perched at the top of the westernmost hill. They had tied the horses down at the southeastern base of the hill so they could get to the horses and to the next hill in the easiest way. This perch gave them a good view of the entire valley, a 360-degree view from every spot on the hill. They all had their rifles loaded and ready. Tom glassed the valley to the west.

"There's some dust off to the southwest, near to Hendricks's place. Could be them, or it could be Hendricks getting a jump on the spring plowing. They ain't behind us, though."

"The barbwire would have stopped them," Sisson said.

"Only long enough for a couple of them to jump out, pull the post, and lay it down. They wouldn't have turned back on account of a barbwire fence. Hell, it ain't theirs; they might have just run it over."

"You don't run over another man's fence," John said.

"Yeah, well, you don't just ride up to someone's cabin in the dawn and start gunning them down as they come out, either. You're the only one going to get held up by that fence. These boys don't care much on manners. The only thing that's going to stop these boys is bullets."

Their perch was also a perfect defensive position. No one could sneak up on them, and they would be firing down from cover at anyone who tried to come up for them. With the guns and ammunition they took from the lawmen, they could hold off a good-sized posse for a long time.

"I don't know where they are, and I figure they do know where I am. I'm not feeling too comfortable here."

"You want to go down and take off again?"

"Eventually. We're tired, and, God knows, the horses are tired. As long as the posse don't show themselves, I think we should stay here for a little bit and then head out."

"Head out where?"

"Hendricks's."

"We can't go showing ourselves all over Cochise County," Sisson said. "We don't know these people that well. Look what happened when we stopped at the old woman's in Pearce. They'll be nice as pie to your face and then go call the law on you. I ain't in favor of paying no more visits."

"Those boys wasn't from the old lady's call. She said she was giving us the night. These boys couldn't a gotten on us that fast. These ones has been out trolling for us."

"You think that old woman told the truth?"

"It's the problem with old women. They mostly tell the truth. Fucks everything up for the rest of us. And speaking of that old woman, there's some of that food left on my saddle. John, why don't you go down and get it."

"Because my leg is banged up," John said. "How's your legs?"

Tom sighed and got up on his knees. "All right. I'll go. You watch out real careful, though. Anything you see, make sure it ain't me or Sisson here. If it ain't and you're positive on that, shoot it."

John glared at Tom making his way down the hill. "Tom. Just in case I do shoot you, let me say 'I'm sorry' right now."

"You shoot me, Johnny, you goddamn well better make a good shot of it."

"Speaking of old women," Sisson said, rolling onto his back and pulling his hat down over his eyes. "If you two would kindly shut up for a bit, I believe I'll grab some sleep and dream about fucking some old woman."

"You dream about fucking *old* women?"

"You take what you can get, John. Even in dreams. You take what you can get."

Down with the horses, Tom surveyed the damage. They were all well lathered, so he took the piece of canvas he had taken at the Johnson mine and wiped them down the best he could. They needed to be stripped of their saddles and dried, but he couldn't risk that. They had been ridden hard for two straight nights, but otherwise they were in pretty good shape. If they could get some rest at Hendricks's, they could go awhile longer. If not, he could probably work a trade with Hendricks for fresh ones. And when worse come to worst, as it usually does, you just steal new ones when you need them.

Back up the hill with the food, he found Sisson glassing the area to the west, sweeping north and south and back again. John was a couple of feet down, already asleep. "Thought it was you going to sleep," Tom said.

Sisson nodded at John. "Went to sleep so fast, he was lucky he didn't just fall off the hill."

Tom nodded. The ones who weren't overburdened with thought slept well. He envied John that ability to just close his eyes and be asleep like a dog. He had a small impulse to walk over and kick John just so they would both be awake. But another impulse held him back, letting John sleep the sleep he needed, that they all needed. "His horse loosened a shoe. Probably at the fence. You got the things you'd need to take care of that?"

Sisson looked at his hands and nodded. "Probably. How bad?"

"I ain't no farrier, but it's something more than I should be after."

Sisson considered this, then nodded toward John. "Want me to wake him so you can grab some sleep?"

"Nah. Let him sleep. He can't see no better than I can, anyway."

Sisson walked heavily down the hill. Any terrain that wasn't flat as a dance floor hurt him, but going downhill seemed the worst. It wasn't as tiring as uphill, but it pained him, hip and knee. He was too old for this but saw no remedy. The fight hadn't started as his, but it had become his quick enough. When people started shooting at you, you didn't need to pause to ponder the imponderables. The fight had chosen him, and now it was his. That's the way with fights. Some of them you chose and were the fool for doing so. The rest just seemed to choose you. Maybe you were still a fool because you made some other choice, some other time, that led to this. He didn't have any answers, except that this was his fight now, whenever he had chosen it or not.

He took the leg of the sorrel mare. The shoe was badly loose. Most likely it had hooked on the fence, and that's what threw them over. He untied the horse from the others and walked it around in a circle. Its gait was off, but it did not seem to favor the leg beyond the loose shoe. He brought it back and tied it to the others.

He took his tool roll from his saddle, where he had rolled it before they left the cabin the other morning. He had a hammer, pliers, file, and, in a cloth pouch, a dozen or so nails. He put the nails in his pocket, walked back to the horse, and laid the tools on the ground next to the leg with the loose shoe.

With his back to the horse's head (so that each got a good view of a horse's ass, Wilson, who long ago taught him shoeing, used to say), he took the foreleg between his knees and held it there while he inspected the shoe for damage. It wasn't too bad. Two of the nails had pulled through the shoe. He could simply pull those out and replace them. The worse news was that the clinches, the ends of the nails that went through the side of the hoof and were then hammered, or clinched, down weren't tight. Whoever shod this horse had been in a hurry. One of the clinches was badly bent, but the end of it was visible and could be filed off. The other was nowhere in sight. Only the hole and the depression it left were still visible.

He tried to see inside the hole, to see if he could detect any trace of metal. It could have broken off from the force of the horse's weight when it went down, but he couldn't be sure. It was also possible, maybe likely, that the nail had bent back toward straight and pulled into the hoof. But even pulled back toward straight was not straight. Pulling the nail out from the shoe would be likely to damage, even crack, the hoof.

He took his file and filed down the clinches from the nails that had held until there were just metal spots on the outside of the hoof, ready to be pulled out from under the shoe. He levered the side of the shoe away from the hoof until he had loosed the nails on that side enough that he could grasp them with the pliers and, levering backward, pull the nails free. When he had done all but one, he went to work on the stuck nail.

He filed the nail with the thin side of the file, working it until he was able to just snap it by prying it up with the shoe. Then he filed the shaft of the nail until it was flush with the sole of the hoof, leaving nearly an inch of the nail embedded in the horse's hoof, but deep inside where it would do no damage. The next farrier who filed the hoof would get an unpleasant surprise, but that was a farrier's lot.

He could remount the shoe, though it was not a good one, a lot worn and a little bent. He would have to leave a nail out, but he saw no use in that. It would be better to let the horse go unshod than to make do with a bent shoe. It would be an uncomfortable ride for John, but it wouldn't hurt the horse much. Confronted with choices of horse and man, he tended to go with what was best for the horse. Horses were expensive, Wilson had told him. People were a dime a dozen.

"See anything?" Sisson asked Tom, who was glassing the lowlands in front of them.

"I'm still sitting here, ain't I?" Tom said. He paused, reconsidered, then, in a milder tone, said, "Nothing. We either lost them, they never saw us, or they've gone to get more men to come and surround us."

"What's your thinking?"

"Mostly, I'm trying not to think."

"Having any luck?"

Tom smiled. "Not much. If they don't know where we are, we're safe up here for a good while. If they do know, they'll come at us from every direction, a lot of them, and then this is just the end."

Sisson picked up a long strand of grass and stripped the seeds from it. He had no thoughts to share with Tom on this particular dilemma, except that he didn't especially want to die, but that if he had to, he would rather get shot than hanged. He had seen a man hanged. It wasn't a good sight. It wasn't a good death.

"I don't know what you're thinking, but I wish you would stop. The look on your face is terrible to behold."

"I'm not thinking nothing," Sisson said.

"You're thinking dying thoughts is what you're doing. I'm trying to think stay-alive thoughts." He rolled over onto his left side so he was facing Sisson. "Here's my thinking so far. We can stay here a little while, rest ourselves and the horses. John needs lots of sleep. But we can't overstay. We stay too long, we die here. This is a dying place. We can put up a fight, but we can't win. Not in the long run. So we got to get out of here and head for better cover, somewhere they won't surround us."

"Where's that?"

"The Stronghold, most likely, but before that I want to try to get to Hendricks's place. We can resupply and rest up there, swap out our horses for new ones."

"John's going to need a new horse if we're to make it very far."

"Then we get John a new horse. Because we're going to make it all the way to Mexico, goddamn it."

They let John sleep and took turns catnapping and glassing the valley. They needed sleep nearly as bad as John did, but this wasn't the time for it. For John, any time was the time to sleep.

It was getting on noon when Tom got up, duckwalked over to where John and Sisson slept, and touched their shoulders. "Let's go. It's time."

"It's time?"

He guessed it was. There was no way to know if this was any better than any other time, except that he was tired of waiting. He needed to move again. "This would be the time," he said.

Tom took a last long look around through the glasses. A full 360 degrees of nothing. He walked down the hill after his brother and the hired man, standing full up this time because it wasn't hide and cover time anymore. Now it was saddle and run time.

John couldn't tell if they were running from someone or toward someone. It wasn't a full-out run, but they were pushing the horses pretty hard, and his had a hard, awkward gait, running on only three shoes. Once they were out of the hills and into the flat of the valley again, they were running pretty much exposed.

If they were seen, they would have to go at a flat-out run, and he worried now that the horses had been run enough and that they wouldn't have much left when it came to a chase. There was no danger apparent in front of them. But the same small convolutions of landscape that gave them temporary cover, that allowed them to come in and out of both sight and fire lines, gave the same to those who hunted them.

The truck had scared him. He didn't like being pursued by a truck full of men with rifles. The truck was too fast, too big, too unrelenting. Still, a man on horseback had advantages in this country, where a sudden cut bank of an arroyo or an outcropping of rock could stop a truck and break it beyond repair. The danger, the greatest danger, he thought, came from men who were on horseback, just as they were. They could go where the trucks couldn't, and they didn't make as much noise or raise as much dust while they did it.

But maybe he worried too much because he was the dumb one. Tom saw things that he didn't, and Tom understood things that he didn't. Or so Tom said. John guessed he had to take Tom's word for it. John had the suspicion that Tom just thought he was smarter than all the dangers that confronted him. He always thought he had a way around things and that when the bad really happened, he could just outthink it. John wasn't so sure. Sometimes he thought that thinking was seriously overrated, especially by those who thought they were good at it.

Chapter Eight
1901

Back in Cliff, New Mexico, after working odd jobs in Texas and New Mexico, Jeff found a faltering cattle ranch looking for an infusion of cash. He bought a half interest in the ranch. Within four months he understood that the ranch was failing because the owner, his new partner, was a drunk and, worse, an ignoramus. Jeff was no teetotaler, but he despised those who were weak enough to have their lives overtaken by a bottle.

He took what little money he had left and half the cattle from the ranch, and then he headed upriver away from Cliff and started his own small ranch. It was good to be living with Granny Jane and the children, but he hated like hell to be leaving Mattie again. He wasn't about to lose all his hard-earned money on the foolishness of a rummy, though. He personally couldn't stand the type. He hated weak.

He prospered yet again. Prospering seemed easy. Holding on to prosperity was a lot harder. It seemed that things just stacked up against a man. By late 1902 he had a herd of 1,145 cattle, which made him neither rich nor powerful but showed him for the quality of man he was, a hardworking, smart operator, able to march right through the tough times. His former partner had sold out what remained of the herd for three years' worth of whiskey and considered himself successful as well.

A drought is a terrible thing. You're deep into it by the time you realize that's what this is. Not that it matters. There's little to be done about a drought. It had started with a mild winter that seemed benign, dropping only a couple of feet of snow in the lower elevations of the Mogollon Mountains. But come spring, the snowmelt was only a few trickles in the streambeds that were gone by June. The clouds built in the summer as they were supposed to do but hung in the south or skirted off to the east. By fall the situation was getting dire. He hired a team to dismantle his windmill and drop dynamite down the well to bust up the rock and free the deeper water to come into the basin. The dynamite merely blew hell out of the rock, and he ended up with a well ten feet shallower than before. The flakes of snow that swirled in January and February seemed only to mock him. He wished he held more with the idea of a kind and merciful God, because he wanted to curse hell out of Him.

He had no choice but to start selling his herd. It was underweight, and the price of beef had gone completely to hell, as everyone else was trying to sell their beef as well. He kept a couple hundred head that could live off the few springs that still ran, and he used the rest of the money to buy alfalfa from southern Texas, where it seemed all the clouds were heading. He had enough cattle, water, and feed to last six months. If the rains started up before then, he was well set to start building the herd again. If the drought continued, he and every other rancher as far as he knew were just waiting to be cut up for silage by the banks.

Then, in February, the rains came. February rains were good rains. They fell light but endured, sometimes falling for a couple of weeks, off and on. There was some snowpack up in the mountains that could fill the streams. And the rains kept up, harder and harder, unrelenting. They melted the snow, and they saturated the ground. The little streams swelled up, and when the river couldn't take any more, the streams overflowed. Jeff went out one morning to ride his fences, plodding through the steady, soaking rain to find a good half acre of his land gone with nearly three dozen cattle.

What forage there had been had been washed away or trampled by the goddamned cows. The roads were washed out, and there was no way, and no money, to bring in more hay. Every day, he found more of his cattle foundered in the mud or just washed downstream. In the early spring of 1904, when the rains finally stopped, Jeff Power was broke again.

He went back to Cliff. It seemed that in the worst of times, the nearness of Mattie was more than just a comfort but the answer to his problems. He had no money to speak of, and he sold the wagon and horses for six months' rent on the same house they had left two years before. But Charlie was now fifteen. A man, basically. And John was fourteen and Tom twelve. He sent them to school because that's what you were supposed to do. He took on jobs cowboying, loading freight, and working on building crews. And when the jobs were plentiful, he pulled the boys out of school and put them to work, too. You had to use every asset you had, if you were going to survive.

So once again he had gone from well-off to dead broke. A poor man couldn't get a decent break anywhere. It was the rich bastards who got everything, mostly from each other. And God was the richest bastard of them all, happy to take from the poor to stuff the pockets of the rich.

Still, this was America, and there was always the chance of doing better. It was the land of opportunity, and if those opportunities were mainly for the rich, there was a chance you could snatch one away when one of the rich bastards was counting another pile of money. He didn't believe in God, and he didn't much believe in America, but he believed in himself, and no matter how many times he got swatted down, he was going to get back up and grab something for himself.

Whatever opportunity there was in Cliff, Jeff never found it. He had a small herd but no land, so the cost of running his cattle on private land was keeping him just about breaking even. The herd was increasing by only three or four every year. That was the slow road to the poorhouse.

In 1908 a letter came to him at the Cliff, New Mexico, post office. It was worn smooth as an old glove, for it had followed Jeff from Cliff, to Alamogordo, to Texas, back to Cliff, always missing him by a couple of weeks or a month. Its arrival seemed a sign that persistence paid off.

The letter was from his brother-in-law, Will, responding to Jeff's letter about Mattie's death. Will was running cattle now, too, in the Horseshoe Mountains of Arizona. By his accounts, he was doing all right. From what Jeff knew of Will's optimism and struggles with the truth, he figured that really meant Will was scraping by, just like him.

Jeff wrote back and in two weeks got a letter by return. In Arizona Will was giving up on the Horseshoe Mountains, but he had found grazing land in Stove Gulch in the eastern end of Aravaipa Canyon. It could support quite a few cattle, and he suggested that Jeff might want to throw in with him and run the cattle together.

There was only a line shack in Aravaipa Canyon. But there was water and grass. The cattle were run down after being driven for seventeen days from the Horseshoes to Stove Gulch. There was enough room in the shack for only two. Will was one of two, and the Powers consulted on who should be the other. Jeff, Charlie, and John all had contacts in Cliff, where they could pick up work. That left sixteen-year-old Tom Power as the best candidate to go to Arizona while the rest of the family stayed in New Mexico. Tom and Will lived in the line shack, and Will became the rancher by default.

Tom rode to the Aravaipa store and post office whenever he got the chance. Usually it was to pick up some supplies or tobacco for Will. He often went, hoping for a letter from the family, though he couldn't imagine who in the family would actually write him one. Granny Jane couldn't write, and neither Jeff nor John was much inclined that way, though both had the skill. He guessed his best chance was Charlie or Ola May, who was now fifteen and the most educated of the family. She did write once every four or five weeks, and it was worth it to Tom to ride in a couple of times a week just in case she got off schedule. Besides, he liked looking at the things in the store that he could not buy.

The post office was one corner of H. F. Firth's store, the only one in Aravaipa and twenty miles beyond that. Firth noticed the good-looking blond boy from the first time he came to the store. The boy would come to the post office window, smile, and ask only, "Power?" Firth rarely nodded "yes." But he kept an eye on the boy, sure that his slow progress around the store was the progress of a thief.

Times were hard, and he didn't need to add theft to his woes. But as far as he could tell, the boy never stole anything but just wandered, picking up cans and boxes and bottles and staring at them as if they were jewels or two-headed cats.

"Are you planning to buy something?" Firth asked one day. He was tired and had a toothache and too many bills to pay. The question was designed to scare the boy off. It would have set any number of boys to stammering and looking for the door.

"No, sir," the boy said. He smiled broadly. It was a good smile, shy, but still welcoming. "You can bet I would if I had any money. Yes, sir. I surely would."

"Then why are you here, picking everything up, looking at all I got. I'm here to sell, not entertain boys."

The smile again. "I ain't going to be poor my whole life. I'm going to get me some money, and when I do, I plan to be prepared. I'm going to march right in here, money in my hand, and buy what I want. What are applecots?"

"Apricots. They're like little peaches, sweeter, though."

"That's the first thing I'm going to buy, then. I ain't never had any, ain't never heard of any until now. But that's what I want. 'Applecots.'"

"Apricots."

The boy smiled again, a broader, brighter smile. "Apricots," he said. "Yes, sir. I'm going to buy me a can of those apricots."

Then, for no reason he could have explained, Firth said, "If someone was handy with a broom and could sweep out this store, I believe I would be willing to give him a can or two."

The boy smiled. "Where's the broom? I'm your man for that."

Tom Power continued to come to the store twice a week, marching in, asking for mail, which he rarely got, then marching to the back of the store, taking up the broom, and sweeping out. When he was done, he would start his slow circuit of the store again, peering at all the cans and bottles. He often chose a can of apricots when he was done, but he also tried spiced apples, quince, and kippered herring.

"You might as well come in on a more regular basis," Firth said. "You're here all the time anyway. You can sweep out and run the counter here so I can take a nap. I'd guess you know my stock better than I do by now. You could tote water up from the spring as well. I'd pay you some money as well as the canned goods."

The customers liked Tom well enough. He wasn't shy and shifty-eyed like most boys his age, and he didn't smirk over jokes he silently told himself. Instead, he looked customers in the eye, smiled the great smile, and, with surprising speed, began to call them by name. More and more, Tom watched the store and handed out the mail while Firth attended to other business, usually his small herd of cattle. At the end of the week, Tom got three dollars and some canned goods. Firth let him take whatever he wanted, which was usually not much.

After one of Firth's steers had knocked him into a fence post, bruising his shoulder so badly he couldn't move his arm for two days, Tom suggested he could save Firth a lot of time and pain if he let Tom take the herd to graze with Will's up in the gulch.

"And what would this cost me?" Firth asked.

"What's fair?" Tom asked back. "I only want what's fair."

"Another couple of dollars a week?"

Tom hesitated.

"And more canned goods," Firth offered.

"Then that's what we'll do."

Tom drove the little herd of twenty cattle back up the canyon and brought them in with the Power and Morgan herd. There was plenty of water and good grass, and the addition of the few cows didn't change that. Tom gave Will a dollar a week and brought him cans of potted meat, of which Will was overly fond. Tom was now, at sixteen, making three dollars a week. And it was easy work, except for hauling the water. Every day he took a string of burros three miles to Turley Springs, filled up ten-gallon kegs with spring water, and loaded them on the burros. Then they trudged three miles back.

"You take those burros back there to that spring empty, don't you?" This was a cowboy named Albee who came to the post office every week.

"I do," Tom said. "That's where the water is."

"That seems a waste, don't it? Taking those burros back there empty?"

"I don't know what I would take to Turley Springs, except kegs for the water."

"Yep. That's right. You would have to find someone who wanted to send something up that way, wouldn't you?"

"I guess I would."

A week later, Albee caught him again. "This here's your lucky day. I found you some folks that want to send stuff back to Turley Springs."

"Who would that be, and what do they want sent back there?"

"It wouldn't be your problem, that's what it would be. We'll be getting some stuff from Phoenix and back east and such, and when it comes in, you just tote it up to Turley Springs and set it there for us, and we'll pay you a dollar a trip. And that's all you have to do. How's that sound?"

There was a movement on for the prohibition of alcohol. People in Arizona were talking statehood, and the argument was that it would be easier if Arizona was to go in a dry state. The argument didn't sit well in the most southern counties—Pima, where Tucson was, and Santa Cruz, which bordered on Mexico. But in largely Mormon Graham, Greenlee, and even Cochise Counties, there was strong support for the prohibition.

Tom figured that that's what this was, a preparation for prohibition. Moonshiners would need a lot of equipment, a lot of good water, and a secluded place. And Turley Springs was a secluded place with good water. The cowboys who wanted to send stuff up there were setting up a still. He was sure of that.

"I don't think it's right," he told Albee. "I think it ought to be a dollar a burro."

"Well, hell, you're driving them up there anyway. It won't even be out of your way."

"I'm driving them empty," Tom said. "You want me to drive them loaded, and you want me to do the loading and unloading. A dollar for each burro I got to load and unload."

"Well, hell. Nothing for the burros that ain't loaded? I guess that would be all right. Don't you go putting a little bitty stick on each burro and claiming for a load."

"I wouldn't do that," Tom said. "I decide how much weight is a load for the burros, though. They're Mr. Firth's burros, and we treat them right."

For three weeks he carted barrels and piping of all sorts, iron, gauges, burners, and boxes of bottles up to the spring. He took all of this well back into the bush where it wouldn't be noticed by anyone just visiting the spring. A happy customer was a repeat customer. He had learned that from Firth. He took a fully operational still up the steep trail in three weeks and pocketed sixty-two dollars. He was coming up on rich. He liked being on his own and making his own money. He had learned from his father that when opportunity knocked in America, you best not be broke.

By 1910 Jeff was growing restless again. The family had scattered—Charlie and Tom to Arizona, John to Lordsburg, New Mexico. Only Granny Jane and Ola May remained at home. He loaded the women into the wagon, got word to John, and moved the family to Arizona, closer to Charlie, Tom, and Will Morgan. They moved to the small town of Klondyke on the eastern end of Aravaipa Canyon.

Jeff didn't approve of Tom's handling of the cattle. Power cattle and Morgan cattle grazed with Firth cattle and some others Tom had picked up while working at the store. Jeff's experience had taught him that no real good came of grazing cattle together. Even when you seemed to be making a profit, you were sowing the seeds of your own destruction to feed the cattle. He looked at the Galiuro Mountains and knew they had found the place he had searched for for so long.

The Galiuro Mountains run perpendicular and then parallel to Aravaipa Canyon, just to the south and west of the canyon. They are rugged basalt mountains, cut by two main canyons running roughly northwest to southeast—Redfield Canyon to the east and Rattlesnake Canyon to the west. Both of the canyons have good sources of water, and Rattlesnake Canyon, which gets its name from the serpentine wanderings of Rattlesnake Creek at its bottom or from the abundance of rattlesnakes, especially the fat, irritable Mojaves that thrive there, striking cattle and cowboys alike until it was hardly worth trying to make a go of it with cattle in that canyon, seemed to Jeff Power perfect.

Jeff made Tom cut out Firth's and the other lease cattle from the herd and return them where he got them. Jeff had the idea that they might be better served by sending Tom to school with Ola May rather than cowboying for pocket change. Tom was the smart one, at least among the boys. Charlie was headstrong, and John was simply strong, but Tom had qualities the others didn't share. While Jeff didn't approve of Tom's business dealings—he had left him in Aravaipa Canyon to watch over his own cattle, for God's sake, not to set up business running other people's cattle—he admired Tom's ability to see money in a situation most people would see as simply drudge work worth a few coins here and there. Tom had Jeff's brains and, just maybe, better luck. Tom could be the one to strike it rich. Jeff had no question that the Power family was going to be rich. He questioned only which one would uncover the opportunity. He wanted Tom to get himself educated, believing, though, as he always would, that smart was entirely preferable to educated.

The situation was not much to Tom's liking. Sitting in a schoolhouse seemed a waste of time. The activities there, the reading and writing and reciting, seemed baby work and unprofitable. He knew how to read and write and add and subtract. Beyond that, education seemed frivolous. But despite his months on his own, being his own boss, his father was back in charge and making decisions for him.

But Jeff sent Tom and Ola May to school some three miles from Klondyke, an hour's walk each day. Then Jeff divided up the cattle. He sent Will Morgan up into Redfield Canyon with his herd and moved his own herd into Rattlesnake Canyon. It seemed better, more agreeable, that way. He liked to say that he had faith in his fellow man except when it came to money, land, love, sex, whiskey, and anything else you could think of. There would be no arguing over whose cattle were whose. The two herds had the rugged peaks of the Galiuros, frequently large basalt boulders, delicately and beautifully balanced, one on top of another, to separate them.

Most of the cowboying was done by Charlie, now twenty and a full-grown man. He was capable. There was no problem with sending Charlie out with the herd for weeks. He could take care of himself and preferred his own company over anyone else's. Jeff never had to tell Charlie what to do. Charlie did what he liked, and what he liked was keeping things safe and orderly.

As summer wore on and Rattlesnake Creek began to dry up at the bottom, the cattle moved to higher ground where the creek still ran. Charlie followed. As summer heat built, air pressure dropped and pulled moisture up from the Gulf of California. The heavy, wet clouds moved north until they encountered mountains, and then they rained, and they rained hard. Ranchers needed to be careful that their cattle did not get trapped in small canyons where a quickly rising stream could drown them. So Charlie kept moving them farther up the canyon. As he kept moving, he ran into Pete Spence.

Pete Spence owned a section of land along Rattlesnake Creek at an elevation of 5,600 feet, close to the top of Rattlesnake Canyon, some four miles south of where the canyon ran into Kielberg Canyon. On a wide cienega, where the creek flattened and spread before heading back into the rocks and downward, under the shadow of Topout Peak, Spence was herding goats.

Spence met Charlie with a double-barreled shotgun broken across his folded arms, barrels down. "These your cows?"

"They are. That your shotgun? You plan to keep it broken, then?"

Spence smiled. "At least until I load it."

"Sorry about the cows, then."

"No real harm done. I was a little afraid they'd gone through the fence and got after the garden. The damned goats just jump the fence, but I don't have to mend it after."

"Looks like you could use a taller fence."

"Damn. Why didn't I ever think of that?"

"I beg your pardon," Charlie said. "That was unmannerly of me."

"Nah. A taller fence would require another trip to town. I been keeping those to a minimum."

Charlie dismounted and extended his hand. "Charles Power. Charlie."

"I heard there was someone running cows down the creek. I figured I would run into you one of these days. Pete Spence."

"That the reason for the 10 gauge?"

"Not really," Spence said. "More for bear and lion. It's pretty much lousy with them up here."

"Are they a great bother to you, running goats and all?"

"Not so much. Summer's pretty good. Sometimes in the fall before the berries and whatnot get going full out, the bears get after them. A bear would rather eat berries than meat, though. Always lose a few goats, usually at the end of summer. Lions is unpredictable. Mostly they leave us alone. Plenty of deer and sheep up in the hills. Lions don't like the smell of people much. Can't say I blame them."

"You're what they call a hermit, then?"

"No. I don't think so. I'm just Pete Spence, goat herder. Used to go down the canyon a lot to sell milk, cheese, and goats. Your Mexican is very fond of goat. Don't go down so much anymore, unless I got an abundance of something. Mostly, I just keep myself fed. I believe I'm more lazy than unsocial. Fact of it is, it's a relief to talk to something that can talk back."

"Well, I admire a man who keeps to his own business. There seems to be a shortage of them," Charlie said.

"What's the news of statehood? Since you was just speaking of people who don't mind their own business."

"Looks like they're going to do it. Lots of fighting about this or that. Should we go in death or no death, wet or dry? All claim their own view will carry us into the United States."

"How's it going to come out, you think?"

"Don't really know. We're already dry. We got that worked out. That will make the Mormons happy and someone else rich. Mostly it's just an aggravation. Whiskey is still around. More expensive, though. It kind of looks like we're going for no death."

"Sorry to hear about the whiskey. That will make it a little tougher up here. I'll be looking at the goats and counting them up against bottles of whiskey. Tough on the goats."

"Not a lot of people willing to deliver way up here, I guess. Of course, you'd want to make acquaintance with my kid brother, Tom Power. That boy would walk on his hands to the moon, rolling a barrel of whiskey with his feet if he thought there was a dollar up there. Summers will still be hot and winters cold. Nothing is going to change much. Of course, I don't really follow the news."

"I don't, either. I didn't ever think I would want to need it, but I'm finding a hunger for it more and more. If I was an ambitious man, I would go to town and hear of the happenings. But, as I said, I'm mostly just lazy."

"This here's an awful nice spot. Real pretty and handy to water and grass."

"I done some work up here. Come on. I'll show you the property. You can see how the poor folks live."

Spence had built a solid cabin out of ponderosa pine and Douglas fir. It was small but tight, and Charlie admired the hand that had put it together so well. There was also a garden and wire pens for the goats. Charlie saw how easy the fences were for goats anxious to get at the vegetables. All in all, it seemed a waste of fence. To the north of the cabin was a long, cleared field where Spence had taken the lumber for his cabin.

"I've always had a mind to plant trees in that field. Apples would be good, I think. Of course, then I'd have to pick 'em and tote 'em down to the store or, even worse, to Safford or Willcox. And I ain't anxious to travel."

"It's a nice spot you got here, that's for sure. I can see why a man would want to hang around. My family's never stayed in one spot long enough to pick a grape we had planted."

"Well, make me an offer. It could be yours."

"I'm not sure I could," Charlie said. "I don't know where I would begin."

"I wouldn't begin no lower than a thousand dollars, if I was you."

"I might not be able to come up with a thousand dollars."

"Well, if I was you, I would begin there. Though that wouldn't necessarily be where it would all end up."

"Not sure I could go beyond that. I would have a hell of a time coming up with the starting sum."

"Well, then," Spence said, "if I was you, I would make an offer of seven hundred and fifty dollars, because negotiations can travel both front and back. But that's just what I would do."

"That's a better figure," Charlie said. "Not sure I could scrape up even that much, though."

"Do you want to name a figure, or would you just prefer I do the negotiating for both of us?"

"Well, I haven't been around here very long. I don't know the area very well. I'm not sure what would be a fair price for something like this."

Spence shook his head and scuffed at the sand with the toe of his shoe. "I don't know 'fair,' either. Seems to me, 'fair' ain't real. It's just something people talk on. I wouldn't offer a man anything less than six hundred dollars for fear he might shoot me for being a jackass."

"Six hundred dollars." Charlie nodded his head and chewed his lip. "Six hundred dollars."

"Next figure I mention goes back in the other direction," Spence said.

"Well, I would think that would be a fair price."

"Especially since it includes two mining claims about a half a mile down canyon."

"Mining claims?"

"Silver and gold around here. Prime country for it. Not that I know anyone who has pulled a good deal of it out. But that may just mean that there's more down there to be taken."

"All right, then," Charlie said. "Six hundred dollars."

"You drive a hard bargain, Charlie Power. You certainly do. I would think you could silent a man out of his own boots. Bring me the money, and I'll be gone by the end of next week. I will require a handshake to seal the bargain."

They shook, and Charlie remounted and went looking for his cattle, which were now grazing land that was as good as his own. He had been close to saying yes to the thousand-dollar figure. Usually, hesitating got you only sorrow and pain. He looked at the cienega, nearly knee-deep in grass—grama and tobosa—and at the fine, spring-fed pool at the other end. It wasn't quite the Garden of Eden, but it would do for Power Garden.

Pete Spence's cabin was too small for the five of them, so even before Spence had moved out, Jeff had Tom and John at work, felling trees while he and Charlie split the logs. "Don't you two little weasel turds drop one of those trees on yourself. Don't drop one on us, either."

John was nineteen, Tom seventeen. They were grown men now, fully capable of felling trees, splitting logs, building fences and cabins, and just about any other thing Jeff might require. John especially had a knack for seeing which way a tree wanted to fall and to either drop it right in that spot or convince it to go another way. He lacked the cleverness of Tom, who was small and had learned early on to trust his wits to avoid the beatings his fists might not save him from, but John understood more than he was given credit for. He knew what he figured he needed to know and didn't worry on the rest. Since Tom was known for being smart, John was content to let Tom handle all the affairs John didn't want to be bothered with.

They built four additions to the cabin—a kitchen where Granny Jane would have the space to do what needed doing and a bedroom for Granny Jane and Ola May, who was now fifteen and needed a place of her own where she wouldn't be seen doing all that she needed to do and so that she and Granny Jane didn't have to look on what they didn't need to see. There were two more rooms—a dining and living area and a bunk for Jeff, Charlie, John, and Tom.

As soon as the kitchen and the women's room were done, the men set to work on building corrals for the cattle and horses. In the meantime, the men slept where they would, often enough outdoors. They tried to keep small fires going to keep the animals back, but one morning, in the weak light just before full sunrise, John woke to a black bear sniffing around his head. When the bear saw John's wide eyes, saw that he was awake, it huffed at John, turned, and ran back into the woods to the west.

They built a tack shed and strung wire in the winter, but mostly they tended the cattle, busting ice off the pool from the spring and taking turns at night watching for lions that could come down from the higher elevations to pick off the corralled cattle.

It was too cold to sluice the creek, and the ground was too frozen to dig at either of the claim sites, so they let the mines be for the winter and spent their time planning ways to make a go of what they were now calling "Power Garden." Charlie and Tom took jobs in town, trudging up and down Rattlesnake Creek in the snow and cold only as often as they had to. John and Jeff tended the stock.

By the spring of 1911, they were working the cattle and the mines steadily. They had sluiced some flake gold from the highest mine, not much, just about a hundred dollars' worth, but a start. They then went in search of the source of the flake. They moved upstream, steadily diverting the stream and scratching at the creekbed, hoping to uncover the vein of gold or at least some nugget.

It was a good area for mining, and they had six neighbors who were mining gold with varying degrees of success. No one had yet uncovered the thick vein of ore they were hoping for, but two of the mines had produced enough to warrant two neighbors buying ball mills to process the rock for more flake gold.

A ball mill was a large, hollow ball filled with small, solid iron balls. The large ball could be turned with the aid of an engine or water, horse, ox, or even manpower. It would be filled with rock and then turned. The iron balls, which started out the size of a child's head and wore down, would tumble inside the ball, crushing the rock so that it could then be sluiced for the gold.

The Power claims were promising but not rich enough to warrant working by hand. Jeff looked on the neighbors' ball mills with envy. He worked out an arrangement with one neighbor, Ed Knothe, to crush his ore in Knothe's mill, carrying the ore to Knothe's on donkeys. But the quality of the ore was poor, and Jeff was barely getting enough gold to pay for feed for the donkeys. He had been a small-time rancher much of his life, and now he was a small-time miner. He didn't see much future in either one, and now he was growing impatient. Wealth, it seemed, was always just beyond his grasp and retreated further as he went closer to it. Bad luck seemed too inevitable to be random. There was some kind of plot going on, and he was pretty sure God was in on it.

Tom and Ola May continued on with school, though Ola was more interested in her schooling than Tom was. If there was something that needed doing at the Garden or on the range, that took precedence for Tom. Likewise, if he heard someone was paying for day labor, he was happy to skip school in favor of money.

Though she was a fine rider herself, Ola May rode with Tom to the Klondyke school. So when Tom did not go, neither did Ola May. Jeff was never overly concerned with appearances, but Granny Jane insisted that an attractive young woman should not ride twelve miles unaccompanied. Ola did not miss the lessons so much as she missed the attention of the boys and the thrill of learning which of the boys had now become a stammering, fumbling idiot in her presence.

She was small, like Mattie had been, and attractive, though not so much beautiful or pretty, though her features were small and regular. There was something about the eyes, though, that rendered her very desirable. She had grown up around boys and men, with only her grandmother's female presence. She knew men. She understood their bodies and their ways, and she had developed a man's interest in the pleasures of the world.

While the other girls cast their eyes to the ground, Ola May would look a man in the eye, the slightest of smiles playing about her mouth, daring him to come closer, to make a play, to follow up on the desire that shone from his eyes. Few did. Rather, it was the boys who looked away, who looked off to the horizon in an attempt to find something there that would redeem them, confirm that they were young men, not boys, and that they were the powerful ones, the ones in charge. They never found it.

The deference was both a pleasure and a disappointment. She wanted to find the boy who would hold her look, who would take the dare and try to show his will was greater than hers. She would find him, but she hadn't yet. She took her pleasure, then, in the rejection, the boyish surrender that inevitably followed. She was a Power, after all, and tougher than the rest, and if she barely held her own against the men of her family, she towered over all other boys, though she was barely five feet tall.

But she was also jealous of the girls around her, the ones who dropped their gaze and reddened their faces when boys looked at them with desire. They got their books carried and extra treats at lunch. And they got to go to the dances at the LDS stake center and at the fairgrounds. She envied them and she wanted them. She wanted them to be pliant and deferential to her the way they were with the boys. She heard the whispering, knew that they called her a tomboy, a puss, a bitch, and a harlot behind her back while they pretended to be nice as pie to her face. She sometimes had the desire to take one of them and push her into a wall or a corner and then push herself onto the now-frightened girl, covering and crowding her like she knew some men did to low women, just to show who was boss. Instead, she reduced their admirers and boyfriends to helpless twits whose fumblings in the dark later would be as tainted with her image as they were awkward.

Tom met Bob Wootan, who made extra cash by putting on rodeos outside of the various small towns of Cochise, Graham, and Gila Counties. Rodeos had been officially banned in Arizona for their inherent cruelty to animals. As Arizona marched toward statehood, it was eliminating all things that might trigger organized protest against its admission to statehood.

But there was also an abundance of wild burros in southern Arizona. Abandoned by miners, the burros thrived in the desert by virtue of their ability to survive on little food and water and a general absence of predation. The state allowed anyone with a mind to to round up and keep wild burros.

Like a few others, Wootan found the burros profitable. Wild, the burros were hard to ride, but they were low to the ground and, therefore, less likely to do damage to their would-be riders. Burro rodeos were becoming a popular, though illegal, entertainment, traveling from small town to small town, setting up for a day or so, and providing the opportunity for various sorts, from leading lights to staggering drunks, to get slammed to the ground by kicking, braying burros and then stand up, wipe themselves off, and try again.

Tom, who could ride anything, was good with the burros, and when his entertainment value waned as he stayed on a burro longer and longer, he was invited to help Wootan out as he moved his stock from one county to the next. The burro rodeos were also perfect vehicles for bootlegged liquor, and Tom was happy to help out with that, too. His old connections near Firth's store were able to supply him with a good deal of bad whiskey at a decent price.

But decent wasn't good enough for Bob Wootan. "The liquor is where the money is," Wootan said. "The burros is just an enticement. We need to make more money on the whiskey."

"How we going to do that?" Tom asked. "We got every cowboy for forty miles around coming out here and riding and drinking all weekend. We can't take out notices in the paper."

"Well, we make more money on the whiskey we sell."

"Can't raise prices too much; whiskey is already twenty dollars a bottle. Cowboys ain't millionaires."

"No. But we can work the other end—get the whiskey for less."

"I'm getting a good price on whiskey," Tom said.

"We can do better. I know where we can get it at half the price we're paying now."

"Stealing it?"

"Better. Buying it from someone else who's stealing it. The marshal's office has been picking up a lot of illegal whiskey coming in from Mexico. Some of it is destroyed, some is held for evidence. The rest just sort of disappears."

"And we could buy the disappeared whiskey?"

"Yes we could," Wootan said. "I got contacts, too. Family connections, you might say."

Tom considered this. "And this is reliable?"

"Full faith of the United States government," Wootan said. "And there could be some extra work helping to move the whiskey from one place to another. Because there are people in high position here in this business, and they're looking for others to actually handle the merchandise. It keeps them removed from the evidence."

"So we would be bootleggers as well," Tom said.

"More 'independent distributors,' I would say."

"And who's involved in this? Who would we be dealing with?"

"I can't name names. But the US marshal's office is the source."

"The marshal?"

"Not the marshal, exactly, but close to it."

"Frank Haynes?"

"You didn't hear that from me."

Tom started picking up cases of whiskey from Bob's cousin, Kane Wootan, once a week. Half he kept for the rodeos; the rest he was free to sell to others. Eventually, he began just picking up the whiskey himself from an abandoned barn near Dos Cabezas. Bob paid Kane for what they took. There was so much whiskey and so much money that Tom began adding a couple of extra cases as a kind of handling fee. The money was good.

Chapter Nine
1915

Robert Franklin McBride had been a deputy sheriff of Graham County, Arizona, for ten months when he could stand it no more. Again, he had arrested two men riding the road from Solomonville to Safford with a load of whiskey. Again, they had been released on the grounds of "insufficient evidence," though there were six cases of homemade whiskey taken from their auto and stored in the basement of the Graham County Courthouse in Safford.

The illegal liquor was poured out on the dirt roads of Safford to settle the dust. It seemed to McBride that a lot less whiskey and gin was being dumped than had been taken in. Whether Sheriff Tom Alger was in on the missing whiskey didn't really matter. It was his jail, and if he wasn't directly involved, he was complicit. It gnawed on McBride. He had risked a good deal going after whiskey runners headed for Safford and on to Fort Thomas on the Apache reservation. Once he had been shot at, and a couple of times he had to physically force runners to the ground in order to shackle them. It was usually for nothing. Runners rarely went to trial, and many, like the latest arrests, spent just a day or two in jail before they were set loose. The prohibition of alcohol in Arizona wasn't a bad law. But enforcement was lacking.

McBride thought sometimes it might be better if there were no law. But there was one, enforced or not. He didn't like alcohol and had never consumed it himself, though most of his friends had at least tried it once or twice when they were boys. The use of alcohol was forbidden by scripture, as was tobacco and other stimulants. But the teaching of the Latter-Day Saints aside, he saw from his own experience that alcohol quickly turned good men into fools and otherwise good women into tramps and slatterns. One of his own friends, a Latter-Day Saint in good standing, had a fondness for the stuff, and McBride had been called on more than once to come to his friend's aid when he was under the influence. Like a true friend, McBride helped to conceal his friend's secret to the detriment of both their souls.

The prohibition law, many argued, was simply a way to entice the United States into granting Arizona statehood, which it had done three years ago. Like the abolition of the death penalty, the law was a good compromise to those who, far away, wished to rule the lives of those in Arizona, a good deal of whom were

Mormon. It would not be seemly to repeal those laws so soon after statehood, thereby admitting that they had been passed to ease the way for statehood. And the church supported the ban, and he respected the authority of the church, whose politics, by revelation, came directly from God. Still, he thought it a terrible charade to pretend to enforce a law when you were actually turning a blind eye to those who broke it.

He wasn't keen on the death penalty, though he had a hard time refuting the argument that the death penalty ultimately saved lives. He had some difficulty, however, understanding how taking a life saved more lives. In his short experience with criminals and with murder, most murders were committed when the killer was out of his mind with rage, fear, or hatred and wouldn't be stopped by the knowledge that there was a death penalty. In fact, the two murderers he did know seemed decent-enough men who had gotten themselves into tight spots they didn't know how to get out of. Still, the Heavenly Father was clear on His commandments.

Personally, he would rather deal with a murderer than a whiskey runner who was driven by a quite well reasoned desire for wealth.

And there was good money in whiskey. Very good money. The prohibition of whiskey had driven its price up to a nearly incredible twenty dollars a quart, when gold itself was eighteen dollars an ounce. An ounce of gold, which would take a man considerable time to sluice, fell short of buying one quart of whiskey. The prohibition dwindled supply, which drove up prices. The high prices drove greed, which drove the illegal production and distribution of the stuff. He was struck by the way the most firm believers in the forces of the marketplace could be convinced that they didn't operate in situations involving ethics and morality.

Maybe he had been better off as a carpenter. He was a decent carpenter, though there were faster and better carpenters than he. But he could build a building to stand, its walls and corners square, roof, door, and windows tight, and it wouldn't be unpleasant to look at. Carpentry was simple when you had learned its secrets and were fastidious and patient. He was all of those. And once a board was sawn, it stayed sawn. Once a nail was driven deep, it wasn't coming back out without a good deal of effort. And bad boards were thrown on the scrap heap, not in jail.

But he liked the law, too. Most of the time. He liked to be out and around, and he was rarely happier than when he was on horseback, which the job required often enough. He had never shot at a single person in his nearly a year of being the deputy sheriff. He often went home at night late but satisfied that he had accomplished things during the day. He aided his fellow man, as directed by the Teachings, and he saw results, where when he built a house, he often could not see what he had done that day for seeing what needed doing tomorrow.

Mostly, the job was settling disputes. Graham County was an open, rural county in the southeastern part of the state. The towns, and there were only a few—Safford, Thatcher, Pima, Solomonville—were small and largely populated with Mormons. The communities were tight and homogeneous. Often enough, it was the stake president of the church who took care of difficulties. The ranchers whose spreads surrounded the towns and made up most of the Gila River Valley were nearly autonomous and tended to keep peace on their own land. For the most part, residents of Graham County got along with each other just fine.

There were isolated trouble spots where the ranchers and the church held little sway. The town of Fort Thomas to the west was part of the Apache reservation, and there the effects of alcohol and poverty led, often enough, to flashes of violence. While no one had been killed during McBride's tenure as deputy sheriff, a couple of residents of Fort Thomas had come close enough to make the possibility of deadly violence nearly an inevitability.

To the south was the town of Klondyke. It was small and remote, and though it fell under their jurisdiction, the Graham County Sheriff's Office tended to leave it be, visiting only when there was real trouble. There was minor trouble in Klondyke often enough. There was a café that had once been a saloon and wanted to be a saloon again and so carried out all the functions of a saloon, including the provision of alcohol. Fights were frequent, sometimes several a week, and a couple of cowboys had been badly beaten for their attentions to one or another of the local women.

McBride had been directly involved in one incident, though it was clear his assistance was neither required nor desired. Klondyke was largely Gentile, and the sheriff's office was considered a Mormon office and ignored, if not despised. He came back from his investigation with a dozen different stories of what had happened and no charges filed by the victims, one of whom had moved on and the other who claimed that he fell from his horse while riding fences at night.

Real violence was usually due to disagreements over money or women. There wasn't a great deal of money in Graham County and even less in Klondyke than in Safford or Thatcher, but in his experience, the smaller the amount of money at stake, the greater chance of theft or brutality. And men always fought over women. It was in their makeup. All animals fought over prized females. Where the church held sway, that instinct was channeled into manners, piety, and love of family. Men tended to behave themselves, though boys fought over girls eternally until they were ready to accept the teachings of the Prophet.

And all men and women, Gentile and Mormon alike, were capable of missing the mark of good behavior and conduct. But while the church could lessen both the possibility and the extent of that, alcohol increased it. It fogged men's minds and made them forget what they knew and believed, and it led them to trouble. Alcohol was a solvent, and it was a powerful one, capable of dissolving the layers of civility and goodness that church and country coated its citizens in. That was the great danger. Instead of rising up through levels of holiness, the drunken fell down through levels of beastliness.

He, for one, wanted the prohibition of alcohol to be permanent in the county and state and, perhaps one day, in the nation. There were enough members of the Church of Latter-Day Saints who would speak with one voice and join with the other righteous that they should have been able to easily defeat any attempt to lift the ban on strong spirits. But there was another great source of unease among men to consider—money. Alcohol had been made more valuable by the desperation of the imbibers, and many of the very men charged with protecting the peace turned a blind eye to the trafficking of alcohol in the state and even in Graham County. How many of the county's and state's governments were involved in the trafficking of whiskey he couldn't say, but there were a lot.

And whether Sheriff Tom Alger was directly involved in the dirty business or not, he did little if anything to slow the whiskey traffic. McBride didn't know whether money came to Sheriff Alger every time he let a bootlegger go or whether it simply kept him employed. In either case, Sheriff Alger was part of the problem, and that was enough to convince Robert Frank McBride that Alger had to go and that McBride was the man to replace him.

In August 1916 McBride filed paper to run for the office of Graham County sheriff on the Democratic ticket. McBride cared little about party affiliation, but Alger was a Republican, so McBride would need to run as a Democrat. It was difficult to unseat an incumbent in a general election but even more difficult to unseat one in a primary.

And the Democratic ticket for the November elections seemed to be unbeatable in the state. The ticket, headed by President Wilson and Governor Hunt, would be able to sweep McBride into office along with the rest of the ticket. The *Graham County Guardian*, the only paper in the county, was sure to endorse the Democratic slate.

McBride was well known in Pima, Thatcher, and Safford, the strongholds of the church in the county. While the three towns were unlikely to provide enough votes by themselves to win him the election, they gave him a solid base to build on, and he would need to carry only a handful of the outlying precincts.

He began riding the southern precincts on his day off, paying visits to Klondyke on the actual but not entirely necessary premise of keeping a lid on things in the wild little town, not much more than a gathering spot for cowboys freed from the constant and often boring work of the ranches.

McBride was paying such a visit to the Klondyke store and café, not really looking for alcohol or much of anything else, thinking that his mere presence would be enough to discourage, though not enough to end, the liquor business there. And by coming by and showing concern without threatening the livelihood of the owners and customers there, he would keep his name in their minds in case they should actually turn out to vote in November. He moved around the store, saying hello and shaking hands with the idlers who gathered there.

One of the layabouts in particular caught his eye. He was young, good-looking in the way that cowboys, unkempt and sun-blasted, could be. He was a little above average height, blue-eyed, with a shock of sandy hair cut at an odd angle, the way hair looked when you cut it yourself, that stuck out from under his battered hat pushed back on his head. There was something compelling, even wholesome, about him. The young man eyed McBride as he moved about the store, and when McBride got to him, he nodded but did not hold out his hand to shake McBride's.

McBride went to the front of the store, where Ike, who had bought the store from Firth, leaned against the counter, studying a paper too intently to be actually reading it. McBride stopped in front of him and stuck out his hand. Ike regarded it for a moment, then shook it reluctantly.

"I think you all probably know me," McBride said. "I'm Frank McBride, and I'm running for sheriff. I know many of you." He stopped and looked around. "Some of you better than others." A few of the idlers exchanged sheepish, knowing looks. "Others of you I'm meeting for the first time today. I just want to introduce myself and ask that you consider voting for me in the upcoming election.

"I've been a deputy in the sheriff's office for a few years now, and I've done my best to do my job without concern over who knows who or what school or what church they've attended. I'm a member of the Latter-Day Saints, a Mormon, if you will, and I don't try to deny or hide that. I know many of you are not members or have lapsed away from the church. That makes no difference to me.

"I try to be right and fair in all that I do. When I'm not, it's a failing, not an intent. I wish no one ill, but I want this county to stay the good place it's always been. There are good people here who mostly mind their own business and stay to the right. That's a good thing, and I don't mean to change it. But there are outsiders here now who are looking to change our lives. They're offering some pretty good money to people willing to break the law. I understand that that's a big temptation. But the law is backed by good reasons and judgment, not just ours but our forefathers' and the Heavenly Father's. Those outsiders would have us sell our lives and happiness for a few dollars. I don't think that's worth it."

"But it ain't 'a few' dollars," someone said.

McBride smiled. "No. I guess it's not. But compared to the peaceful, happy lives we lead here, it's not enough, I wouldn't think."

"What are you going to do about bootlegging?"

McBride smiled again. "I believe I've heard about that. Some of it may even be pretty close by. Bootlegging is against the law, and I'm for the law, so I'm against bootlegging. I'm not going to go busting into people's houses or their businesses, either, if I can help it." He stopped and glanced back at Ike. "But when we find a bootlegger, we'll arrest and try him. I won't lie. I would like to see the practice wiped out. I know others disagree, but I think the prohibition is a good law that helps to keep things peaceful. Like I said, I'm not a crusader, and I won't go around breaking down doors, but I'll try my best to put an end to the illegal business when I find it."

Ike stopped him before he could go further. "We've a good, long history with Sheriff Alger, Mr. McBride. I'm not sure we want or need to change that."

"I do understand, and I understand that I probably can't say much to change that. Sheriff Alger has let you be, and I mostly will, too. Though, if I know of illegal goings-on, I'm duty bound to try to put a stop to them. If you do change your mind and want to elect a sheriff who's fair and who won't favor one side or one man over another, you'll want to consider Frank McBride."

"I guess you've had your say," Ike said.

"Yes. I guess I have. I would also like to leave a few of these with you." McBride took a small stack of 3-by-5-inch postcards with a photograph of himself atop his dappled horse, Big Boy, McBride's sidearm and rope in clear view. It could have been a publicity still for William S. Hart.

Ike motioned to the right side of the store's counter. "You can leave them right there."

"They're postal cards," McBride said, smiling. "You can send them to your friends, if you want. A note to your mother won't be a commitment to vote." Ike simply glared, and McBride, smiling again, walked out, nodding to the idlers he passed.

He was climbing into the truck he had borrowed from a neighbor when he heard his name. He turned, and the sandy-haired cowboy from the store had come up behind him. McBride hadn't heard a thing.

"Mr. McBride," the man said, "I just wanted to make your acquaintance. I'm Tom Power."

There were a few names that caught the attention of every lawman in Graham County. Wootan was one, Power another. They weren't necessarily troublemakers, but they always seemed to be around when trouble happened. Trouble seemed to follow them like a cloud of dust followed a truck.

"And I didn't want you to waste your time."

"Waste my time?"

"In there." Power nodded toward the store. "You ain't going to win many votes in there."

"I believe I knew that," McBride said.

"They ain't your kind. Not many of your kind down here." Power went on as if McBride hadn't responded.

McBride wasn't sure what Power meant by his "kind." Mormon? Certainly, this southern district wasn't a Mormon stronghold. Or did he mean something else?

"You ain't got a Chinaman's chance around here."

McBride nodded in comprehension but also uncertainty. This was all pretty obvious, and he wasn't sure why Power was letting him in on the obvious.

"And you can't win with just the Safford and Pima bunch, either. You got to get votes out of the rest of the county."

This, too, was fairly obvious, though he was impressed that the young cowboy was smart enough to understand that. He would have a big lead in the major towns in the northern precincts, but Alger was going to be strong in the south. He had determined early that they were nearly evenly matched, and to win, one would have to cut into the other's territory. But Klondyke was beyond a long shot. It was an impossibility. He was here only because he wanted people to see that he didn't give up on things. He would come into a bad situation and try to turn it to his advantage, whether he could or not.

"Yep," Power said. "You got to carry some of this part of the county or you ain't going to have a job come November."

"I believe I understand that, too. That's why I'm here."

"Wasting your time."

"I don't know about that. I guess we'll see in November."

"You can see right now. You got only one chance around these parts. And you're looking at it."

"You?"

"Yes, sir. Me. I can win you votes around here. People know me, and they know I'm the real business. They listen to me because I'm one of them."

"So you'll stump for me?"

"That's it right there. I'll ride this whole damned county, and I'll ride on a horse, coming up to people's ranches and houses the way you're supposed to. On a horse, not in a truck." Power nodded at McBride's borrowed truck.

"I've got a lot of territory to cover."

"You don't need to. I'll do that for you."

"That would be quite kind of you."

"I like to help out where I can."

"And I might be able to help you out in return?"

"It's what neighbors do. You help me buck hay, and I'll help mend your fences. Country life."

"What do you have in mind?"

"You're going to need an undersheriff."

McBride nodded as though he were considering this. He knew where this was going, but he wanted to see how Power was going to get there.

"Like I said, I just want to help." Power eyed McBride, trying to gauge a reaction. McBride did not react. Power went on. "If I was to help, maybe swing a few votes down here, you might see what a valuable addition I could be to your staff."

"And I could appoint you undersheriff."

"You could, yes. I could help you. I would like you to see that."

"Help me how?"

"I know a lot. I know more than most people think I do. I know what goes on down here, and I know who is involved in the goings-on." Power nodded, confirming this for McBride and himself. "A lot. I know a lot."

"I've heard you know a lot about rodeos, too."

Power smiled. "Rodeos are illegal now." McBride nodded and Power went on, still smiling a small, wry smile.

"Yes, they are. They are illegal."

"A lot of stuff is illegal these days. But rodeos. Rodeos are a great tradition. Cowboys are dying out. No one in the world is going to know about them in the next fifty years. It's going to be like the free Indians, just a memory. Rodeo keeps cowboying alive for a little while longer."

"That it does," McBride said. "And it gives the cowboys, Indians, and everyone else a chance to gamble and lose their money."

"Well, not everyone loses." Power's eyes were darting, and the sides of his mouth occasionally betrayed a small twitch as he tried not to smile. He was clearly enjoying this. McBride was, too. Power wasn't as dumb as he looked.

"Most do. That's why it's illegal."

"Only the ones who believe in luck lose. A lot win. And I'm thinking that it's illegal because people seem to enjoy it, and there are those who just can't stand to see others enjoying themselves. Not that that means you."

"Of course not. We support the prohibition of alcohol, too, but not because we don't want people to enjoy themselves. We want them to enjoy themselves without getting hurt or hurting someone else."

"You can't stop people from hurting themselves. It's what some people are good at. Hurting others, too. Same things. I just ain't sure the government needs a say in that. I know something about the whiskey trade."

"I had heard that you might know a thing or two about that trade. I know something of it, too."

"I'm sure you do," Power said. "But I know more. I know who's involved and who's not."

"I know a lot of that, too."

"If you know, you ought to be doing something about it, which I don't see you doing. Unless you're involved in it, too. Which you ain't, because I would know that. And, of course, you ain't giving all the orders."

"No, I'm not. Yet. But I think you're probably right. You do know more about it than I do, though I suspect I know more than you think I do."

"You don't play cards, do you, Deputy? I mean, real cards, for money. It's like this. You'd probably enjoy it."

McBride smiled. "We believe that just because you enjoy it doesn't mean it's good for you."

"Can't always have what's good for you. Life ain't like that," Power said.

"You see, there's another place we disagree." He held his hand out to shake. "It's been a pleasure talking to you, Mr. Power."

Tom took his hand and shook it. "Likewise. You mix blue and yellow paint, and you got green. If you don't mix them, you just got blue and yellow."

"I understand that." McBride opened the door to the truck and retrieved the crank.

"Nice truck."

"Borrowed."

"Someday you'll likely have one of your own."

CHAPTER TEN
1918

Tom pulled them up to a line shack on the Hendricks ranch. They had ridden most of the day, not seeing anyone, as though the pursuit of them had just stopped. The line shack was small, more a pile of sticks than a building. Most of it was made from boards that looked like they'd been pulled off of packing crates. The roof and the doors were ocotillo stalks wired together. And the door was wired to the shack, fencing wire on both sides, for hinges on one side, a latch on the other.

Inside was mostly rolls of barbed wire, stacked out here to save riding all the way back to the main ranch to run new fences or repair the old. There were cans of staples and an assortment of tools—shovels, picks, axes, a couple of come-alongs for stretching wire, hammers, and pliers. There was a stack of wooden crates back in a corner under some wire and canvas.

"I want you and Sisson to stay here," Tom told John. "You'll be safe here. I'm going to take the horses up a ways, then ride on into Hendricks's. He'll let us stay here a couple of days, maybe help us reprovision. At least we can get some good sleep around here before we head into the mountains."

"Which mountains?" Sisson asked.

Tom pointed to the southeast. "Chiricahuas. Then from there into New Mexico and down into Old Mexico. I think when we get across the Chiricahuas, we can rest a little easier. They ain't going to follow us up there. Then it's down into Mexico, and we're free."

Sisson snorted. "They're going to follow us to hell."

Tom scowled. "Well, then, let's avoid going to hell for a little while yet. What do you say? Besides, Mexico ain't hell. It's where we can get a fresh start. Mexico is going to be Power Heaven. We're going to own that place."

"What if someone comes out here?" John asked.

"No one's coming out here."

"But what if they do?"

"Well, John, you could invite them in, maybe see if they would be interested in playing some cards or such. Or you could just goddamned kill them. You decide."

Tom led the two horses about a mile from the shack before tying them off to a mesquite tree. It would be a hard run to go get them, but if the horses were found closer to the line shack, there wouldn't be much mystery about where John and Sisson were. Likely the shack would be so blasted full of holes that the two wouldn't know they were found until they were already dead. Better to make a long scramble to the horses than a quick trip to the grave.

Tom rode on alone at a slow pace, plodding along like any cowboy who wasn't anxious to come upon further work. Halfway into the ranch house and barns, he saw another lone cowboy off to the south. Or, likely, it was a cowboy. If he were mistaken for one, he could mistake a searcher for one, too. Cowboys were no threat. A lot of them were vaqueros, up from Mexico. The United States was a good place to work. Other than that, it meant nothing to them.

Even American cowboys had little interest in the events of the world around them. They were laborers who took what they could get. They were solitaries who intentionally cut themselves off from the world around them. As long as they could eat, sleep, get drunk, and fuck once in a while, the world held little more interest to them. Mostly they were not antisocial but asocial. Cowboys were their own society. But there were some Mormons among them, and Mormons could never cut themselves entirely free of Mormondom.

But, he figured, searchers would be going together, not out riding alone. Whoever you were, whatever allegiances you might have, you did not want to come up on three armed fugitives alone or even in a pair. You always wanted the advantage of numbers, and that advantage gave Tom the advantage in pursuit.

He came on three cowboys before he found Billy Hendricks. Two of them were Mexicans and simply pointed when he asked, "¿Dónde está señor Billy?" The last was Jedkins or Judkins or something damned closed to that, whom Tom had run into a couple of times before. The Mexicans had stared at Tom's swollen eye. Judkins didn't. Tom figured that meant Judkins knew who he was and what he had done. But Judkins just pointed to a windmill a couple hundred yards away. "See that windmill yonder? That little dot up at the top is Billy."

"Hell," Tom said. "Billy's too old to be up top a windmill."

Judkins smiled. "The way I look at it, I'm too young."

Tom nodded and headed for the windmill.

"You better come down before you kill yourself, old man," Tom yelled.

"Hold on there, Tom. It will be a couple more turns up here. I ain't coming down just to go back up."

Tom sat his horse while Hendricks tightened, pounded, and muttered at the top of the windmill. Finally, Hendricks moved down a step. "Watch below. Tools coming."

Tom turned his horse and backed off a few paces as a ball peen hammer, pliers, wrenches, screwdrivers, and a small roll of baling wire came sailing down, setting up puffs of dust as they hit the ground.

Billy came down the built-in ladder in a series of lurches, his left foot landing heavily on the wooden slats of the ladder. Billy had no doubt broken the leg a couple of times and, at least once, hadn't gotten it set right. He was old, maybe fifty, gone to gut mostly but still strong through the arms, legs, and shoulders. His face was the color and texture of an old saddle. He was dressed as he dressed every day of his life—canvas pants, a cotton shirt, and a battered hat that was once probably a pretty good Stetson. His boots were old. You knew he was a successful rancher, as far as success could ever be counted in ranching, because he had boots good enough to get old before they completely fell apart. He extended his hand to Tom. The fingers were grease-stained, cut, and bent at odd angles from breaks and arthritis. Tom took the hand, which was a preview of his own if he could stay alive a few years longer.

"You look like hell," Billy said. "What's with your eye?"

"Glass, I guess. Maybe wood, probably glass. Did you hear what happened?"

"More or less. I guess pretty much everyone's heard something. Can't outrun that damned telephone."

"They been looking for us?"

"A couple of times. They'll be back a couple more, that's for sure. How much do you know?"

"Just what happened. The Old Man's dead. So are McBride, Kempton, and Wootan."

"All dead. They've had posses out since Sunday evening."

"Who got away?"

"Haynes. Got away clean. Called it in from Klondyke. That's how they's on you so fast. You didn't know that?"

"It was a hell of a fight, Billy. There could have been a circus set up ten feet away, and I wouldn't have noticed."

"It don't make sense, though. None of it."

"I'm guessing it was the gold they was after."

"They're saying it was that draft business, Tom. Most around here ain't in favor of that story, but that's what they're saying. It just don't make much sense, the way I see it. It would have been a damned simple thing to take you boys in Safford."

"We didn't go to Safford much. Usually Sisson went."

Billy Hendricks shook his head. "Well, there it is. You wait for Sisson to come to town, and you arrest him. Aiding and abetting. Pretty soon, Old Jeff comes wandering in, looking for Sisson. Aiding and abetting, again. Then, when they don't come back, you and John come in looking for them. Pretty simple. You got all four of you without any unpleasantness. Not a shot fired. Anyone knows that firing a shot at a Power is going to get you a bunch of shots in return. No. It don't make no sense at all."

"The way you had it makes sense, all right. Except that wasn't what they wanted. They was looking for a fight. We took six hundred rounds out of their saddlebags. They wanted us dead. Six hundred rounds."

"You don't say? That casts a light on things, don't it? Six hundred rounds is the start of a small war."

"And that's what they got," Tom said.

"Well, that was my point, Tom. You can't go in and try to buffalo an outfit like yours. They was counting on a fight, and they got one. Odd thing, though. I wouldn't want to start a fight with you Powers evenly matched. Hell, to take out four of you, I'd bring a dozen or so with me."

"They was thinking on surprise. They came up right at dawn. It was light, but just barely light. Shot the Old Man soon as he opened the cabin door. Wasn't even dressed yet. Gunned him right down in his underwear."

"See. The word is, he fired on them."

"Never had time. He was shot before he could jack a shell into that Winchester."

"Damn. Did they announce themselves?"

"Not intentionally. Spooked our horses, which was belled. I heard the horses go by the cabin and woke up. Next thing, I heard a shot and I seen the Old Man fall out the door. I just jumped up and grabbed my gun. John, too. I took the window, John took the door. There was no pleasantries exchanged."

"Hell, that's not what they're saying, but there's no surprise there, is there? Still, I think you got a pretty good case for self-defense there."

Tom snorted. "You think so? You think there's even going to be a trial? I don't. I think that unless we can outrun them and get to Mexico, we got two choices—shot in the back, or hanged. Neither is a prize, but given my druthers, I don't really want to be hanged. We got to keep riding."

"There's a lot of bad feeling, Tom. It ain't a good thing to go shooting the law."

"It ain't a good thing to shoot three of Thems, either. Thems don't pay a lot of heed to that 'forgive and forget' business. That don't seem to be in Thems' Book. Thems don't forgive, and Thems sure as hell don't ever forget."

"I wouldn't argue that, Tom. They do hang together. It's their history. I know that, but you can't hold to history forever. They'll swarm like bees if you bother just one."

"It's the gold, Billy. It's the gold."

"You really think so? Not the whiskey?"

"Yes I do. We was on to something, Billy."

"No lie? I hadn't heard that. Normally something like that would get around faster than the squirts after the church picnic. You was really pulling gold out of that hole up there?"

"Hell, yes. I ain't going to make more of it than it was, but we was taking some good-grade ore out of that thing. Not a lot of it. But we was coming on to more and more of it, like we was coming at a good-sized vein of it. We had it assayed. It was high concentration."

"You had it assayed? Where?"

"Well, in Safford, of course."

"Well, that there's another side to the story, ain't it?" Billy took off his hat and scratched at his head. "Had it assayed in Safford. I would have gone to Lordsburg, myself."

"Thinking back on it, I'd be hard-pressed for argument. But we was digging and finding more, and we didn't want to run at a third of capacity while someone rode to Lordsburg. So we took it to Safford. Had it done there."

"Right in the middle of Thems."

"Right in the damned middle."

"No offense, Tom. But that wasn't sterling thinking."

"Yeah. I guess I know that. But I had good relations up there in Safford. Hell, I campaigned for McBride when he first run. I figured that bought me something."

"Of course it got you something, Tom. I mean you been doing your whiskey business more or less right out in the open for over a year now. Did McBride ever lay a finger on you?"

"Well, no, Billy. He didn't. It just seemed to me that that was all business, and everyone done OK on it. I didn't see a reason for McBride to have got upset over it."

"No. I wouldn't figure he would. He would most likely just not want to be bothered with any of it as long as you weren't upsetting the general peace. You know, Tom, and I don't mean any offense by any of this, but there is a lot of questions going on about how you all came into that mine."

"We bought it. Fair and square. You know that, Billy."

"I know and most of the people in the valley know, but we ain't the ones that count. We ain't the ones asking, 'How did the Powers get all that money?' Not that it's our business."

Tom's jaw began to flex the way it did when anger took him over. "You're right about that. It ain't your business."

"I agree on that. But there's lots of questions. Hell, Tom. Gold is eighteen dollars an ounce, and whiskey's twenty dollars a bottle. That's a lot of money, there. And whiskey's got a bigger, easier market than gold. Everyone knows that."

"All right," Tom said. "It ain't a good-kept secret, but it ain't coming fully out, either. Whiskey's big business, and it's big business for nearly everybody. Hell, there ain't a soul in the state that ain't got some whiskey money in their pocket. You're making out all right on this, ain't you?"

Billy nodded. "Yes. Yes I am. People like to be able to put beef on the table every now and again, and it seems like more and more people are able to do exactly that. And that's put money in my pocket."

"And that ain't the only part."

"I'm aware of that, too. And I know that where there's big money, there's big feelings. If you're looking to get yourself killed, you can fuck a man's wife or steal his money. Each is about equally effective. I, myself, am trying to keep out of this as much as I can. Maybe you ought to think the same."

"That would have been good advice awhile back. Right now, it ain't worth shit, Billy."

"I ain't trying to add to your misery. Just trying to keep you alive is all."

"I guess I know that, Billy. And since we're onto that subject, can the three of us stay here for a while until they get tired of looking for us?"

"You know you can. Don't even have to ask."

"Well, John and Sisson is back at the line shack. Can't stay there very long. It's too small and too out in the open. They stumble on that, and we're nothing more than targets."

"I can put you out in the horse barn on the west eighty. They won't likely search that."

"It's the same problem, though. If they do, we're stuck. We got to be someplace they can't look for us at."

"Hell, Tom, I'd put you in the house, if I could. But there ain't room for the three of you. We'd all be crashing into each other. But you can stay in the big barn next to it. I'll lock you in."

"They'll want to search it."

"Yes, they will. But they ain't going to. There's only so much intrusion a man can abide. You'll be safe there."

"All right, then. That will be good. Obliged. I need to swap out some horses, though."

"They ain't the law's horses, is they? I don't want to get found with them."

"No. I swapped them out back at Carlink. They's out in the pasture back there. These are ones we got from Poke."

"Well, that's all right, then."

"One of them threw a shoe."

"You got Sisson with you, don't you?"

"Yeah."

"Ain't a better farrier in these parts. I got all the gear he'll need."

"Well, I'm obliged again."

"We got to stick together, Tom. Even when we don't especially want to. Thems stick together like they was glued. Like they was one person with a thousand arms and legs. They force us to stay together just to survive."

"What's taking him so long?" John asked.

"I don't think it's been that long. It's just the accommodations is pretty damned cramped."

"I don't believe I would be comfortable in here if I was a fence post."

"Roomier than a coffin, John. See if anyone has left some food out here. Sometimes they do. Check that pile in the corner."

"My Lord. Look at this," John said when he had pulled back the canvas to reveal stacks of whiskey boxes.

"Son of a bitch," Sisson said. "That there's a lot of whiskey."

John pulled a bottle out of the open box. He uncorked it, sniffed, and took a pull at it.

"That ain't ours," Sisson said.

"It ain't all that good, either. But the only thing worse than bad whiskey is no whiskey. They's plenty. They won't miss one bottle." He held the bottle out to Sisson.

"Someone will miss it. This one bottle is twenty dollars or so. That's near to a week's pay for most folks."

"You going to fret or drink? Billy Hendricks is running whiskey. I'll be damned. I never would have thought it. Not Billy."

Sisson sighed and took a pull. "Once you get it past your mouth, it feels pretty good going down."

"Yeah," John said. "You get stuck out in an old line shack, there are worse things to get stuck with."

Sisson looked at something he had seen earlier—a little thumbnail scorpion, the kind that sting worse than the ones ten times their size, hanging on to the boards of the shack. He stoppered the bottle and pressed the bottom of it onto the scorpion, grinding it into the wood. "I guess that's right."

"Sisson? Tom knew right where this line shack was, didn't he? Like he had been here before, right?"

"I know what you're thinking."

"This here's Tom's whiskey. It ain't Hendricks's. He's just letting Tom store it here."

"That's a probability."

"How much you think this whiskey is worth? There's, what, fourteen cases of it? And part of another."

"I don't know, John. A lot. I know that. It's a lot."

"Is all of this, all of this—Old Man, the law we shot, this running to Mexico, and hiding out and all. Is this all part of Tom's whiskey business? I mean, is all this trouble, all this killing just business, Sisson?"

"John, I don't know. I just don't know."

"But it could be, right? I'm right, ain't I? It could be."

"It could, but I don't know. It's Tom's business. That's all this is."

"I know," John insisted. "I do, too, know. It's Tom's business. That's all this is."

Sisson shook his head. "No, John. You don't know. You think you know it all. It's a possibility. You got to admit that, but it ain't a certainty, just a possibility. Don't go jumping on conclusions. Don't go putting everything at risk on a possibility."

"I know. I know for certain. This is all Tom's doing. This whole business just stinks of Tom."

"John." Fear and anger were finding their way into Sisson's voice. "Tom's your brother. He ain't as good as you thought he was, once. And he ain't as bad as you're thinking he is now. He's your brother. That's all. Now get ahold of yourself."

"We're going up into Hendricks's place," Tom said. "And put that fucking gun down, John."

"I ought to shoot you. That's what I ought to do. And maybe that's what I'm going to do."

"Find yourself some whiskey, did you?"

"Tom," Sisson said, "he's pretty upset. You take some care now."

"He's pretty drunk. That's what he is. We still got business to take care of. Thems ain't out there having Themselves a party. Thems's still looking for us. We got a hard ride to Hendricks's barn, to put up there for a bit. Now let's just get ready to ride."

"Whose whiskey, Tom?" John was still holding the gun pointed more or less at Tom.

"I don't know, John. Might be Hendricks's or one of his men. Right now, it looks pretty much like yours. Or you're its."

"It's yours, Tom. I know that, and I know that's what this whole thing is about. It's all about whiskey. Not the draft, not gold. Whiskey. Your whiskey."

"John, shut up," Sisson said. "Would you please just shut up? Come on. Let's get out of here."

"You know I'm right, Sisson." John turned toward Sisson in a big, sloppy gesture that put the barrel of the gun pointing to the ground. Tom stepped in, pulled the gun, and kicked John in the knee. When John went down, Tom took the gun, which went off, blowing a hole through the roof of the line shack.

Tom handed the gun to Sisson. "Take this. Don't let him have it until he's sober." He looked down to where John was on the ground, holding his knee up to his chest. "And brother, you best remember, drinking don't ever improve stupid." And back to Sisson. "Help him to his horse or shoot him. I don't much care right now."

Hendricks's barn became heaven. They stayed in the hayloft, where they built a fortress of hay bales against the chance someone would come up looking for them. But no one did. The hay-bale fortress was a labyrinth, so that they could travel from the sleeping and eating area to visit the slop bucket without being seen. Several times they heard voices raised outside, and Tom, pressing his good eye to the spaces between barn boards, saw a group of riders who were certainly part of a posse that remained mounted beyond the barn not four rods from where they were concealed. No one but Manuel, Billy Hendricks's foreman, who came in morning and evening to bring them food and water and poultices for Tom's and John's eyes, tried the labyrinth. Each morning, whistling the same five notes to identify himself, he brought them a fresh slop bucket, though he did not take the old one. That he left for the boys to empty themselves under cover of darkness. For a day and a half, they slept, coming awake for only short periods, rarely awake together.

Tom woke in the night from a bad dream in which a posse set fire to the barn. In the daylight he understood that not even Thems would burn a rancher's barn to get at them.

"That whistling he's doing, that ain't the 'Degüello,' is it?" Sisson asked, referring to the song Santa Ana played all night outside the Alamo. It meant "massacre."

When they were awake, they were eating or talking to Manuel, once to Billy himself, though he stayed out of the barn as much as possible, letting Manuel, who was supposed to spend a good deal of time in the barn anyway, tend to the boys and Sisson.

Their food was prepared by Manuel's wife, Rosalinda, who cooked for both the family and the hands. Once Manuel placed a plate of cookies next to the tamales and said with a wink, "From la señora, who does not know you are here."

"If we were here," Sisson said, "we would thank her."

"And if you were here, she would say, 'De nada.'"

In the afternoon of the third day, heaven became simply an open area amid hay bales in the loft of a cold barn. They could not have a fire, though Manuel brought them small piles of heated bricks in a canvas sling. Mostly, they huddled in their coats and in blankets brought from the house, and they walked, as quietly as possible, from one part of the hay labyrinth to the other. There was little talk, and when there was talk the brothers talked to Sisson, not to each other.

"It's getting cramped in here," John told Sisson.

"Enjoy this now," Tom told Sisson. "We need to get out of here soon. We're imposing on Billy Hendricks and putting him in danger as well. We'll be moving on."

"When?" John asked.

"When the time is right," Tom told Sisson.

"Where?" John asked Sisson.

"Where Thems ain't," Tom told Sisson. Sisson, meanwhile, looked glum in his role as intermediary.

In the afternoon of the fourth day, they heard the familiar whistle, but instead of Manuel, Billy Hendricks himself came through the opening in the hay bales. "Afternoon, boys. I got your horses downstairs. I'll take your saddles and gear down and pack you up with provisions. Manuel's getting a fire going in the forge. Sisson, you can attend to that thrown shoe there. Anything you know you're going to need?" He did not ask if they were ready to ride.

"No, sir, Mr. Hendricks," Sisson said. "You've been kind. I'll tend to the shoeing."

"Manuel will come and get you when it's time."

"Where are the posses?"

"Can't say for sure. They's several of them. About four have been by here, looking around and asking questions. The general notion seems to be that you all must have took off to the west, around Tucson, and then down toward Mexico through Papago country. That's the notion as I take it."

"That's some good news," John said.

"Well, you'll remember that the general notion was that the war in Europe was none of our business, too. General notions are made out of tar paper and spit."

"Newspaper and ink, I'd think," Tom said.

"In that case, you would be about right. What's your plan?"

"I was thinking to go up to the Stronghold for a while. Maybe go up through Rock Creek."

"Well, they been nosing around Rock Creek quite a bit. Maybe they'll come back there. Maybe not."

After Hendricks had left, Manuel came in, whistling his five notes. "El fuego," he said, "está listo. ¿Estás?"

Sisson got up heavily. "Estoy listo. As listo as I'm going to be."

It was the work Sisson loved. It had aspects of all the best jobs—the careful measuring of the hoof and the iron to be attached to it. When the measuring was done, not once, not twice, but three times, because to misshoe a horse was to risk destroying the animal, came the hammering and the beating of the iron to his will, then the measuring again, and more hammering. He thought of it as work that used all sides of a man—his thoughtful and deliberate side, which projected out into the future and did what was necessary to prepare for that future, and the side that had an immediate need to bend things to his will, to force himself on a world that did not see a man's will as anything of consequence.

When the shoe had been fitted, he placed it, after cooling it in water, and began driving the nails into the white line of the hoof and outside of the hoof. He then clinched the nails down along the outside of the hoof and rasped both the clinchers and the hoof for rough spots. He let the horse's hoof go and stepped to the side and let the horse work its weight onto the newly shod hoof, which, no doubt, felt odd to it, since it had been going shoeless for days.

He led the horse around outside the barn and watched it walk, its gait smooth and even again, though it was unused to the shoe. It was ready to go, and so were they.

"No one has seen any searchers since early morning," Billy said. "I can't guarantee that they won't be back."

"Never been much for guarantees, anyway," Tom said. "Seems they never quite work out like they're supposed to. I wouldn't want to get caught here, anyway. It would cause you a world of hurt. I been thinking how easy it would be for them to just burn this barn down with us in it. That gives me the shivers. I don't want to be hanged, but I'd sure rather be hanged than burn to death."

"Well, Tom, I don't think you got to be thinking so much on those kind of choices."

"This would seem to be the time," Tom said. "Sometimes you think on that, and it's just idle fiddling in your head. Other times, it takes on a seriousness you better damned well think on. This is one of those times."

"I guess I can't argue that."

"Billy, I ain't looking to die, and I ain't looking to take you with me, either."

"Oh hell, Tom. I know that. And I don't think it would ever come to that. I might catch a little hell, but I been catching that all my life. Don't go worrying too much on me. I'll be all right. It ain't like I'm going to lose a lot of friends. Thems talk a lot about loving their fellow man and such, but it's mostly just tolerating, and more often than not, less than that, even."

"Well, we ain't going to get you in trouble, Billy. I hope you know that. When we leave here, no one is ever going to know we been here, at least not from us. I understand you could be looking at jail if Thems was to find out you hid us."

"Thems ain't going to find out."

"And you got our appreciation. It was a fine thing you done for us. I hope you don't ever need help as bad as we needed it when we got here. But if you do, you know you got it."

"We stand together, Tom. When Thems is standing together, the rest of the world better stand together, too. It seems to me Thems's like dogs. Just one of Thems can be as fine and loyal and sweet as you can imagine, but you get Thems all together in a pack, and everything changes so much you wouldn't recognize the sweet mutts."

"Well, maybe we's all dogs, Billy. Listen. There's whiskey out there in the line shack. Pretty sure that John and Sisson has been in it already. But what's left is yours. Do with it what you will. It's some good money out there."

"How much is there?"

"About fourteen cases."

"Damn. That's a lot of money. Is someone going to be looking for that whiskey, Tom?"

"Someone's probably looking for it right now. Ain't going to find it, though. You and I are the only ones that know it's there. You just keep it. I ain't going to need it anymore."

"Can I ask just who's looking for this whiskey?"

"I'd guess you'd say it belongs to Frank Haynes. Of course, he won't come looking for it himself. Probably Kane Wootan would have been looking for it, but he's no worry. Kane couldn't find his ass with his fingernails most of the time anyway, no matter how bad it itched. You're all right with it, Billy. No one knows that you and I been doing business. You just keep that whiskey and prosper for your kindness."

"Tell you what, Tom. It don't ever hurt to have cash money on you. I believe I got some back to the house. I'll just buy that whiskey off you."

"No, Billy. You done enough. You just keep it, or sell it."

"I don't need fourteen cases of whiskey hanging around. I try my best to stay away from it these days. I don't so much see the pleasure anymore, just the trouble. And if one of my boys gets his hands on it, there's no end to the damage that it's likely to cause. No. I'll sell it. I'll give you what I got for it, and that will leave me with a nice profit when I sell it. You go on back to the barn. I'll be out there in a minute or two."

"You all ready to ride?" Tom asked John and Sisson.

"Guess we are," John said.

"How's your knee? Sorry I had to kick you."

"It's all right. It ain't broke."

"Good. Wouldn't want to have to shoot my own brother for a cripple."

"Here you go, then, Tom," Billy Hendricks said, walking into the barn. "Two hundred dollars and a couple more. It's what I had. You fellows take care now. If you got to come back this way, I don't want you hesitating on that."

"We won't be coming back," Tom said. "Can't see that happening."

"Well, vaya con Dios, then. Cuidado, amigos. Cuidado."

"What was that?" John asked as they rode toward the last fences and Rock Creek.

"What was what?"

"Two hundred dollars."

"Going out of business sale, brother. Going out of business."

"I knew it was you, Tom. I knew it."

"Listen, brother. You want to know so damned much, you just listen. Whiskey comes in from Mexico, and it gets stopped. Some of it gets dumped, the rest of it gets lost or broken. That's the whiskey you found. It's lost whiskey. It bought us the mine."

"And got the Old Man killed."

Tom said nothing. He turned his horse and spurred it.

The Cochise Stronghold is located in the eastern side of the Dragoon Mountains. Named for the great Chiricahua Apache leader in the nineteenth century, the Stronghold features a series of spires of eroded granite rock that provided cover for the Apaches during the wars of the middle and late nineteenth century. It's difficult terrain to traverse and thus gave the Apaches, the indigenous mountain people, significant strategic advantage over anyone, especially the army white men, trying to search them out or pursue them back into the mountains. Much of the Stronghold is passable only on foot, and the granite spires afforded the Apaches both lookout and cover and allowed them to easily repulse anyone who tried to come up into the Stronghold after them.

It was a short ride from Billy Hendricks's ranch to Rock Creek and then up into the Stronghold. The brothers and Sisson dismounted and set the horses to graze what grass remained on the banks of the creek as they began the steep ascent into the Stronghold. They took only what they needed—food, water, guns, ammunition, and rope. Tom wore his shoes, leaving his boots with his horse at the creek. John, unwilling to give up his boots, struggled up the slippery rocks and scree. Tom Sisson, older, in worse shape, simply struggled.

John was further burdened with his saddle, which he refused to leave behind, though both Tom and Sisson had abandoned theirs in the first outcropping of rocks, pointing out that it was an unnecessary burden that would prove useless in the Stronghold.

It was the hardest climbing Tom had ever done. It became vertical almost from the outset, a scramble from one rock to another, often with a branch or exposed root for a handhold that threatened to give out at any second. He led the way with John behind him, lugging the saddle, and Sisson last, forcing his aged body up through the granite by sheer will. They went nearly a hundred feet up before they came to the first level ground. Tom kicked rock and gravel on John, and John kicked it onto Sisson. Neither complained but only tucked their heads down to protect their eyes and mouths and kept climbing.

When they hit level ground, they were able to make their way walking rather than scrambling, but they still had to squeeze around and between and over granite boulders. Tom hoisted himself to the top of a boulder. On the other side was a drop of nearly ten feet. He sat there and waited for the others. It was still cold, and they needed their coats and would need their blankets at night, but the rock was warming in the sun and comforting.

"Here," he said to John when he had come up alongside him. He handed John his bedroll, gun, canteen, and a canvas bag of food and ammunition. "When I get to the bottom, throw all this down to me, then throw your stuff and follow me."

John looked at the drop-off. "How we going to get back up?"

"Not the problem right now. Getting down is." Tom rolled over onto his back and spread his arms, pushing himself across the rock like a swimmer doing the backstroke. After a few pushes, gravity took over, and he slid about four feet down the face of the rock before he fell away, landed and rolled over, then got to his feet again. "It ain't that bad."

John threw down Tom's stuff and then his own. He rolled over onto his back and followed Tom down.

Sisson was giving the drop a bad glare. He rolled over onto his back as the brothers had done, though he looked more like a steer struck by lightning than a man preparing to jump off a boulder. "Fuck me. I don't want to do this."

"We could leave you there," Tom said.

"Yeah," John agreed. "We'll pick you up on the way back."

"You'd be our first line of defense if they follow us up here."

"Yeah," John said. "He looks like he could be right dangerous if someone was to trip over him."

"Yep. Fall down that boulder and break his neck or something."

"All right," Sisson said. "When you morons are done amusing yourselves, you might want to give me a hand so I don't break my neck."

"Aw, Sisson. It ain't that likely."

"Yeah," John agreed. "I'd think he'd break his leg, not his neck."

"Probably right."

"All right, then. Goddamn it. Shut up. I'm coming down." Sisson pushed himself across the arc of the boulder with his hands until gravity had a grip on him and pulled him down the face of it, then dropped him into the arms of the Power brothers.

"You looked right graceful coming down, Sisson."

"Shut up."

They continued the climb, bushwhacking through chaparral, including oak and, farther up, rock-hard manzanita stands that were nearly impenetrable. They went through the first granite spires back into a second ridge where smoke would be hidden from passersby below. What didn't require bushwhacking required scrambling. John was having trouble with that, coming up vertical faces without getting good purchase with his boots, coming down chutes of scree and falling, sending debris onto Sisson and Tom.

Near the top of their climb, Tom came out of a clump of hard, sharply broken manzanita right to an outcropping of granite, vertical for nearly eight feet. He was able to jump enough to get his hands onto the top of the outcropping, something he didn't like to do—putting his hands where he couldn't see. He pulled himself up with his arms, digging as best he could into the granite with his shoes.

They brought Sisson up together, John boosting him with a foothold of interlocked fingers while Tom reached down, took Sisson's wrist, and pulled him up. When they had Sisson on flat ground, Tom threw himself down on the ground to catch his breath.

John jumped for the top of the rock but couldn't get purchase against the rock face. "Tom," he yelled. "Give me a hand up here."

At the edge of the ridge Tom looked down at his brother and shook his head. "I told you not to wear your boots. Take them off."

"I ain't going to. Reach down and haul me up like you done Sisson."

"The hell. You're liable to pull me off the top here, and then I got to do it all over again. Take off the damned boots."

"You can take his arm, and I'll hang on to you so you don't go over," Sisson said.

"The hell with that. Let him take off his boots."

"You'll throw my damned boots down into that canyon there. You think I don't know that? You think I don't know you?"

"I ain't going to throw your boots away. That's just stupid. You need to be able to walk, and boots are better than nothing. Throw them up here and get on up. We need to keep moving."

"Oh, hell. You throw these boots away, and I'm going to damned kill you." John tossed the boots up over the top of the outcropping one at a time. Then he took another jump, scrambling against the granite in his stocking feet and up onto the top with his brother and Sisson. When he got to the top, Tom was threading a length of rope through the pull straps of John's boots. "All right, then. I'm here. Give them back."

"No," Tom said. "You'll move faster without them. Not all that slipping and sliding you been doing."

"No. Give me my damned boots. I ain't going to go walking around here in my stockings, getting them all full of rock and sand and crap. Give me my boots."

"Then take off your stockings."

"Goddamn you, Tom. I don't know why Ma ever had you."

"Because after she had you, she knew she could do better. That's why."

"All right. All right, damn you." John took off, scrambling down a short chute of sand and gravel. They were coming to another vertical face. His feet, stockinged, must have hurt him as he stepped on rock and dry sticks and other plant matter, but he didn't give any sign of it, just moved quickly ahead, reinvigorated with anger at his brother. He leaped up, grabbed the top strata of rock, and lifted himself up, coming over the top of the escarpment in a rush so that the speed of his body propelled him over the leading edge and down the slant of the other side, a smooth slope of granite pushed up out of the earth.

He continued to slide, trying to find traction with his feet and hands to slow himself down, but the rock face, scoured by wind, washed by rain, was smooth and unbroken, and he kept going down, picking up speed as he went. His own motions threw his body into a spin, and he ended up barrel rolling down the escarpment to the ground below.

He came out of the chaparral bruised and scraped. He rose slowly, testing his arms and legs, both of which seemed bruised but not broken. He looked back up at the top of the escarpment for a sign of his brother or Sisson. Neither was there. His right wrist hurt him quite a bit, but he could move it, and he knew it wasn't broken.

He hunkered down at the base of the escarpment and caught his breath. He reached up and touched his face and brought his hand back bright with new blood. He touched himself gently around his eye, cheek, and brow. There were a couple of scrapes, but the blood was coming from the eye again. He rose up, then leaned back onto the granite and lay back, letting the sun warm his face. Now he wished Sisson had just taken the damned eye out.

He heard thrashing in the brush to his left and jumped upright. He looked for his rifle and realized he had left everything, rifle, bedroll, provisions, back on the other side.

"Oh, brother," Tom said, emerging from a small stand of oak and brush. "What did you do that for?"

"You took my goddamned boots."

"I guess there's some sense in there that I'm missing." Tom took the lashed boots from around his neck and threw them to John. "That was one hell of a scramble, though."

Sisson emerged from the oaks.

"Brother busted his eye open again." John's face was again half covered in blood.

"Don't worry about it." John was struggling to untie the lashing from the boots, holding them up close to his good eye.

"Don't plan to. You ain't going to die on us, are you?"

"Ain't died so far. I guess I don't plan on it."

"And speaking of plans, it wasn't hard to just walk around that chunk of rock you went over."

"It wasn't that hard to go over, either."

Tom smiled and tossed John his canteen. "Wash your face."

They kept a small fire. They were far enough up that there was some tree cover to break up the smoke as it rose rather than leaving a single column of smoke that could be seen from miles away. It was a small area, big enough for a fire and room for the three of them to sleep, though they never slept at the same time. The only way in was the way they had come, and they took turns guarding that entrance. It was barely necessary. Only a fool would come up into the Stronghold after them. It was the most strategically defensible site in southern Arizona. Still, they kept a watch. There is never a shortage of fools.

Sisson didn't keep his eye on the opening in the brush where any possible pursuers would have to come. If you kept your eye on one spot long enough, it would entrance you and, finally, put you to sleep. Instead, he picked up a good-sized chunk of Douglas fir and began stripping the bark from it in preparation for carving it into something he hadn't yet decided on.

Escaping and hiding were new experiences for Sisson. He was used to being the pursuer, not the evader. Still, he had learned a lot in his years of scouting Indians for the army. There were two basic strategies in pursuit. In the first, you kept pressure on the prey and kept them from finding shelter, and you kept that pressure on until they faltered and you caught them. In the second, you pressured them to go to ground where you wanted them—some location that gave you good access or trapped them in such a way they would have to come at you fighting or die of hunger and thirst.

This seemed uncomfortably like the second. They had food and water and could forage for a good deal more of it, but their only real way out was the way they had come in. A good hunter would just wait them out. But this bunch, these bunches, for he couldn't tell how many there were, didn't seem so good. They were amateurs who knew something of hunting deer or javelina, even bear, but not men. They were outraged citizens, determined to administer justice as they saw it. They were on the side of right, and, in their world, right was always destined to prevail, despite evidence to the contrary.

Sisson's world didn't seem so simple. It wasn't right and wrong but the belief that there was right and wrong that drove events. Years after he had left the army he had wondered about the rightness of driving the Sioux, the Apaches, and the Paiutes to ground. He had never considered the question while he was doing it, because his job was to do it, not to think about it. They paid him to track and find Indians and only that. He was employed by the United States Army, but he was no soldier. Once he had done his job, he stepped aside and let others do theirs.

Sisson did not fear prison. A return to it would be an inconvenience but not a tragedy. What he feared was rope. Arizona was not a death penalty state, though it had a deserved reputation for quick and fierce justice, full of retribution but not remorse. The lawmen they had killed were Mormons. Most of the law in Graham County and much of adjoining Greenlee and Gila Counties were Mormons. And Mormons were clannish. They had survived and prospered by banding closely together and fiercely protecting one another. After their prophet, Joseph Smith, had been killed by a mob in Illinois, they came together under the protection of Brigham Young and his thug, Porter Rockwell, and made their way across the continent to the more desolate places in the West and set up camp there. Young understood that flight was only a temporary refuge from persecution and that, eventually, it offered no refuge at all, only more persecution. So the Mormons fought, and their neighbors learned the high cost of opposing them. Rockwell was thought of as something of an avenging angel, prepared to shed the blood of the unrighteous to protect the righteous.

And so Sisson had no illusions. If the posses, made up mostly of Mormons and Wootans, caught them, the posses would kill them. And so the pattern that the Mormons had followed became theirs. They would flee as long as they were able, because to resist could lead only to death. But that was just the first part of the pattern. Once they fled, they set in motion an inevitable stand that would be made somewhere at some time. Just as the Mormons knew they would never entirely escape persecution, Sisson and the Power brothers knew they would never escape the Mormons. The pursuit would be relentless.

He did not understand, completely, why they were headed to Mexico, though Mexico had always meant refuge for the hunted north of the border. Under normal conditions. But the Mormons would not be stopped at the border the way a usual posse would be. Mormons had colonies in Mexico and were more familiar with the country and welcome than the Power brothers would be. The legal posses would turn back at the border. The Mormons and Wootans would not.

They would continue to hunt the Powers and Sisson because political boundaries were illusions, and only the boundaries of blood and faith were real. They would be required to fight. Outcomes were always paradoxes that took you by surprise, though they were always inevitable. Only when and how it would happen were unknown.

Sisson would continue with the brothers because he had no other options. And Tom believed, in a way Sisson didn't, that there would be justice or prosperity in Mexico. They would evade the posses as long as they were able. Like the Indians before them, they had resources—an understanding of the country, a toughness shared with their pursuers, and also the will to live, the drive that gave them the tiniest of edges.

They had been in the Stronghold for two days. The swelling in Tom's eye had abated, but it still hurt like hell and didn't work at all. John's eye seemed better. It was still swollen but no longer oozed pus. Tom thought that a good thing, but he wasn't positive. Often enough things that seemed good weren't. The bridge of John's nose was completely scabbed over now, and it had not bled in two days. That was a good thing. The nose was starting to heal.

They were rested. The days in the Stronghold and the days at Hendricks's had allowed them to eat and sleep well. The strength they lost in the initial days of pursuit was pretty well back. Tom figured they had another four days of riding before they reached Mexico. They would go up over the Chiricahuas on a line just east-northeast of where they were encamped. The way would be steep and snowy now, and it would be tough going, but tougher on the posses, who would have to abandon their trucks and cars and follow on horseback. Tom was pretty sure they could outride anyone in pursuit. The tougher the climb, the more it favored them over a larger group of riders. The larger the group, the greater the chance that trouble from the mountains or the horses or the inexperience of some of the riders would slow the pursuit. All in all, he was beginning to like their odds now. They had one more dash across the valley to reach the Chiricahuas, thirty or thirty-five miles, but that would be a day, not much more. Once in the foothills of the Chiricahuas, they could slow, rest, and prepare to go over the heights of the mountains.

Tom started down the way they had come up. Their food supplies were holding out all right, but they needed water. About two-thirds of the way down, the creek flattened out and formed a nice pool where he could fill the canteens and bags. He would go on down and check on the horses to make sure none of them had become entangled in the brush or got stuck in the mud. With water and some decent grazing through the light snow, the horses should be ready to go as well. All in all, things were going better than expected.

The first sound of a voice froze Tom. He wasn't sure that it was a voice, just a sound, but a sound that didn't belong with the other sounds he was hearing. He stopped, instinctively reaching down to keep the canteens from banging into one another. He bent his knees and slowly lowered to a crouch.

"Shut him up," someone said. "He's louder than a brass band."

They weren't far away. Probably at the same pool he was headed for. Slowly, he lifted the straps of the canteens from his shoulders and placed them carefully on the rocks next to him. Then the water bags. When he was free from the containers, he slipped the Colt automatic from his belt. He tried to remember if he had chambered a round before he left. He didn't think he had. He didn't trust automatics the way he did revolvers. He liked things simple. He liked being able to tell what was what just by looking. You couldn't do that with an automatic. But it was a big gun, and it put people down the way a revolver couldn't. No one would run through a bullet fired from this big .45 Colt. He pulled the slide back, just slightly, an eighth of an inch, no more, and saw brass. There was a bullet in the chamber. He eased the slide back into position.

"You think they're up there?" This was another, different voice.

"Maybe. Probably. I don't know." This was the first voice again, the one that had told the other to shut up. "Three horses. It would seem likely."

"We're going on up after them, ain't we?"

"Look up there. You want to climb up there, over all those rocks, with three armed desperados waiting for you? You do, you go right ahead."

"It ain't what I want, it's what Braz Wootan wants. He's the one deciding. It's his brother that's dead."

"I ain't sure how much Wootan decides for me. Everyone's got to die someday. I understand that. I don't particularly want to die today. How about you?"

"Of course I don't want to die. Still, I'd like to know if it's them up there. I'd like to know if we got them."

"We ain't got them. In fact, it's more like they got us if we go up after them. If we can wait them out, down on the other side of the creek, maybe then we got them. The last time someone thought they had them, they got themselves killed. All they had to do was march on up to that cabin and haul them in. Now they're all dead. It don't seem such a good idea now, considering. I believe we should just wait them out, just like the others should have."

"They's eight of us. Three of them."

"Eight's a good number, but every step we take closer to where they's holed up, they's going to be less of us."

"But we can pin them down."

"And what then? Who's going to know we got them pinned?"

"We can send someone back. It don't seem all that hard to me."

"I believe Custer said much the same. If those is their horses down there, they'll be coming down for them sooner or later. We got food, we got water. I don't know what they got, but I'll bet it's less. Waiting is a lot safer than going up after them. Up there, they got all the advantage. We got it down here."

"If there's enough of us, we can take them."

"That's what the last bunch thought. They're dead. We go up after them, it's all bound for glory for us. You want to end up perforated, you just be my guest."

"There's cover for us up there."

"Yes, there's cover all right. But we won't get to it. You feel rifle sights on you yet? Because I'm starting to feel them on me. I ain't going up there."

"Well, hell. I ain't going up without you and a bunch of others. Let's send someone back to get the others. We'll wait here and then go up after them."

"All right, then."

Tom heard them talk and then didn't hear them anymore. He was still crouched between the rocks, the .45 in his hand. He stayed still until the birds and other sounds started up again. Likely, the talkers had moved back. He couldn't stay there much longer. His legs were cramping, and Thems was sending for reinforcements. He had to move. He rose up uneasily, slid the gun into his belt, and gathered up the water bags. There wasn't a lot of time left.

"This all the water you got?" John asked.

"That's it. They're here. They found the horses."

"Damn."

"We got to go. They're sending for the others. I heard them."

"But the horses."

"No horses. They're gone. We're going that way." He indicated the taller spires of granite behind them. "We got to get south of here and then cut across the range at night."

"On foot?"

"Yes. On foot."

"And if we make it across the range, what are we going to do about the Chiricahuas?"

"We got to cross them. We can't risk the border until the other side."

"We'll cross them on foot?"

"No. We'll find some horses along the way. Horses ain't hard to find."

"I ain't no horse thief."

"And you was always a disappointment to the Old Man."

"We better go down and get the saddles, then," Sisson said.

"No. Too risky. Thems'll be right below us."

"They'll find the saddles and know we're here."

"Won't be here. We're leaving now. We got rope. We can make hackamores. It's a bad task before us. We best get on it."

"They'll know we was here, and they'll track us."

"They'll know anyway. Who do you suppose made this fire? Squirrels? They going to know we was here, and we don't want to stay and fight another fight. We won't get out of the next one."

Sisson scowled. "Bury the goddamned fire and scatter the rocks. Maybe they won't see it."

The way out was harder than the way in. There were more tiers of granite to work past. The first tier to the southeast had a fifteen-foot vertical ascent. Tom threw a rope over a bit of scrub oak, getting solid purchase on his eighth try. Being the lightest, Tom belayed his way up the rock face and onto the flat of the ridge. He tied the rope around his waist, looped it around the scrub oak, and sent the free end down to John, who slipped and skittered his way up the rock with his awkward boots.

When John was up and safe, they threw the rope down again and began the arduous haul of Tom Sisson, who was heavy and, though strong in the arms, weak in the joints. John grabbed Tom by the waist, and they both leaned back, pulling Sisson up. Once at the top, they began the search for a way out of this small canyon.

The columns of granite that had not washed away as the surrounding softer rock had formed small canyons with tight inlets and outlets. In some cases, they were able to scramble out of the inlets, but twice more, they had to make vertical ascents with the rope and then rappel their way down.

Going down turned out to be worse than going up. John made his way quickly down chutes of sand and scree, but Tom and Sisson made their way slowly, slipping and staggering their way down. Tom slipped again, fell a few reeling steps, then caught himself on a bit of creosote bush and steadied himself before he could slip more. Sisson came up from behind and handed him a length of sotol, a light but fibrous and strong stalk of the highland agave family. It was a favorite of the Apaches, themselves a mountain people, who favored its light strength for arrows and the framing of their wickiups. It made a fine walking stick.

"You need it," Tom said, handing it back.

"I'll find another."

"No. We got to keep moving."

"We got time," Sisson said. "Would you climb back in here if you weren't being chased by a bunch of shoe salesmen thinking they're Wyatt Earp?"

Tom smiled. "No. Don't guess I would."

Sisson nodded. "Let's take a little time and not kill ourselves."

"Yeah," Tom said. "We'll have some horses, too."

"I took a few horses in my life," Sisson said. "Maybe you have, too. Usually, I just happened on them. You steal a horse because it's there, not because you're looking for one. And, generally, there ain't three for the stealing unless you walk right into someone's ranch and gun sights. I'm thinking we may steal a horse or two. I'm not thinking we're going to find us three right off the bat."

"We'll find three. I don't much like the idea of the three of us going into Mexico on less than three horses. It makes a bad impression."

"I don't think we need to worry much about impressions," Sisson said.

"Always got to worry about impressions. An American generally does all right in Mexico because the Mexicans know he's got money. An American without a horse is sure to be a broke American. They don't have much use for broke Americans down there. A broke American ain't no better than a Mexican when it comes right down to it."

"Let's steal some horses, then."

They came down into the foothills of the Dragoons in the late afternoon. They had walked a lot of miles, a lot of those vertical, rarely speaking. Tom had scrambled up rocks and then let the rope down for his brother and Sisson nearly a dozen times. In midafternoon they had found a small pool where the ground dipped to lower than the water table and let water collect. They had rested for nearly half an hour, drinking their fill and filling the water bags, which John and Sisson carried now.

There was not a lot of light left. Again they were facing the long, broad prairie of the Sulphur Springs Valley, which they would have to cross at night. Where they were going was just beyond where they had been nearly a week ago. They would have to go back past Pearce, where the old lady would surely have called the law. Then, in the dark, they would have to find Ash Creek and follow that up and into the Chiricahuas. Each carried a rifle and a sidearm. They had filled their pockets with as much ammunition as they could stuff in them. It was going to be a hell of a trip across the valley.

Chapter Eleven

1916

Lee Kirby was on duty at the US Forest Service office in Safford. It was a slow day, as most were, and Kirby was talking with T. T. Swift, who was off duty but hanging around the office because he could think of nothing else to do that held any interest. Both men turned their attention to the man who had just barged through the door.

"Forest land is government land, right?"

"I beg your pardon?" Kirby asked.

"Forest Service land is public land, ain't it? It belongs to all the people, and anyone can graze cattle on Forest Service land, ain't that right?"

"Well, pretty much," Kirby said. He picked up a ponderosa pinecone that was sitting on his desk for no reason he could remember.

"'Pretty much' my ass. Belongs to everyone."

"Is there something I can help you with?" Kirby asked. His interlocutor was a rangy kid, light hair and eyes and a look more serious than you'd expect from a kid. "You're one of the Powers boys, right?" Kirby turned the pinecone over as if it might have some answer.

"Thomas Power. And I'd like an answer to my question."

"Most of the land is open range, yes. There are places that are closed for one reason or another and some private leases. But most of it's open."

"Aravaipa Canyon. That open?"

"That's open if you want to run cattle there. It's some rough country."

"My family, we're running cattle there, and there are some others, too. They's the ones doing it."

"Doing what?"

"Running off our cattle, chasing them all to hell and back. That ain't right. That ain't what the federal reserve is for. What are you going to do about it?"

Kirby looked over at Swift, who raised his eyebrows and turned the corners of his mouth down in a look of mock consternation. Mostly, it was a look that said, "You got yourself a dandy here."

"I need to know."

"Do you know who's running off your cattle?"

"The others that are grazing herds in Aravaipa. They act that it's theirs, and it ain't. It's everybody's land, and they got no rights to be running our cows off. We got to go down there a couple of times a week and round up our cattle, which are scattered all over hell and back, just because the others think they got a right to the grass and water, which they don't."

"No. They do have a right to the grass and water. Same as you."

"That's what I'm saying, only it ain't no 'same as.' It's 'mine and mine alone,' and that ain't right. Can you buy land in Aravaipa? Can you lease it?"

Kirby shook his head. "No. You can't buy or lease it. It's federal land, and it's open for grazing."

"Which is what I was saying. Now what are you going to do about it?"

Kirby picked up the pinecone again. "Not sure. I'll look into it, though."

"What's that mean—'look into it'?"

"I get out there every once in a while, check on things. I'll talk to the ranchers about respecting other people's cattle. No one's got more rights than anyone else in Aravaipa Canyon."

"When's 'once in a while'?"

"I was just out there last week. I wasn't aware of any problem while I was there. I'll get back that way in a week or so."

"Meanwhile you got your backside in that chair."

Kirby set the cone down carefully, deliberately on the desk. "Now hold on a minute, son. You have no right to be talking to me like that. I'm a government employee, not your servant. And I'm your elder. You need to show some respect."

"And I ain't your son," Power said. "But I'm a citizen of the United States, so you are my servant. We got a mining operation going up in Kielberg Canyon, and we can't be riding over to Aravaipa all the time just to round up our cattle. That ain't right, and you know it. We're miners and cattlemen, and we got a right to be both."

Kirby stared at the kid, who was staring right back and not backing down any. Power held Kirby's gaze, calm and collected, like a man older than the boy he was.

"I got a lot of territory to cover, and I can't be in two places at once. You talked with the other ranchers?"

"The other ranchers don't want to talk to us. But they'll listen to you."

"And maybe they'll listen to you, too. If we do this the right way. What if you were acting on direct orders from me?" He looked over to Swift, who was knitting his brows in puzzlement.

"You mean, like a deputy?"

"Well, sort of."

"Could I have a badge?"

"Well, only for the time being. This all has to go through Washington."

"Washington." Tom scratched at a scab on the back of his hand, causing it to send a thin course of blood down his hand and between his fingers.

"It's a federal post. Everything has to come from Washington. You'd be an officer of the United States government. I can't just hand out badges for that. Your appointment would come from President Taft himself."

"Could I have a gun?"

"Haven't you got a gun?"

"Hell, yes, I've got a gun. I got a couple. Plenty."

"Well, then, I guess you wouldn't need a gun. Not from us, anyway. But if President Taft says to give you a gun, I most certainly will. Do you know President Taft?"

Swift got up and shot a glance at Kirby before quickly shuffling out the side door, saying only, "Crapper." Kirby smiled broadly and then looked back at Tom Power.

"No," Power said. "I don't know him."

"That's all right. It would speed things up if you were a friend of the president, but it's not essential."

"I could arrest people who were driving off my cattle?"

"Yes," Kirby lied. "Yes, you could. You could arrest them and bring them to me, but you've got to have evidence. Evidence is the key. You got to have evidence before we can charge anyone with anything. I wouldn't want to see you dragging some poor soul through here without evidence. Here." Kirby pulled a badge from his desk drawer. "You got to get me evidence."

"Oh, I'll have evidence," Power said. "You can bet I'll have evidence."

Swift was just coming back into the room, letting out some of the laughter that he'd held in while Kirby toyed with Power. The front door of the office swung open, and Power walked back in, not acknowledging Swift, who turned to go back out again.

"Obliged," Power said with a wink. "Obliged. I forgot to say that. Now I'm going out and get some evidence." He turned and went back out the front door, closing it behind him. Swift poked his head back into the room.

A week later, when he went to check on the cattle, Power found them missing again and only Cleghorne cattle grazing the creekbed. Cleghorne owned a big ranch just south of Klondyke and seemed to think he had a special right to the prime grazing land.

Tom Power spent the better part of the day riding up Aravaipa Canyon into the tree line, trying to round up all his cattle. Most of them he found together a mile up the canyon; the rest he had to pick up, one or two at a time, from the hillsides. Some he never found but thought they might find their way back when they found the rest of the herd missing.

He had missed a full day of digging for flake gold back up Rattlesnake Creek. He, Charlie, John, and their father were working their way up the creek, still looking for the source of the flake. When they ran out of flake, they determined that the source was now below them, but then a few more flakes showed from up above them. It was erratic that way. Some days there was a lot of flake, other days none or hardly any.

It was never enough to be worth the energy they were putting into it. But that was mining. There was a lot of labor and money invested in the early days of an operation, with little reward. So you rode hope, figuring that somewhere, up above you, ahead of you, there was a payday that would return more than you had invested. It was an operation that ran on hope and a belief in a future that was little evident in the present or past. Your own past was forgotten, and the present became only days that pushed you further into the future when you would be rich enough not to care about the days you had lost.

Still, their day-to-day living was being bought by cattle, and now someone was driving their cattle off the best range, making them climb up into the hills with their sparse grass, where the cattle fed on brush that put no weight on them at all. Climbing through that rugged country, looking for feed, the cattle were likely to lose weight rather than gain it.

Now that he was an official deputy of the US Forest Service, Tom meant to put an end to Cleghorne's dominance of the Aravaipa Canyon area. No rich bastard had the right to keep Power cattle off the sweet grass.

He took provisions for four or five days, a week if he took it easy and slow, and he headed down out of the Galiuros for Aravaipa to watch over the cattle. He had a lever-action Winchester .30-30 and a hundred rounds of ammunition. In his belt he had a Smith and Wesson .38 six-shooter, so worn in the action that he didn't dare carry it loaded.

He stayed in the hills above the creek, watching the cattle graze the grass and broadleaf weeds of the creekside for two days and nights, eating only enough to keep him strong, and heading upcreek to fill his water bag in a small, protected pool where the cattle couldn't crap in it. He thought about how it was to be one of the little guys. None of the other ranchers were camped out watching their cattle, only him. And he was doing it because no one was afraid of him, no one feared insulting him or stealing from him. And that was the way it was. If you had no money, you had no respect. People thought poor was its own fault. Famine, flood, and disease meant nothing for the rich because their money would float them through those times. Plagues were the province of the poor, whose cattle starved or bloated and died or got run off by fire. The poor couldn't protect themselves against what went wrong, and that was their own damned fault.

The Power family would be different, though, if trouble would let them be for a while. Their land on Rattlesnake Creek was fine land, and there was gold there.

They knew that. They couldn't tell how much, but there was gold. They had seen flake, had sluiced it, and had taken small bottles of it to town and sold it. And there was more than just flake. Folks had known for years that the Galiuros were good gold mountains. It was true that, so far, none of the mines had amounted to much. But there had to be big veins of ore no one had found yet. It was rough and remote country that didn't give up its treasures easily. It was good country for the Powers because they were as hard and rough as the mountains.

And people in Safford were taking notice of them. While they didn't step off the sidewalk to let the Powers past them, the townsfolk didn't push them off the sidewalk, either. The Powers were poor, undereducated Gentiles, and they were outsiders. But people were starting to think that they were outsiders that had to be reckoned with.

He was sleeping on the afternoon of the third day when he heard the whistling and shouting from the creek below. He heard cattle scrambling and crashing through the brush, making their way up the hillside as the riders came through, driving them from the creek. He had to put himself behind a tree to keep from being trampled as a couple of steers came his way.

He made his way to his horse, dodging frightened cattle. He had dealt with bears and a lion or two and all kinds of snakes, but there was little that scared him quite so much as a frightened cow. A thousand terrified pounds coming at you, trying to get away from something behind it, and you were just an obstacle in its way, an obstacle small enough to just run over. And if you did get run over, you were in terrible trouble.

The horse was unsaddled but bridled with a hackamore so it could graze. He could ride it with the hackamore, but he needed the saddle and the Winchester that was in the scabbard of the saddle. The horse was no less worried about the charging cattle than he was, and he had the devil's own time getting the saddle cinched to the belly of the shying horse. But when he got it cinched, he was up and off, heading for the creek, the cattle now separating and making way for the charging horse.

The first rider he came to didn't even hear him coming with the noise of the cattle all around him. Tom simply swung the Winchester by the barrel, catching the man across the shoulder, likely breaking it, sending him crashing to the ground and rolling into a ball as more steers came running past him.

When Tom got to the creek bottom, he fired off three shots in quick succession into the air. The shots added to the general confusion, but the other riders stopped what they were doing and wheeled and turned toward him. He shouldered the rifle and moved the sights from rider to rider as they brought their horses to a standstill and, one by one, raised their hands, none of them seeming to be armed, though only a fool would ride into Aravaipa Canyon without some kind of firearm.

"Just what the hell do you think you are doing?" he yelled. Then, "Stop. You're under arrest by the United States Forest Service. This here is open range, and you got no right to do this. You're all under arrest."

He held the Winchester in his right hand, the stock trapped under his right elbow. He swung the barrel from rider to rider. There were four of them, five if you counted the one he knocked down and who was still down, perhaps steer-trampled, Tom didn't know. He kept his eyes moving, waiting for some movement from another one he couldn't see.

"There's no need for a gun, Power," one of them said.

Tom swung the barrel of the Winchester in search of the voice. When he saw who had spoken, he lowered the rifle. "Ranger Kirby," he said. "What are you doing here?"

There was a long pause, then Kirby said, "I'm finding the men who've been driving off your cattle." There was another silence, then a snort from one of the other riders. Tom swung the rifle in that direction. "Laughing boy," he said. T. T. Swift shook his head and raised his hands shoulder-high in submission.

Power turned back to Kirby. "What are you doing?" he asked again.

"I told you," Kirby said. "I'm arresting these men for running off your cattle."

"You ain't," Tom said. "You ain't arresting no one. You're running off my cattle. I ain't stupid." There was another snort from T. T. Swift. Tom brought the barrel of the rifle back to him. "You got an annoying habit I can cure for you." Swift raised his hands again.

"Why would I do that?" Kirby asked.

"That's what I was asking. Why would you do that after you give me this badge and everything? I ain't stupid." He swung the rifle back to Swift, who just shook his head and looked at the ground.

"I think I'm arresting you. You better give up your guns." He heard a noise behind him and wheeled his horse to see the knocked-down man back on his feet. He was covered in dust, and his arm hung limp, but he looked all right. He was trudging over to where the others were.

"You can't arrest us," Kirby said. "I'm a United States forest ranger."

"And I'm a deputy United States forest ranger."

"No," Kirby said. "You ain't taken the oath. It don't count if you ain't had the oath."

"Who can give me the oath?"

Kirby said nothing.

"You can, can't you?"

Again, Kirby remained silent.

Tom brought the Winchester up to his shoulder now and took aim at Kirby. "Let's get on with that oath, then."

"I—" Kirby said. "Say your name."

"What?"

"I'm giving you the damned oath, even though it doesn't mean a damn thing because you're holding me at gunpoint. But you got to say 'I' and then your name—Tom Powers."

"Power," Tom said. "Not Powers. Power."

"Power, then. Say that, say, 'I, Tom Power.'"

"I, Tom Power—"

"Swear to uphold the laws of the United States of America and defend her lands against all interlopers—"

"Against all what?"

"Interlopers. It means 'intruders' or something."

"Why don't it just say that, then?"

"I don't know. Hell, I don't even know the goddamned oath. I'm just making this up because you have a gun pointed at me."

"Is it going to be official, then?"

"I guess it is."

"It better be, because I got to arrest you boys. That's better for you than the other thing I got in mind."

"All right. 'I, Tom Power, swear to uphold the laws of the United States and to protect her against intruders—'"

"Before it was 'defend.'"

"'Defend,' 'protect,' it don't matter. Say what you want to say."

"No. It's got to be right. I got to arrest you."

"You got us with our hands up, standing in the middle of the creek. How goddamned arrested do you want us to be?"

"This has to be right. That's all I'm saying."

"All right. 'I, Tom Power, swear to uphold the laws of the United States and to protect her against intruders.'" He paused, obviously grasping for some other thought. "So help me God."

"Did you take that oath?"

"Something like that. I can't remember all the words. No one was holding a gun on me."

"It didn't work, did it?"

"Pardon?"

"The oath. It didn't work. You didn't uphold the laws. You busted them."

"Tom," Kirby struggled. It was like talking to a child, an armed child. "I didn't steal your cattle or hurt them in any way, did I?"

"I guess not."

"I just moved them."

"Away from the good grass."

"Yes. Away from the good grass."

"That ain't the law, is it?" Power asked.

"No. But it ain't exactly against the law, either."

"Does the law say I can graze my cattle on open range?"

"It does. Could you please put that gun away?"

"I could," Tom said. "But I won't. I got you talking to me like I somehow matter, and laughing boy over there," he motioned toward Swift, "he ain't laughing. I figure that's all the gun. Now, if the law says I can graze my cows on open range, and you come in and chase them off, that's against the law."

"Not exactly, is what I'm saying—"

"And how is it different? Is it different for a Cleghorne than a Power?"

"No. No, it ain't."

"Yes. Yes, the hell it is. It's always different for the rich. You would think the law would try to help the poor, to sort of even things out, at least keep the rich from shitting on them. But it don't. The law's on the side of the rich. Always. The law's for making the rich richer."

"Well, Tom, I take your point. But Cleghorne, he's a powerful man in these parts. He makes a lot of money, and he does a lot of good, too. He sells a lot of beef, he hires a lot of hands, and he buys a lot of supplies. He paid for the library, too. Cleghorne cattle don't flourish, Graham County don't flourish. That's all it is."

"And we should just raise us some more beans and be happy about it. Ain't that right?"

"I know. It don't seem fair. But you got to see the big picture."

"It ain't fair, no matter what the size of the picture. And here's what else ain't fair. You got to go tell Cleghorne that you ain't running any more cattle off this creekbed and that he better not send anyone else to do it, either. I'm a miner now. I got a going concern up in the Galiuros, and I ain't got time to sit out here protecting my cattle. So the next time I come up here and find my cattle all scattered to hell and back, I'm going to come looking for you." He swung the rifle to Swift. "And laughing boy here, too. Now that ain't fair. Is it?"

"No, it isn't."

"Well, there you go then. See how you like it. Now you get on out of here and let my cows graze in peace. I got to go back up Rattlesnake Canyon and get me some more gold. Maybe, when I get enough, I can buy you next time you all come up for auction. But I'll be back, and you won't know when. But, by God, I better find my cattle right here. Now go. You ain't under arrest no more. But I will shoot you if needs be."

Tom Power headed back up the hills and waited to be sure that they were gone. They were, riding steadily east, out of the canyon and back toward the Safford road. He was satisfied for now. He had won, but it wasn't over. The rich believed the poor were created just for them to use any old way they wanted.

When the Powers found the source of the flake up in the canyon, then it would be over. They would ride into town, maybe in one of those automobiles, and they would have a lot of money. Maybe they would ride in on horseback and then buy an automobile and drive it back to the canyon. However way it worked, people would see that they were the Power family, and they were rich, and they were not to be fucked with.

Gold kept turning up, but only in small bits of flake, never more than a few dollars' worth at a time, hardly worth the effort, except for the promise of a big strike as they moved farther and farther up the canyon and into the rhyolite and quartz country that held the promise of some rich veins.

The most promising gold claim seemed to be the Gold Mountain lode in Kielberg Canyon in the central part of the Galiuros, just north and parallel to the head of Rattlesnake Canyon, some six miles from the Power land in Rattlesnake. First opened by the Consolidated Gold Mountain Mining Company in 1902, it had seemed to play out early, producing a disappointing amount of ore and profits well below the estimated $85,000 per month the company had projected in its prospectus.

The Consolidated Gold Mountain Mining Company had quickly failed, unable to produce enough ore to break even on its operation. Since the mine showed little promise of good profits, it was sold to three men operating as their own mining company. Half interest was owned by a Mr. Bowman, and a quarter each belonged to C. P. Tucker and R. C. Elwood, an investor. Tucker and Bowman worked the mine together. They pulled out a modest amount of ore, enough for the two of them to survive on and an indication that there might, indeed, be a rich vein in the mine yet untapped.

In the summer of 1911 the Powers were working their small farm at Power Garden. They had cleared a couple of acres of decent soil to the north of their cabin, planted a decent-sized garden, and then sown the rest of the field in grass for cattle feed. Needing another cash crop to keep them going while they grazed the cattle and sluiced for gold, Jeff sent John and Tom along with Ola May down Rattlesnake Creek, looking for seedling Arizona walnut trees. These they dug up, brought back to the Garden, and transplanted into the fields. In two weeks they planted over sixty trees, which were of little value for their nuts but of greater value for their wood. The nuts would be sold in town, but they would mainly become fodder for the cattle—entirely free, except for the labor of the children.

Jeff was digging a small channel from the field up to the spring where he was going to build a concrete-and-wood gate to open and close the springwater to the field below. The grass and trees could be watered year-round, regardless of when the rains came. Jeff was used to hard work, and so were his sons. He and Charlie were digging the irrigation ditch when C. P. Tucker rode into their tiny empire to rest and water his horse on his way from the mine down the canyon and into town.

"How you doing up at that mine? You rich yet?" Jeff called to Tucker.

"If aggravation at Bowman was worth anything, I'm a goddamned millionaire already," Tucker said.

"You two getting on each other's nerves?"

"Well, I hope I'm getting on Bowman's nerves, because he sure as hell is on mine and pitching a damned tent and thinking about putting up a house."

"I'd guess it would be hard to partner in an operation of that sort, wouldn't it?" Jeff asked.

"It is with Bowman. He's always got a better idea. If we was to just find gold laying on the ground, ready to pick up, which we ain't, Bowman would devise a plan to include eighty steps and forty days of work just to bend over and pick it up. I ain't never seen the like of the man. I think he would rather plan about it than to breathe. He just ain't natural."

"It does sound like a pretty good nuisance," Jeff agreed.

"And that ain't the worst of it. We take turns riding the ore we dig into town, and he always comes back with less money than I do. 'Price of gold is down,' he'll say. Or 'wasn't the best quality.' When all the while I know some of it's going direct into his pocket. I bring the money back, fair and square, except maybe for a drink or two in town to help get back up the canyon, and I know he stops at the bank along the way and sticks a portion of the profits there. I know it as well as I know my own name, C. P. Tucker. He's got a woman down there, too, who's getting a share just for laying still a couple times a month. I tell you, it's aggravating as all hell."

"It does sound like a rotten deal to me," Jeff said.

"And when I get back from toting the ore down, how much work has he done? How much ore we got ready? None."

"That was going to be my answer," Jeff said.

"Sits on his damned hind end, dreaming about that woman or some other one. That's all he does until I get back, and then it's 'I got us a new plan on going at that gold,' and the nonsense just pours from him like milk from a bucket. You know what, Power? You ought to come in with us."

"Well," Jeff said, "you do make it seem like an attractive bit of work."

"No. No. No. Think about it. I do believe Elwood would be willing to sell you his quarter interest in the mine. We're making money, but not enough to keep Elwood occupied. If you and I was to own half the mine, we could do things our way, and by and by we could force Bowman out."

"And how would that work? He owns half of it. We would own half of it. It's a standoff. I don't think much of that plan."

"But you don't know what I know, which is that Bowman's got a silent partner. We could go around Bowman and buy out the partner, and we'd own three-quarters of the mine, three-quarters of the ore, and three-quarters of the profit, and we would pretty much own Mr. Bowman, too. He'd have to sell us his share because we could just vote him right out of any profits at all."

"And how much would this cost me?"

"I believe I could get you Elwood's quarter interest for just about twenty-five hundred dollars. Are you interested?"

"That's a lot of money."

"But I'm pulling in near to two hundred dollars every month, averaged out. And it would be more if we was to keep Bowman from taking the gold into town. You'd make your money back in less than a year. Now that's a good investment. And you got those boys. We could move a lot more dirt with four extra men working. I'm telling you, Power, this here is opportunity."

"Let me think on it. I would want to talk to the boys about it."

"There you go. I'll get in touch with Mr. Elwood while I'm in town, find out how much he'll take for his share. This is opportunity. Golden opportunity. The only thing better than gold for making money is whiskey, and that's illegal. This ain't."

They had, all together, a little over a thousand dollars, earned with the strenuous and sporadic efforts that only the poor can exert. Jeff thought the mine was a good risk. Charlie, always the cautious one, had grave doubts. That thousand dollars would go a long way toward making their cattle ranching prosper. The thousand meant new fences, corrals, new stock, and a means of surviving a weak market without selling off the entire herd.

The one Jeff could count on was Tom. Tom had inherited Jeff's vision and the gambler's instinct to try to make big money out of little money. If they were to lose everything, Tom would simply start over, as Jeff would. All gambling involved risk. Anyone who didn't know that was a fool. But any man who was unwilling to gamble was a bigger fool.

And that left John. John, unlike Tom, didn't like to think. He wasn't good at it, and he was smart enough not to fool himself. John was muscle and determination. Once someone told him what needed to be done, he went forward, always straight ahead, never complaining or giving up. But both Tom and Charlie had long ago figured John out. It wasn't hard. And they could control John easily. He never questioned their arguments, however arcane or thin. And both Tom and Charlie moved John first one way, then the other. Either Charlie or Tom would figure out how to do something and then set John to work at it. It was an arrangement that seemed to satisfy them all.

But John was mercurial. Since he took orders from everyone, he had little allegiance to anyone. He loved, in his own way, both Tom and Charlie, and he believed in them. Charlie had the upper hand because he was the oldest, where Tom was the youngest. But Tom was the smarter. When Charlie and Tom were at odds, and they seemed to be at odds more and more, John would side with Charlie, and then Tom would convince John that Charlie was wrong or taking advantage of him. Since they both took ample advantage of John, he was easy to convince.

John was merely afraid of Jeff. Charlie had outgrown his fear, becoming bigger and stronger than Jeff, and Tom had learned and invented tricks to get around Jeff and to head off Jeff's anger. John simply took what Jeff dished out, though he was stronger and tougher than even Charlie. More and more, he had been siding with Tom, who protected John as best he could.

They were still fifteen hundred dollars short of the amount Tucker thought they would need. Jeff was ready to just let the whole deal slide by when Tom handed him a leather pouch.

"What's this?"

"Two thousand dollars."

"Where'd you get it?"

"I got it is all. I got a little side business. Now we can get that mine."

"You doing some bootlegging?" Jeff asked.

"Like I said, I got a little side business."

Jeff looked at the two thousand dollars. "It's damned profitable, that bootlegging."

"Now we can buy the mine."

"I don't know. Charlie ain't keen on the idea."

As Jeff saw it, it was two to two in the family. He and Tom were the right side. Charlie and John would block their way. He could try to exert his authority as head of the family to weight the argument to his side, but, lately, that brought only grief. The brothers would turn against each other, and at least two of them would turn against him. His ally would be Tom, and Tom looked out for himself first. It was no good. If they were going to buy that mine, John had to join with him and Tom against Charlie. And he told Tom that. And Tom nodded, understanding completely.

"What if we was to split the money from the mine three ways instead of four?" Tom asked.

"How we going to do that?"

"Well, we ain't going to give up the cattle operation, are we? After all the work we put into it, we ain't going to just turn our backs on it, are we? If the gold doesn't come through, we got to have a backup, right?"

"There's going to be gold. There's gold there now, we know that," Jeff argued.

"Yeah, but what if there ain't? What if that little vein doesn't lead to a bigger one but just plays out? What then? We're going to need cattle then. And someone's got to keep that operation going. And I think that's Charlie. We make the cattle his job, and the three of us work the mine. He gets the whole share of the cattle operation, and we split the mine money three ways. That would work, wouldn't it?"

"Well, yeah. I guess it would."

"Then that's the way it will be," Tom said.

"You see, John. Charlie wants to be a rancher, while we want to be miners. And there's more money in mining than ranching. So if you throw in with me and the Old Man, everybody gets what he wants. If you side with Charlie, then Charlie's happy, and me and the Old Man are just left out in the cold. You don't want that, do you? Of course you don't. Our way works out for everyone. Charlie's just all for Charlie. Do you see what I mean?" Tom took a step back and cocked his head.

"That's not how Charlie sees it," John said.

"Of course it ain't how Charlie sees it. Charlie's afraid he's going to lose his cows, and that ain't going to happen, because he's our brother. We're Powers, and the Powers stick together, don't they?"

"Yeah," John agreed.

"So that's what we're doing. Sticking together. Our way keeps everyone in the family happy, and we all work together. Charlie's way has Charlie in the catbird's seat and all of us—you, me, the Old Man—working for Charlie, and that's going to break up the family. You see? You don't want the family broken up over this, do you?"

"No, Tom. I don't want us broken up."

"Then you side with us. Charlie will have him one of his little fits, but he'll get over it and see that we all make out real good. All right?"

"All right."

Three months later, Charlie left for New Mexico, where he started his own cattle company. The last word they had from him was that he had lost his hand in an accident.

Three days after they had paid C. P. Tucker $2,500 for his share of the mine, Jeff, John, and Tom were camped on Rattlesnake Mesa. They had a small string of horses they were taking to Willcox to replenish their supply of cash, and the horses were grazing the grass below the mesa before heading to market. Horses were bringing good money, and the Powers were more concerned with their cattle and mining operations. It seemed like a good time to get out of the horse business.

It was dark, and the three of them were huddled around the fire, about to turn in for the night, when they heard brush rustling and footsteps coming up the hill. They scrambled up and over to their saddles, where their rifles were scabbarded. They stood armed and ready as the footsteps got closer.

"Hello," a voice called. "Just a friend, coming through." The voice was weak and quavery. But the speaker was coming from Rattlesnake Canyon, where he would have just made the steep, difficult climb out of the canyon. "Is that you, Mr. Bowman?" Jeff asked.

"Yes. Yes, it's me. I mean no harm."

He stepped into the light. It was Bowman and, right behind him, Ranger Kirby. "Is it the Power boys?" Bowman asked.

"It is."

"We're coming down from the mine. Just coming down from the mine," Bowman said.

"You're welcome to sit by the fire for a bit," Jeff said.

"No. We're heading on, trying to make as much progress as we can."

"Not a lot of moon tonight. It's a hard walk in the dark."

"We're going to Klondyke. It's not far. We know the way." This was Ranger Kirby. "You boys are camped out pretty close to home."

"We set up camp when the light began to fail. That was here," Jeff said.

"Well, we're going on. You boys pass a pleasant evening."

"What do you figure that was all about?" Tom asked.

"Bowman likes to take a deer every now and again. Maybe he just got himself arrested by Kirby there. That's the reason they were walking in the dark and didn't want to stop for some rest. Bowman was being marched off to the jailhouse in Klondyke. I'll tell you, that's for sure what that's all about."

"Don't see how Bowman got himself arrested," Tom said.

"The way people do."

"No. I mean Bowman's got money. Ranger Kirby's got more interest in money than in arresting people. I'd think it would be hard to get yourself arrested by Kirby if you had money."

"Maybe he's too tight to get hisself off," John said.

"Maybe. It don't add up good, though."

On their way to Willcox they came on a group of riders also heading south. Rube Wootan, a justice of the peace, was at the head of the group.

"Where are you boys headed?" Jeff asked. "Rodeo in town?"

"Better than that," Wootan offered. "This here's a coroner's jury headed to Willcox for a swearing in."

"Coroner's jury? You don't say. Who got hisself killed?"

"C. P. Tucker. Got hisself shot by Ranger Kirby yesterday."

"Ranger Kirby? We saw him last night, heading out of the canyon."

"Probably on his way to report the killing. He did that last night in Klondyke. They're holding him and Bowman in jail in Willcox this morning until we can get this jury here to sit and hear the evidence."

"Why the hell did he kill Tucker? Why would anyone kill Tucker?"

"Hell," Wootan said, leaning over to spit. "Why do most men kill other men? A woman. It was Bowman's woman, and Tucker was running his mouth about her. Nothing a man cares about as much as new pussy, I guess. They'll do just about anything for it. You headed to town to sell those horses?"

"We are."

"You should get some good money for them. That's a good-looking string."

"Say, Wootan. You know the law. We was in the middle of a business transaction with Tucker. We're on our way to pick up the deed to some land we bought."

"My guess is you'll be cooling your heels for a bit. Once this inquest is done, they got to read the will, if there is one, and make postings for all who have claims against Tucker. I guess that includes you. You can probably do that today. But you won't get nothing until the estate has settled."

"How long will that take?"

"It's law. It'll take awhile. A long, damned while."

They went back to their various operations, running their small claims and grazing cattle in Aravaipa Canyon. Tom went on with his rodeos and his booming whiskey business, moving through Cochise, Graham, Greenlee, and Pima Counties, always a couple of steps ahead of the law, whose officers were often enough riding in the rodeos themselves.

Ola May stuck with Tom. She was almost twenty now, and the rodeo life was the best life she had known. She continued to work at the cabin in Power Garden, raising small crops and tending to the sapling walnut trees they had scavenged and set out on the north side of the cabin. She helped Granny Jane, who was visibly slowing down, with the cooking, housekeeping, and general chores. Ola was a hard worker and strong for a small girl, but she did not complain. Life was hard for everyone. At least as far as she knew. But when Tom rode in on Friday night or Saturday morning, she was ready.

She wore her work clothes—jeans and heavy shirts and boots—but carried dresses, stockings, and makeup. She rode, often enough, in the back of the truck, bouncing along country roads that weren't much more than trails, and she worked the stock with Tom and the boys from the time they arrived at some ranch or another to set up until the rodeo was over and the money had been split up amidst arguing and cursing, which she took her part in, along with her split. Then she was on her own until Monday morning, when Tom would fire up the truck, and she would make her way back to the camp from wherever she had spent the night. She never volunteered where she had been, and Tom never asked. It was all rodeo business, and rodeo business didn't bear a lot of looking into.

Still, her business was obvious. While they were readying the stock and while the rodeo was going on, a fairly steady stream of cowboys came to call on her. She was friendly to all. Someone who had spent all week isolated with only her grandmother and a few mules was unlikely to turn down any company or contact that came her way. And she was a pretty girl, small and comely, who could even look delicate in her dresses and powder.

She welcomed them all and considered them without the appearance of comparing them as they chattered and bantered. But everyone knew she was eyeing her choices for the weekend, comparing them exactly as the men compared horses, with a quick eye and good judgment. All this was done while she worked alongside Tom and the others. If she stopped her work to chat or to look over some new cowboy or some old cowboy with new prospects, Tom would be at her. Lately she had been favoring Kane Wootan, a tough little cowboy who was not unlike her brother Tom.

Tom would watch her talk to Wootan, standing closer than she needed to be for conversation, hunkering down with him next to the fire at night, or wandering off into the brush with him. When there was dancing after the rodeos, she was likely found at the end of Kane Wootan's arm.

"You stay away from him," Tom would say.

"I'll stay away and go with whoever I please."

"But not him."

"Why not him?"

"Because he's nothing but cheap trash."

"They're cowboys, Tom. They're all cheap trash. We're cheap trash. I'll see who I please."

"He's shiftless, lazy, and stupid. You don't want him."

"Shiftless, lazy, and stupid are fine for what I want him for."

"Yeah. And he'll knock you up because he's too shiftless, lazy, and stupid not to. And then I got me a shiftless, lazy, and stupid brother-in-law that's just another burden I got to attend to. Find you someone better."

"I don't see you spending a lot of your free time trying to improve the Power bloodlines," she said.

"It's different."

"How's it different? You just tell me how."

"I ain't going to saddle us with a worthless man, that's how it's different. I've known Kane Wootan a long time, and I haven't found one soul more worthless than Kane."

"But a worthless woman is all right?"

"It's not the same."

"Because a woman is not worth what a man is? That doesn't seem to be how it is when you take out after some of these gals, limping along with a lump in your pocket. And stay away from Sallie. She's a dead end, and you're going to spend the rest of your life trying to get that lump out of your pocket, because she ain't going to help."

"And you know this how?"

"I just know. It's free advice, brother man. Think on it."

"How do you know what you say you know?"

"It ain't always dicks and slits, Tom. It don't work that way all the time."

Tom took her by the arm and yanked her to him. "You tell me how you know about that."

Ola May smiled. "You're so damned smart, you figure it out."

He grabbed and yanked again, harder, pulling her off her feet and into him so her face was right up against his. "Goddamn it, Ola. If you're one of them, I will purely kill you, just to save the Old Man the trouble of doing it himself. I mean that. You can count on it."

"You afraid I'm going to spoil the good Power name?" Ola laughed, though he could see the fear in her eyes as well.

"I mean it, Ola. This ain't no fooling around. You get those notions out of your head. It would be hard to do worse than Kane Wootan, but I believe you may have just found the way. You get those thoughts out of your head."

"It ain't my head they're in, brother man."

They continued on, not speaking of the incident. Ola went with Tom to the rodeos each week, helping with the money and liquor. In the day, she outworked most men, and at night, after the rodeo, she outdanced everyone else. There was no letup on Kane Wootan as far as Tom could tell, but there was always a line of cowboys waiting to dance with her, and when she went off into the corners with the other girls, the laughter got louder and, somehow, warmer.

Tom kept his eye on her. She moved around, unlike the unpopular girls, who were always nailed to the floor in some dark corner, hoping some cowboy, drunk or hapless enough, would seek them out and turn their lives around. Ola would be at the punch bowl one moment, gone the next. Then she would reappear in some other part of the building.

Tom took Sallie Reynolds by the arm as she came back into the barn.

"Why, Tom Power, are you looking to dance with me?"

"What was you doing out there with my sister?"

"I beg your pardon?"

"What was you doing with my sister?" He repeated the question, pausing and stressing each word, putting the greatest stress on "sister."

"I don't believe that's any of your business, Thomas Power."

He moved up on her, standing over her, though he was, himself, a short man. "You tell me."

"All right. We were doing what women do, and that's private."

"You don't need no help, doing that."

"Well, Mr. Power. You go out and squat down on a rattlesnake." She started to turn away but turned back to him. "Please." She turned again and was gone.

What right did Ola May have, he wanted to know. What right?

Chapter Twelve
1918

Tom woke to the rush of wings above him. The sky was nearly dark, streaked with slender bands of rose and orange, and in the middle of it all, a long, dark spiral like the funnel of a tornado, only mottled and full of movement, soared high above them and deep into the night sky. Free-tailed bats. With the coming of the night, the bats were leaving their den and traveling in a great spiral, nearly vertically, into the darkening sky. He had seen bats before, but not in these numbers, not this close.

He shook John, and when John woke, Tom, without speaking, pointed up to the spiral, which showed no sign of letting up but rather got darker and louder as more bats came out of the mountains and up into the sky.

"Holy Jesus," John said.

Sisson had come awake now, and he looked up at the great funnel of bats rising ever upward. None of them said anything, just watched the funnel rising and filling with more dark, leathery wings. It seemed to have no end, as if the earth were transforming itself into a steady stream of bats. It was as if when all the bats were in the sky, the earth would be gone.

"They're going. Guess we ought to, too," Tom said.

"How far you think they're going tonight?" Sisson asked.

"Far as they want to, I guess," John said. "Look how fast the little bastards are. How far are we going tonight?"

"Far as we can. Far as we can," Tom said. "We can't make it across the valley, but we might make Ash Creek and find cover for the day. Then we can get up into the Chiricahuas tomorrow night. We get to there, we're in pretty good shape." He believed that, more or less. Perhaps more than he should, less than he wanted. They had been able to traverse the valley from hill to hill, so far. But now, this far south after running from the posse, they were going to be heading into more than thirty miles of open country.

The valley was pretty flat, and that would increase their speed. He thought they should be good for two and a half, three miles an hour. Maybe, if it was just him and John, they could push four. But they had Sisson, and Sisson was wearing down some. He moved all right, but he needed more rest than either of the brothers did. They would have to stop every hour or so.

And then there were the obstacles of flat country, because, in the end, there was no such thing as flat country. There were washes and creeks, rocks and hummocks that had to be negotiated. And fences. Always fences. It wouldn't be as dark as when they had left the Galiuros. The moon was not quite half now. There still wouldn't be a lot of light, and they wouldn't be able to see long distances. They would be forever climbing over barbed wire and either jumping or slogging through irrigation ditches.

They, all three of them, had been cowboys. And they owed part of their lives to cattle. But it was easy to see that cattle were killing the country. The old ones talked about long fields of grama grass, stirrup-high. And it was that grass that brought the cattle. Those first ranchers thought they had unending grazing lands of sweet grass that would go on forever.

But cattle just eat grass. They don't replant it. And the grass had given way to cactus and the tough, thorny plants of the new valley—creosote, catclaw, Russian thistle, the scrubbier lower grasses, and saltbush, jojoba, and greasewood. The ground dried, cracked, and got rockier. The rainwater wasn't held, and runoff cut arroyos and streams across the land.

They would come across the land of cattle. It was a good thing, he thought, that cows were so damned tasty. Because there wasn't another good reason to have them out here. He had loved them when he was cowboying because cows create work, lots of work. But now he was a miner, and cows were mostly a big, shitting annoyance.

They slowed as they came down from the mountain. The Dragoon Mountains were formed by the swift upheaval of rock as tectonic plates shifted during the Mesozoic era and seemed to have simply erupted from the ground. The foothills were small—low and short—and gave small transition from the mountain to the valley below. But they were wooded foothills, and that provided plenty of cover. The moon gave some light, but not enough that the men's movements would stand out.

The advantage to them was a similar advantage to those who were pushing them. In the near darkness, it would be possible for a man, or even several men, for that matter, to hide themselves behind trees and rocks. And as long as they stayed quiet and still, it would be possible for the brothers to walk right up onto them without being aware of their presence.

It was all, finally, a trade-off. The advantages of the foothills and the weak light of the half moon became disadvantages if you simply looked at the situation from the other side. It seemed to Sisson that the disadvantages outweighed the advantages because the men had to be on the move, and movement was easy to spot and to hear. The waiting posses, if they were here, would have the advantage of stillness and perpetual cover, while he and the boys would have to move from cover to cover. They were not Apaches, and they did not wear moccasins. They could not move silently even two or three steps. The hard soles of their boots and shoes would draw complaints from the earth under them.

With both Tom and John half blind, Sisson again took the lead. They moved slowly through the heavily treed foothills, moving from scrub oak to scrub oak, slowly. Slow was key here. But slow also entailed the need to resist running from one point of cover to the next. That was instinct—spend as much time under cover as you could. But three men sprinting from one tree to another were loud and easily seen, giving back the advantage that the weak moonlight gave them. Sisson was again aware how much he hated being the quarry rather than the hunter and how little he actually knew about it. Tom, he thought, probably knew more.

Each time they stopped, they listened. The sounds of night were just starting to rise. Though winter was quieter than summer, when crickets, cicadas, and night birds were out, there was the hiss of a barn owl that seemed to be following them and, farther off, the hoot and who of a great horned owl. The coyotes were just starting up. There was plenty to hear, but also plenty to cover up the stray sounds of men.

So Sisson listened for horses. Horses heard better than men did, and horses would hear movement before the men who had ridden in on them. And when horses heard sounds, they reacted to them, often nickering or neighing and almost always moving restlessly, knowing that when men were moving, horses would soon be moving as well. Horses were also louder than smart men. Nothing was louder than a stupid man.

In the peering into the dark, the creeping from one cover to the next, the listening, the efforts to control breathing, there was nothing. They all felt the eyes on them, the rifle sights, even, but there was nothing. Sisson thought of deer, the way they moved, cautious, alert, then began or resumed grazing until the next stray sound or smell reached them, and they stopped, came alert again, and listened, tense and ready to spring and bolt.

Sisson was pretty sure that they were all right. He was almost positive that no one had come this far south in an attempt to cut them off. They had been on the run for more than a week now, and many members of the original posses would have given up, the desire to catch and kill them waning and the hope of blood sport losing out to the desire to sleep in a bed and eat good food, to rest against the breasts of their women, and the desire to see their children. And that, Sisson understood, was the advantage he, Tom, and John had over their pursuers. Their desire to stay alive was stronger than Thems's desire to kill them.

Except, that is, for Wootan. He would still be out there. And he would have others with him, feeding off his need to shed blood for blood. The strength of that desire was enormous and frightening. A man who had caught the desire for blood and had blended it with righteousness was a man to fear. Sisson had seen in the army, years after the Little Big Horn, how men could still hold on to a desire to smash, destroy, and exterminate in the holy name of Custer. A man they had not known, a man they had never met or even seen, and, often, a man who had not even lived in their lifetimes held sway over them and demanded blood sacrifice. Blood of the Indians, blood of the soldiers who had been taken for some reason they didn't fully understand. It didn't matter. It mattered that blood was required of someone, anyone, maybe everyone.

He didn't know how smart Wootan was. He didn't actually know him that well, though he could recognize him on sight. But he knew the Wootans in general. There were a lot of tough cowboys, not unlike himself and the Power boys. Wootans were the type to claw and scratch their way not to the top but to the lower rungs, where there were scraps to be picked up by those who were smart and tough enough to take them from the others. Sisson reckoned that the Wootans were tough and smart enough.

Sisson didn't want to take on another Wootan in a fight. He hadn't wanted the first one, and he figured they were lucky to have come out of it as little wounded as they were. It hadn't been his fight, but he'd been pulled into it simply by location and the turning of events. Not that it mattered too much. But this time it would be his fight. People had been killed, and he was on the side that had done most of the killing. He wasn't just the hired man anymore, he was one of the Power boys now. And he guessed that was all right. When you signed on, you stayed on. It didn't do anyone any good to pretend that their fights weren't your fights. They were, or, at the least, they were going to seem that way. It didn't matter which way you stepped or which hand you shook. In the end, you were dead. The only questions were when and how. And those didn't matter a whole hell of a lot.

They continued down the foothills, and the tree line continued to thin until they were sprinting long yards from one tree to another, fanning out as the trees spread and grew shorter and scrubbier. They went down an arroyo and back up the other side. On the east side was the beginning of the plain, and the few trees along the banks of the arroyo quickly gave way to the rock and grass of the plain. The Chiricahuas were so far away, you couldn't make them out in the looming dark.

Two or three nights. That's what it would take to cross the plain of the Sulphur Springs Valley. That was if they were lucky, if they didn't get chased back again and have to start over from some other, more southerly point. You could walk it in two nights if you kept up a good pace and walked in a straight line. They could do neither. Sisson was too busted up in the legs to move as fast as they needed to. And you couldn't walk a straight line, anyway. You needed to work with the land, following ridges, arroyos, and rocks that offered cover. If there were hills a couple of miles off your line of flight, you went to them, because hills meant safety. And it was harder to track men who moved in random directions. Hell, anyone could track three men moving in a straight line. So there were no straight lines.

John was still bothered by the discovery of the whiskey. Tom had headed straight for it, just like any man who knew it was there. And John knew that Tom knew it was there because he had put it there. It was his whiskey, though it had probably belonged to someone else before Tom got his hands on it. And that could be the cause of the killing. Whiskey. John hadn't seen Haynes. Haynes wasn't one of the dead. But Haynes could have been involved. Kane Wootan was involved. And so Haynes would have been involved, too. And now Kane was dead, and they were being chased by Wootan's brother and, maybe, Haynes as well. Wootan wanted revenge, and Haynes wanted money. Both were good reasons for getting yourself killed.

It was trouble to have a brother like Tom. Bad trouble. But there it was. Tom was his brother, and there was no doing anything about it. He thought of Charlie, off in New Mexico somewhere. Maybe Charlie was the smarter one. He'd just got the hell out. The Old Man's dreams and notions had just never stuck with Charlie. Charlie only wanted to live a quiet life, to marry, to have kids, to get called "mister" someday. It wasn't that he didn't like the Old Man, it was more that they just didn't match up on each other very well. The Old Man had no use for the simple life. He always figured he was destined for more, but he had never found where "more" was at. He was hell-bent on finding it, though, and he figured he would. One day, he would.

Now the Old Man was dead, and Charlie was in New Mexico. John guessed that at some point he'd had a choice between going with Charlie or staying with the Old Man and Tom. He didn't remember making the choice. He didn't actually remember that there had been a choice. Charlie had never offered to take him along when he went. He'd like to have that choice now, but it was gone, and, if it wasn't, Tom would make it for him anyway. He was here with Tom and Sisson because he was John, and that's what John did. Maybe there were no such things as choices. Maybe you just looked back and believed they were there.

Traveling at night was fine in the summertime. And in the times of big moons, too. But in February, with little moonlight, night travel had little to recommend it, except the dark. That and that smart people didn't travel in the dark. Only fugitives and idiots. It was damned cold. There probably wouldn't be any snow tonight, and that was good, because it would make tracking harder. But the clear sky with all its bright stars made the air sharp as nails against their skin, especially their ears and noses.

John had a wool coat and a wool blanket that was getting thin. The others had much the same. John kept the blanket around him as they walked, though the stray branches of mesquite, creosote, and catclaw kept pulling it off him. He had tried running rope through two corners of it and tying it around his neck, but that was worse. The thorns caught the blanket and pulled him up short, and then he had to go back and free the damned thing from the vegetables.

He had a hat and gloves, but it was getting colder. They hadn't really seen snow since leaving the Galiuros, but there would be plenty in the Chiricahuas. The others were dressed much the same, wearing their blankets rather than carrying them. Tom had a scarf wrapped around his head, over his hat, and Sisson wore a kerchief over his mouth and nose to take the sting from the air he breathed. John had a kerchief, too, but he didn't wear it. He reasoned that he would need it more later, and it would be a comfort to finally put it on. Each carried a couple days' rations and two or three gallons of water at eight pounds a gallon. They had a total of six firearms, and each carried two hundred rounds of ammunition. They could hold off a good-sized posse if they could get to cover.

It wasn't rough going, and the farther east they went, the more the sense of danger from hidden posse members diminished. The terrain presented few obstacles. There were rocks and bushes and occasional arroyos and washouts, but there was nothing to compare to what they had already been through in the Dragoons. It was the length, not the terrain, of the trek that presented the problems now.

Visibility was surprisingly good with the small moonlight. There were few clouds, and that made it easier to see the near distances, though it also made the cold air more cutting and painful. The riders would be bedded down for the night now, since it was too dark to follow tracks and too dangerous for the horses. While horses generally see better than their riders do at night, they have a blind spot directly in front of them, so they can't see where their front hooves are landing. So it's easier for a horse to step into a gopher burrow or other hole at night, especially if the rider, whose night vision is relatively poor, can't see the hole first.

So what they had to watch out for was the truck or the trucks. And the trucks had to move with their lights on. The trucks had an advantage in speed and firepower, carrying a number of men, but they were at a huge disadvantage in being seen and heard a long way off.

Perhaps the greatest danger was the uneventfulness of the long trek. They simply walked, keeping their eyes open for distant lights. With no real problems to occupy them, they could think, and, thinking, their thoughts turned to the pain. John's left eye was swollen to the size of Sisson's hammy fist. The bridge of his nose was crusted half an inch deep in blood. Every so often the scab would break open again, and a new rivulet of blood would course down his face to dry and harden. Tom's eye was less swollen, though it was shut tight and had turned a bright purple, like a baby bird's.

To keep their minds off the big pains, they thought about the small ones. Their feet hurt and would keep hurting. Tom had developed a small limp that John figured meant blister. Sisson was a plodder anyway, but now he looked like an old horse shuffling through the chute to catch the hammer between the eyes. Dog food. John's feet just hurt, and his legs had progressed through burn into the dull grind of fatigue that was going to go on for hours more.

Their gear, in leather and cloth bags, banged against their backs and ribs. The roped and leather lacings cut into their hands and shoulders. Their rifles, though slung, were in their hands because there was no more room on their shoulders to carry them. The water bags were the worst. They steadily thumped against their bodies, John's bumping his ass with every step, sixteen pounds of slow, soft tapping that was threatening to break him.

They rested every couple of miles. They took two kinds of breaks—standing breaks, when they could rest their hands from carrying the guns and unsling the water bags from their shoulders, and full breaks, where they dropped everything, sat, breathed, and felt what it was like to not lug weight. The full breaks they allowed every five or six miles. Tom called the breaks, but Sisson occasionally overruled him, declaring that he had to rest or he wouldn't be able to go on much farther.

The rest was the soft concussion of step after step. The slow chewing of the landscape. The Chiricahuas were still too far off to really see them in the dark. The only indicator of how far they had traveled was the Dragoons, steadily diminishing. Every time John looked back, he found them harder to see.

And then they were easier to see. John moved up to tap Tom on the shoulder. Though the sunlight hadn't come over the tops of the Chiricahuas yet, it was starting to faintly light the ragged spires of the Stronghold. "Yeah," Tom said when he saw what John had seen. Then he turned and walked forward again. He stopped and turned. "Still too dark to find a good hiding place, but we should be getting the light in a couple of minutes. As soon as you can see, start looking for a place to stop for the day."

"Bless Jesus," Sisson said.

They tucked into an arroyo some four feet deep. There were no clouds, and it was February, way too early for snow thaw. They were secure and out of sight. It was just coming dawn, the light weak and hazy. Tom took first watch, just up on a small rise, amid a clump of prickly pear that didn't hide him but broke the sight lines well enough that someone would have to get pretty close to get a clear view of him. He could see for miles in every direction. If there was trouble, he would know in time to get them moving toward better cover, though he was not sure where that would be.

"Sisson?" John was exhausted and sore from the walk and wrapped tightly in his blanket, waiting for the sun to come fully up and warm the air and ground.

"Yeah?"

"You asleep?"

"No, John. I'm talking to you. I'm awake."

"This is about Tom, ain't it? I mean, all of it."

"All of it?"

"The law, the shooting, the Old Man, the running. It's all tied in, ain't it? It's Tom and that whiskey back there in the line shack."

"I don't know."

"Sure you do, Sisson. I know you know. I'm right, ain't I?"

"John, I don't know. It could be about the whiskey. There's a lot of money in whiskey, and most killing is about money or pussy. That's what I know."

"So it makes sense, right?"

"It does make sense, John. But you want to be careful about sense. A lot of times, especially when there's killing, sense don't have a lot to do with anything. It would be easier if sense was all there was to it, but that, generally, ain't the case."

"I think I'm right."

"Could be. Or could be you're wrong. Or, likely, the truth is somewhere toward the middle."

"So you saying it ain't the whiskey?"

"John, I ain't saying. I'm saying it could have been. That's all. Could have been something else. Could have been the gold just as well. I don't know. And, you know, it don't make a hell of a lot of difference right now. They're after us, and it would seem likely they would hang us if they can. I'm focused on not getting hanged. That's all that matters at the moment. I don't care why they want to hang me, I'm just trying to make sure they don't succeed."

"You think much about dying?"

"I'm against it for myself. For others, I'm pretty much neutral on it."

"I really don't want to die."

"I know that. None of us do, I don't think. Except crazy ones. Seems to me we all get exactly the same amount of time for living—not enough. You don't want to die, that just means you ain't crazy or stupid."

"Tom says I'm stupid."

"In Tom's book, everyone is stupid except him and, maybe, the Old Man."

"He is smart, ain't he?"

"According to him. But look here. He's at exactly the same place we are. All his thinking ain't saved him from the rope yet. Ain't made him rich, either, though I don't have a good handle on such conceptions."

"I ain't smart. I know that. Tom's the smart one. I rely on him for that."

"Some would say that knowing you ain't smart makes you pretty damned smart."

"I wouldn't know about that."

"Me, neither. Probably."

"You think they're going to hang us, then?"

"They're going to try. We got to make it as difficult as we can."

"Did you shoot one of them?"

"John, it don't matter. It purely don't matter."

"I guess I'll sleep."

"See, you ain't stupid at all."

Tom woke John at midday, the sun near its peak, though far south. "You all right, brother?" John nodded his head. "I think we ought to let Sisson sleep as long as he can. He needs it more than us. In a couple of hours, we can wake him, eat some, and go. You OK with that?"

John nodded.

"All right, then. If there ain't difficulties, we'll make the Chiricahuas tonight, and then we all can sleep tomorrow. You doing all right? You ain't going to go back to sleep, are you?"

John nodded.

"All right, then. You fall asleep, maybe none of us ever wakes up."

John took his blanket off, though he was still cold. He would need it later. He reasoned that if he kept it off for a while, he would be more likely to feel warm when he put it back on later.

He looked out in all directions and saw nothing. But that gave no comfort. He had a bad feeling. Maybe because he really was stupid. He sometimes felt things that Tom didn't but failed to see what Tom saw. He was starting to get that rifle-sight feeling again, and he couldn't shake it.

There wasn't much to do when it was your lookout. He would scan the horizon with the glasses every few minutes but see nothing. There were good sight lines to the north and west, and that's why Tom had chosen this spot. It was most likely that any posses would come from either the north or the west, but they had been running long enough that one could come from any direction. No doubt some had scattered and scouted along the Chiricahuas and even down toward Mexico. So there was no lane of sure safety.

There were a few hawks and an occasional vulture drifting high in the winds above them, too high to be actively hunting but just moving around trying for a sight or scent. Around him, the insects were at work, too. Ants mostly. They were also scouting and occasionally walking across his hands. He made a game of it, seeing if he could just sit there and watch them go without trying to brush them off. And many just walked across his hand as if it were just another obstacle and crawled off the other side and kept going. The ones that wanted to go up his shirtsleeves he brushed off or grabbed and crushed with his fingers.

They were black ants, and mostly they didn't bother you. But a bite from one stung real bad. The old-timers knew you could suture a cut with them, pressing their heads into the wound until their jaws snapped shut around the cut. Then you squeezed their bodies off, leaving the heads on the wound, holding the edges together. He had done it a number of times, but he mostly remembered the Old Man doing it to him when he was only a kid.

He was playing near the corral back in New Mexico. He had come up hard against the corral and opened his upper arm on a piece of snipped wire that was holding some of the branches together. He opened a pretty good gash. The blood flowed freely, and that scared him bad.

The Old Man came then, answering his screaming. The Old Man tried to calm him, but the blood kept coming, along with the screaming. The Old Man dragged him to the trough at the far end of the corral, washed the blood off, and looked at the ragged cut. "Jesus, look what you done, you little turd monkey." And when John looked and saw the cut, the blood already welling and starting to spill again, he began to cry again. The Old Man went from what might have been a touch of tenderness to anger. He reached down, picked up an ant, and mashed it into the cut. When John felt the fire of the bite, he began to yell and kick at the Old Man.

"That don't hurt," the Old Man said. Then he slapped John hard across the face. "That there hurts. This—" He mashed another ant into the cut. "This don't hurt." John kept crying.

"You need to learn what hurts again?"

John shook his head violently from side to side, fighting against the blubbering tears. The Old Man kept mashing ants onto the cut until there was a ragged line of ant heads getting covered in coagulating blood. The Old Man pushed John roughly away. "You don't want me to help you, don't get yourself hurt, you little moron."

When the Old Man had gone, John saw Tom on the other side of the corral, peering through the rails, his face a combination of fear and fascination. John walked over, still sniffling a little, and showed Tom the scabby line of ant heads and the rapidly puckering wound. Then he slapped Tom hard across the face. "You going to live with us, you best learn not to cry." And he didn't remember seeing Tom cry again after that.

He was about to wake Tom when he saw the dust. At first, he thought it might be a dust devil, a spout of sand and dirt like a tiny tornado, though it was the wrong season for wind to swirl like that. But it wasn't a dust devil. If it was, it was three of them. And dust devils were solitary things. They didn't come in threes. He scrambled up and scuttled back to where Tom and Sisson were sleeping.

"Get up. Something's coming. I think it's Thems."

Tom was on his feet almost as fast as he got his eyes open. He had that knack. He came out of a deep sleep, immediately, ready to go like a startled cat.

He grabbed the glasses out of John's hand and scurried over to the little ridge where John had taken the watch.

"Goddamn," Tom said. "Goddamn it all and everything. It's trucks. Three of them, and coming right for us. Go get Sisson on his feet. We're going."

Sisson was already awake, though still on his ass, blanket around his shoulders, looking like a big Indian chief in a picture book.

"They coming, Sisson. Trucks. Three of them."

"How the hell did they find us?"

"Stay and ask if you like."

"Fuck it all." Sisson shook his boots and began pulling them on. Tom came back, hunched over so low he was nearly bent double.

They gathered up their small belongings—guns, ammo, water, blankets, rope, the bit of food that was left.

They were moving nearly due east, alternating between a trot and a fast walk. The Chiricahuas loomed in front of them, quite visible, but still a long way off. They wouldn't be able to outrun the trucks to the mountains. They would need to find some cover or some canyon or rockfall where the trucks couldn't go.

Sisson had already slowed to a moderate walk when Tom came springing past him. "They've split up. One's going southwest, and another's going due south." He didn't need to fill in the information that the third was going southeast.

"Out ahead of us?" Sisson asked.

"Looks like it. We're going to need to find a place to hide out and let them go past. It's our only real hope, to go behind them. Any way you look at it, it's bad."

John was stopped ahead, waiting for them. "Any chance of just outrunning them?"

"Always a chance of everything. But this don't look good. That truck's coming up fast. There's got to be some kind of road up there. It ain't running across bare ground like that. It would have busted an axle or something by now. You know of any roads out this way, Sisson?"

"Hell. They're all over the place. They just throw their wire and poles and stuff into the trucks now and ride out to do the fences. Just sitting on their asses. It's too easy. They got roads all over the damned place."

"What are we going to do?" John asked.

"I don't know," Tom said. "I just don't goddamned know. I been down through this country, but I can't say I know it. We can try to Apache it—go as far as we can, then curl up into the landscape and hope they don't see us. I think we got to keep going forward. I don't much like just sitting here, waiting for them to pick us off."

"That worked back up in the Dragoons."

"It's low percentage, and I think we done shot our wad with that one."

Chapter Thirteen
1916

In the days before and after the election, McBride thought about his strange encounter with Tom Power. The expected Democratic sweep hadn't happened. He, President Wilson, and Governor Hunt were the only Democrats who won, and Hunt lost Graham County by over two hundred votes. And McBride's election was closer than he expected or wanted. McBride took 730 out of 1,600 votes cast, less than 50 percent. McBride thought he may have to rethink some things, including the offer by Power. Power was an odd figure in Graham County. He was never in actual trouble, but he always seemed nearby when it happened. He was a likeable, good-looking kid. Oddly, it seemed to McBride, Power might have had a point about his value as a deputy. Power did know the southern boundaries of the county, and he knew the cowboys and miners who populated it.

And Power wasn't a Mormon. That could be a benefit. McBride had carried the Mormon vote, and the Mormon vote had carried him. It would be good to pick up some additional strength before the next elections. On the other hand, he did owe the Mormon community for his victory, and they would want a Mormon, not a Gentile, in the undersheriff's office. Though Mormons were the majority in Graham County, their history was that of a minority, an outside-the-mainstream religious sect, viewed with suspicion and distrust. The killing of their founder and leader, Joseph Smith, in 1844 and the fear that people held for Brigham Young and his protector, Porter Rockwell, still echoed into the twentieth century. The massacre of 120 people by the Mormons at Mountain Meadows and the whole business of polygamy, which had been largely, but not completely, left behind, seemed to the Gentiles clear proof that the Mormons were a sect led by a succession of madmen. And McBride had won only the northern section of the county, which was Mormon. He didn't have a lot of support in the south, where he and all Mormons were likely to be seen with some distrust.

Though he continued to think about Power and the odd meeting, McBride never really considered Power. He knew that Power was involved in the illegal rodeos that moved through the southern reaches of the county, and he was fairly sure that Power had some connection to the bootlegging that plagued the state. People were already talking about the probability that the law was entangled in the bootlegging, whether simply turning a blind eye or actively running the operation.

McBride himself had suggested that Sheriff Alger's connection with various bootleggers, evidenced by the lack of convictions of arrested bootleggers, was the largest legal problem in Graham County. And the church, which had put its resources behind him, was adamant about the necessity of prohibition in the county, in the state, and, soon, in the nation. He wanted support from the Gentiles. He wanted to be the people's, all people's, sheriff, but he understood that it was the Mormon vote that allowed him to win despite the surprising success of the Republicans in the state elections. It was the Mormons to whom he owed the greatest allegiance.

So he chose as undersheriff someone he could trust, young Martin Kempton, a Mormon from a good, long-established Graham County family. Realizing that Power's argument had made some sense, McBride offered the post of occasional deputy to Thomas "Kane" Wootan, who, like Power, knew the southern part of the state. There were rumors about Wootan as well. In fact, they were the same rumors that stuck to Power—rodeos and bootlegging. But Wootan lived in the north, and McBride could keep an eye on him. And Wootan had connections to US Marshal Frank Haynes, and it made sense to use those connections, though rumors put Haynes in the bootlegging business as well. All in all, McBride thought it better to be able to keep track of Wootan and Haynes than to have them operate behind his back. It was just smart law enforcement.

Mart Kempton got the responsibility for cutting down on the bootlegging. Young, energetic, and ambitious, Mart threw himself into the task. By the spring of 1917, it was impossible to pick up a copy of the *Graham County Guardian* without finding an article on the exploits of Undersheriff Martin Kempton. He was arresting one or two, sometimes four or more, bootleggers a week. He posted himself out on the Solomonville road and just waited for a car or truck he didn't recognize. He then simply pulled into the middle of the road and stopped the car for a friendly chat. The *Guardian* and the good people of Graham County loved the stories of his exploits.

On August 17, 1917, Kempton arrested four bootleggers, three men and a woman. The following Sunday, Kempton similarly took off after a man and woman riding in a Jeffery Six Roadster. Again he followed the car until it stopped and then arrested the couple and confiscated twenty-one cases of whiskey. The *Graham County Guardian* reported: "They were given apartments in Hotel McBride and were arraigned before Judge McAlister Tuesday afternoon."

Not only was the jail filling up, but the evidence closet in the jail was filling with cases of whiskey confiscated from the arrests. Deputy Kempton was becoming a local hero for his efforts, which were frequent, and frequently successful. Kempton was getting more press than McBride was, and he was beginning to entertain ideas of turning his celebrity to his advantage in the next election by opposing McBride for sheriff. McBride was well liked and respected, but Kempton was a celebrity, young and ambitious. He had a presence that McBride lacked. It seemed to Kempton that in many significant ways, McBride was still a carpenter, always measuring twice before cutting. Kempton didn't need to measure twice. His gut instinct served him well. He acted, and acted quickly, and that was the key to his success.

Kempton, who kept a careful eye on his own reputation and its possible value, also kept an eye on the whiskey in the evidence closet. The stack of wooden cases seemed to him visible testimony to his prowess as a scourge of bootleggers and as a lawman. He had no particular plans for his future. He liked and respected Sheriff McBride, and he liked his position as deputy, though, more often than not, McBride seemed to favor Wootan when it came to doling out responsibility, and Wootan wasn't shy about shoving responsibility in Kempton's face. Kempton thought that maybe, one of these days, he would like to have more responsibility, just to see how Wootan liked those apples.

Where McBride was hesitant to put himself in the public eye, Kempton didn't shy away from the newspapermen who frequented the diner on Main Street and even sought them out, buying them coffee, which, as a practicing Mormon, he did not approve of, but he was willing to abet others in the indulgence. It was not so much what you did as what people thought you did.

The troublesome aspect was the whiskey in the courthouse evidence locker. Or the lack of it. Kempton would transport whiskey seized in an arrest to the courthouse two days before the case went to trial. The whiskey was to stay in the courthouse for a couple of months after the trial, then be given back to the sheriff's office to be destroyed. Trouble was, it wasn't coming back.

And it wasn't piling up in the courthouse. It was disappearing. Someone was taking the liquor from the courthouse evidence locker. And that wasn't causing a great deal of concern because there had yet to be a need to bring the evidence back for a retrial. That seemed to show that whoever was taking the whiskey, and, surely, someone was taking the whiskey, knew what cases were open and what ones were closed. Kempton couldn't help but think of Kane Wootan. It was generally accepted that when there was trouble in Graham County, there was a Wootan nearby. They were like moths to the flame, except that they carried their own matches.

When US Marshal Frank Haynes came in the door, McBride was not happy. He was never happy to see Haynes. Haynes was a snappy dresser, his shirt always pressed, his tie secured by a silver tie bar, and his "gig line," formed by the tie, the front seam of his shirt, and the flap of his fly, always straight. He wore knee-high laced boots, shined to near brilliance. He was a good-looking, middle-aged man with a square jaw and a quick smile. He had an eye for the ladies and a taste for whiskey. He was well connected and had made his way through the ranks of lawmen in central and eastern Arizona quickly and smoothly without leaving much trace of accomplishment. He looked good and prosperous, and he made a show of being active in the faith despite his habits. McBride assumed that was enough to keep him as the federal presence in the area.

Haynes came in smiling, his hand extended, eyes bright and eager as though he were an elected official coming up on a new race. "McBride. How are you? Winning the war on demon rum?"

"Wish it were so, Frank. For every one we catch, Lord only knows how many get through. We can't stop every car and truck that comes through Graham County."

"I don't know, McBride. That Kempton boy seems pretty intent on doing just that. You watch yourself around him. That young man has a future, and right now, you're sitting right in the middle of his chosen road." Haynes spoke with the authority of a man who, not a politician as such, understood power and how to get it. He was a glad-hander and a probable fraud but damned good at both.

"What's on your mind, Haynes?"

Haynes flashed the big smile again. "Maybe I'm just here to pick up tips on putting a halt to the hooch business. It's starting to look like the amendment is going to pass and that it's going to become my job to stop it, not yours."

"I would be happy to turn it over to you. I believe in the amendment, and I think alcohol is one of the greatest problems mankind faces, up to and including the war in Europe. But just from our experience, it strains the resources, badly."

"But it keeps us in work. It keeps us in work. Law's a good business if you like steady work and don't mind getting shot at."

"You ever been shot at, Frank?" McBride asked.

"I've heard some gunfire," Haynes said. "But I can't swear any of it was aimed at me. I do accept the possibility of a shooting, though. Not anxious for it, you understand, but I accept the possibility. And you, Sheriff?"

"Never have. Never want to."

"If I was a drinking man, still, I would toast that." Haynes had been promoting his sobriety despite his reputation as a drinker. He made himself out to be a reformed man, though that was surely a sham. He had just become more careful about hiding it. And there were persistent rumors that Haynes was himself involved in the bootlegging business, though no one had come forth with any proof. McBride suspected that the rumors were true. There was not a direct line from the disappearing liquor at the courthouse, but there was one if you just added Kane Wootan into the line.

"And what can I do for you, Frank?" McBride asked.

"Well, I'm getting pressure from above about the draft resistors. 'Slackers.' That war over there just keeps eating up the troops. A terrible thing. The

Germans and the British are just stalled over there in France, killing each other in bigger and bigger numbers. Washington wants us to start rooting out slackers and getting them enlisted or to jail. I need your help with Graham County."

"Graham County has an admirable record for enlistments, Frank. I would venture to say this county has more enlistments per thousand men than any other county in Arizona. Certainly way more than Maricopa and Pima. Why aren't you after them?"

"Who says we're not?" Haynes replied. "Everyone knows Graham County has signed up a good share of its eligible men. And this is not about Graham County. It's about this whole state, the whole country. We all got to do what we can. We got to get the war over and the Kaiser out of town. We all got to do our part. Hell, if I was younger, I'd sign up."

"No, you wouldn't."

Haynes laughed. "Guess you got me there. But it needs to be said. Got to let the young ones know we all share the burden."

"So I'm supposed to round up all the young men in this county who haven't enlisted yet? How am I supposed to do that? Are you going to give me additional men to help find these fellows? Isn't that your job? That's federal, Frank, not state or county."

"Like I said, McBride. We all do our part. It's not your job. But I'm spread thin. I can't cover Graham, Gila, Pinal, Greenlee, and Cochise Counties with the staff I got. I need help from the locals."

"But we don't have the authority."

"We can fix that. I can deputize one of your deputies, and you can use his authority to make the arrests and then just hold them for me. It will all be well and proper."

"You want Martin to round up slackers?"

"No. Kempton is a born temperance enforcer. I'll deputize the other one— Wootan. That will give him something to do. I understand he hasn't got an excess of ambition."

"He's not as enthusiastic as Mart Kempton, but he's all right."

"Kane Wootan ain't after your job. And if he was, he wouldn't get it. It's Kempton you want to watch. Don't give him a lot of power. If he's a nice boy, he might offer to let you be his deputy someday. 'Cause he's going to be sheriff if you let him. We'll spread the authority around. I think Wootan's my man."

"And how are we going to identify those slackers?"

"It's a tight community. People here know who's signed up and who hasn't. You let it slip around the church that you're going to be looking for slackers, and they'll be lining up to register. That's all we ask. And I'll give you your first leads. Power. John and Tom Power."

"The boys up in the Galiuros?"

"That's them. I think they deserve the opportunity to see France. Where the ladies don't wear no pants."

Two days after his talk with Haynes, McBride saw the battered flatbed truck outside the tack and hardware. He passed it, then came back, thinking that this could be one of the Powers. The truck, like a lot of others, had had hell beaten out of it, the way a truck would if it went up and down Rattlesnake Canyon regularly. He couldn't ever recall having a conversation with a Power other than Tom, but he knew who they were.

The Old Man, not actually so old, a little more than McBride but weathered hard on the face and hands, maybe ten years beyond his actual age, leaned on the counter of the store where his goods were being tallied. Someone had told a joke, and there was laughter, but it died out as McBride walked in.

"Mr. Power? Mr. Jeff Power?"

The Old Man turned to face McBride, leaning back into the counter. "That would be me."

"Frank McBride. Sheriff." McBride extended his hand, and Power took it. Power's hand was remarkably calloused and strong.

"What did they do?"

"Pardon?"

"My boys. I ain't done nothing that would be of interest to you, so I figure it would be one or both of the boys you're interested in. What did they do? Tell me, and I'll beat hell out of one or both of them for you and save you the trouble and expense."

"Not so much what they've done but what they haven't done. They haven't registered for the draft."

"Couldn't. Went to Redington and got turned away. Wouldn't sign 'em up there." Power turned back toward the layabouts he had been talking to.

"I don't know about that. They're not registered, and the law says they have to register. They can come here. Right away. Today if they can. Tomorrow at the latest."

Power turned back to McBride, looking him up and down as if seeing if he were worth bothering with or maybe seeing if he could take him if he needed to. "They'll get on it. One of these days. Maybe not soon enough for your liking, but they'll get on it. We got gold to dig."

"It's not my liking you need to worry about, Power. It's the federal government's liking that counts here. Things are going hard on boys who don't register. There are mobs beating them up back east, killing them, even. I don't want to have to rescue your boys when they come downtown and get set on by a mob that thinks they're slackers, whether they are or not."

"First of all, my boys ain't slacked on anything. Second, God help the mob that sets on a Power. If the boys don't handle the situation, and that ain't likely,

I will. Third, what my boys do is their business and my business. It's not any of yours. You got any paper that says my boys broke any laws here in Graham County, show it to me. If they have, I'll take care of it. We're running a gold operation up there, and we don't need disruptions. We work, and we work hard. We don't bother folk, and we expect not to be bothered."

"It's the law, Power. The law says they have to register for the draft and serve if called. That's federal law."

"I say they got to bust rock up to the mine. That's Power law."

"They have to serve their country. That's the supreme law here. They must defend their country."

"Their country. I presume that's the United States of America?"

"Yes, sir."

"That ain't our country. That's New York and Pennsylvania and Kansas and whatever the hell other states they got now, including this one. That ain't my country. You can have the whole damned bunch of it for all I care. I wouldn't lift a finger to stop you if you was to burn it to the ground, because I don't give a damn. Rattlesnake Canyon. That's my country. Bought and paid for. And I will defend that. You send someone up to take what we got up there, and you will see some defending. And you won't want a lot of it."

"Mr. Power. I'm doing you a kindness here, warning you that those boys need to get registered for the draft, like all the fine young men in this country are doing. If they do that, there's no trouble as far as I can see. But if they don't, there's going to be a warrant on them, and the next time they come to town, they'll be arrested and sent to the deputy US marshal in Globe for trial. You don't want that, and neither do I, particularly. You can save us a lot of trouble, you, me, and the boys, everyone, if you'll get them down to register."

"The deputy US marshal wouldn't be Frank Haynes, would it?"

"Yes. That's him."

"Well, where's the profit for Frank? Frank don't wipe his ass unless he sees it profit him. How's this business lining Haynes's pockets? What the hell is he fishing for now?"

"He's the marshal. It's his job to enforce federal law here. And the draft is law."

"Well, he's got a problem, Sheriff. You tell him something for me. It will be a kindness, and I understand how you are always looking to do a kindness. Tell him the boys won't be coming into town. And tell him he doesn't want to come up Rattlesnake Canyon. That's a kindness. I would appreciate you passing that on to him."

"Don't make trouble where there doesn't need to be trouble, Power."

Jeff raised his hands, palms up, shoulder-high. "I ain't got trouble, Sheriff.

But those of you who do got trouble don't want to be handing it off to me. I don't need it, and I won't take it."

"Get the boys to register. Let's stop this foolishness right here. Get the boys to register and be done with it." McBride turned and walked out of the store. He listened. It stayed quiet in the store for several seconds, and then the laughter broke out. Nervous laughter, like when men don't know how to react to something, so they just laugh.

McBride was stung by the dismissiveness of Power's answer. And the laughter was directed more at him than it was just nondirected laughter. It was true that Power often gave a smart answer, one that almost everyone in the room could appreciate. McBride wasn't interested in smart answers. He was interested in justice, law, and truth, and Power had little use for those. He could let go a lot where the Powers were concerned. They were rough customers, but they weren't great troublemakers, no matter how often trouble found them. But this was just wrong. Everyone owed support to the war. No one should be exempt. Men were called on, periodically, to give themselves over to the higher power, and this was one of those times. He had no use for men who shirked their duty.

An hour later, he was restored. Trying to control the Powers was like trying to control the wind. There was little use trying to enforce laws when the Powers were involved. It was better to just leave them where they were, far away, deep in the Galiuros. You didn't reach into a rattlesnake den to explain to the snakes that they needn't strike at everything that passed their way. No. You just gave them a wide berth. And he was content to do just that.

Keeping the law wasn't a bit like carpentry. Carpentry was exact. If you cut a board too short, it was simply too short and, therefore, useless. Precision and patience were the keys to good carpentry. And that didn't work in law enforcement. If you tried to be precise, to follow the law to the letter, you were bound to fail, same as if you had used a rule that was mismarked. People were not boards, and they weren't suited to precision, and you couldn't recut them to make them that way.

But other people didn't see it that way. If you missed a cut on a board, you slapped some molding on it. If someone violated the law, either the state's or Heaven's, you punished him, no matter why he had done it or what the outcome. People were odd that way.

Chapter Fourteen
1916

They were riding fences some two miles below the Garden when they saw the rider approaching them. None of them spoke, but they all dismounted at the same time, and they all pulled rifles from their scabbards.

The rider saw this, stopped, turned, put up his right hand to show he wasn't armed, and started toward them, picking his way. "Would you be the Power family?"

"That's right," Jeff called.

"R. J. Samuels, deputy clerk of the Cochise County District Court." Again, nearly in unison, the Powers pulled their rifles up across their chests. "With good news," Samuels added. "Good news."

"And what good news ever comes out of Cochise County?"

"It's the matter of the Tucker estate."

"Is that settled?"

"It's about to be." Samuels rode up to where they stood, started to dismount, but looked at Jeff, and only after Jeff had nodded his assent did Samuels dismount fully. "Documents in the bag," Samuels said, motioning with his head to the big canvas bag behind his saddle. He retrieved a small bundle of papers. Unfolding them and pressing out the creases, he said, "You were in the midst of a business transaction with Mr. C. P. Tucker at the time of his unfortunate demise, I believe."

"We were buying a share of a gold mine," Jeff said. "One-quarter of it."

"Right, right," Samuels said. "There's a complication."

"We bought it outright. Paid money to Tucker. In full. I got papers," Jeff said.

"Yes. Yes. That's right. Not all complications are bad. Sometimes they're just complications."

"What's that mean?"

"Well, you signed and Mr. Tucker signed a contract stating that you were buying, and these are the exact words of the contract, 'that share of the mine owned by Mr. C. P. Tucker.'"

"That's right."

"Yes. I know that's right. I just said it. Now. Here comes the complication. As he was selling his share to you, he was also buying another one-quarter share from a Mr. Elwood. He had paid for it and had a receipt for it. Not sure why he was doing that, but that's what he did. That's a mystery not yet solved."

"And that means what?"

"Remember what I said about the 'that share of the mine owned by Mr. C. P. Tucker'? Since he had paid for the quarter share owned by Mr. Elwood, and even though the purchase had not been recorded, Mr. Tucker was then the owner of Mr. Elwood's share."

"We would be interested in buying that share as well, if that's where you're going."

Samuels smiled. "That's not where I'm going. You already own that share. You bought the share owned by Tucker. Legally, that share is his one-quarter share plus Mr. Elwood's one-quarter share. That makes you half owner of the mine, and for no more money than you had already spent."

"Half owners?"

Mr. Samuels smiled. "You are. Yes."

"And no extra money?"

"None required, sir." He handed over the papers to Jeff. "Your deed to one-half interest in said mine. I require only your signature on this piece of paper."

Jeff took the papers and leafed through them, trying to read but too flummoxed to actually comprehend. "Half owner. And if Mr. Bowman is found to be guilty, you're three-quarters owner."

"Well, I'm obliged to you." Jeff looked around at his three sons and Samuels. "Sorry about the guns," he said.

Samuels tipped his hat. "I get those all the time."

The Powers now owned half interest in the mine in Kielberg Canyon. Another quarter was owned by Bowman, who was now in jail for the killing of C. P. Tucker. And the final quarter was owned by Ed Lyman, a butcher in Bisbee. The mine was now in the control of the Power family, as Bowman and Lyman were both absentee owners.

The family began spending more and more time at the mine. On any given day, at least one would be working it. They sold a portion of their cattle to buy another string of burros, and they used the burros to power a stamp mill that crushed the rock and separated the ore from the bearing stone by simple gravity. They could then load the burros with ore and take them down the trail through Rattlesnake Canyon to Klondyke, where the ore could be moved to Safford by truck.

They had not struck it rich, but the burros allowed them to increase the amount of ore the mine was delivering to the extent that Jeff could see that if they had more transport, they could make decent money off the gold, which was a much more stable commodity than cattle.

What they needed was a truck to take the ore out and directly to Safford without the expense and time-consuming unloading of the burros and loading of the truck. The burros could be put on the arrastra full time, and their production would be much higher.

But for a truck to get down and then up through Rattlesnake Canyon would take a road, a real one, and some bridges to cross the creek where the siding cliffs were too steep and rocky to cut through. It would take men. A lot of them.

Men, fortunately, were cheap. Arizona's prosperity had proved somewhat less than originally thought, and a lot of men had traveled there, looking for work and opportunity, and had found little of either. Jeff posted a notice at the Klondyke store that he was prepared to hire a gang of laborers. He would return the following Wednesday at noon to interview prospective workers.

He thought he might find three or four that first week, but when he arrived, there were several groups milling about. His notice had attracted more than twenty men. He shook hands with each one, using the handshake as a gauge of strength and history of hard work. Anyone with soft or weak hands was immediately dismissed. Men with hard grips and calloused hands were taken on.

One man, in particular, stood out. He was a big man, old, nearly as old as Jeff himself. He had large, drooping moustaches that gave him a somber, melancholy air. He was both strong and well used to hard work. Jeff asked his name.

"Sisson. Tom Sisson."

"What kinds of work are you used to?"

"Most of it," Sisson replied. "I've been a ranch hand, a deliveryman, and a night watchman. I'm a first-rate farrier, and I was an army scout for nearly twenty years."

"How about the last couple of years? What have you done the last two years?"

"Road work, mostly. Digging and scraping."

"And who did you do that for?"

"The state of Arizona."

"And where?"

"Florence. Arizona State Penitentiary."

Jeff smiled. He liked the man's candor.

"You would have found out anyway. Save the trouble of an argument later on."

"What was you in for?"

"Horse stealing."

Jeff scowled.

"It was fair pay for what was owed me. I just evened things out."

"But you stole them."

"I did. You going to turn me down on that account?"

"Where did you steal them?"

"Apache reservation."

"So those was likely stole horses anyway?"

"I don't know," Sisson said. "I had some horses stole. Figured they was on the reservation, but those wasn't the ones I took. I took other ones. Figured it all come out pretty even."

"No. I ain't going to turn you down for that. That sounds all reasonable to me. But you got other things going against you. You're old."

"So are you. You figure many of these fellows could outwork either one of us?"

Jeff looked at the group he had separated out to join his road gang. They were the usual—worthless cowboys, busted-up laborers, and kids who still had a lot to learn about the hardness of the world.

"How'd you like the army?"

"Fine. Wasn't a need for scouts anymore. They cut me loose. I would have stayed on if I could."

"You ever been foreman of anything?"

"No."

"Well, figure it out as you go. Between the army and prison, you been told what to do enough in your life that I guess you'll get the hang of telling others without much trouble."

"All right, then, Tom Sisson, army scout. This is your crew. I want to have them here at sunup tomorrow. We'll load into the truck and drive where I need to go. When we can't go no further, we get out and start building a road." He turned to the men. "This here's Tom Sisson. He's foreman. You do what he tells you to do, and you got some steady work. You don't do it, you got a long fucking walk back home."

They scraped a road from near Klondyke up to the top of Rattlesnake Mesa, cutting it along the edges of the mesas there until they reached the peak by scraping it with a mule team and by busting up the rocks by hand, rolling them out of the way when they could, blasting them with dynamite when they couldn't. The rhyolite of the mesa and canyon was soft and flaky. Breaking it off wasn't difficult, and they made good progress, reaching from Klondyke to the entrance to Rattlesnake Creek at the bottom of a steep hill in less than two months.

Once in Rattlesnake Canyon, they did less hammering and scraping and more felling trees and pushing rocks out of their way. It was easier work, and it was cooler in the canyon, and the water of Rattlesnake Creek was cold and clear. There were abundant pools where the men could swim and bathe to rid themselves of the day and its dust.

Jeff and Sisson got along fine. Sisson did his work, making steady progress through the canyon. His men seemed to like him, and while a couple of the kids and a few of the drunks quit early on, the rest of the crew stayed. Sisson insisted that the men be paid every Friday. Jeff would have preferred paying them every other week to get some Saturday and Sunday work out of them. Men paid on Friday headed to Klondyke or Safford and were lost for the weekend. Sisson argued that men who could have a couple of nights to themselves worked better during the week. He demanded that the men return to camp Sunday night to be ready for work on Monday morning, and mostly they did.

Sisson and a couple of the teetotalers stayed in camp during the weekend, cleaning up, doing their laundry, swimming and lounging at various pools. Sisson usually went to town Saturday morning and brought back supplies, including good meat, potatoes, and a couple bottles of good bootleg whiskey for them to drink through the week. Sisson stayed away from town in the evenings, fearing the kinds of trouble that generally got started there. He had had enough of prison and had no desire to ever go back. He reasoned that if it was difficult to resist temptation, it was easier to avoid it altogether.

When the work routine had become established, Jeff took to sending Granny Jane and Ola May down from the Garden to the camp with food—biscuits and pies, chickens and vinegar slaw—hoping they would entice more of the men to stay in camp over the weekend and do more work. Granny and Ola came down in a one-horse carriage, picking their way down the small trail they had cut earlier. Ola, a capable horsewoman, took charge of the trip down and back.

It had some effect. A couple of the younger boys stayed on because of Ola, who was a pretty girl with a lot of history that might or might not be true. What they did know was that she looked a man over without apology and stared him right in the eye as if she, and not he, were the pursuer. While the boys and the men were willing enough to complain about Ola May's "brazenness," they did nothing to avoid her and everything to encourage her.

One Sunday, with a borrowed horse hitched to the carriage, Ola and Granny Jane made their way down the canyon with fried chicken, potatoes, biscuits, and wild raspberry pie. They delivered the dinner to Sisson and stayed awhile, Granny talking with Sisson, Ola May keeping an eye on part of a pool she could just glimpse through the sycamore cover and catch the occasional glimpse of a couple of boys swimming and playing in the water.

When the boys came from the pool, wet but dressed, Granny Jane became anxious to get started back toward the Garden, though Ola May had taken a sudden interest in hearing Sisson's account of the week as the boys began picking the covers from the baskets of food she and Granny Jane brought. The more interested Ola May became, the more anxious Granny Jane was to get going on their way back up the canyon. Finally, Ola May relented, and they started back.

"You needn't be eyeing those boys like that," Granny Jane said.

"No harm in it," Ola May replied.

"You'll find out about 'harm' if you keep it up. Nothing in the world glitters quite like a useless man."

"Glitter ain't so bad, and there's no harm in looking."

"Glitter and looking ain't trouble. But they're what brings the trouble. Looking leads to wanting, and wanting leads to having. Having is a particular thing. And having something useless, especially a man, is a life's worth of sorrow and aggravation. And looking never gets better, only worse."

"Granny Jane, you're just old. You've forgotten all about how it is."

"I haven't forgotten. There are some things you never forget, no matter how you try to do it. I remember all too well. Ola May, rein in that horse!"

They were approaching the gate to their house when the horse shied and reared from something seen or imagined. Ola May reined it hard, but that only panicked it further, and it put down its head and lunged forward, toward the house. Ola rose in the carriage, pulling at the reins and trying to calm the horse, which became nearly impossible as her own sense of the urgency and danger increased.

The horse turned abruptly from its course as it neared the house, throwing Ola May out of the carriage and onto the ground, where she lay still. The horse wheeled again, tipping the carriage and dragging it on its side away from the house some hundred yards until the weight of the tipped carriage brought it to a halt.

Ola May never lost consciousness, but she lay dazed for a bit, coming to wonder what, exactly, had happened. Her shoulder hurt her, and there was a sharp pain in her leg, though she thought there would be nothing broken. She slowly regained her senses and pulled herself up on an elbow. Then she remembered. "Granny? Granny Jane?"

Granny Jane lay on the ground some fifty yards away, barely conscious. Ola lifted her head, which was bleeding, and tried to wake her. Granny would come to consciousness for a few seconds, try to focus her eyes on Ola May, then pass out again. Ola May yelled for help.

A young cowboy, Elmer Gardenhire, was passing by from visiting family farther up the trail. He came down as fast as he dared, tied up his horse, and ran to Ola May. Between the two of them, they were able to pick Granny Jane up and carry her into the cabin. She regained consciousness one more time, but the pain of what proved to be a broken hip took her back into unconsciousness.

Gardenhire, seeing there was nothing more he could do, remounted and rode down the trail toward the road crew. He had just reached the crew and Sisson when Jeff, back from Klondyke, rode into camp. Jeff rode on up the trail to the cabin, and Gardenhire continued down toward the mesa and Klondyke to call for help.

It was a terrible scene when Jeff reached the cabin. He saw Ola May first, bleeding from her head and arms, her clothes torn and tracked with smears of dirt. She waved him off. Hers were superficial wounds, scrapes and cuts from sliding across the ground after she had been thrown from the wagon.

Granny seemed to look better. Her clothes were bloodstained, but Ola May had bound up the wound in her head with some linen, and she lay still, sleeping. Her breathing was shallow, and she groaned in her sleep, reacting to the pain of her hip.

They sat with her for three hours, waiting for a doctor to come, knowing that it was too early for a doctor to cover all the distance he would have to get to the cabin. And it was unlikely that Gardenhire had done much more than reach Klondyke and a telephone by this time.

As it grew dark, Granny Jane's breathing became more shallow and ragged, becoming the full death rattle shortly after dark. She died without regaining consciousness. The doctor arrived in the morning and did a quick examination—concussion likely, skull fracture possibly, and broken hip certainly.

Jeff took Granny's body down to the road camp, where he and Sisson salvaged enough good pine lumber to build a decent-enough coffin, the joints sealed with pine tar to keep it, at least temporarily, watertight. Then they loaded it onto the back of the wagon Jeff had brought her down in, tied it in securely, and started down the newly cut road toward Klondyke.

They reached Klondyke by midafternoon. Working together, changing off the pick and the shovel, they dug a grave in the hardpan and rock of the small mesa above Klondyke and buried her before dark. There was nothing to mark the grave with, so they erected a crude cross of sticks wired together with fencing wire.

Ola May had not expected the onslaught of loneliness that caught her up after Granny Jane's death. The old woman had been quarrelsome, abrupt, and imperious, but she had been company. Now Ola May lived at Power Garden alone, the sole keeper of the family's small cabin and farm.

She made trips nearly every day up the new road to the mine shack in Kielberg Canyon where Jeff, John, Tom, and Sisson, who was the only one of the road crew to stay on when the road was finished, worked the mine seven days a week. Some days, one of her brothers or Tom Sisson would bring a truckload of ore down the road, heading for Safford. Frequently, the driver would stop for lunch, or at least water and biscuits, and a small part of the day would fill and quickly pass. But then, just as quickly, time would stall and seem to stand still as Ola May worked the afternoon away, dreading the coming of evening and dark.

In the dark there was little to do. She took up the mending that Granny Jane had done in the evening, but she could not do the knitting. Granny Jane had offered to teach her, but she had no interest in learning. Granny Jane had a Bible that was more frequently used for the recording of family information than for reading, but Ola started to read it anyway, though she had little aptitude for it.

She was further burdened by the sense, instilled in her by both Granny Jane and her father, that kerosene was not to be wasted by staying up in the evening. And the work in the mine, going deeper and deeper now, required more lamplight. Daylight was for work, and the night was for sleep. There was no need to prolong the day with artificial light. One went to bed when the sun went down and rose when it came up again. And as the late fall pushed into early winter, the days shortened, and sleep became harder and harder to come by.

Had she asked her father, he would have told her she needed only to work harder to be ready for sleep in the late afternoon and early evening. None of the men at the mine shack were troubled by wakefulness. They put in exhausting days digging the ore, milling it at the arrastra, and moving it down the road to town. But there was always whiskey, too. And the men finished their days with whiskey after the evening meal, and that led them more quickly to sleep.

And it was not that Ola May did not work during the day. She took care of the animals—two horses, the string of burros that the men no longer used to haul ore down the mountain, a cow, two pigs, and fourteen chickens. The population of chickens was always in flux according to the ability of the predators that abounded in the Galiuros—mountain lions, black bears, wildcats, coyotes, and occasional Mexican wolves, expanding their territory farther to the west.

There was water to haul from the spring and wood to split for the stove and fireplace that heated the cabin and cooked meager meals. She also looked after the men, cooking for them twice a week and packing it up the road to the mine shack. The rest of the time they took care of themselves, which usually meant beans from cans or some unlucky bird or mammal that had wandered through the camp when a gun had been handy. In winter there was not enough daylight to work the mine and hunt, too.

But it was less the work and the boredom that went at her than the loneliness. Granny Jane had been Ola May's constant companion since the death of her mother when she was still an infant. Most of what she knew about the world she knew from Granny Jane, and though the old woman's ways had grated on her more and more as she got older, she missed her dearly. She was twenty-four and had been out of school for over twelve years. Granny Jane had been the center of her life, the tether, and now Ola had come free.

Most of the girls her own age down in the valley were long married and burdened with children. She was past prime marrying age, though she had no real desire to marry. Her whole life, it seemed, had been spent in the service of men—father and brothers. She was often enough glad to be away from them with their quarrelsome, demanding, and self-righteous ways. And younger men were no better. They thought themselves emperors and acted like squalling, demanding babies. And the attention required to keep their little pricks taut grew irksome. She was less fascinated than irritated by the things. Married girls, she thought, lived a burdened life, constantly attending to the needs of children and husband. It wasn't for her.

She craved company, seeing only her father, brothers, and Tom Sisson when she ventured up to the mine or when they came down to the Garden for some rest or supplies. She thought often of the rodeo days and the dancing. She thought often of Kane Wootan and the other cowboys, and she would give a lot to have those days back. And she thought about the girls who attended the rodeos and dances and laughed and whispered funny things.

She craved the company of women.

She took to leaving the Garden on occasion, right after she had delivered the men's food. She would turn her horse around, head back toward the cabin but past it, and ride down the road through the canyon, past Klondyke and toward Safford.

It was a three-hour ride, and it brought her to the small Richards ranch at the base of the Pinaleno Mountains, some ten miles southeast of Safford. There she met Sallie Richards, a woman she had known when they went to school together and, later, at the rodeos.

Sallie was a big-boned girl, solid and hearty, a girl who, like Ola, had worked her whole life. The Richards ranch had a small acreage at the base of the mountains, but it extended up into the foothills, where they had planted apple trees. They harvested them in the fall, storing them in a stone cellar at the foot of the mountain. Then they opened the orchards up to the public, who came through in the fall, picking bushels of apples that built the Richardses' cash reserves for the year.

Spring and summer were the busiest months, clearing the ground around the trees, pruning the dead branches, clearing the deadfall, and maintaining the small irrigation ditches from the stream that coursed down the mountain a quarter of a mile away. It was strenuous. The winter rains and freezes uprooted rocks and crumbled banks. Then the spring rains brought the weeds and grasses, the tough mesquite, and, higher up, the ironlike manzanita that had to be cleared from the ditches first by axe, then by shovel, until the ditches once again flowed, at least until the summer rains began obliterating them.

That had been Sallie Richards's life, a tender of the orchard. She worked along with the men—her father, uncle, and brothers—through the warm seasons, side by side, and, often enough, alone while the men rode fences, branded cattle, and cut the calves. She was strong, her arms as hard as any man's.

She was known as "boy crazy" among the townsfolk and the cowboys who followed the rodeo. But Ola May knew it was not boy craziness that drove Sallie to follow the rodeos and the cowboys who rode in them. It was a fundamental loneliness. Sallie was a woman who lived the life of a man, who worked with men, fought with them, tolerated and imitated them. If she was a tomboy, it was because she lived that life, hard and tough, self-reliant and distant. On the weekends, she wanted the company of anyone who would talk to her, dance with her, and know that she was a woman, not a cowboy.

Sallie and Ola had barely known each other in their earlier years. Ola was outgoing and popular, and Sallie was shy and withdrawn. But as they grew, their lives taking up similar tracks of living the life of men in the world of men, they became friends, and Ola sought out the shy, quiet girl who smiled the sweetest smile, the smile that hid nothing and laid bare her loneliness.

Tom had discovered her, too, as recognition of her grew among the cowboys. A woman who demanded little of anyone, who was glad to share whatever she could with anyone willing to spend some of their time with her, to pay attention to her, all their attention, if only for a while, and who would not demand some recompense for that time. But Tom, like the others, spent time with her, got tired of her quiet and obeisance, and moved on to the livelier girls who offered challenges and dares.

But Ola moved closer and closer to her, and when Granny Jane was killed, Sallie occupied more and more of Ola's thoughts. In the daytime and especially at night, Ola constructed conversations in her head with Sallie, who would listen and understand, not scoffing at or ignoring Ola's complaints about the isolation of the cabin in the Garden deep in the Galiuros. She would talk to her, listen to her, and touch her, and there would be no judgment, only the reciprocation of one whose needs mirrored her own.

So Ola took to riding to the ranch once, occasionally twice, a week when she knew that the men were taken care of and were not yet ready to bring another load of ore down the road. And she would work alongside Sallie, digging the weeds from irrigation ditches, talking and laughing with her, happy to broil in the bright sun, sweated and weary, beginning the ride home in the late afternoon, and arriving at the Garden deep in thought. She enjoyed the company and the warmth, and, best of all, Sallie was glad to see her.

In the early fall of 1917, Sallie told Ola not to visit anymore. It was harvest time, and they would be in the orchard. Soon the townsfolk would come to pick apples and picnic under the trees. Sallie's time would belong to the apples and the orchard. It would be that way until deep into winter, after all the apples had been harvested and cellared.

It had begun to snow in midafternoon, just before the sun set behind Topout Peak. Ola May had spent the last hours of daylight moving wood into the cabin to keep the fire going. It was likely to be a light snow. December snows generally fell light and did not last. But it would do whatever it would do. She did not take chances. She washed out the enameled chamber pot in case she was not able to get out to the privy. She watched the first flakes of snow whirl to the ground in the fading light. She looked at the flakes stuck to her sleeve and tried to catch new ones on her tongue.

As it darkened, the snow turned to sleet. She heard it against the windows and door and roof. She was cooking a rough stew of rabbit she had shot, carrots from the garden, and greens she had gathered on the hunt that had bagged the rabbit. She stayed close to the fire, both for the heat and to save oil in the lamps. The few square feet illuminated and warmed by the fire were a little paradise in the storm. She would later pull the quilt off the bed and wrap herself in it and sleep in front of the fire so that she would wake and be able to restoke the fire as it burned down.

When she heard the first scratches at the door, she assumed it was more sleet, coming harder and faster now. But as it kept up in a ragged rhythm, she knew it was not weather. When she opened the door, the huddled figure started to fall inward, caught itself, and remained upright. Ola took it by the sleeve and pulled it in.

It might have been a small tower of cloth, wrapped in oilskin, and topped with a hat encased in rime. A scarf covered the nose and mouth and nearly blocked the ice-lashed eyes. Who or what it was, man, woman, friend, or stranger, Ola May couldn't tell. It was nearly frozen and unsteady on its feet.

The scarf did not want to unravel, the windings of it frozen to each other. When she took off the heavy iced hat, she saw. "My God, Sallie. My God. You're near froze."

Sallie Richards's eyes stayed steady and unfocused, and Ola was not sure Sallie knew where she was or who was unwrapping the scarf frozen to her face. Her breathing was shallow and hoarse as though she were coming to the end of her breath. Her hair was iced, too. The water had soaked through her hat, soaked her hair, and frozen. Pieces of it stuck to the band of the hat.

When the scarf unwound from Sallie's face, Ola kept going, struggling to remove the oilskin from Sallie, who seemingly could not unclench her arms from her bosom. Ola stripped off a sweater and three shirts from under the oilskin. She put her hand just under Sallie's left breast, feeling the skin as cold as a dead woman's, but Sallie's heart was still beating weakly.

"Can you sit?" Sallie's eyes wavered, as if trying to focus, but then went back to their distant glaze. Ola had loosened Sallie's belt from her canvas britches, but she could not get the pants down because of the thickly iced and muddy boots Sallie had tucked them into. Ola draped a quilt over the frozen girl.

"Please, Sallie. Sit. Please sit." Ola had brought a small rocking chair up close to the fire and had set it behind Sallie. Her eyes fluttered again, and then, to Ola's surprise, Sallie let herself go and sat in the chair. It was the first sign that Sallie had life left in her.

The boots were a terrible struggle. They were tight and crusted in ice and mud. When the ice melted, Ola couldn't get a good grip because the mud on them had softened. She was astride Sallie's extended right leg, her back to Sallie, trying to move the boot with small, hard tugs and little twists. She bent down and held the boot to her chest and pushed forward, and, for the first time, the boot budged.

Sallie's feet were white with cold. Ola rubbed them in her hands, alternating right to left, left to right. She pushed Sallie closer to the fire, then pulled her back again, afraid of the pain that would grab Sallie when her blood began to flow through her feet again. When her feet began to barely pinken from the warmth of the fire and Ola's hands, Ola went after the canvas britches, which covered yet another pair of pants, this one denim.

The canvas had not been treated, or had been poorly treated, and in several places the pants were frozen together. She had a hard time tugging them down from Sallie's waist because she could not get Sallie to raise her bottom from the chair. Ola had to pull the pants and try to lift Sallie with her shoulder at the same time. When the pants finally tugged down, past Sallie's knees and, finally, over her ankles, Ola saw that Sallie's lower lip had begun to tremble, a sign she was starting to chatter, a sign that she was coming around.

Ola tried to pull Sallie up on her feet, but Sallie went back down, heavily, into the chair. Ola took a piece of worn burlap and began rubbing Sallie's skin with it, easily at first and then harder and harder, trying to get her dry, trying to get her blood to move again and course through her body. On the third attempt, Sallie stood while Ola wrapped her in the quilt. She gently but firmly pushed on Sallie's shoulders until Sallie let her knees bend and slowly knelt before the fire.

Ola still feared letting her frozen friend warm too quickly. She pulled Sallie the rest of the way down until she was prone on the planked floor of the cabin, and she rolled her away from the fire and toward the middle of the room. Quickly, she took off her own clothes and crawled under the quilt and held Sallie to her as you should with people near frozen.

They lay like that for a long time, Ola May holding Sallie to herself, rubbing her back, repeating her name over and over. She tried to stay like that, holding her body still, squeezing tightly, trying to press the heat of her body into Sallie's. When Sallie began to shiver down the length of her body, Ola May ran her hands up and down Sallie's back and legs, feeling the fine hair over the cold flesh. The fire was starting to die down now, but Ola didn't dare risk letting go of her friend to stoke the fire.

Finally, Sallie came to full consciousness, repeating Ola's name in a voice just above a whisper. Ola crawled from the quilt, picked up two lengths of cordwood, and pushed them into the fire. When she came back to Sallie, Sallie was holding the quilt open for her. They held each other and rocked until, lulled by the fire, exhausted by effort, they both fell asleep.

In the morning, they were embarrassed to wake up naked, Ola holding Sallie's back to her chest and stomach. Neither was willing to crawl from under the quilt to find clothing. Ola would start to get up, pulling the quilt with her, Sallie holding on to her side of the quilt, and then Ola would give up and lie back down, and they would laugh, embarrassed about being embarrassed.

Finally, Ola May slithered out from under the quilt and crawled on hands and knees to the woodbox to gather kindling for the few remaining embers of the fire. She crawled over to the trunk, where there was a thick flannel robe of Granny Jane's. Always she felt the eyes of Sallie on her, too bold and curious to look away.

Ola put water on to boil. "There's no other robe," she said. "But I have a heavy coat you can wear." Sallie was sitting upright now in front of the fire, the quilt pulled around her.

"I'm all right," she said.

They sipped tea and looked at each other, neither quite sure what to say. "You gave me quite a scare," Ola said at last.

Sallie smiled and reddened. "I didn't think it would be that bad. There was only some clouds when I set off, then a bit of snow. I didn't think much of it. I was over halfway into the canyon when the ice came. Here was the closest place. I sat under a tree for a while and tried to wait it out, but when I saw it wasn't letting up, I came on up."

"Thank God for that."

"No. Thank you for that. I would have died. I know that. I don't remember much. Seeing the cabin in the clearing. You talking to me, though I don't know what you said, only that you talked. And then the fire, and you holding me. I remember that."

Ola May reddened further. "You were just ice."

"And you were fire. And you saved me. You melted me."

"I didn't know what to do. I was afraid to let you go. I was afraid you would die."

"No. No. You wouldn't let me die. You kept me here." Sallie rose from the chair she had been sitting in and took a step toward Ola, who rose, too, and tried to turn the other way, away from the fire, toward the open room when Sallie stepped in front of her. "You saved me. You're my true friend, you're my life."

When Sallie let the quilt fall from her shoulders, Ola wasn't sure what to do. Sallie was directly in front of her, naked, and Ola seemed unable to turn away. "You'll freeze," she said to Sallie. "You'll freeze again."

"And you will save me." Ola was startled and shaky when Sallie reached out and pulled the cord that held the robe together, but she did not resist, nor when Sallie reached her arm in the front of the robe and pulled it around the both of them. She let Sallie pull her into her embrace and felt her skin tighten as if it would soon split.

"I saved you."

The sleet and rain had stopped, and a small, steady snow had come again, helping to coat the ice until it was walkable. They dressed, though Sallie's clothes were still slightly damp, and they went outside to empty the chamber pot into the privy and to break the ice on the spring pond and draw fresh water.

The land had grown beautiful in the storm, and there was still ice sparkling on the tree limbs, and the snow was untouched by anything, save their footprints and the tracks of a lone rabbit. They stood together outside the cabin, only their shoulders touching, and looked at the scene before them, and smiled.

They sat together much of the day, usually not talking, always touching, but just barely. They drank tea and ate corn bread before the fire. They would look at each other and smile and look away, though sometimes Sallie, always Sallie, would take Ola's jaw in her hand and angle Ola's mouth up for kissing.

Sallie's clothes were off and in front of the fire again, and Ola took hers off as well. They sat and lay in front of the fire, touched, kissed, and dozed.

Ola May came wide awake to the sound of the door opening. She jumped up, grabbing at the quilt to cover herself, but Sallie was lying on it, just coming from sleep herself, leaving Ola with only her hands and arms to cover her body. She crouched next to Sallie and stared wide-eyed at her brother, who stared back, wide-eyed.

"Get out," Ola yelled, but her brother simply stood and stared at the two naked women. "At least turn around," she said. "Let us get some clothes."

And he did, slowly, uncertainly, while Ola May got her robe and Sallie wrapped herself in the quilt.

"What?" he asked. "What are you doing?"

"Doing what we're doing. Now get out of here. What are you here for?"

"To see if you're all right."

"I'm all right. Don't I look all right?" She immediately wished she hadn't said that, having just stood before her brother stark naked.

"The storm," he said. "Was worried about you in the storm."

"No worry. No need to worry," she lied. She had a quick image of Sallie standing at the door, nearly dead, the night before.

"You have no clothes on."

"I do. We do. I have a robe, and she has a quilt. We have clothes."

"Why is she here?" he asked.

"She's here. She's my friend."

"You don't have no clothes on," he repeated.

"Yes. Yes. We had clothes on."

"No. No, you didn't. You was both naked."

She saw the light begin to rise in his eyes. Her heart and breathing quickened.

"My God," he said. "Oh my God. You two—" He stopped as if he could not formulate the rest of the sentence or finish the thought. "Daddy's going to kill you."

"Not if he don't know. He won't if he don't know."

"You," he said to Sallie. "You get yourself out of here. Get on home."

Sallie had come full awake now. She stood there, still wrapped in the quilt, her chin up, and a brazen stare, unblinking, right at him.

"I said go."

"No."

"I will kill you myself. You get the hell out of here. Whore. Queer. Whore."

"Why do you always got to poison every good thing that happens?" Ola May asked. "I get something that does the tiniest bit of good for me, and one of you just pours poison on top of it." She reached for her dress, and her brother looked away, toward Sallie, who still had the quilt around her.

Then Sallie moved, back, away from him, toward her clothes. The quilt fell as she reached for her shirt.

The sight of her naked back, her naked backside, seemed to incense him, and he moved toward her, his hand raised to strike her. Ola May rushed between them, and his arm coming down caught her across the shoulder and sent her down to the floor. Sallie, who had put the shirt on but not buttoned it, stared at him, then down to Ola May on the floor. His gaze followed hers, and she bent to Ola, whose eyes were open but moving side to side in the attempt to focus. She picked up Ola May's head and cradled it in her lap, smoothing the hair away from her face.

Ola lost consciousness, then came around again, though her eyes would not focus. Her brother was still hanging back, near the door, his face a register of confusion and, maybe, panic. He did not take his eyes off Sallie as she cradled Ola May's head and spoke to her at just above a whisper.

And then he ran at her, jaw set, waving his arms, windmilling the air as he charged her. "Git," he yelled. "Git. You go and git," thrashing at the air and stomping the ground, yelling like she was a steer that had gotten at the garden. He took Ola May by the arm and pulled her, and Sallie held on to her, and for a few seconds they were having a tug of war with Ola's limp body. Then Sallie let go, and John gathered Ola May to him, picked her up in his arms, and carried her to the bed, dropping her there, too hard, Sallie thought.

Then he turned back to her. "Now you get out. You get out of here and don't come back, or I'll let the Old Man have you, and you won't like that. Now go on."

She was still in the unbuttoned shirt, and now she nodded toward her clothes spread out in front of the fire. "I'm naked," she said. He said nothing, just looked from her to his sister on the bed. "She could be hurt bad. Let me stay with her."

"No," he said. "You go on. Don't you never come back here again."

Ola May let out a low moan, and they were both quiet and watched her. She did not wake or make another sound.

"I'll go for a doctor. She's hurt bad."

"No. No doctor."

"You hurt her, John Power. She's bad off."

"It's what you done. You done it. You and her all naked. That's wrong. What's wrong is what you done. I just tried to set things straight. I was just making things right." He picked up the hatchet they used for splitting kindling and raised it to her. Sallie ran out the door.

He knelt beside Ola May, smoothing the hair away from her face exactly as Sallie had done. "You done wrong, Ola. You done real wrong. I'm sorry, but the Old Man would have done a lot worse than I did."

It was nearly dark when Jeff Power began to wonder about Ola May. They were working a small vein of gold that had promised to lead to a lode, though in the days they had worked it, it had shown more signs of playing out than paying off. Ola May should have been there an hour ago to fetch them their supper so they could get on up to bed and out early the next morning to have at the vein again.

He called John over. "You saw her this morning?"

"Yes, sir."

"And she was all right?"

"Yes, sir. Said she wasn't feeling too well, but she looked all right."

"Not feeling well? Where?"

"In her stomach. And head."

"Why didn't you tell me?"

"She just didn't seem sick."

They found Ola May on the floor next to her bed. Her spine was curved so that her feet pointed back and up at an angle they had never seen in a human before. They rushed to her, kneeling beside her as the Old Man shook her, trying to revive her. Her eyes came open but rolled as if untethered, unable to focus.

"Ola May. Ola. You wake up now. You stop this foolishness. It's your daddy. Wake up."

And her eyes did stop their rolling then, and she looked up at Jeff and held his gaze for a second. "Poison," she said, just above a whisper. "Poison."

They put her back up on the bed, and as soon as she lay flat, they knew she was dead.

A slow, dismal procession to the cabin began. Tom took the truck down the canyon to the nearest neighbors, the Boscos, and asked them to come help. He then went on down the canyon and over to Klondyke, where he reported Ola's death. When he made his way back to the cabin, the men—his father, brother, and Mr. Bosco—stood in the cold outside the door while Mrs. Bosco cleaned the body.

Mrs. Bosco was having a difficult time of it. The joints of Ola's body had already begun to stiffen as the joints of the dead do. She was unable to get Ola's unbuttoned dress over her arms, which were tightly crossed in front of her, so Mrs. Bosco found scissors in Granny Jane's sewing kit and began cutting the dress away.

Two things seemed particularly odd to Mrs. Bosco. Ola May wore nothing under her dress. It was odd enough that Ola, who favored britches and shirts, would be wearing a dress when she was not going to town, but to wear nothing under it in December, in the mountains, was most peculiar. And though the joints of Ola's arms, legs, hands, and feet were rigid in the death clench, Ola's head moved easily from side to side and back and forth as Mrs. Bosco moved her.

As the men waited, Sisson rode up from the mine. "I knew it was trouble. When you didn't come back, I knew it was trouble."

"Ola May is dead," Jeff said, his face a gray mask, his eyes distant as if figuring the loss the world had given him, or just trying to sort out what else he could possibly lose. First his wife, then his mother, now his daughter. The women of his life removed, one by one. He thought probably he would never again know the world of women.

"What happened?" Sisson asked.

"Rattlesnake," John said simultaneously as Jeff said, "Poison."

Sisson and Jeff both looked at John.

"Spooked her horse and throwed her," John said.

"How do you know that? She said it was poison."

"Rattlesnake is poison."

"Kind of the wrong time of year for rattlesnakes," Sisson said. "They sleep the winter."

"Don't have to," John said. "One could come out."

"I don't think so," Sisson said. "I ain't never seen one in the winter unless it was in a long warm spell. Snakes is cold-blooded. They can't move in the cold."

"Maybe they can, maybe they can't."

"John, why are you so all-fired certain she got throwed from a horse? It don't even look like that happened. She was in her bed, or next to it. She said it was poison, and I think it was."

"Like I said, snakes is poison."

"You know something you ain't letting on?"

"She told me," John said. "I put her horse away. She got throwed. Maybe it was a stick. Horses get snake mad and shy at sticks. I only know what she told me. I'm only saying what it is that she said happened."

"Well, why didn't you say that? And why was she going on about poison?"

"Snakes is poison."

"She didn't get bit, though, did she?"

"Snake's still poison if it bites you or not."

They turned in unison, hearing the hooves of Tom's horse coming over the rise by the orchard. "Doctor's coming," Tom said. "In his car. Guess he ain't in no hurry."

Dr. W. E. Platt examined the body. He noted no external signs of struggle or fall, though her neck did appear dislocated. Nor could he find any signs of poisoning or any poison on the premises. In the death of any young woman an immediate suspicion was botched abortion. But a quick pelvic examination showed no signs of an abortion and, in fact, showed that Ola May was a virgin. He concluded that the death had come from "unknown causes."

Tom took the truck to Safford, where he bought an inexpensive pine coffin and brought it back. They wrapped Ola in quilts and nailed the coffin shut, then lashed it to the back of the truck and started down the road through the canyon toward Klondyke. Jeff drove while Tom, John, and Sisson rode behind the truck. Mr. and Mrs. Bosco followed in their wagon.

When they reached Klondyke, they found Dr. Platt waiting for them with Sheriff Frank McBride and his deputy, Kane Wootan. McBride approached the small funeral procession. "My condolences on your loss," he said. "We cannot know the ways of the Holy Father." Jeff simply stared at McBride as if he were speaking in French. "I'm afraid," McBride said, "that since the cause of death here is undetermined, an autopsy may be necessary."

Jeff Power just stared straight ahead, his face an index of grief and anger that went far beyond the reach of words. Finally, he simply shook his head. "No."

"We have a death of unknown causes here," McBride said. "Dr. Platt is uncertain, and he agrees that maybe another eye might see something he missed."

By now the entire funeral party had gathered around them. "Enough eyes," Jeff said.

"Beg your pardon?"

"There been enough eyes on my daughter. She don't need your eyes, or his eyes, or anyone else's eyes on her. Eyes, hand, anything else. It's enough."

"I understand," McBride said. "But the law is clear on this."

"No. No, you don't understand. This is my daughter, and I say what happens to my daughter. And more looking and prying and poking ain't what she needs. She needs to be buried now, and that's what we're about to do."

"We don't know how she died, though," McBride said. "We have to know."

"I think her neck is broke," Mrs. Bosco said. "Her head just rolls about."

"Neck isn't broken," Dr. Platt answered. "I checked that. It's not broken."

"She said she was poisoned," Sisson interjected. "That's what she said. The words of the dying. Her last words."

"You see," McBride said slowly, measuring his words. "We don't want to disturb the dead, but we have to know. Some say 'neck,' some say 'poison.' We want an answer."

"That there is a dead girl," Power said. "A dead girl. Not a Power. A poor dead girl. You all have never given an ounce of respect to any Power. But she's not just a Power now. She's a dead girl, and you owe respect to the dead. Even you should understand that. Give her her justs. Leave her in peace. She's a dead girl."

"I'm sorry," McBride began.

"You're sorry? Well, you'll be a lot sorrier if you try to stop us from this burying. I am going to bury my daughter, and you can go to hell if you don't like that. This poor girl is done with all your law nonsense."

"Mr. Power, I am sorry. You can believe that or not. But if you bury her, we're going to have an inquest, and that requires us to dig up the body. Wouldn't it be better to hand over her body, let an autopsy be done, and then let her rest in peace?"

"She's going to rest in peace. She's going to rest in peace right up on top of that mesa there. And she's going to start in just about an hour. And I won't have you digging her up. I'll sure to God camp out on that mesa with a shotgun for the rest of my days if that is what it needs."

"I won't argue with you in this terrible time. You do what you need to do, and I will have to do the same. I'll try not to do any disservice to any of your family, including your late daughter. My condolences to you and to your entire family. It's a very sad day."

The sheriff turned to Deputy Wootan, who was involved in some whispered conversation with Tom Power that neither seemed to favor. He turned back to Jeff. "I really hate to do this, to bring this up. But your boys have to register for the draft. That's federal law. I have no say."

Jeff, his jaw still set, continued to stare straight ahead. He turned slowly to face McBride. "You take your law and get the hell out of my life. I don't give a damn about federal or state or local. I care about Rattlesnake Canyon, and I care about my boys. All the rest of you can just go to hell. Soon."

McBride stared back, then nodded. "Deputy, let's ride and leave these people to their grief."

A week later an inquest was held in Safford. The jury heard the testimony of Mr. and Mrs. Bosco and Dr. Platt. A grim-faced Jeff Power stood at the back of the courtroom, but he was not called, and he did not speak. The jury ruled that an autopsy was not necessary and returned a verdict of "death by unknown causes." On hearing the phrase, Jeff Power turned and left the courtroom.

He tried to think of the losses of Granny Jane and Ola May as inconveniences, their chores now his. It was a way to avoid thinking of those losses as the deep and dear ones they were. He had thought that the day the roof fell in on Mattie was the worst day of his life, and in terms of pure pain, it was so. But it was also the first day of a lifetime of pain and loss. It was an announcement that the hardest times were to come, but he had been deaf to that.

Whether by the hand of God, or fate, or plain old happenstance, or just by the nature of the world, his life had turned that day. He had had a good run of getting—finding Mattie and marrying her, building up herds of cattle, the birth of three sons, and then, finally, the birth of his daughter. But then it turned to a progression of loss—Mattie, the ranch, then Charlie off to New Mexico without a damned look back, Granny Jane and Ola May within two months of each other. The getting had been slow and graceful, the giving up had been hard, swift, and unrelenting. How people could keep kneeling and praying to a God they thought loved them, and protected them, and occasionally tested them he could not understand. The God he conceived was a mean, vicious old man who cared for nothing beyond His own damned amusement. He wished that God would come to him as He was supposed to have come to others. He would love to give that son of a bitch both barrels of a 10 gauge and then piss on the corpse.

Chapter Fifteen
1918

They weren't running, just walking at a good pace, trying not to make enough motion to be seen. There would be a time for running, but it wasn't yet. Once you started running, the game was pretty much over.

"Tom," John said. "You sit on your ass on a horse or a wagon, too."

"What?"

"You said that them in the trucks just sit on their ass. That's what you do on a horse or in a wagon. I don't see it's that much different."

"John, did I ask your opinion on that subject?"

"No. I thought on it and needed to say it."

"Did you think I needed to hear it?"

"No. I didn't think on that part of it."

"You and the rest of the world. Always in a worry about what you need to say without giving one damned thought to what people might need to hear."

"How am I supposed to know what other people need to hear?"

"Why don't you think on that for a while and then tell me if you think I need to hear your answer."

It was hard work, walking as quickly as they could, never really coming to full upright so they could take natural strides. Instead, they did something like a duck walk most of the time, the lactic acid building and burning in the muscles of their thighs. Tom had surrendered the glasses to Sisson, who needed to stop more often than the brothers did. The glasses gave him both an excuse to stop and something of value to do while he caught his breath.

The trucks were still coming, the dust spires looming ever larger. On one stop Sisson saw the bad news that it wasn't three trucks, it was six, and now they were splitting again to cover more territory as they got closer.

They found a small arroyo, and that gave them modest cover from a distance. But it was only about three feet deep, and as the trucks got closer, as they did steadily, it was going to provide less and less cover as the sight lines got better. There were two trucks coming their way now. They had split some minutes back and were steadily moving away from each other. One of them would clearly cross their path behind them. And that was not a great worry.

The other, however, kept veering east, which gave them a little more time to run and hide, but it was going to cross their path ahead of them. As they pushed forward, toward the Chiricahuas, their path was getting inevitably closer to a crossing with the truck.

"Let's slow down," Tom said. "We keep going at this pace, I'm afraid we're coming too close to that one." He pointed to the truck to the north and east of them.

"They got us surrounded," John said. There was no fear or resignation in his voice. He said it as a matter of fact, which it was.

"That don't necessarily mean a lot," Sisson said. "Being surrounded. There's still a lot of territory between the two of them, and if they keep widening out, they're just increasing it. As long as they don't see us, it don't matter where they got us."

Tom reached for the glasses, but Sisson pulled them back. "They're too close now. Sun's far enough in the sky that we could catch it in the glass and just signal them just where we are. Don't really need them that much, anyway."

That was true. Now they could actually see the truck. They couldn't really make it out, but it wasn't just a plume of dust anymore. It was a truck, coming their way, no doubt full of men with rifles and ropes and the hopes of being the ones that caught the Power boys.

"If we're going Apache, I would guess this would be the time to start finding hidey holes."

John pointed northeast about fifteen degrees. "There's a stand of mesquite."

"Nope," Tom said. "Too dangerous. I'm not sure we would make it there before we were in sight for them."

"It's also the first place they would look," Sisson said. "When you're chasing, you look for the likely cover. No, if we're going Apache, we better do it right. Go to ground. Go into the ground. Get yourself behind a little cover and dig yourself in. Throw dirt on top of you and make yourself small, and then don't move. It'll be a hard thing. And don't look up. Use your ears, not your eyes. Find yourself a little cover. And let's do it now."

"There's rocks right over yonder," John said.

"Rocks is no good," Sisson said. "All the dirt's going to be washed away from them. You won't be able to get yourself tucked in. Just split up, look for yucca or cactus or saltbush. Whatever you find to break the sight. Then start digging. Then throw branches and leaves and stuff over you. And make sure you cover anything shiny, like the breech of that rifle. Nothing gets attention like some metal shining in the sunlight. And don't be a rabbit. Rabbits always give themselves up when they start running. Just stay still. Even if they're coming right at you, you still got a chance. You get up and run, you ain't got no chance."

They broke in three directions then, each scuttling for separate cover. John dove behind a small creosote bush. Diving into a bush was something he wouldn't have done in any other season, but in winter there wouldn't be many things willing to fight for the protection of the ragged little shrub. Everything was hibernating.

Tom tucked in behind a stand of barrel cactus, next to a clump of yucca. He threw handfuls of dirt over himself, trying to stain his clothing the color of the sand and clay around him. Sisson ripped up saltbush, then got in the middle of a patch of it. He covered himself with the leaves and branches he had taken. He stuck a couple of small branches into the band of his hat and carefully placed the hat over his face as he lay in the scrubby chaparral.

The worst part was not looking. That was real hard, and John fought against it. He knew that Sisson was right. Sisson was right more often than Tom was, and that was a strange thing, because Tom was smarter than Sisson. But Sisson knew things because he had lived a long time outdoors. And even Tom listened to Sisson, sometimes, and the only one Tom ever really listened to was the Old Man.

No one went against the Old Man. Charlie might have, but he was smart and just picked up and went. Tom would take a beating from the Old Man. They all did. Tom had beat the Old Man once when he was just a kid, maybe seventeen or eighteen. John, who was older, had never even attempted it. Tom and the Old Man had gone at it for nearly half an hour before the Old Man lay in the dirt, wheezing and unable to get up.

Tom, though he was pretty bad banged up, cut and bleeding, his face puffed, strutted, or did whatever it was you did when you tried to strut with a limp, around the property for a couple of hours, feeling like he was the man of the house now, until he came around a corner and caught an oak limb, four inches thick, across the back and shoulders.

The Old Man stood over him, his face a puffy mask of rage, the oak branch held high over his head. "Get up," he said. "Get up so I can hurt you."

Tom was still conscious, but he didn't move, not even a twitch. John could see him struggling to breathe on the ground. His eyes would blink open, then shut again as if the effort to hold them open was just too great.

"Now the next time you think to take me on, you best kill me. And I mean that. Because if you don't kill me, I will surely kill you. A son of mine tries something like you done back there, he going to be my dead son. And you," the Old Man pointed at John, "you don't help him. When you get up," he said to Tom, "you know where the guns and ammunition's at. If we're both still alive come suppertime, we'll know who the boss is around here. No need for asking or telling. We'll just know." And to John again. "Don't you touch him. He's a big man now. Let him get up on his own."

Tom lay there a long time, struggling to get his breathing right, to adjust it to the pain he was in. Finally, his right arm folded against his stomach, he rolled up onto his shoulder and knees, then pushed himself up with his left arm. John reached out to lift him, but Tom flailed his arm, keeping him back. "You don't think he's watching you? I got to do this on my own." Tom struggled to his feet, still holding his left arm out to keep John away. He stumbled and shuffled over to the open paddock for the horses and lowered himself down into a pile of straw.

He stayed there three days, with Granny Jane and Ola May bringing him food and drink. John didn't think they really tended to him. That would risk the Old Man's fury. But they fed him, and John did all his own work and Tom's, and the Old Man never even mentioned Tom's name until the fourth day, when Tom staggered back out from the paddock, still limping, still favoring his right arm, which hung stiffly at his side, and resumed his chores.

"Tom," the Old Man said when he saw Tom emerge. "See to the tack over there in the shed." And Tom had simply done it, no questions.

So John fought to be a horned toad instead of the rabbit his instincts demanded. He lay motionless, concealed, or hoping he was concealed, and did not look up, but he did fight the urge to jump up and run. It was tough not to run. It wasn't natural. It wasn't right, but he understood it was the way to survive.

He felt the truck coming before he heard it, the soft shudder of the earth as the truck rolled across it. His muscles began to twitch out of his control. He needed to get up and run. And then he heard the truck, and he heard it get louder and more distinct the closer to them it got. He was stiff as a board now. He couldn't relax his muscles, which were tensed for the run, so he went the other way and tensed them further until they were so tight he couldn't move.

He heard the voice then. "Tom. John. Sisson." It repeated the names over and over again, and now he wasn't fighting the impulse to run. He had fought it down, and now he was just waiting. There was a small stick just in front of his face, but he didn't dare to move an arm or hand or finger toward it. So he stuck out his tongue, stretching it as far as he could, then forcing it down into the dirt. It did hurt just a little, not being used to stretching that far, but he caught the stick with the tip of his tongue, and he kept at it until he was able to work it back and into his mouth, where he could bite it with his teeth and exert all the force of his body onto the stick.

"Tom. John. Sisson. Tom Power."

John's teeth snapped through the stick with a crack he thought could be heard another county away. Still, he did not move.

"You. There by the cactus. Come on out. We ain't going to hurt you. Just come on out."

He couldn't remember who was by the cactus. Not him. They hadn't seen him yet, but for the first time in what seemed like hours but was really only minutes or seconds even, he moved. His fingers crept down the receiver of the rifle until he found the trigger guard. When he came up, he was going to come up shooting. They had found someone, and, having found someone, they were going to find the rest of them. Their only chance now was to try to shoot their way out once more.

"Tom. Tom Power. Get up. It's Poke. You're safe. We ain't going to hurt you. Tom Sisson, John Power. Get up."

And then John got up. He came to his knees under the mesquite tree and brought the rifle up. He was moving too fast to aim, so he brought it up to hip level, ready to fire.

"Jesus Christ. Don't shoot. We're trying to help. Don't shoot."

John could see little through the branches and feathery leaves of the mesquite, only shapes. He saw a lot of movement and fired off a round, still not bringing the rifle up to his shoulder or aiming it. He was just pointing and shooting.

"John. John. Goddamn you. Stop shooting."

He swung the rifle to where the voice came from until he understood that it was Tom's voice he heard.

"Stop shooting, John. It's Poke. We're all right."

And he did stop shooting. But he did not get up. He tried, but as soon as he pulled his knees up to get some purchase, he fell flat again. His mind was racing as if it was going all over the place like a dog with a confused scent. He heard his brother telling him to stop, and he did that. But he couldn't understand what was going on.

He tried to get up again, and this time he got his right leg up high enough that he was able to get some weight on his right foot. His heart was pounding, and it sounded indescribably loud in his ears.

"John. You goddamned nitwit. Stop shooting."

And then he was down again, face into the dirt, wrapped and smothered. "John. John. Calm down. It's all right. It's Sisson, John. I got you. We're all right, John." Sisson was whispering into his ear, the way you would to a child or to a horse you were trying to gentle. "It's all right. All right. We're safe. Safe now."

And then it was over. "Sisson?"

"Sisson," Sisson said. "It's Poke. He's going to help us. Come on. Get up."

"Poke," John said. "I'm sorry. I shouldn't have shot."

"You didn't hit no one," Poke said. "It's all right. But we got to get going. The others will be on us directly. Climb into the back of the truck with the boys. Don't do nothing. Don't say nothing. Let me take care of this."

John recognized the boys as hands from the ranch. Poke's boys. They were mostly Mexicans, and none of them had a stake in what was going on. When

John and Tom and Sisson scrambled into the back of the truck, the boys pulled them in and moved around them so they were hidden in the middle of the bunch.

"Damn," Poke said. "Here they come."

Tom scooted around the front of the truck and into the door that Poke had opened and crouched on the floor in front of the seat.

"Don't move. Don't say a word. This is going to be close."

Tom said nothing but pushed his head down farther into his arms. Poke pushed a blanket and some trash over him. He listened as Poke opened and then shut the door of the truck. He could see out of the corner of his eye that Poke had exited the truck. He heard another truck approach, stop, and cut its engine.

"They was here," Poke said.

Another voice mumbled words that Tom couldn't make out.

"No guarantee it was them, but who the hell else could it be? Found a blanket over there. Bootprints all over the place. No sign of horses, though."

"We heard shots."

"Coyote. Missed. You see any signs?"

"We got their horses."

"You got their horses? When was that?"

"A day ago."

"Can't be that far," Poke said, "if they're on foot."

Tom couldn't make out the response.

"Where do you think they're headed?"

Tom heard "Mexico" and "Chiricahuas."

"It was me, I would go straight to Mexico," Poke said. "I wouldn't want to be up in those mountains in February. Of course, I ain't a Power. I do things the reasonable, easy way. And that ain't the Power way."

"They don't gain that much going to Mexico," the voice said. It was closer now, more distinct, and Tom recognized Braz Wootan's voice. "Mexican border ain't going to stop me any more than it would stop them. You afraid to cross the border?"

"Nah. Hell, most of my boys here cross it all the time. Far as they're concerned, it don't really exist. It's like they say, they no cruzan la frontera, the frontera cruza them. There's only here, no there."

"There's a there, and them boys is probably headed for it. Course, you're right. Them Power boys isn't going to do the logical thing. There's just as good a chance they'll head for the Chiricahuas just because no one in their right mind would do that."

"What's your pleasure, then? East or south? I'll take the other."

"You going to kill them if you find them?"

"Not unless I have to, no."

"Then I want to get at them before you do, Poke. I don't want them sitting on their asses up in Florence while my brother rots in his grave."

"I understand that, Braz. The choice is yours. If I find them, I'm not giving them over to you, though. You got to understand that."

"I know that. You ain't got blood in this fight. I don't expect you to do anything you don't feel right about, though it's an easy thing for a man to just turn his back, walk off, and take a piss or such. But we got to move on this. The army's in it now. Detachments from Tucson and Hachita. I got to find them before the army does, if I'm going to put the end on this thing."

"The law don't give us the right to kill, and I'm not going to be responsible, and if I got to piss in my pants, then I got to. But I ain't going to interfere with you, either. It's your call. South or east?"

"Them damned ignoramuses. If it was anyone else, I'd just head south, but I wouldn't put it past Tom Power to head east just to drag our asses through the snow. Of course, he could be figuring that's just what we would figure. Hell. I don't know. They could be heading north for all I know."

"Anything's possible. You got a preference? Otherwise, I believe I'll just head south."

"Well, that would be all right, I guess. No. Wait. Hell. I don't know. I'll go south, which is the way any reasonable man would go, and completely ignore the fact that Jeff Power never sired a reasonable man."

"All right, then, I'll cut to the east."

"Done, then. Good luck."

"Thanks. I don't believe I can wish you the same, not wanting any more killing."

"Not sure I exactly understand that, Poke. But I know it wasn't your blood got spilled."

"No. No, it wasn't."

"I almost had you to Mexico there, Tom." Poke spoke quietly like a voice in the stillness of the dark. "He turned one too many on me, or I turned it on him. Guess it don't matter. We're heading for the Chiricahuas."

Tom poked his head out from under the blanket.

"You just stay put," Poke said. "We're almost out of sight, but we ain't going to be full out of danger for a while yet."

"We appreciate this, Poke."

Poke laughed a small, rueful laugh. "Yeah, I suspect you do. I don't think I ever had anyone who seriously wanted to kill me. That can't be a real good feeling."

"Really? No one ever wanted to kill you? Hell, it's happened to me a bunch of times. How do you live a life like that?"

"I don't know. You just do."

"Well, I don't want to ruin your morning, but if Wootan was to figure that you had us in this truck, sitting right next to him, he'd want to kill you. Probably would, too."

"I was right, then."

"What's that?"

"It ain't a real good feeling."

CHAPTER SIXTEEN

1918

Frank Haynes came into the office with only a quick nod to McBride, then strode to the back and peeked around the corner at the empty jail cells. "What did they do, escape?"

McBride didn't bother to ask what "they" Haynes referred to. "And a pleasant good morning to you, too, Marshal Haynes."

"It would be more pleasant for me if there was a Power or two back there. I could just load them up and drive back to Globe, and that part of my job would be done. But I guess that's wishing on rainbows, ain't it?"

"Apparently so. I had a talk with the Old Man. I told him that the boys had to come down and turn themselves in."

"And a fine job you did on that, Sheriff. They must still be packing for their trip to France."

"I'll give them a couple of days. If they don't come in, I have a plan. A contingency sort of thing."

"That's a big relief to me. Soon as I tell the district marshal we got us a contingency, he'll stop gnawing on my ass every time he sees me. You've taken a great load from me."

McBride sighed. "If you really want those boys, go up and get them yourself. You don't need me or mine. It's your jurisdiction, not mine. This is purely federal."

"You know I don't know the country, McBride. If I was to find them, they'd be old and the war over."

"Marshal, you just head up Rattlesnake Canyon. Follow it to the end. You'll pass their cabin down at the Garden. It might be a worthwhile stop for you. Then just keep going the way you were. When you hit the end of Rattlesnake Canyon, take a right into Kielberg Canyon. And there's the mine. You can't miss it."

"Don't be giving me all that sass, McBride. I don't know the country. I can't go traipsing up there alone to confront three of them, four counting that old horse thief Sisson. Might as well just shoot myself down here and save wear and tear on my horse. I need someone to go up there with me. I'm not lazy. I'm not scared. But I ain't going up there alone, either."

"You could hire some of the locals to take you up there. There's plenty around who know just where that mine is."

"Funny you should mention that, because that's the marshal's and my opinion, too. And you're the local I'm going to hire. I got authorization to deputize you and Kane to come with me and arrest those boys. If there's going to be shooting, I want someone I can trust to get my back."

"Who says there's going to be shooting? I don't see any reason for shooting. And I'm not going to be deputized, either."

"Oh yes you are. McBride, do you understand what's going on in this country? All over the country, vigilante groups, gangs, are looking for slackers. Back east, they're hunting them down and beating them to death on the street. Around here, where things are tidier, we're hanging or shooting them. Is that what you want in your county? You want a mess like Wheeler had in Bisbee last summer when he had to go against the Wobblies down there?"

"No. Of course not. It's not going to happen here."

"It is going to happen here. You got no less than Teddy Roosevelt out riling up the public against slackers. He's saying this is a form of treason. I don't want to open up the paper and see news of lynching or riots in my district. I don't want people beat to death on the streets of Safford, and I'm pretty sure you don't want that, either."

"And you're not going to get it. That won't happen in Safford or anywhere else in Graham County. There aren't many places that respect the law like Graham County does. We'll get them, arrest them, and hand them over for trial. There will be no riots, no killing. Not here."

"You know what else I don't want to see in the paper? Come November I don't want to see that you got your ass handed to you in the election because you refused to be deputized and bring criminal slackers to justice. I don't think you want to see that, either. Though young Martin over there, he might enjoy the story."

"You can't scare me into this, Haynes. It's not going to happen."

"All right, then. I'm heading back to Globe for a bit to get ready. That'll take a day or two. If I was you, I would work on my excuses why I didn't do my job, why I didn't support my country. Because I might not know where that goddamned mine is, but I know where the *Guardian* office is, and I know the editor. Call me when you change your mind."

"Thanks for stopping by, Marshal. Always a pleasure, and I will be calling you, but it won't be for help. I'll be calling to let you know that I have your prisoners and that you can come and get them at your leisure. I'll keep them safe and warm for you."

Haynes slammed the door on his way out.

"Sheriff," Mart Kempton said, "we really should go after those Power boys. I think the marshal was right. We need to bring them in. There's talk around, and it's not doing us a lot of good. I think we should go up there and get those Powers."

"You do?"

"Yes, Sheriff, I do. They're slackers who have no respect for authority. And that makes us look weak. And we'll seem even weaker if we lie in wait for them to come down and pick them off one by one."

"The way that gets no one hurt."

"No one's going to get hurt. We'll go up. Four of us. You, me, Marshal Haynes, and Kane. More, if we think we need more. Haynes can deputize more for the posse. Those Powers will see they're outmanned and outgunned and just give up. And we'll come riding back into Safford with the Power boys in tow, and there will be a big commotion, and we'll all be heroes. There's nothing to it."

"There's a word there I don't like—'outgunned.' I don't want any guns involved in this. It's a bad deal when guns get involved."

"Not all the time."

"All the time. Every single time. And just because you have to use a gun doesn't mean it's right. If you have to use a gun, something's gone wrong. If the idea includes a gun, it's a bad idea."

"Sheriff, I don't think you're really looking at the whole situation here. It would be good for us to do something like this, to make people notice what a good job we're doing. This is an election year. And if you have to defend yourself, you must defend yourself. Remember Nauvoo."

"And Mountain Meadows."

"We have jobs, Sheriff. I want to keep mine."

"And mine, too?"

Kempton began pacing back and forth, chewing his lip—a man trying to find something to say while he was trying not to say what wanted to come out. "If you just hand the job to me, I guess I'll take it. I don't want to take it from you, but you're acting like you don't want to be sheriff anymore. It's all about how people see you. That's what it is, right there. How people see you."

"I prefer how the Heavenly Father sees me."

"Of course. That's the only way. But those Power boys are disrupting the natural order of things. And to attack the order of things is to attack the Heavenly Father who created it. And I, for one, don't want to let that go on."

"Did you just come up with that argument, or have you been working on it? It would make a fine campaign speech."

"It's the truth, the way I see it. And here's more. I'm not running for sheriff."

Martin did want to be sheriff. That was as clear as a June morning. And Haynes was even more self-serving than Martin, and his service took less honorable avenues. Martin was right that the people would want the Power boys brought in—at least, the good people would. They would want them brought in and thrown in jail or worse.

And the "worse" bothered him. Without the death penalty, which the state had forgone in order to get into the Union, a lot of people would find the process too slow, too weak for their liking. People didn't like deliberation. They liked action. And they might well come for the boys or even the Old Man, and they would come with ropes and an earnest desire to show that they would not be trifled with. There was, certainly, the possibility of a riot or a lynching at the end of this business. McBride couldn't shake the feeling that all this was because Tom Power had somehow bested Haynes and Kane Wootan in some illegal whiskey business. McBride wished, vaguely, that he had chosen to remain a carpenter.

Chapter Seventeen
1918

It was no more than a walk through Bonita Canyon, through the scrub oak and mesquite, a steady uphill pull they were able to do standing up, not crouched, not looking back over their shoulders. Poke had given them a good lead on their pursuers. Ahead of them lay more than twenty miles of mountain to climb and scramble through, but Poke was right. A few miles in, and they would be mostly free from pursuit. The mountain would turn the others back, except for Wootan, of course, and whatever lackeys and crazies he would talk into climbing into the mountains with him. Tom couldn't even think how many times in his life, when things seemed to be going his way, a damned Wootan showed up.

There was still some water running in the creek, and they stopped and ate, drank, and filled their water bags at the creek. It was a nice spot here—sheltered, clear running water, not too cold. They would have trouble getting up and out of this spot, but it was vulnerable, and easy country wasn't good for them. They were hard men, and hard country favored them.

John's eye was beginning to putrefy. The smell was awful, and John moved in and out of consciousness regularly now, though he still kept pretty much on his feet, walking even when sleep overtook him. They had two bottles of whiskey left from the line shack, and nearly all of it was going onto John's eye. John's awareness of his own predicament was fading in and out as well. Often enough, he forgot what the whiskey was for, and Sisson would have to grab him from behind and wrestle him to the ground and hold him for Tom to pour the alcohol into the eye, sending John into a fit of screaming rage and pain.

Other times, he took treatment with a stoic calm, the working of his jaw muscles the only clear sign of the pain that engulfed him. The eye less and less resembled a human eye. The swelling covered the entire eye socket to the size of a plum and roughly the same color. The eyelids had now lost their elasticity and pulled back from the ruptured eyeball so that Tom was no longer required to pull them open to get the whiskey in. The yellowish ooze that came from the eye continued to darken, and everyone knew that things were getting worse as time passed.

They were in the oak and pine of middle Bonita Canyon now, well hidden unless someone rode right up on them. John was useless as a lookout, so Sisson and Tom took turns down in the lower reach of the canyon in a nest of rock with two rifles and a sack of ammunition. The other tried to watch John and sleep at the same time. John was prone to coming back to consciousness without warning and, disoriented, getting up and running.

Tom Power was just starting to nod off, the rifle jammed between two rocks, when Sisson came up behind him. "You need sleep," Sisson said. "Go on back there. I got this."

"How is he?"

"Sleeping. You sleep a bit, too. You need it."

"I don't want him waking up and running on us."

"Not to worry."

When Tom got back to the camp, John was curled at the base of a pine. A length of rope was wound several times around his ankles and knotted. The rest of the rope was wound around the base of the tree. John had maybe six or eight feet of freedom if he awoke.

Tom went at the knots, his hands shaking in fury so that he gave up and used a knife on them. When he had the rope off, he gathered it up and went back down the canyon to where Sisson was awake and watching. Tom threw the rope, now in four sections, at Sisson. "You do not tie up my brother like a steer, goddamn it."

Sisson looked at the pieces of rope littered at his feet. "We need sleep," he said. "We're not going to get it if we're worrying that John is going to wake up and rabbit on us. It's for his own good. Ours, too."

"There ain't no good a rope can do a man. A man puts a rope on any other man, it's a bad thing. You ain't going to do it to John or me. There are enough men trying to put ropes on us. And as many as I can send are going to hell for their trouble. Don't be one of them."

Sisson shook his head as if trying to shake the nonsense off this exchange with Tom. "No harm was meant. No harm was done. We're in this together. If you boys get hanged, so do I. I tied him so we could get some sleep and so's he wouldn't hurt himself. I was looking out for all of us."

"From now on, you look out for your own self. I'll look out for me and John. It needn't be your bother."

"It's all my bother. I didn't choose it, but it is. If we're going to get sleep, we got to get somewhere else."

"Like where?"

Sisson nodded toward the top of the canyon. "They come after us, and they're going to, they'll come through the canyon. We need to be up there."

"No water up there," Tom said. "Ain't a lot of cover, either."

"There's rock and there's height. When the shooting starts, I want to be shooting down, not up. Up is a hard shot. We can stay together, watch the canyon and John while the other sleeps."

"That might be a way to go."

"Not 'a way,' 'the way.'"

Tom said nothing, just stared at Sisson as though trying to figure whether to shoot him. He nodded and got up, ready to go get John and get started up the canyon wall to the top.

They had to move back the way they came to where the walls of the canyon were not so steep. But John was nearly dead weight to be hauled up with them. He could manage for a few minutes on his own, then, despite the exertion, he would fall asleep, stumbling blindly forward, sometimes backward, and Tom, walking behind him, would have to prod him forward and awake. Sisson, in the lead, scouted the easiest route, but with a man sleepwalking, no route was easy.

"This would be easier if we could rope him between us," Sisson said.

"We could do that."

"We don't got a lot of rope left," Sisson said.

Tom started to object, then remembered cutting the rope off John's ankles and wrists and realized now that was a bad decision. "We could walk closer together."

Sisson nodded. "We could. More dangerous, though. One of us slips up there in the snow, all of us are going to go."

"Let's not slip, then."

Sisson nodded and tied a length of rope around his belt and tied the other end to John's belt. Tom did the same. "Watch him he don't fall," Sisson said, "and take us all down."

"I got him," Tom said. "He's my brother."

By halfway up the canyon wall, they had a good look at the floor of the canyon and the small, iced stream. With the leaves off the oaks, they could see fifty yards or so to both the east and west. If they had to, they could hold off a fair number of pursuers on the floor of the canyon. Walking was difficult and would stay so, but the climb was the right thing to do.

They reached a small, flat ridge by early afternoon where the walking was easier. They were still below the snow line but close enough that they could see it in the distance. A thin, light rain, barely a drizzle, had begun to fall and to freeze on the rocks, which made passage slower and more treacherous. That made footing a bit less secure. They were still at the beginning of the passage over the mountains. They had a long way to go.

They were anxious to get deeper into the mountains, farther from the posses and farther from the places the posses would likely stop. John was getting worse. The pain in Tom's eye was nearly unbearable, and he tried to imagine how John felt. John's lapses into delirium and unconsciousness must be a blessing, Tom thought.

They camped for the night under a small outcropping that shielded them from the rain and then the snow. They slept huddled together with a cover of pine branches and brush. John slept but moaned in his dreams and woke with starts that woke both Tom and Sisson. When John lapsed back into deep sleep, Tom and Sisson dozed.

Their shoes and boots were nearly gone now. They used the last of the canvas they had taken from the Johnson mine to wrap the thin, worn soles. It would keep some of the snow and wet out, but it wouldn't last long.

All night the cold came at them in waves. They could feel the cold rolling down the walls of the canyon and engulfing them, sending them, shivering, tighter and tighter into each other. When their bodies had adjusted to the new drop in temperature, another wave of cold would roll down. Both Tom and Sisson held on to John, both for security and warmth. He was burning with fever.

At dawn, Sisson scrambled back down into the canyon floor for water while Tom stood sentry on the ridge. When Sisson came back, he had three canteens full of water and his shirt stuffed with wet green plants.

"What are those?" Tom asked.

"Skunk cabbage. You can eat them. Won't hurt you."

Tom took a tentative bite, chewed slowly and carefully, and then spit out the mash. "I ain't eating that."

"Won't hurt you," Sisson repeated. And when Tom said nothing, Sisson added, "Give you some heat. Long, cold walk. Might be more of it up the canyon, but I don't know. Suit your ownself, but it's probably the best you're going to get, and it's the only heat you're going to get, too."

Tom scowled but took another bite. This time he chewed quickly and swallowed. "Not so bad if you don't actually eat it."

"Guess it don't matter, long as it gets into your stomach."

Tom went on taking small bites, chewing a few times quickly, then swallowing. When John next came awake, Tom put a leaf into his mouth. John spit it out. "I know. I feel much the same, but you got to eat it." John's good eye rolled a bit, failed to focus, and then closed. Tom put another leaf into John's mouth, and again John spit it out.

"Oh, the hell." Tom took a big bite and chewed it well, leaned over, pulled John's mouth open, and spit the mash into it. He pushed John's jaw shut and held it while John coughed and tried to spit, and he did not let go until John had finally swallowed.

"Damned cold," Tom said.

"Better than the night," Sisson said.

"Not that much, but some. Maybe we should go back to walking at night and sleeping in the day."

"No," Sisson said. "Too dangerous. Can't see where we're going, and there's a lot of ice. Not much moon anymore, either. No, we got to walk in the light and try to sleep at night. We ought to get going."

The ascent got steeper, and they struggled with John. They were getting closer to the snow line now. Tom dreaded it. It would be slower, even more miserable, and once into it, they would be in it for a long, grueling time. By afternoon they had made their way over the ridge, into another canyon, and back up to still another, shorter ridge. They climbed into the snow and back out of it and then into it again. By the time they had come down out of the snow for the second time, Sisson estimated they were four, maybe five miles from the entrance to Bonita Canyon, and he set about gathering wood for fire and shelter.

There was no wildlife to be found. There were, no doubt, rabbits, raccoons, bobcats, deer, bears, and lions, but they would require serious hunting. While Sisson built shelter and got the fire going, Tom took the .30-06 and made a wide circuit, hoping to find a deer. The big rifle wouldn't leave much of a rabbit or raccoon if he found one.

He found the tracks almost immediately. He tracked the deer for only a hundred yards or so before he found the tracks of the lion, which was also tracking the deer. He hoped it was a young adult cat and not a starving old cat, one smart enough and quick enough to bring the deer down quickly. They could share the deer with the lion, driving it off or killing it with the .30-06. Hell, he'd eat cat if he had to. A fed cat posed no danger to a lone hunter who was moving slowly in the snow.

He followed the tracks, deer and cat, for another half an hour or so, until the sun was clearly going down behind the tree line. He found the pile of lion scat, rough with deer hair, not far from the trail he'd been following. The lion had brought down the deer, but though the scat was still pretty fresh, the carcass was probably still a ways off. It would have taken hours for the deer to make its way through the cat's stomach and intestines. He walked farther, looking for blood on the ground, but he found nothing as the afternoon light began to fail.

He turned and went back, following his own tracks in the snow. There was still enough light to see by, and after he had stepped in one track and had it give way as the snow underneath continued to melt, he walked a half pace off his earlier tracks, hoping the dropping temperatures would keep the ice crust thick.

By the time he was losing sight of his tracks, he caught the scent of pine smoke in the air. He couldn't see either the fire or the smoke yet, but the smell was strong, and he could follow his nose back. He was starting to guess where the tracks were when his right foot went through the snow.

He went down hard, catching himself with his hands and his left knee, both of his hands breaking through the crust of snow and down almost a foot. His right leg was stuck nearly to the hip. He was able to lift his left leg up enough to straighten his knee. He was now caught by his right leg and both hands. The weight of his rifle and water bag on his back pushed his face into the snow.

There was no way to extract his leg from the snow. When he tried to push himself up, he succeeded only in driving his hands deeper into the snow, and his own body weight pinned his hands under him. He was able to move his face to his left and free his mouth and nose from the snow, but the snow muffled his voice as he called out for Sisson.

The urge to panic came on slowly. He kept trying to move parts of his body without worsening his situation, but every motion only seemed to make things worse. He called again for Sisson, though he knew Sisson was even more likely to struggle through the snow and less likely to be able to free himself than Tom was.

He began a slow rolling, rocking his body from side to side. Gently he made a depression with his right shoulder that gave him a little room to try to extricate his left hand. It took several tries before he felt the snow give for the first time as he pulled his hand up. In a few more tries, he was able to pull it from under his body and the snow.

It was fully numb now, and he put his arm down at his side and grabbed the cloth of his pants with his hand and began another series of rolls to his left until he was able to free his right hand. He was stuck now by only his right leg. He tried moving his right foot back and forth laterally to clear some space around it. Every time he was able to get some space and move the foot farther, the wet snow crumbled and fell around it again.

He began to slowly inch his left leg out to his side, pulling it with his left hand. When he had it at a good angle away from his body, he was able to reach back with his hands and scrape some snow away from around his trapped leg.

When he had dug down only six inches, his body position rendered his efforts mostly useless. He needed to get himself upright in order to get his hands deep enough into the snow to dig himself out. He pushed his hands down as if he were doing a push-up, only to have them break the ice crust again and sink into the snow. He would have to pull himself upright by the strength of his stomach and back alone.

He gave one big heave and brought his body upright, only to have it pass the vertical and, by the weight of his water and rifle, flop him onto his back. Again when he pushed himself with his hands, his hands broke through the snow and gave him no leverage. Finally, he was able to slowly, by concentrating and gritting his teeth, get his stomach and back muscles to gradually bring him upright and let him put his arms out to either side to steady himself.

He began the tedious process of digging his right leg out of the snow. Every few inches, he would try to pull the leg up, and he was nearly down to his knee when the snow around his foot and ankle gave and the leg came free.

With all four limbs free, he was still trapped by the brittle crust of the snow. He tried, gingerly, to rise, but it gave way under him. Finally, he laid himself out prone, face down on the snow, legs spread behind him, and began to crawl, using his elbows and feet to propel himself across the snow crust.

Because he had to stay prone, he used his nose to guide him, inching forward through the snow. The lion, wherever it was, was likely not hungry, certainly not desperate, but Tom, moving forward slowly on his belly, knew he looked more like an injured animal than a human being. He must look that way to the cat as well. It would be all instinct now, and the cat would do whatever it was that cats do in that situation. He pushed his elbows farther out in front of him and increased the pace of his crawl.

It was colder down here with his whole body, rather than just his feet, in contact with the snow. The softened crust of snow flaked off and pushed its way inside his jacket, his pants, and his boots. It was almost fully dark now, and the temperature had begun to fall noticeably. He didn't know how much longer he had before the chill took him.

Carefully, he rose up on his elbows and yelled for Sisson, waited, and then heard the answering call. He was fairly sure he was moving in the right direction, but the answer from Sisson confused rather than clarified his bearings. They were still forty yards from the peaks of the canyon walls, and the sound bounced. He couldn't tell if it came from ahead or behind him.

Sisson would come looking for him, but without light it would be impossible for him to track Tom in the snow without stepping in Tom's footprints and risk falling through the crust himself. If Sisson foundered, it would be up to Tom to find Sisson and rescue him. And Tom knew neither where he was nor how he was going to rescue himself. He raised his head and sniffed the burning pine and juniper. It seemed stronger now.

Keeping prone made it difficult to maintain a straight line. He could pick out landmarks like trees and rocks, but they were only close ones, and then he would have to find a new one and hope that he was maintaining a relatively straight line. His hands were numb now, his thin leather work gloves wet with snow and freezing against his skin.

Sisson called out again, louder this time, and Tom yelled back for Sisson to stay where he was and keep calling out. The sound was clear, but it still echoed off the rocks, and then, through the trees ahead, he saw the small flicker of light. It came and went, and he knew it was fire, their fire, inside a ring of rocks, the flames jumping up, then falling back down. He put his head down and kept crawling.

Next to the fire, which they had to keep small, Tom dried an article or two of clothing at a time—his gloves first, then his shirt, and after that his socks and shoes. There was not enough time or fire to dry or warm them completely, and he wouldn't be able to avoid the chills of the night, only lessen them.

"He came awake," Sisson said, nodding to John asleep in his blanket at one end of the fire. "He was clear. He wanted to know where you were, and then he wanted to go after you. Clear as could be. Like he wasn't sick at all."

"Maybe the fever broke?"

"Might have. Wouldn't count on it, though."

"I don't count on nothing. We get through these mountains, though, we're in for a clear run to Mexico."

"Tom? What are we going to do down in Mexico? There's a million vaqueros down there. Ain't a lot of need for cowboys in Mexico."

"Guess that's right. I been thinking that maybe we could hook up with Villa, do a little fighting against the government down there."

"Villa is a son of a bitch."

"Well, that Zapata fellow, he seems pretty good. He's little folks like us."

"Yeah, but he's way down to the south. It's a big country, Mexico."

"But it's a good country. I don't know a soul who wants me dead down there. Mexico is going to be good for us. Any country that hates its government seems like a good place to me."

"Unless the government wins."

"Ain't going to. It's going to be good in Mexico. It's Mexico for us and us for Mexico."

"You're the boss, I guess."

"Sí. El jefe."

Chapter Eighteen
1918

McBride knew who it was even before the door fully opened. Frank Haynes marched straight to McBride's desk and dropped the papers onto the desk.

"We're going up," Haynes said. "And I do mean 'we.' You been deputized by the US marshal. Kane, too."

"When?" McBride asked, feeling defeated and deflated. "When are we going to do this?" He looked at the papers as if there would be some clue to the thought process that had brought this about. There were official deputizations of himself and Kane Wootan and two warrants for the arrest of the Power brothers, one for John and one for Tom.

"Tonight. We go up early evening so they don't see us. We make the arrests in the morning."

"Tomorrow? Tomorrow's Sunday."

"No day of rest for us."

"It will likely snow."

"Sheriff," Haynes said evenly, "what kind of job, exactly, was it you thought you were getting here? This here's a seven-day-a-week job."

"When there's a need," McBride said. "And I don't see the need. I don't see the need at all, and I certainly don't see the need to do this on a Sunday with a storm rolling in. It will likely be rain here, but you know it's going to be snow in the mountains."

"Well, that's the federal government for you, isn't it? Wants its work done regardless of the inconvenience to the locals. I got my orders, and now you got yours. I thought we'd head out about four this afternoon."

"I don't have animals ready. That's a long, hard climb. I'd like to have my horse reshoed."

"Been taken care of. We'll take my truck. We'll have horses waiting for us at Klondyke, at Haby's place, courtesy of the US government. What have you got in the way of weapons?"

"The usual." He nodded back toward the gun cabinet. ".30-06s, two shotguns, an assortment of handguns."

"Bring what you want, but bring rifles and a couple of handguns. And bring plenty of ammunition. Don't bother with the shotgun. This isn't going to be a short-range affair. We want to knock them down, kill them if we can."

"I thought we were going to arrest them?"

"That's the plan. But they might not go along with it. This is 'dead or alive,' whatever way they want it to go. If we have to lay siege to that cabin, that's what we're going to do."

"This is crazy. These aren't violent criminals. They're not murderers. I can have them safely in my jail by the end of next week. We don't need to be doing it this way."

"Government says we do. You answer to who you answer to. I answer to the one that pays my bills."

"It's crazy. It's stupid."

"Think what you want. I don't really care what you think. Your opinions here don't carry much weight, I'm afraid. I'll be back at four. You be ready."

"And Kane."

"Kane will be with me."

"Frank," Martin Kempton said, "take me with you."

"I need you here, taking care of the office. It's Saturday night."

"But it's going to rain. It will be slow. The cowboys won't make much of a presence here. No one wants to ride twenty miles in freezing rain."

"You need to stay here. Haynes has already chosen Kane. I didn't have any say in it."

"I want to go. You need me. If it comes to trouble, you're outgunned up there. There's four of them up there. You don't want to be going after them with three. You need me. You could get killed."

"Well, Martin, that would leave the door to my office wide open for you. It would be a stroke of good fortune."

"I'm not after your job, Frank."

"Martin, we all tell lies. All of us. It's just what people do. And mostly, it don't make a lot of difference. Mostly it's harmless. But when you start telling lies to yourself, that's when the trouble starts. And that's what you're doing right now. You're lying to yourself so that you don't have to lie to me. You most certainly are going after my job. You've been going after it since before I hired you."

"All right, but I don't want to get your job because you got killed. I want to be sheriff someday. But I don't think this is my time. I didn't have any plans to run against you in the next election."

"But now you do."

"Not yet, Frank. Not yet."

McBride didn't want to damage Martin's chances at a future career, for Martin would be sheriff one of these days, soon enough, but he didn't want to put him in the way of danger, either. Between the weather and the evidence that Haynes and maybe Kane as well had blood in their eyes, it looked like a dangerous piece of work. It was more than duty for Haynes and Wootan. This was personal. It had the stink of money.

Perhaps it was fear or moral failure that held him back. He was being tested by the Lord. And tests were always difficult. A man had to bolster his faith until it was the strongest force he had at his command. "Screw thy courage to the sticking point." He had heard that somewhere. It wasn't in the Book of Mormon but probably the Bible. And he recognized that those were the words of the Lord being spoken directly to him. "Screw thy courage to the sticking point."

"Get ready, Martin."

Kempton looked at him as though he had said something in French or Martian.

"Really?" Kempton asked.

McBride nodded. "You're going. Get your stuff together. I'll get word to our wives that we won't be home tonight and will likely miss services tomorrow. But I'll get you home."

"You sit up here with me," Haynes directed McBride. "Let the young ones ride in the back."

"I don't mind riding back there."

"I mind you doing it. Come up here."

It was a nearly new flatbed truck with wooden rails, a light-duty International Model H. McBride climbed in, and when he was settled, the truck lurched forward, headed northeast out of town, then south toward Klondyke.

"You don't seem to understand that I'm doing you a favor," Haynes said. "You're going to owe me for this one."

"I suppose I don't," McBride answered. "I don't see the advantage to this. I don't see why we're doing it on a weekend. I guess I don't see it at all."

"That's because you still think like a carpenter. And don't get me wrong. I appreciate carpenters. When you need a carpenter, you need a carpenter. But most of the time, you don't need a carpenter."

"Jesus was a carpenter."

"Well, I guess that's right, isn't it? He surely was. But where did that get him? Nailed up on some other carpenter's handiwork. It may not have been his best choice of jobs."

"That would be blasphemy."

"And I suppose that's right, too. Didn't really think of it that way. Things work out the way they work out. You make a wrong decision, and you get nailed to the wall—or the cross—for it. Good Lord. Sorry about that. I wasn't keeping a good eye on the road when I hit that rock there. My God. Feels like my kidneys swapped sides. Count the bodies in the back, would you?"

"They're all there," McBride said. "But they're not laughing. Now I'm glad I'm up here. Though I would prefer a new topic of conversation."

"Start it. Your choice."

McBride fumbled with his thoughts. He could think of nothing to talk about with Haynes.

"Or we don't have to talk. It's getting cold. Reach under the seat there and hand me what you find."

McBride found something wrapped in burlap. As he pulled it out, he knew—a bottle. "Evidence, Frank?"

"Of the weather, my friend. Of the weather. Not of a crime." Haynes pulled the cork with his teeth, then took a drink. He offered the bottle to McBride.

When McBride refused, Haynes took another long pull, tapped on the truck's rear window, then reached the bottle out the side window for Kane Wootan. "Going to be a long night, Sheriff. Long and cold."

They reached Haby's ranch after dark. Haynes had arranged to have three horses saddled and ready for the trek up Rattlesnake Canyon. "Need four horses," Haynes told Haby.

"You said three," Haby replied, watching the men pull firearms and ammunition from the truck.

"Yeah, well. Things change. Need four."

"I don't know," Haby said. "Bad ride up there at night." It was clear to Haby that the lawmen had been drinking. Certainly Haynes and Wootan, maybe McBride and Kempton, too. "I'm not sure you're in any condition to ride up there. You been drinking."

"We're lawmen, Haby. And we can ride."

"I don't think so. I can't risk four horses on men who been drinking and men who've got more weapons than anyone could ever need."

"I judge what we need."

"No," Haby said. "No horses."

"There is a road up there," McBride said. "We could just drive."

"Too much snow, too much noise from the truck. Kane. You got enough horses at your place?"

"Yeah, I got horses. And a mule."

"Then let's go." They piled the guns, ammunition, and liquor back into the truck.

Access to Rattlesnake Canyon is best gained from Rattlesnake Mesa rather than from the exit of the creek some miles to the south. Rattlesnake Mesa is a ridge of hematite a few hundred feet above the canyon floor. The road, cut by the Powers' work crew, winds up the side of the mesa and around several cutbacks until it flattens out at the entrance to the canyon. The last descent from the mesa is a steep, sudden drop from the last rim of the mesa, all the way down to Rattlesnake Creek and the narrow floor of the canyon.

Coming down that last descent, McBride wondered about the ascent coming back, presumably in the snow or, at least, frost, with prisoners in tow, whether two or more. On the way down, the horses' hooves skidded on the scree that inevitably piled onto the trail from the surrounding walls of the canyon. The mule, ridden by Mart Kempton, did somewhat better. The Powers took the hill by truck, he knew, and imagined the labored drive up the steep slope, surely in the lowest gear and winding the engine to the max, and then, later, the descent, which necessarily required no use of brakes and must be a wild ride, the truck giving over to gravity, gaining speed steadily until it hit the bottom of the canyon, surely with a sigh of relief from the driver.

Rattlesnake Creek was a strong body of water, running high and fast in the spring but still running now, even in the middle of winter, when much of the supply was frozen. They heard it before they saw it, not the fierce rumble and rush of a spring but steady gurgling as the creek made its way down the canyon in a series of small drops over the stones from one icy pool to another.

Riding at night, they would be guided by the creek. As long as they were close enough to Rattlesnake Creek to hear its sound, they were not lost. The road, more trail than actual road, crossed and recrossed the creek as it made its way up the canyon, counter to the flow of the creek.

It took them nearly two hours in the dark to pick their way up the trail, crossing and recrossing Rattlesnake Creek five times. The temperature continued to drop, and the creek water, splashed up by the horses, was nearly ice. McBride, dressed in a heavy wool coat, gloves, and denim pants, was beginning to feel the cold bite through the clothes.

Kane Wootan came up on his right side, slowing his horse until the two horses paced evenly. "We're going to get us some Power boys."

McBride kept his silence.

"Come on, Sheriff. We're going to have a good time. A hot time. They're going to get about all that's coming to them."

"And that would be what?"

"All we can give them. All they deserve. Same thing. You know they got it coming, especially that weasel Tom Power. He's going to be one sorry son of a bitch come soon enough."

McBride spurred his horse away from Wootan and up to Mart Kempton. "I don't like this one bit," he said. "They're drunk and spoiling for a fight. I'm calling this off."

"Don't do that, Sheriff. We can handle this. You and me. Those two are still passing that bottle between them. By the time we make the mine, they'll be ready to pass out. You and I can take the Power boys, and Haynes and Wootan will have to see if they have the nerve to take credit for it. This is the reelection, right here. Tomorrow, we'll be heroes."

"It's a bad deal, Mart. Powers got the high ground, and they know the area. If these two do end up passed out and it comes to shooting, we're outgunned. There's nothing good about this."

"We're making good time. We can get there before daylight and take them while they're sleeping. You and I will be the only ones alert. We have surprise on our side."

"Surprise can cut both ways, and it can cut deep."

"Come on, Sheriff. This is our big chance. We're going to be famous. We're going to be the top lawmen in the state, and think of what we'll have over Haynes the next time he tries to push his weight around. We have to do this, Sheriff. We have to do it."

They crossed the creek again, gaining its left side. Haynes stopped, and so did the rest. Haynes turned his horse and came back. "We need to go on foot a bit." He nodded his head. "The Garden is a few hundred yards ahead. They could be there. We don't know. We should lead the horses up just a bit and tie them and go on our own until we see if they're there. Kane, you go on up to the cabin and take a look."

"I thought they were at the mine," Kempton said. Haynes gave him a contemptuous glare.

"Probably they are," McBride said, "but we can't be sure. If they've come down for a bit, we don't want to get surprised."

"That's right," Haynes said. "Surprising them is good. Them surprising us is bad."

It was farther than Haynes had led them to believe. Power Garden stood at 5,800 feet, and they were climbing forty feet or so every hundred yards, walking and stumbling in the dark.

"There's good water over that way, quarter of a mile or so, but there's a nice spring up at the Garden where we can water the horses when Kane gets back," Haynes said when the canopy of trees had begun to thin.

"How come Kane got to go up there?" Kempton asked, though his voice didn't betray a lot of envy.

"Let's put it this way," Haynes said. "When that boy's around, you want to keep stuff locked up good. He comes in and out mouse quiet. What he wants he takes. He's good at that stuff."

McBride gave a snort of assent.

Kempton said nothing more. He knew Kane, and he knew Kane's reputation. He didn't like what Kane did, but it was hard not to give him some small admiration. He was, as Haynes said, good at what he did.

There was a small, low whistle from up ahead. "Let's go, then," Haynes said, untying the bag of ammunition from the mule.

McBride asked, "What kind of war you expecting?"

"Just careful. Always careful."

They moved up in the dark. Something kept rolling and cracking under their feet as they walked.

"Walnuts," Haynes said. "They been planting them for years. Growing them for feed and sale down in the valley."

Kempton wondered briefly how Haynes knew so much about the Power family.

Beyond the orchard of walnut trees they could just make out the cabin. There had been six Powers when they had moved up here, and they had, obviously, lived in tight quarters. But now Charlie was gone. Granny Jane and Ola May were both dead. There were only three now, four, counting Sisson, the hired man.

They took prone positions some thirty yards from the cabin, loaded the rifles, and prepared. They could just make out the door and windows of the cabin, so they would have the advantage in the low light until the Powers were able to get a fix on their muzzle flashes. Until then, the Powers would be firing blindly, unlikely to hit anything.

They could not see Wootan making his way to the cabin, but they knew he was, and Kempton jumped when he heard Wootan hit the door and yell. "Tom, John, it's Kane Wootan. Get up! I need you." Then there was silence and, after that, a long, low whistle.

They rode up to the cabin, leading Wootan's horse. Past the cabin, they tied off the horses at the corral and walked back to the cabin, which was ablaze with light. Kane was going through boxes, trunks, and the few cupboards there were. He had lit every lantern in the cabin.

"What are you looking for?" McBride asked.

"My stuff. Your stuff. Other stuff. I want to see what's here. Mostly, it's female stuff. Looks like the men moved themselves up to the mine shack. That's what I think."

McBride snorted again. Boy would steal the coins of the dead.

Wootan looked up. "Tom Power done stole a lot from us. We're going to get it back."

"Shut up," Haynes said.

"Not sure we want to get up there before daybreak," McBride said. "That's about four hours from now. It's a two-hour ride. We probably ought to take a rest here and get back to going about five, a little before, maybe."

McBride and Kempton watered the horses at the spring behind the cabin, breaking ice off the pool. When the horses were done, they corralled them and moved back to the cabin. There was no fire going, just in case the Powers were near enough to see or smell the smoke. Haynes held a bottle up for McBride and Kempton. "I understand your desire not to offend your church, but it's cold in here. You really ought to put some warmth into yourselves."

"I think I'm plenty warm inside," McBride said.

"You know, Sheriff, I don't know you real well, but I don't sense that much warmth in you at all."

"But then, you don't know me real well."

Haynes nodded. "Probably a blessing for us both."

McBride wasn't unhappy to see the bottle out again. In the two-or-more-hour wait there was plenty of opportunity for Haynes and Wootan to overdo the whiskey and end up passed out. He could wait and waken them in the morning light, claiming that he, too, fell asleep. They would have to scuttle the plan for a while. That would give McBride his chance to take the Power brothers into custody in Safford one or two at a time. It would be easy. And no one would get hurt. He thought it a good plan and watched the bottle go from one to the other.

"Sheriff. Sheriff." It was Martin. "Sheriff, Marshal Haynes says it's time to get going if we're going to reach the mine before daylight."

McBride came fully awake. He could not remember getting sleepy, though he had been tired from the events of the day and the ride up the canyon. It was still dark out, and he and Kempton were the only ones in the cabin. Haynes and Wootan were readying the horses for the last push through the canyon and out, over the ridge to Kielberg Canyon and the mine. That settled it. They were going. There was no question now.

His only recourse was to make the operation go as smoothly as he possibly could. They would move in swiftly and occupy the mine shack before the Powers were fully awake. They would be calm and professional, not throwing down on the Powers and starting a fight but letting them know that they had the upper hand and that there was no use resisting. He was pretty sure the boys would come quietly. He wasn't so sure about the Old Man. Jeff Power was stubborn and bent on making his fortune with this mine. The Old Man was a tough old bird, and taking his boys or his mine would not be easy. McBride's misgivings about this whole episode were surfacing again. Quick and easy, he thought. Quick and easy was what was needed here. They could do it that way.

The way out of Rattlesnake Canyon was easier than the way in. The road rose slowly, winding around hills and outcroppings of the canyon until it reached the summit of Rattlesnake Canyon under Kielberg Peak at 6,900 feet. Then the slow turn to the right and the descent into Kielberg Canyon.

They started down, hugging the right side of the canyon wall, descending at a slow but even pace. It was less than a mile and a half to the mine. They rode for a couple hundred rods, then dismounted. The sun was not yet up, but the sky was steadily lightening. They could make out the outlines of trees and rocks now. Wootan led the way, with McBride and Kempton behind him. Haynes brought up the rear.

Wootan slowed and turned in his saddle. He held the palm of his left hand up, questioning whether it was time to dismount and start walking the horses down the road until they could find a place to tie them and continue on foot.

McBride nodded but saw that Wootan could not pick that up in the dim light, so he swung down from his horse, and the others stopped and dismounted as well.

"How far?" McBride asked Wootan.

"Hundred rod. More or less. Maybe less."

"Tie up here? Walk the rest of the way?"

"There's a small spring pool down there. We could leave the horses there. It's a ways from the cabin. No one would hear us."

"Unless they're up and about."

"Then," Haynes said, "let's get on it."

"Marshal," Wootan said, "dibs on the mine."

"Shut up."

They walked down until they could see the roof of the mine shack below them, and there they tied off their horses at the spring. It was barest daylight now but light enough that they could see the shack and the rest of the mine camp. There was no smoke coming from the chimney on the far side of the shack. Haynes spoke first in a voice barely above a whisper. "Load 'em up." He put the bag of ammunition on the ground. McBride and Kempton checked their handguns, and each took a handful for their long guns. Wootan and Haynes stuffed boxes of cartridges into their pockets and inside their shirts.

McBride tried to get them together to plan this out, to note the strategic positions and the available cover to be prepared before they approached the shack. He imagined stationing himself and one other, maybe Mart or Wootan, on either side of the door and taking the Powers one by one as they came out the door, pulling them to the side and down to the ground. There would be no reason for anyone to fire a shot. There should never be a reason to fire a shot if you plan your strategy beforehand.

But before he could get them together, Wootan took off, scrambling down the ridge behind the shack, holding his rifle high in his right hand. McBride saw what was happening and stood, for a second, stunned. Then he motioned for Kempton to follow and started down the ridge behind Wootan. He could hear Martin coming right behind him. Haynes, he presumed, was behind Kempton.

McBride saw Kane Wootan reach the bottom of the ridge, right himself, and head from the back of the shack, then around to the front. McBride followed, with Kempton right behind him. Then from the back, McBride heard someone lose his purchase and go down on the ground, giving out a yell of surprise as he fell.

There was a clatter and ringing of bells as horses rushed past them. McBride threw himself to the side of the trail and let the horses get by. They must be Power horses, he thought, spooked by Haynes, who had fallen behind him.

"Throw up your hands," McBride heard, and knew that it had all gone bad.

Chapter Nineteen

1918

Through the night, the cold came in waves. When Tom thought he couldn't bear to be any colder, his body would adjust, and he would fall asleep for a short while. Then another wave of cold rolled in, dropping the temperature even farther. He was happy to get up and take his watch and let Sisson try to deal with the cold while he huddled in his blanket next to the fire.

He woke as the sun came up, still sitting by the dying fire, which he was supposed to be tending. He looked around at Sisson, who was still wrapped in his blanket, though moving, and at John, who was staring at him.

"Good morning, brother," John said, as he had said every morning of their lives. They sat at the rebuilt fire, melting snow in their tin cups, waiting until the water began to steam before they drank it.

John walked the rest of that day, not seeming any worse for the spell of fever and delusion he had gone through. The snow had picked up, and above the tree line, the rock got more and more treacherous. Both Tom and John had worn holes in their shoes—boots, in John's case—and Sisson had lost the heel of one of his shoes. He had tried to nail it back on with a farrier's nail, only to have it stick into the bottom of the shoe. He pried the heel off, threw it away, and walked the rest of the way limping heavily on his right side. The pieces of canvas they had tied on were already shredded and tattered. By late morning Sisson's knee and hip were stiff and painful from the odd gait.

But they kept walking, moving nearly due east, and, as they neared the end of the Chiricahuas, the danger grew again. As unlikely as it was that any of the posses would pursue them through the winter mountains, it was just as likely that they would be camped and waiting for them at the eastern side of the Chiricahuas.

It was nearing dark of the fifth day in the mountains when Sisson stopped suddenly, holding his hand up as a signal for them to stop, too. He put his hand flat to his mouth, pointed into the canyon below, and then pointed to his ear. They stopped breathing then, listening hard to the silence. And it was only silence until the wind shifted a little and they heard a man's disembodied voice.

"Fourteen mile, maybe more."

Tom was wide-eyed with the desire to run, but he held his ground. Sisson listened, trying to pinpoint the location. John stared ahead, impassive. Sisson held up two fingers, waited, then held up three. After a few minutes, four. They waited. Sisson nodded and put up four fingers again.

Four of them. If it came to a fight, they could probably take the four simply by surprise. But there was no good reason for a fight. They had water, and they could wait out the four below. They crouched, waiting, not moving or talking.

Within the hour, they heard what they had not wanted to hear—the clanking of tin. The ones below were getting ready to cook. They were staying for the night. Soon the smell of smoke drifted up to where they were. They would have no fire tonight, nor would they be able to build any substantial shelter. They would sleep where they were, by turns, waking the snorers who might signal their presence. None of that needed saying. Slowly, quietly, they dropped their packs, unlashed their blankets, wrapped themselves, and went to ground. With hand signals, they set the watch—Tom first, then Sisson, then Tom again. John shook his head vigorously. He would take third watch. Tom shook his head "no." They could not risk John falling asleep if the fever spiked again.

The smoke from the fire below picked up again before the sun was up. Those below were going to make an early start, get a jump on the brothers before sunrise. Tom woke Sisson, who rolled over and immediately understood the situation. John was still asleep, not moaning in his sleep anymore but breathing with an odd, pulsing rhythm as if he were trying to sing in his sleep.

Tom and Sisson listened to the sounds from below, the voices still sporadic, carried on shifting winds that rose up from the canyon floor—"east," "noon," "newspaper." And later "sons of bitches" carried up on a current so clearly that Tom spun around to confront the invisible speaker. Within half an hour they could hear the tack being moved, then the sounds of horses' hooves. The men were heading deeper into the canyon, trying to catch the brothers sleeping.

They woke John and rerolled their blankets, picked up their packs, and continued east, away from the pursuers. But those were only four. There had to be more, probably quite a few more. They had no delusions. The pursuers were not about to give up, and they had to know that the brothers weren't far away, though, certainly, not how close they actually were.

By midmorning they were back into the heavy tree cover, which gave them visual cover but multiplied the possible sounds they could make—snapping branches, startled animals. It was a trade-off. Everything was. To gain one thing, you had to give up another. Watchfulness was one sense traded for another.

They came down into the low hills of Portal. Though Portal was south of their best-known territory, Tom had worked some for a ranch just southeast, between Portal and Rodeo, New Mexico. He was pretty sure they could get provisions there. They stayed in the hills as long as they could and kept moving east, now angling south toward Rodeo and, eventually, Mexico.

They stayed at the base of the Chiricahuas as long as they could. Once they cut east toward Rodeo, New Mexico, they would be back in the open again, protected only by the low, rolling hills and the scrub of the desert. By noon they were pretty sure they were now due west of Rodeo and not far from the Blakely ranch, where Tom had worked, branding and cutting for a couple of seasons.

They made the ranch with daylight to spare. Sisson and John waited in a clump of mesquite a few yards from a stock tank. Tom walked on into the ranch. No one was in the barn, the tack room, or the corrals. Tom made his way to the house, stood by the door for a while, then, ready to run, gave a tentative knock.

It was the missus who answered. "Miz Blakely," Tom said, taking off his now-battered hat. "I'm Thomas Power. Done some work for you all a couple of years back."

"Tom Power, you get out of here. You'll get us all hanged. Go on. Go."

"Miz Blakely, we're in bad need of a little food, some water. Then we'll be gone."

"Half the state is after you. We get found out that we're giving you comfort, they'll hang us or burn us out. Something. You go."

"Please, Miz Blakely. We haven't eaten in many days or had clear water."

She came out the door with a broom and brought it heavily down across Tom's shoulder. "You go. You'll get us killed." She drew back the broom and brought it down again. Tom retreated a couple of steps, holding up his hand to ward off the broom.

Herb Blakely appeared at the door. "What's going on here?"

Miz Blakely took another swipe at Tom. "You git now."

Herb stepped into her and took the broom with one hand. "Tom? Tom Power?"

"Herb. I come looking for a little food. Water. Don't want to start trouble."

"He's going to get us killed, Herbert. They will come here and find him, and they will hang us next to him. We got to get him out of here."

"Yes, Momma. But not with no broom. We ain't turning our backs on him. We know this man. We don't turn away the hungry or the hurting. Where's the rest of you at, Tom?"

"Yonder." Tom pointed back the way he had come. "By the stock tank."

"You go on out there and wait. I'll be along directly, and we'll take care of you."

"I appreciate it, Herb."

"I know you do."

"You sure we can trust him?" Sisson asked.

"Herb Blakely is good people. I've known him a long time. He wouldn't lie. If he didn't want to help us, he would say."

"All right. Going to be dark soon."

It was dark when they heard the engine chugging toward them, then saw the faint glow of the lights behind the hill. They moved back into the mesquite, their rifles cocked. The small truck crested the hill, came up to the stock tank, and shut down. "Tom. Tom Power. It's Herb. I got provisions. Come on. I'll take you to Mexico."

Blakely had moved in front of the truck so that his body, though not his head, was illuminated by the truck's lights. Tom gave his rifle to John, though he wasn't sure John was awake enough to get himself pointed in the right direction. He moved slowly away from the mesquite in case it was a trick, drawing fire away from John and Sisson, giving them the chance to take out whoever it was in front of the truck.

"Herb?"

"Yes. It's me. Come on."

Tom walked to the front of the truck. He still could not see the man's face. He assumed it was Herb Blakely but wasn't sure. Sisson was back in the darkness, out of the range of the truck's headlights, with his rifle trained on the man.

"Got you some bread, some pork smoked in the fall, a jar of cooked beans, and some pie. The missus didn't want to give up the pie, but I took it anyway. And I got water. And I'll drive you to the border."

"Herb, can you duck down a little so your face is in the light? No offense, now. Just caution is all."

"I understand, Tom." Blakely knelt and turned so the truck lights lit his face. "All right for you?"

"Yes, sir, Herb. Can't tell you how grateful we are."

"Don't even think on it. I was a little jealous when Hendricks told me he saw you boys and helped you on your way. I knew I would do the same, and here I am. You all climb into the truck, and we'll be on our way."

"I hear there's army after us."

"Out of Hachita, yes. They was through here early this morning. Cavalry. Come on, get in the truck."

"If there's army down there, I'm not sure I want to be in a truck."

"It'll be fine. Come on."

Sisson came out from his dark cover. He came up even with Tom and spoke just above a whisper. "I don't like it. Truck will draw the soldiers."

"Hello, Mr. Sisson. Herb Blakely." Blakely held out his hand, which shook in the light of the truck headlamps.

Sisson merely nodded.

"Who else you got back there?" Herb asked.

Sisson stepped forward. "Why you nervous, Mr. Blakely? This is Tom Power. You know him."

Blakely laughed. "Hell, yes, I know him. But I knowed him when he was just a cowboy, not when he was a famous desperado."

"Let's take the food and go," Sisson said.

"No, no. Let me take you in the truck. Tell you what, I'll drive up about ten mile and let you off, and you can walk the rest of the way if that's what you have a mind to do. I could cut off to the southeast. If they saw me, they would come after me."

Sisson leaned into Tom and whispered, "He's working way too hard at this." Tom nodded.

"Herb," Tom said, "this is a terrible thing to have to do, but it sure sounds like you got plans for us." Tom stepped toward Blakely and grabbed him by the arm. Then Sisson jumped, knocking them both to the ground. Soon, Blakely was trussed in baling wire from the back of the truck, including a piece that passed through his mouth like a bit, keeping him from spitting out the rag they had stuffed in there. "Not sure this is right. You did bring us food and all, and I'm not sure why you would do that and then turn us in, but we can't take chances. You'll be all right here for a bit. I think we're going to borrow the truck, too."

"No," Sisson said. "No truck. They'll be looking for it."

"Well, then," Tom said, "we'll be saying good-bye. Hope you don't spend an uncomfortable night out here, Herb."

They moved as they had learned to move—tree to tree, bush to bush, stopping when they reached cover, looking to see if there was anyone anywhere, then moving quick to the next cover and beginning again. They favored the sides of hills and under ridges where they had sight but would be difficult to spot. They moved as fast as they could, which was not fast. John was fading in and out of consciousness again.

They moved in a semicrouch, which gave them no advantage except the illusion of more security. They watched the ground as they went, looking to avoid loose rock and pieces of wood that would crack like gunshots in the night. They saw no signs of the patrol, but they knew it had to be near. Likely the soldiers were bivouacked somewhere close by, but the lack of sign was more unnerving than knowing they were close. They kept walking until the sky began to barely lighten in the east.

"Where do you think we are?" Tom asked.

"Mexico. Or damned close. Mexico, I think."

"Doesn't look any different, does it?"

"No," Sisson said. "You want it to, but it doesn't. We don't know where the border is, and neither does that patrol there. We got to just keep walking. Sooner or later, everyone will figure it's Mexico, and then we're all right."

"Why haven't we found those soldiers yet?"

"I don't know," Sisson said. "Maybe they're pretty far ahead of us."

"In Mexico?"

"I don't know. They should be turning back if they think they're at the border. Maybe we haven't gone as far as we think. I just don't know."

"We couldn't have passed them, could we?"

"I don't see how, but maybe we did. Maybe they cut off to the east, or went farther up into the mountains, thinking we wouldn't risk the flat land."

Even though John was getting worse again, they kept walking the best they could. Tom walked behind John, grabbing him by the belt or shoulders when he started to slump or to drift off the trail. John was moaning and mumbling now, walking in his sleep. Tom grabbed him by the belt and pulled him back when he started to quickstep forward.

"Let me go," John said. "I got to go see Ola."

"Ola ain't here, John."

"Up there. She's right up there. I got to go to her."

"You can't go, John. She ain't here. You got to believe me."

"No, Tom. She's here. She's right there. Right there by that bush. She's telling me to come to her."

"You ain't going to Ola, John. Not while I'm here, you ain't."

They kept walking. John stumbled several times, and once it took both Tom and Sisson to pick him up and get him back on his feet. By late afternoon they were spending more of their energy on keeping John moving than on moving forward.

"There," Sisson said. "Up there. Smoke."

"The army?"

"Shouldn't be. We're well into Mexico by now. It's likely a posse. Wootan, probably."

"That son of a bitch just don't give up, does he?"

"Would you give up if it was him killed your brother?"

"No."

"Well, there you go."

Tom moved up, still crouching, keeping toward the ground, moving in short bursts, forward from one side to another, never in a straight line, always prepared to turn and run if he stumbled on the posse. He came up a low ridge piled with stones. The stones were loose and scattered, but he could see it was the remains of an old revetment, probably from the Indians, where they used to hide themselves from game that came through the low valley below.

The smell of smoke was strong, and Tom figured that he was right on top of the posse now. He got flat on his belly and crawled up, pulling himself with his arms. He didn't like moving this way, hands and face toward who knew what. He was glad it was still winter and the snakes and other menaces were still in hibernation.

He found a low spot in the stone wall, and he slowly poked his head between two rocks. There were a lot of them. Some milled around or sat in small groups, while others tended the fire. They were all alike in their khaki uniforms with the tall, peaked hats and the tan gaiters. He counted twelve, but there were certainly more.

"We found the army," Tom told Sisson when he had crawled back.

"Damn. Followed us right into Mexico."

"They must want us awful bad."

"Maybe," Sisson said. "Maybe."

"Why else would they follow us?"

"They don't want Thems to hang us."

"Don't seem like that would matter. They're in Mexico, where they ain't supposed to go. Might as well hang us or shoot us far as I can see."

"I don't think so. And there's something you better see over here." Sisson led Tom to where John lay on the ground asleep. "Here," Sisson said. "Hold him and look at the eye."

Sisson struck a match and brought it close to John's swollen and festering eye. Tom saw it then, the small movements under the stretched purple skin of John's eyelid. With his other hand, Sisson reached out and peeled the lower lid back. The eye was infested with maggots.

"Well, shit." Tom said. "Fuck me."

"Yeah. Well, fuck us all. We got to decide."

"What?"

"Go on or save John. Can't do both."

"We spend a month walking to Mexico, almost get caught three times, and we end up here just to give up? We're in Mexico, Sisson. We're here. We just got to get around these soldiers."

"It's a choice, and it's yours," Sisson said. "Whatever you decide. This can't be my decision, got to be yours."

"It's your life, too, Sisson."

"Your insides tell you to keep running. That sooner or later you'll get away and be all right. But it won't be free. It's got to cost something. That, I figure, is your brother. His eye is rotting. The eye's connected to the brain. He ain't going to live through this. He just ain't."

"Not sure we will either."

"No," Sisson said. "Nothing's sure, I guess. You just wait for the next card to turn, and you hope it goes your way."

"What ever goes our way?"

"It's all been some pretty bad luck, I'd say."

"It ain't luck, Sisson. The fucking deck is stacked. It always has been."

"Probably so."

"Listen, Sisson. You can do all right in Mexico. You're a farrier. There's always work. John and I are just cowboys. That's lugging oranges to Florida, if you ask me. You go on. I can hold the army here for a while. Hell, we still got enough ammunition to fight a small war. I'll stick with John. You go."

Sisson looked off to the south as if he could see what awaited him in Mexico. "I been in prison," he said. "It wasn't much good, but I could do it if I have to. I'll stay here. You go to Mexico. It's what you want. I was never that keen on it."

"They might just kill you."

"Well, I ain't ever been killed, but I suppose I can do that, too."

"Hell. Damn it all. Can't stay here, can't leave my brother. It wasn't your fight, Sisson. Hell, I'm not even sure you ever got a shot off."

Sisson glumly stared ahead. "I signed on with you boys. I guess I'll stay with you boys. If you're staying with John, I am, too."

"What I'm telling you is you don't have to stay. There's no reason. It's all over for us. But it wasn't your fight. The Old Man never said nothing about dying for the family when he hired you. You're the hired man, is all. John and me, we're blood. Go on, get out of here. Find you a ranch with good horses and a nice señora and live out your days a free man."

"I can't decide. You go on. I'll wait here. Time will decide. It always does."

Tom stood up and began walking for the ridge. Halfway there, he put up his hands.

Afterword

The Power brothers and Tom Sisson surrendered to the US Army's Third Squadron of the Twelfth Cavalry, headquartered at Hachita, New Mexico, on March 8, 1918, some twenty miles into Mexico. They had been on the run for twenty-eight days.

The army brought them back to Clifton, Arizona, in Greenlee County, just north of Graham County. John's eye was treated, then removed. Tom's eye healed, though it was permanently blind.

On May 20, 1918, Tom and John Power and Tom Sisson were found guilty of three counts of first-degree murder. The testimony of Marshal Frank Haynes was central to the state's case. He swore that the first shot had been fired from the cabin. The three were sentenced to natural life in prison at the Arizona State Penitentiary in Florence. As their train moved them from Clifton to Florence, people lined the tracks to see the three killers. Many of the people waved to them, and at every stop someone brought them food.

The gold mine in Kielberg Canyon was given to the widows of the slain officers. Clara McBride eventually bought out the others' share of the claim, and the McBride family operated the mine for the next three decades.

Tom Sisson died in Arizona State Prison in 1957. Tom and John Power were paroled in 1960. They both lived in Graham County, and both were reported seen up in the Galiuros where they had lived and mined. Tom Power died in 1970, and John died in 1976. They are buried with their father, sister, and grandmother in Klondyke, Arizona.

Acknowledgments

I would like to express my gratitude to Dr. John Sellechio, OD, for his counsel on eye trauma. To my graduate students—Jane, Amanda, and Adam—and Rod Siino, Rusty Barnes, and Katie and Brian Laferte for reading and advising well. To Bob Carey for reading and helping with the title. To the late Barry Briggs, who first suggested the idea for this novel. To the Arizona History Society in Tucson and the Graham County Historical Society in Thatcher, Arizona, for the use of their resources. To Rhode Island College for the time to research this book. And, as always, to Amanda Urban and to Randy for their help and unflagging support.

About the Author

Thomas Cobb is the author of *Crazy Heart*, *Acts of Contrition*, and *Shavetail*. He grew up in Tucson, Arizona, and lived for a number of years in Graham County, where he learned the story of the Power boys. He is professor emeritus at Rhode Island College and lives in Foster, Rhode Island, with his wife, cat, and dog.